"WONDERFUL . . . CAPTIVATING . . .

In THE PAST IS ANOTHER COUNTRY, Lois Battle has labored on a huge canvas: from the first pages I was swept into the heat and light of her Australia."

MARION MEADE
Author of *Dorothy Parker*

"Lois Battle has written the best kind of novel—full of characters who really live and a story I didn't want to end. Witty and full of wisdom, THE PAST IS ANOTHER COUNTRY is a superlative book."

LEONA BLAIR
Author of *Privilege* and *A World of Difference*

"Engrossing . . . This poignant exploration of women's needs, goals and choices resonates with insightful implications about women's roles in modern society."

Publishers Weekly

"Compelling . . . A genuine pleasure."

VALERIE SAYERS
Author of *Due East* and *How I Got Him Back*

THE PAST IS ANOTHER COUNTRY

Lois Battle

FAWCETT CREST • NEW YORK

A Fawcett Crest Book
Published by Ballantine Books
Copyright © 1990 by Lois Battle

Library of Congress Catalog Card Number: 89-40775

ISBN 0-449-22117-2

This edition published by arrangement with Viking Penguin, a division of Penguin Books USA Inc.

Manufactured in the United States of America

First Ballantine Books Edition: February 1992

To my Aussie family

> *You cannot imagine what a queen of the earth I was when I was twelve years old. . . . Ah, how you would have loved me, and how I miss myself.*
> —Colette

Western Australia, 1958

The screen door slammed shut as she raced to the front gate. Freedom at last. She clasped her bookbag to her chest and suddenly it became her illegitimate child. The hollyhocks, zinnias and nasturtiums blazed in the morning sun, but in her mind it was night. She must escape before the guards detected her absence. She ran across the street to crouch near the rear wheel of the old pickup truck. Glancing furtively over her shoulder, she pulled down her hat, then dashed to the eucalyptus tree. Another quick look back, then a zigzag to the camouflage of the lantana bush. She pressed herself into it, breathing hard, calming the child. Would she be able to reach the harbor before her lover's ship set sail?

"Ah, if it isn't Megan Hanlon, our own Sarah Bernhardt." Mrs. Whitehead, her hair still in clips, her singlet poking up around the neck of her housedress, leaned on her broom. Megan drew herself up. She mustn't be cheeky, but she wouldn't be intimidated by the likes of Mrs. Whitehead, who was known to sing, or rather bay, at the moon when she'd taken enough spirits.

"Good morning, Mrs. Whitehead. Your garden's looking lovely."

"It would if the likes of you didn't nick off with the roses. Don't think I haven't seen . . ."

Megan looked back at her house. The cousins were piling out, Auntie Vi following, yelling at Moira that she'd forgotten her lunch.

"Sorry, I'm late for school." She nipped off through the lane and into the main street, which was out of her way but a more

1

interesting route even though the shops were still shut. She passed the greengrocer's, the Greek's fish-and-chips shop, the newsagent's, the pea-green doors of the pub, the alleyway where the men played two-up, and stood for several minutes outside the Regal, studying the poster for *My Foolish Heart* and admiring Susan Hayward's cleavage. She broke into a trot, up past the railway station, over the bridge, through the open paddock to the church. She slowed down and crossed herself as she passed it, then ran across the road and paused again at Corcoran's sweet shop. Smudge, Mrs. Corcoran's pure-white, one-eyed cat, lazed in the window beside jars of licorice whips, gum balls, toffees and a bleached and fly-specked photo of the queen. There were only a few girls in the shop so she knew she must be late. She pulled at the stocking that had been sucked into her shoe and hurtled down the hill to St. Brigid's. The playground was teeming with navy blue uniforms. One of the girls yelled hello and, feeling that her talent had been called upon, Megan became the March Hare, raising her index fingers to the sides of her hat, forcing her front teeth over her bottom lip in a rabbity smile and muttering, "I'm late, I'm late." She reached the entrance and blinked into the darkness of the school foyer, taking in the smell of wood polish, fruit peels and books. There was a shuffling from the alcove next to the hat pegs. "Have you got it?" her friend Aileen whispered.

"Yes," Megan said in a normal voice, wishing Aileen would grasp the fact that conspiracies should be conducted with a certain nonchalance. "I saw the pale grey light of dawn, but I finished it."

"You mean you were up all night?"

"Not really." Aileen had such a literal mind. "I went to sleep around midnight."

"And your aunt and uncle didn't mind?"

"They were dead to the world by then. My silly cousin starting whining about the light being on, but I know how to deal with her." She'd put a pillowcase over the bedside lamp. "I am desperate for privacy, Aileen. Just desperate."

"But what did you think of it? Didn't you just love the part where . . ."

"It thrilled me in every fiber of my being." The author had

used those words in several of the love scenes and Megan had repeated them as she'd dropped off to sleep, and again this morning, during the usual chaos of breakfast when cousin Jeremy had a nosebleed (because he'd been picking it, she was sure), cousin Moira burned her fingers on the toasting fork, and Auntie Vi left off spooning the coddled egg into Great-grandmother Kathleen and threatened to lay into them all with the bread knife.

Aileen smoothed her thick blond plaits. "The part I liked best was where Aurora had to undress in the captain's room and he discovers that she's not a boy."

"But I think he should've noticed that sooner, don't you? Because she's described as having voluptuous breasts and . . ." A roundness already pushed out the cloth at the front of Aileen's uniform. Megan's own uniform still hung straight from the yoke. Until a few months ago she'd been forced to take her bath with nine-year-old Moira because Auntie Vi said it saved on the hot water and Megan "had nothing to hide." Now Auntie Vi bowed to modesty and let her bathe alone, but she joked about Megan's "knobs" and with what Megan thought unforgivable crudeness said that they'd grow faster if Megan soaked them in a thimbleful of gin. ". . . and besides, she's got those long eyelashes."

"Sometimes boys have long eyelashes. Look at Kevin Stokes."

"Kevin Stokes," Megan said with disgust. "He's such a drongo." Last Saturday at the Regal, Kevin Stokes had left his crowd of boys and given Aileen half of his Carmello bar. Megan had not noticed his eyelashes, but she had noticed that his fingernails were dirty. Sometimes Aileen was indiscriminately eager for male attention. "And I don't see how the captain couldn't have noticed Aurora before, because—"

"But he's engaged to Lady Sheltingham."

"But men notice other women even when they're engaged. Even when they're married. Haven't you seen the way, when men are standing around, they . . ." Her rebuttal was cut short. Mona Gallagher had come out of the office, carrying the brass bell by its clapper. "Ask not for whom the bell tolls," Megan said, and got the expected laugh from Aileen. Mona paused, her eyes demanding to know why they were loitering in the forbidden territory of the foyer when they were supposed to be out on the playground. Aileen smothered her laughter and Megan, affecting a look of hauteur she'd practiced in her mirror, busied herself with her bookbag. Mona was a prefect. She had special responsibilities and privileges that the other girls both envied and despised. She rang the bell to call the girls to order, collected the nuns' mail and ran errands for them. Outwardly, Megan had nothing but contempt for her—Mona was a toady, an informer, what Uncle Mick would call a scab—but secretly she didn't begrudge Mona her favored status as the nuns' pet. With her high forehead, long upper lip and spotty complexion, Mona was clearly destined to become one of them.

"Quick, give me the book," Aileen insisted, when Mona had swanned past. "If my mother notices that it's missing, she'll skin me alive. And take off your hat. It's almost time for the bell."

Megan handed over the book, which she'd taken the precaution of covering with the same brown paper that protected their school texts, and grasped the elastic beneath her chin, yanking off her hat. She hung it on the peg with "M. Hanlon" printed beneath it on a piece of adhesive tape and patted down the live clump of red hair. "I put a creme rinse on it last night. Does it look any better?"

"Yes," Aileen assured her. That was only a white lie, a venial sin for which she could gain forgiveness with a quick prayer. Megan's hair, as usual, was a fright. "Hurry up," she said, stuffing the contraband book into her sack. "Pull up your stockings and fix the knot on your tie."

They managed to get outside just as Mona rang the first bell. All activity on the playground stopped. The younger girls, who'd been skipping rope, playing knucklebones or catch, froze into exaggerated positions. Older girls closed their books and ended their conversations. A tossed ball rolled down the hill. In the sudden quiet, the heretofore unnoticed chirp of birds was heard, and the labored rendering of "The Merry Peasant" tinkled from the practice rooms that separated the school building from the convent garden. After a moment, even the piano stopped. Mona, with the smugly placid face of a petty bureaucrat, clanged the bell a second time. The nuns walked in dignified procession from a side door, their hands hidden in the loose sleeves of their habits, and the girls ran to form their lines, right arms extended to touch the shoulders of the girls in front of them. Megan was first in her class line. Sister Bruno, who had a drill sergeant's obsession with order, periodically rearranged the girls according to height. During the last term Megan had stayed in the front, while Aileen had been moved farther and farther to the rear. Sister Bruno referred to them as Mutt and Jeff and was delighted with this excuse to separate them. On the third bell the girls dropped their extended arms and stood at attention while Sister Bernadette, the Mother Superior, walked among them, on the alert for the uncontrolled whisper or the hand undisciplined enough to scratch an itchy knee or ear. Once Sister Bernadette had passed, Megan, still standing at attention, let her eyes slide over to Sister Mary Magdalene. Magdalene's head was not bowed. She stood at parade rest, her grey eyes focused on the mid-distance. Her mouth had a tantalizing quiver, as though restraining a smile.

For Megan, Sister Mary Magdalene was special. She was the youngest of the nuns and also the most intelligent. She taught with a newcomer's verve, demanding thought instead of rote response, and had little patience with the dim-witted. Once, in a fierce burst of temper, she'd hurled an eraser across the room because Eleanor Pujoli couldn't explain the difference between the Spartans and the Athenians. And there were countless clues that Sister Mary Magdalene daily did battle with her true nature. Sitting in the garden, she was as likely to be reading as fingering her rosary. When not walking in lockstep with the other nuns, she had an energetic stride. She held her head high and not even the heavy serge habit disguised a slight movement of her hips. Her laughter was light and spontaneous, exposing strong, irregular teeth, and sometimes her eyes grew troubled and her hand would absently caress her cheek. Her very choice of a name suggested a sinful past.

The goody-goody prefects, who had access to the nuns' quarters, were grilled for information. Were letters to the nuns ever addressed with their real names? Where were they sent from? Was it true that the nuns' rooms looked like cells and that they ate only cabbage and dry bread? Scraps of information were collected and lavishly embroidered upon: the bottle of eau de cologne discovered in Sister Claire's room became a secret cache of cosmetics (how else to explain her rosy cheeks?); Sister Bruno, who was portly, was whispered to have a hidden supply of food; Sister Cecilia, who was pious and had dark circles under her eyes, must stay up all night praying. Speculations about why various nuns had taken the veil fell into three categories: the prettier ones were believed to have locked themselves away after blighted love affairs (breach of promise, untimely death of the lover, and family interference were favorite themes). The less attractive ones had been forced to take vows by pious or unloving parents who wanted to impress the priests and assure themselves a lifetime of surrogate prayer. The third group (the disciplinarians like Sister Bruno) had joined the Order because they wanted to be in the police force or the army but weren't allowed to because they were females. But Sister Mary Magdalene didn't seem to fit into any of these groups. Megan was sure that one day, or more likely one night, Sister Mary Magdalene would "leap over the wall."

Though the girls prayed, as directed, to be called to a religious vocation, it was impossible to understand why anyone would leave the world and take vows of poverty, obedience and chastity. Aileen said poverty would be the most difficult for her. Her family was well off and she was used to pretty dresses and spending money and riding in a car. Megan knew she'd have the most trouble with obedience. She hated rules, even when they made sense. About chastity they were both undecided. They scoffed at younger girls who thought you got pregnant from kissing, but the particulars of sex were murky, alternately fascinating and appalling. Reading love scenes in forbidden books or watching them on the screen at the local pictures produced a diffused excitement. But Aileen's older sister had told them that her fiancé put his tongue in her mouth when he kissed her, and that was too disgusting for words. Though they talked endlessly about a future of dances, handsome men and weddings (Aileen had already decided on a magnolia satin dress with a long train), Megan reminded Aileen that after marriage came children, and you never knew how many you'd get. From the pulpit, Father Coffin spoke about the blessing of large families, but most of the women who had them didn't look particularly blessed. Mrs.

Henning, for example, who'd had eight, looked haggard, played out. Even Father Coffin looked at her as though she wasn't quite clean. And how could she be? She'd spent her entire adult life wiping bottoms, noses and chins. So there was something to be said for chastity.

Sister Bernadette joined the other nuns, giving Mona a nod. Mona rang the bell a final time and the girls began to file into the building. Just before she got to the door, Megan glanced back and, keeping her hand close to her side, gave Sister Mary Magdalene a little wave.

". . . and of the Son and the Holy Ghost. Amen." The morning prayers concluded, the girls crossed themselves and slid into their seats. Sister Bruno's catechism class. What a way to start the day! Megan leafed through her catechism, desperate for a last-minute look. Her stomach grumbled. Eleanor Pujoli giggled and Megan pulled a face at her. Sister Bruno cleared her throat. "Megan Hanlon, since yer fidgetin' y' no doubt want to be first," she said in a brogue as thick as porridge. "Close yer catechism and tell me, what is free will?" Megan got to her feet and parroted the answer. The vertical line between Sister Bruno's black brows creased in disfavor as her eyes, magnified by thick lenses, blinked once, then slid to another victim. "Kathleen O'Hare. What does St. Thomas Aquinas tell us . . . you may be seated, Megan . . . what does St. Thomas Aquinas tell us about the nature of free will?"

Megan smoothed the back of her skirt and sat down. She searched for a loose piece of paper that could be quickly destroyed and began to write her name, first in shadowed block letters, then in flowing script. Last week Sister Bruno had given her three swats of the cane after seeing "Life is hell" scribbled in the margin of her book. Life was not hell, Sister Bruno had insisted. Hell was hell. And where Megan would likely end up if her conduct didn't improve. Sister Bruno said hell was a place of torture but Sister Mary Magdalene said that hell was a sense of perpetual loss, like never being able to see the face of a loved one again. At first Megan had thought that tolerable, but upon consideration it was really much more frightening. What if she never saw her parents again?

She turned the paper over and began to write her parents'

names: Thomas Shelby Hanlon and Irene Hanlon. The sun
poured in through the open window and warmed the back of
her neck. She could hear Sister Claire's elocution class reciting
"Aw to be in England naow that April's there . . ." and Sister
Claire stopping them to say impatiently, "*Oh, oh,* push the lips
forward to make the round vowel!" Hours were spent learning
the round English vowel, expunging any hint of Aussie twang
from the great-great-granddaughters of convicts, publicans,
bushrangers and rebels who'd spat at the name of England.

She enclosed her parents' names with a heart and thought of
last week's movie at the Regal: Vivien Leigh as Anna Karenina,
throwing herself under a train because Count Vronsky had deserted her. But Thomas Shelby would never desert Irene. They
were married and they were Catholics. Besides, they loved each
other. It had been so long since she'd seen them that they'd
become like lovers in a movie, distant but more intensely real,
and certainly more glamorous than anyone she knew. Irene was
beautiful, Thomas Shelby was darkly handsome. Photographs
were proof that this was not something she'd just imagined.
Of course they fought. She could remember them fighting.
And sometimes submerged, ugly memories threatened to sur-
face—of screams and shouts, doors slamming, Irene sobbing
and getting into bed with her. But all exciting couples fought—
look at Spencer Tracy and Katharine Hepburn—and they always made up.

She stopped writing and stared at the inkwell as the questions
and answers droned on. What *was* the nature of free will, she
wondered? You were supposed to be born with it but she didn't
have a hint of it yet. She hadn't been able to give up sweets for
Lent, though she'd vowed she would, and she couldn't stop bit-
ing her fingernails either. Perhaps you got it as you got older,
like the privilege of coming and going as you pleased. But even
adults didn't have free will. Look at Uncle Mick. He couldn't
give up his cigarettes even though he said they were a nasty
habit and cost too much money. And free will wasn't just about
habits. It was more important than that. It meant the power to
make a moral choice, the power to direct your life. If she had
that sort of power she'd choose to go back to America and live
with her mother and father. But probably by the time she had

free will she'd be married, and what good would it do her then? Because then she'd have to do what her husband said. So it might be better never to marry and just have a life of adventure. She twisted a strand of hair, felt it resist the control of her finger and spring back. No matter how much creme rinse she put on her hair she'd never get it to look like Susan Hayward's. But perhaps she wouldn't get to see *My Foolish Heart*. Uncle Mick and Auntie Vi would pile them all into the old pickup and drive up to the property. She would have to go with them. Uncle Mick really wanted to live up there in the bush and only stayed in town so that the children could go to school. And it would be good fun to help clear the mallee, cutting and burning it up in a bonza fire, and to sleep on the veranda in the old iron bed. If it rained . . . She was aware of a cessation of sound and looked up, realizing that she was the center of attention. Sister Bruno must have called on her again. She covered the sheet of paper with a book. "Yes?" Sister Bruno inquired.

"I was . . . thinking."

"And no doubt yer thoughts are of such importance that you should share them with us. Thinking about . . . ?"

"Free will."

"Up. Stand up. And straighten that spine. And share with us, if y' will be so kind"—Bruno's voice was coated with sarcasm—"yer original thoughts on free will."

"How is it possible for us to have free will if God is omniscient? That is, if He knows all and sees all, can even see into the future . . . I don't see that we have much to do with it."

Sister Bruno affected a look of strained patience, as though she were a saleswoman indulging a customer who was returning perfectly good merchandise and claiming it was faulty. "I'll explain it to y' again," she began. "Suppose yer sitting on top of a hill . . ."

"I wish I was sitting on top of a hill," Megan heard Aileen whisper. Aileen had perfected the ability to speak without any apparent movement of her lips—yet another of her remarkable talents. Megan caught her lower lip between her teeth to stop from smiling.

". . . and from yer vantage point, high on the hill, y' see two cars approaching each other from opposite directions. Y' can see that if neither driver turns his wheel they will crash. Each driver is *free* to turn his wheel, but he does not. Yer knowledge of the impending disaster does not prevent it. You, like Almighty God, have the power to see what will happen. Now do y' understand?''

Megan, always quick to turn stories into vivid images, saw the smashed windshield, the buckled metal, the crushed and bleeding bodies. ''But if God is so powerful—omnipotent *and* omniscient—why wouldn't He prevent the crash? Why would He let it happen?''

Sister Bruno was so exasperated with the denseness of Megan's mind that she was beyond so much as a sigh.

''I only meant that . . . ,'' Megan began. But the bell rang. Sister Bruno motioned to her with a crooked finger. ''Megan, y' may clean the blackboard.'' On the face of it this was an act of forgiveness. Most girls liked to clean the blackboard. Megan was not one of them. Once Sister Bruno had heard her say that she hated the feel of chalk, flour, crumbling pages, indeed anything dry. So it was really a punishment; and as Megan walked to the front of the room and Sister Bruno gathered up her books, they shared a quick glance that acknowledged it as such.

''Old Boldface,'' Aileen said, when Sister Bruno had left. Taking up an eraser, she began to help her friend clean the board. Geography was next and she reached up and pulled the string that lowered the map of the world. ''I'll go to Paris on my honeymoon,'' Aileen announced. ''Then we'll sail down the Nile and climb the Himalayas.''

''The Nile isn't anywhere near the Himalayas,'' Megan told her.

''Where do you want to go?''

''Away from here.'' Megan's face felt heavy as a pudding. Her discontent was so enormous that it enveloped the entire continent. Australia was not important. Not famous. It was ''down under.'' Nothing marvelous could ever happen here. And to think she'd lived in Texas (though she couldn't remember it) and in California, too. And her mother and father, and a brother she'd never seen, were *there*, where she'd put a pinhole on the southern California coast because this map was so old that Hollywood wasn't marked on it. It was only a matter of time before her parents rescued her. Only a matter of time before they—how did Irene put it?—"straightened things out." Of course, they'd been straightening things out for years. She couldn't understand how things had become so messed up in the first place. But lately there'd been strong hints, almost amounting to promises, in her mother's letters. Her father hadn't written in years, but then, men weren't supposed to. Women took care of correspondence just as they took care of babies, cooking and washing. She still had the photo of her father. In it he wore plaits, and his bare chest bulged with muscles, and his eyes— oh, he didn't have to kill with an arrow or a spear. His eyes could do it. Her mother hadn't mentioned him for ages, though that—she wiped her chalky hands on her backside—hardly bore thinking about. She would practice her free will by not thinking about it.

The girls moved their desks closer together so that they could share the limited number of atlases. Sister Claire bustled into the room, crossed herself quickly and said, "Aw right, yesterdie we tawked about the Aurora Borealis. Who'll 'ave a go at telling me about that?" When she wasn't teaching elocution, Sister Claire sounded like everybody else. Hands shot up. "Yes, Mona."

"Luminous bands . . ." Mona stopped and started again, getting a good run on it the second time. "Luminous bands of light sometimes appearing in the night sky of the Northern Hemisphere."

"Good girl. Now, Ellen . . ."

Megan's stomach grumbled again. She could smell the Vegemite sandwich in her lunch bag. Only two more classes before lunch: geometry (Aileen was bound to have worked out the theorems), then Sister Mary Magdalene's history class. She could get her teeth into that. The glory of the Greeks (though of course they were pagans), the battle at Thermopylae. (How tragic Magdalene had looked when she'd read the elegiac couplet chiseled on the tomb of the fallen: "Stranger, tell the Spartans that we lie here, obeying their orders.") Just to think of it! Those heroic men, fighting and dying, the great generals, the epic poets, the philosophers who'd laid the foundations of science and medicine, though, Magdalene reminded them, the women didn't have much of a go of it. There were exceptions: Aspasia, Pericles' consort (and didn't "consort" sound so much more intriguing than wife?); but they couldn't hear more about her until they were older.

"Would you like half of my cucumber-and-tomato for half of your Vegemite?" Aileen asked. The rule against swapping lunches was honored in the breach. Megan nodded.

They sat at the far end of the wooden trestles, depriving themselves of the shade of the gum trees. It was the only place where they could have a measure of privacy. The younger girls were like a herd of wild animals, neighing and bellowing, wolfing down fruit and sandwiches, slurping milk, even tossing food about when the nuns who patrolled the periphery of the grounds turned their backs. "What will you wear to the pictures tomorrow?" Aileen asked.

"That old green dress, I suppose. When I wore those jeans my mother sent, word got back to you-know-who." Slacks or jeans were considered immodest, and since even the prefects went to the Saturday pictures, the nuns usually found out about the conduct and dress of their pupils. "And speaking of spies . . ."

Mona was approaching them. She carried a small cardboard box shaped like a native hut. There was a drawing of a black child on it, sitting near the door of the hut, which also served as a slot. "Don't forget these mission boxes are supposed to be turned in on Monday," Mona reminded them. "If our class collects the most money for the missions, we'll get—"

"A dinner of witchty grubs," Megan interrupted.

"I suppose that means you haven't collected any money," Mona sniffed.

"Aw, heaps. I've knocked on every door on our street. I've solicited men outside the pubs and bashed old Mrs. Whitehead into the gutter so's I could nick her pension off her."

"You always have to act the fool, don't you? Just think how humiliated we'll be if the junior girls win the portrait of St. Maria Goretti," Mona said.

Maria Goretti, Virgin and Martyr, was that year's celebrity saint. Holy pictures bearing her likeness had been liberally distributed, and the class that raised the most money for the missions would win a larger reproduction of her portrait. She was an Italian girl who'd submitted to death rather than yield up her virtue. Her attacker had stabbed her several times, but in the holy pictures she appeared unharmed, a lily clasped to the bosom of her pink-and-gold robes, her dark eyes cast heavenward, the trace of a smile turning up her full lips. Looking at the holy card, even Uncle Mick had said she was "a bit of all right," though when Megan told him Maria Goretti's story, he'd said he didn't think it right for the nuns to be filling the girls' heads with a story that more properly belonged in the *Police Gazette*.

"But I don't suppose you care about St. Maria Goretti," Mona continued.

"She does care about her. She's her favorite saint," Aileen insisted, "because she's got red hair, just like Megan's."

"Maria Goretti's hair is *auburn*. Megan's hair is more like the color of a boiled prawn."

Aileen got up, offering her arm to Megan. "Miss Hanlon, shall we take a stroll around the grounds?"

Megan curtsied. "I'd be delighted, Miss Ingpen." As they walked off Aileen said, "Don't worry, I got some money from my father. I'll give you half for your mission box."

"Oh, no. I couldn't. It wouldn't be right."

"What are friends for, Miss Hanlon. What are friends for?"

"Who are those kids over there?" Megan asked, looking at the two dark-haired girls sitting on the bench near the front doors. Their backs were pushed up against the baking bricks. The younger one was chewing on a chunk of homemade bread, the older had an unopened brown paper bag on her lap.

"They're new. Their parents are DPs or something. And they have a funny name that's about fourteen letters long."

"Imagine sitting in the sun in winter uniforms."

"They're Greeks. They don't feel the heat."

"Why would some people feel the heat more than others?"

"It's like natives in Africa. God gave them dark skins because they live closer to the equator."

"But dark colors attract the heat," Megan reasoned, then fell silent as they walked by.

Greta Papandreou lowered her eyes and wished she were invisible. Her ears burned and her skin felt damp and prickly. She'd been so happy when her mother had taken her and her sister to buy the uniforms, even though there'd been some embarrassing moments. Her mother, who couldn't speak much English, had kept insisting on larger sizes and Greta'd had trouble translating "grow into" to the salesgirl. There'd been more confusion when her mother had said they only wanted winter uniforms, but then the salesgirl had understood: she'd smiled as though lack of money had nothing to do with it and said that yes, it was better to be a bit warm in the summer than to shiver through the colder months. Now, after only a week at the school, Greta knew the uniform wasn't the protection she'd hoped it would be. Even if it hadn't been two sizes too large and out of season, she would still have been spotted as a misfit. The other girls had their friends, their secrets and superiorities. She was always afraid that she would do something wrong, that there would be some signal, known to the rest of the tribe but not to her, and she would be exposed, as though she weren't wearing any clothes at all.

When the two girls had passed, she looked after them. They walked arm in arm, like grown-up women sauntering through King's Park on a Sunday afternoon. The skinny one with the untidy red hair was at least a head shorter than her friend, who had thick blond plaits tied with navy taffeta ribbons, and the milky skin and pink cheeks of the coveted English complexion.

"That red-haired girl's father is an American film star," Greta's younger sister, Loukia, told her.

"Don't be stupid. How can he be?"

"He is. Everyone knows it." Loukia stared after them in slack-mouthed fascination.

"Close your mouth when you eat," Greta ordered. She was hungry but didn't want to open her lunch. Their mother had given them all the wrong things: a hunk of bread, a chunk of feta cheese wrapped in newspaper, and a bunch of grapes. She'd noticed that the other girls ate Vegemite, jam or tomato sandwiches wrapped in slick waxed paper. The pretty blonde who'd just walked by had had sandwiches cut into triangular shapes with the crusts trimmed off. She'd looked so dainty eating them. But how could you look dainty if you had to gnaw on half a loaf of bread and a slab of smelly cheese? The grapes were probably all right. She opened the crumpled paper bag and took a few.

"If you're not going to eat your cheese, can I have it?" Loukia asked.

"I said close your mouth when you eat!"

Loukia brought her face close to Greta's and opened her mouth to show a gummy paste of half-masticated bread and cheese. "Aaa-ah."

"You're disgusting! You're acting like a baby. Stop it or I won't sit with you."

"Who will you sit with?" Loukia demanded, knowing a hollow threat when she heard one. But her own fear of abandonment and the approach of a sallow-faced girl caused her to close her mouth and swallow. "Do you want to play Simon Says?" the girl asked. Loukia nodded and ran after her, leaving the remains of her lunch on the bench. Greta wrapped up Loukia's cheese in the newspaper. She knew the sallow-faced girl had only come over to get a look at what they were eating, but Loukia was too dumb to notice that.

She stared up at the sun, then closed her eyes. Great orange and red swirls appeared behind her lids. The swirls, and the heat and shouts from the playground, reminded her of the beach. Last Saturday in the dressing stalls, when she was touching herself down there to wipe sand from between her legs, she'd heard a woman cry out, "Don't do that!" then a man's laugh. Then the woman had laughed, too, as though she really wasn't angry, and Greta's mother had started talking, loudly and quickly, saying she was going to report the man for being in the women's stalls. She'd yelled at Greta to hurry, pushing her out the door before she'd even had a chance to put on her sandals, warning her that she must be very careful at the beach. She needn't have yelled because by then there was only a soft, bumping sound coming from the adjoining booth. Outside there were all those half-naked bodies crowded together, children crying, and lifeguards with their big chests and legs and arms like hams and . . .

"And why aren't y' eating yer lunch?" It was the fat one, Sister Bruno. Greta tried to answer but her throat had dried up. "Don't you know it's a sin to waste food?"

"I don't like . . ."

"Sure, there's nothing wrong with what you've got." Sister Bruno leaned forward but straightened up when the pungent smell of the cheese hit her. "Now come along and take a bite," she ordered. She touched Greta's head for the briefest moment. "Sure, it's all God's food and we must give Him thanks and not waste it."

Greta bit into the cheese and, under Bruno's watchful eye, took a mouthful of bread. Bruno nodded and walked away. But Greta couldn't swallow. She tilted back her head and sniffed so that her tears would go to the back of her throat and help wash the food down. She mustn't cry. Absolutely mustn't. She was too old to cry. But holding back tears was harder than holding back pee. She squeezed her eyes shut. When she opened them the red-headed girl was standing in front of her, frowning. She smiled quickly and offered Greta a Granita biscuit. "Would you like to swap for some of your grapes?" Greta made the transaction with silent gratitude. "Righto, thanks for the grapes."

"Thank you. My name . . ."

But Megan had already run off, pleased that she'd performed an act of charity.

"What time is it?" Megan whispered. Aileen pulled the purple embroidery thread through her doily and turned her wrist so that Megan could see the face of the watch her father had given her for her birthday. A quarter to three. Friday afternoons were interminable, given over to artistic pursuits: penmanship, water colors and, finally, embroidery. Sister Bernadette sat on the dais, reading from *Lives of the Saints* so slowly that she could look at the girls over the tops of her glasses without losing her place. Today, it was Maria Goretti again. Sister Bernadette was talking about Maria's attacker.

"I wonder what he looked like," Megan said, *sotto voce*. Sister Bernadette droned on, "And the shame and contrition with which this sinful man began to comprehend the horror of his act and—"

"Who?"

"Her attacker. I wonder if he was ugly and couldn't get a girlfriend, or if he was really . . ."

Aileen shook her head in warning and bent over her sewing. If they were caught talking again, they'd definitely be separated.

Megan sighed and looked at the bunch of pansies Aileen had almost finished. Aileen had agile fingers and made neat, tiny stitches, so the pansy petals looked like satin. Her own embroidery was an execrable mess. Sister Bernadette said she had hooves instead of hands and her stitches looked as though they'd been made with an upholsterer's needle. A quarter to three. She looked out the window at the yellow blossoms of the wattle tree. Their scent made her drowsy. Only a few more minutes until the bell rang. Then they'd put on their hats and be out in the afternoon sun, marching down the hill to the church for choir practice.

Since Christmas was approaching, they'd sing carols, as well as hymns. Megan loved choir, not only because Sister Ursula appreciated her voice but because Sister Ursula, when conducting, was a show in herself. Normally a soft-spoken, unobtrusive woman, Sister Ursula became transported by music. An off-key note seemed to cause her physical pain. Urging them on to a rousing crescendo, she would wave her arms, tap her foot, strike the music charts with her cane. The Sanctus of the Mass almost sent her into a swoon; her arms floated like feathers in a breeze and her eyes would almost cross with rapture. If there were such a thing as a musical saint, Sister Ursula was it. Ouch! Megan pricked her finger with the needle. A tiny blood spot stained her already grubby doily. She knew she would have to do without sweets when she went to the movies in order to buy Aunt Violet a proper Christmas present. She certainly couldn't give her this.

The bell rang. Megan quickly folded her embroidery. Sister Bernadette lumbered to her feet and started up the aisle. Smiling, Aileen held up her handiwork. But instead of complimenting her, Sister Bernadette said, "Little vanity. Aren't we too proud of ourselves, Miss Ingpen?" Megan felt a flash of resentment. Even when you did things well, you still couldn't gain their respect. Mediocrity, that's what they wanted, Mona's lopsided bluebird or Eleanor's uniform daisies. Aileen's beautiful pansies, like her good looks, put her on a dangerous precipice of Pride, so Sister Bernadette tipped her off.

They marched two abreast down the street toward the church,

past the corner shop, where someone had painted NO AUSSIE SONS BEHIND YANKEE GUNS shortly after the outbreak of the Korean War. It always embarrassed Megan to see that. If her father saw that it would wound him to the quick. It made her feel terrible, too; after all, she was part American.

Father Coffin was standing on the front steps of the rectory. He nodded as they passed. Sister Ursula bent her head even lower and hurried on. On their right was a wild, open paddock, partly hidden by rows of tall hedges. After school, boys from the state school lurked in those hedges and when St. Brigid's girls came by, the boys ran out. They did bicycle tricks, beat their chests like Tarzan, tried to hit birds off the telephone wire with slingshots. If that failed to get attention they yelled, "Catholic dogs, sitting on logs, eating maggots out of frogs" and little girls who'd spent their day learning about Christian charity countered with "Protestants, Protestants, march to hell; while the Catholics ring the bell." Girls of Aileen and Megan's age did not sink to that level. Boys, especially heathen boys who still wore short pants, were beneath contempt.

The vestibule of the church was cool and quiet. There was a lingering smell of incense and rotting flowers, since old McConnell, the caretaker, often forgot to open the doors and left the disposal of flowers to the Ladies' Altar Society. The girls dipped their fingers into the holy water and climbed the stairs to the choir loft. The red panes of the stained-glass window cast a pleasingly rosy glow over Sister Ursula's freckled face and the music charts printed on sheets of butcher paper.

They practiced the carols first, which put everyone into a good mood, then Sister Ursula said they'd played enough and that they must get down to some serious work and perfect the harmony on the Agnus Dei. "We are singing about the Lamb of God, who taketh away the sins of the world," she explained. "Like the Lamb, this is a gentle hymn. It must be sung with reverence. If you cannot find the appropriate reverence in your heart, then don't sing." Since no one wanted to admit she was lacking in reverence, each face was drawn into a simpleminded, dour expression that was the closest approximation that each could imagine. Aileen thought that Mona looked more like a sheep than a lamb, and said as much in Megan's ear. The need to laugh, which became a compulsion in church, seized Megan.

"Megan Hanlon!" Sister Ursula commanded sternly. Megan bit the inside of her cheek and fixed her eyes on the music chart. "Now, one, two and . . . A-a-agnus Dei-i-i-i, open your mouths so that the sound can come out. A-a-agnus. Keep the mouth open, Kathleen." Kathleen O'Hare looked as though she were in a doctor's office, gagging on a tongue depressor. Someone broke wind. Megan was sure it was Eleanor Pujoli because she had such a sanctimonious look. Again her laughter threatened to erupt, but she heard her own voice, high and pure, cresting the note. "Yes," Sister Ursula encouraged, making sweeping motions with her arms and throwing back her head. The pin that held her veil to her wimple had worked itself loose, the veil was slipping off, but Sister Ursula was oblivious. The girls were transfixed, waiting for the movement that would free the veil and reveal that great secret: the color of a nun's hair. Megan, reaching for the high note, stopped abruptly, thinking to warn Sister Ursula of her impending exposure.

"Megan Hanlon!" Her patience at the breaking point, Sister Ursula picked up her cane. Her veil slid back, exposing close-cropped hair. From some of the girls there was an intake of breath. A few kept on singing. Megan was thunderstruck. Sister Ursula, though quite an old woman, had tufts of short, curly hair almost the same color as her own. Her amazed laughter could not be contained.

"Sister, your veil . . ." Mona finished the sentence in dumb-show, scratching at her head like Stan Laurel. But Sister Ursula did not see Mona. She advanced on Megan, eyes flashing, cane raised. The other girls, even Aileen, stepped aside. "Put out your hand," Sister Ursula commanded. Megan did so. The cane slammed down across her outstretched palm. "The other hand." Megan tried to comply but pulled back reflexively. If you did not hold your hand still for the initial blow you got two hits instead of one. Summoning all of her willpower, she held her hand steady. Whap. Whap. Stinging blows. Sister Ursula turned away, reaching for her veil, her own hands trembling. Megan felt all eyes on her. She was rigid with indignation. Suddenly she pushed past the other girls and ran from the choir loft, down the stairs and into the blazing sun.

She ran at full tilt into the open paddock. Her hands were stinging but she hardly noticed that. The humiliation of it! She'd bragged that she would rather be caned and get it over with than suffer the more grinding punishment of being kept after school. But that wasn't true. It was horrible to be hit. And in front of the younger girls, too. Her hat had fallen back and she felt the sun burn her head. The dry grass swished against her stockings. She would ruin her stockings and Auntie Vi would be angry with her, but all she could think of was the urgency of her escape. Being hit like that! And by Sister Ursula, who never caned anybody. Sister Ursula, whom she'd always thought was an ally. When she got home she'd tell Uncle Mick and Auntie Vi and they'd be angry, too. They'd stand up for her. They'd . . . no, they'd ask what she'd done to be punished and they'd decide that she'd probably deserved it. Though they made jokes about the nuns and rarely went to church, they wouldn't back her up. Uncle Mick, who'd been a prisoner of war in New Guinea, would tell her to toughen up, show that she was a battler, tell her that she was as good as anybody and could take anything they could dish out. All right. She had deserved it. She had been rude. She had laughed. But still . . . perhaps it wasn't a good idea to go home.

She stopped running. She looked back at the church, then sat down at the base of a peppercorn tree, staying close to the trunk so that she couldn't be seen, and began to pick the grass and burrs from her stockings. One day she would leave here and no power on earth would be strong enough to bring her back. When she grew up . . . when she grew up, she'd fight all injustice. She'd stop cruelty to animals, and wars and . . . her head was aching. She probably had sunstroke, and she'd faint here in the middle of the paddock, and when they found her, what remorse they'd feel then, what shame at having treated her so badly.

She wiped a hand across her cheek and it came away wet. She was making shameful, soft blubbering sounds that puffed her mouth and made saliva drool down her chin. One day she would have a lover, a marvelous lover, who would horse-whip anyone who dared to utter the slightest slur against her. Someone like her father, only more aristocratic. Someone who would never leave her alone and unprotected. But how would she, so miserable and ugly, ever be able to win such loyalty?

She sniffed back her tears and wiped her nose and eyes on the hem of her uniform. She would have to go back to the church, she supposed. First she would go into the lavatory and wash her face, so that they couldn't tell she'd been crying. And she would take the punishment for laughing and running out of choir with a composure that would cut them all dead. And tonight she would write to her mother and father and pour out all the humiliations of her life, all her unhappiness. She plucked at the weeds. It might be best if she didn't mention her feelings in a letter. She wouldn't want them to think she was a whiner. She would just tell them that she'd come in top of the class in the last exams and wish them a Merry Christmas.

She got up and wrapped her arms around the tree trunk, resting her cheek against the bark and staring at the spire of the church. She wouldn't let any of them, not even Aileen, know how she felt. She would never confide in anyone, not ever again. After all, she didn't really belong here. They were bound to write soon and say they wanted her back, in Hollywood where she really belonged. And one day she wouldn't even need them. She put her hat back on, set her features into the mask of noble indifference Sydney Carton had worn when approaching the guillotine in *A Tale of Two Cities,* and began to walk across the paddock. "I wonder what we'll all be when we grow up," Kathleen O'Hare had mused one day in class, and Sister Bruno had said, "You'll all grow up to be good Catholic women." No doubt they would. Aileen would wear magnolia satin and marry a man who could buy the church another stained-glass window, and that toady Mona would become a nun, and Eleanor Pujoli would be a shopgirl at Meyer's and then have seven children and run the Ladies' Altar Society. But she, Megan, would not be good. Perhaps she would not even be a Catholic. One day, when she grew up, she'd be a poet or an opera singer or a stateswoman, because you didn't have to be beautiful or come from a good family to be any of those things. You just had to have talent and grit and . . . yes, she would show them. Show them all what Megan Hanlon could do.

CHAPTER
ONE

"MEGAN HANLON? WASN'T SHE . . . ?" A BREEZE STIRRED the branches of the jacaranda tree in the convent garden under which Sister Ursula's wheelchair had been parked. She brought the Arts section of the newspaper close to her face, her rheumy eyes blinking against the dappled sunlight. "Megan Hanlon," she muttered again. Her memory was now as sluggish as her circulation. She put the newspaper on her lap, which, despite the heat of the day and the ample protection of her habit, was covered with an afghan, rolled her wheelchair to the flower bed that encircled the statue of the Virgin.

Sister Bruno was rooting out the last of the zinnias, the sleeves of her habit rolled back to expose the fish-white flesh of her arms. "Didn't we have a Megan Hanlon?" Sister Ursula asked. "Ginger hair? Lovely singing voice?" Sister Bruno continued to turn over the soil. Her eyes, magnified by thick lenses, narrowed as she uncovered a large worm. "Megan Hanlon," Sister Ursula tried again. "I believe the Hanlon family made a contribution to the building fund when . . ."

"No, no." Sister Bruno straightened, brows knit with impatience. Her double chin had escaped her wimple and formed a fleshy ruff that looked as though it were choking her. "Megan Hanlon's family never contributed to anything but her tuition, and sometimes we had to send a letter to get that. You're thinking of Eileen Hanlon's family. They were . . ."

The crunch of footsteps on the gravel path caused both women to look around. Sister Mary Magdalene, who, since the liberalization of the Order had chosen to be known by her christened name of Joan, came toward them carrying a tray of scones, tea and barley water. In her print dress and sandals, her chestnut

22

hair trimmed just below her ears, she might have been mistaken for a suburban matron. She set the tray on the wooden table beneath the jacaranda tree and passed her hand over her forehead, which was beaded with perspiration. "Aren't you just sweltering in those . . ." She broke off. She had been one of the sisters who had voted that "civvies" should be optional, understanding that for the older nuns, the physical comfort of discarding the long, black serge habits could never make up for the emotional discomfort of being without them.

"You've made scones. How lovely," Sister Ursula complimented her. She knew that Joan would rather be reading than cooking. "Come, Sister," she urged Bruno, who had bisected the worm with a thwack of the trowel and was patting its halves into separate graves, "do take a rest and enjoy your morning tea. You look quite flushed."

When they had arranged themselves around the table, Sister Ursula asked again, "Didn't we have a Megan Hanlon? Years ago, Joan. When you were first with us."

Joan unfolded her napkin. "So you've seen the article. Yes. That's our Megan. Isn't it wonderful that she's made a name for herself?"

Sister Bruno pulled off her gardening gloves and rolled down her sleeves. "I remember Megan Hanlon only too well. Bold as brass, she was. Always had too much to say for herself."

"She was exceptionally bright," Joan said, and hearing the edge in her voice, added, "At least in history."

"Challenged everything on principle. Always made a shambles of the religious instruction class," Sister Bruno insisted, picking up a scone and inspecting its burned underside. Joan offered the butter but Sister Bruno put up her hand as though she were a policewoman stopping traffic.

Sister Ursula looked from one to the other. Oil and water, that's what Sister Bruno and Sister Magdalene—she meant Joan—were. She'd prayed that something approaching understanding might support the rule of charity to which they were all bound, though if it hadn't happened in all the years Joan and Sister Bruno had lived beneath the same roof, she knew it wasn't likely to happen now. "So," she said, "Megan Hanlon is in films. Imagine that!" She pronounced it "fi-lims" and since her acquaintance with them had stopped around the time of Rudolph Valentino, she pictured a girl in jodhpurs, violently struggling as a leering seducer in a burnoose carried her into a tent.

"She's not a film star," Sister Bruno corrected. "She directs and writes films. She made this documentary that's up for some award."

"Ah, then . . ." Sister Ursula was relieved. Documentaries were the things the education department sent around: instructions on the causes of the Boer War, or how to harvest rice or prevent tooth decay. She wondered, briefly, how Sister Bruno, who complained that newspapers were an intrusion into convent life, had managed to get the jump on her and read the article first. "Yes. Now I remember her quite well. A skinny little thing with frizzy hair. Used to chew her nails. Had an angelic singing voice. She sang the solo in the Angus Dei. But wasn't there some sort of difficulty in the family? I seem to recall . . ."

"Oh, yes. The father was an American serviceman," Sister Bruno said, implying that was difficulty enough. To her mind, the hordes of Americans who'd occupied the country after their defeat in the Philippines were only secondarily concerned with winning World War II; their first objective was despoiling the virtue of Australian girls. "The father," she said, scraping the burned part from her scone, "left the mother, I believe."

"No," Joan corrected. "The mother was Australian and went to live in America, then she sent Megan back here to live with relatives."

"If the girl was sent to live with relatives there must have been trouble in the family," Sister Bruno insisted, making her point.

Sister Ursula squeezed cold fingertips against her palms, took up the paper again and found her place at ". . . beautiful and outspoken writer-director is on the verge of major success." The pouches under her eyes constricted as she scanned the rest of the article. "It doesn't say anything about her family," she said finally. "They don't say if she's married or if she's still a Catholic."

Joan lowered her head and smiled as she poured the tea.

"I believe they say she's a feminist," Sister Bruno put in.

Sister Ursula was confused again. "I never quite know what . . ."

Sister Bruno grunted. "Don't worry. They don't know what it means either."

"And she's nominated for an Academy Award," Joan put in, "for this documentary on runaway girls." Sister Ursula's expression begged further explanation; runaway girls didn't seem to be a likely subject for a documentary. "I do wish I could see it," Joan went on. Sister Ursula nodded dubiously. Joan's graduate work at the university seemed to have increased her appetite for the unpleasant. "And she's made a feature film called *Chappy*. They're going to show it at the film festival. That's why she's coming back to Australia. That and to scout locations for her next film. Well, you read the article. Imagine her making a film here. Yes," Joan concluded, "Megan was very bright."

"But very . . . emotional . . . ," Sister Ursula muttered. She strained to remember some incident . . . Mother of God, what had happened to her memory?

Sister Bruno captured a crumb with a quick flick of her tongue. "Rather more arrogant than bright, I should say. Sure, I had to punish her more than once and I know it did her no harm."

Joan made sure that the glass of barley water was secure in Sister Ursula's grasp, then squeezed some lemon into her own tea. She brought her fingers to her nose, comforting herself with the pungent citrus smell, wondering how many souls had been lost to the Church because of Sister Bruno's heavy hand, exhaustive lectures on purity and elementary grasp of theology. Bog Irish, that was the only description of Sister Bruno. It was a blessing that Bruno had been retired from her teaching responsibilities.

Despite the rule against personal attachments to students, Joan had been very fond of Megan. There was only an eight-year difference in their ages, though the gap between twelve and twenty had been almost as vast as that between nun and pupil. She could still picture Megan lingering in the classroom after the other girls had rushed off to the playing field or the sweet shop, her ink-stained hands gesticulating or patting down her wild hair, her face screwed up quizzically. Megan would usually begin with sly questions about what Joan's life had been like before she'd entered the convent and when Joan, secretly flattered and therefore adamantly unresponsive, tried to shoo her away, the girl would launch into a discussion of what she called her "crisis of faith." Megan had difficulty with the doctrine of papal infallibility: didn't anyone who set themselves up as infallible commit the sin of pride? And how could it be that animals didn't have souls? Surely everything in God's creation had a soul. That, Joan told her, was the pagan belief called pantheism. But, Megan argued, what was the point of trying to get to heaven if there were no dogs or horses there? And another thing: why was Sister Bruno always on about the saints welcoming their martyrdom? Surely there was something a bit off about anyone who wanted to be shot full of arrows or boiled in oil, even if it was for the love of God. And why were there so many interesting books and movies on the forbidden list? And . . . and . . . and . . . Joan would surreptitiously scratch the eczema on her legs and end the discussion by saying that they must pray for the gift of faith, to which Megan would answer, "Does that mean we have to leave our brains at the church door?" Well, it was true that Megan could be cheeky. Had she been a boy, they would have packed her off to the Jesuits.

Looking back on it, Joan could see that she'd been almost as naïve as Megan. She'd been afraid of older nuns like Sister Bruno, even more afraid of her own weaknesses—her terrible temper, the way her mind wandered when she prayed, her suspicion that her eczema was the manifestation of psychological problems rather than the "test from God" the Mother Superior thought it to be. "I had rather hoped," she said, taking up her teacup, "that Megan would become one of us."

Sister Ursula dabbed a drop of barley water from her chin, her fingers lingering on the lone whisker that had appeared a few years ago and whose presence still surprised her. "Yes. I believe she had the beginnings of a vocation. I shall always remember her child's voice reaching for the high C and capturing it with such grace. And"—she nodded in Sister Bruno's direction—"I believe Megan once said she wanted to be a missionary."

Sister Bruno swallowed the last of her scone and reached for another. "No doubt that appealed to her sense of self-dramatization. With that family of hers . . ." She heaved a sigh. "The uncle was an atheist, that I know."

A silence ensued, broken only by a torturously slow rendering of a Chopin waltz coming from the window of the practice room.

Joan's cup rattled against her saucer. Realizing that she was shaking, she put it down and steadied her hand against her cheek, sniffing the lemon on her fingertips and remembering how touched and surprised she had been the day before when Professor Ferzaco (he told her to call him James but she did so only in her mind) had given her the book for her birthday. It was the only birthday gift she'd received for her actual birthday, not her saint's day, since the party for her seventeenth, just before she'd entered the convent. She had no recollection of ever having mentioned the date to him, so he must have looked it up in the university files. She was flattered by his thoughtfulness, even more pleased at his understanding of her taste. The book, *Parallel Lives*, was a study of the marriages of famous Victorian intellectuals, and she'd stayed up, or rather gone to bed with it, reading long after the convent was quiet. And this morning, when she'd heard the first bell, she'd rolled over, found it close to her breast and stared at the inscription (*To Joan from James, with respect and fond regard*) until the second bell had rung. As she'd hurried to dress, her mind kept going back to something he'd said over a year ago, when she'd first attended his history seminars: "Radicals are never satisfied with reforms. Reforms merely unleash the rebellious spirit." He had been talking about the Bolsheviks taking over the Kerensky government, but the remark had taken on a more personal significance. Though outwardly she still conformed, she could no longer deny her rebellious spirit.

After Vatican II, when the Order had become liberalized, even she'd had some trouble accepting the reforms, but very quickly she'd wanted more. She'd liked driving a car again and wearing civilian clothes had pleased her. Either because of the increased sense of freedom or the healing rays of the sun, her eczema had cleared up and she'd noticed that despite lack of exercise she still had a shapely body. She'd been delighted when given permission to attend university. She'd decided it was best if she didn't tell the other students she was a nun, though the more insightful ones might have guessed because of her conservative dress and the fact that she overcompensated for her lack of ease around men by looking them straight in the eye and talking in a businesslike voice. Gradually they came to accept her, borrowed her notes and invited her to the delicatessen around the corner, where she developed a taste for argument and strong black coffee. Often, after class, she wanted to sit on the lawn or linger in the library when she was supposed to be back at the convent. But it wasn't until Professor Ferzaco became her graduate adviser that she became acutely and painfully aware of her dissatisfactions.

On first meeting Professor Ferzaco, she'd thought him an ugly man. He was barrel-chested, somewhat bowlegged and slightly shorter than she. He had bushy eyebrows and a self-possessed, almost arrogant demeanor. When he questioned her in class she was reduced to stammering irrelevancies, even when she knew the answers. Later she realized that they were much alike. Neither of them suffered fools gladly, both were demanding, though she was more likely to fly into a rage with ill-prepared pupils, while he pricked their egos with witty and sarcastic remarks. He'd really gotten her back up with an offhanded remark that "Catholic" and "intellectual" were mutually exclusive terms. But a few days after that he'd called her into his office. He'd poured each of them a glass of sherry (she supposed she was being treated as an equal because they were close in age), and begun to discuss a paper she'd written. A sleepy-looking dog lay under his desk. She'd followed Professor Ferzaco's eyes and lips and gesticulations, then focused on the dog. It came out from under the desk, first nosing her foot, then her hand. It had been a long time since she'd petted a dog. As she stroked its head, a wave of affections and associations swept over her, and she blurted, "I used to have a dog."

"What was his name?"

"Blue. My brother christened him, with the garden hose. He had very black fur, so black that when wet it looked almost blue, so Blue." When she'd first entered the convent, her mother had written to say how Blue had pined for her.

"During the Middle Ages there was a papal letter concerning nuns having pets. Apparently some became so attached to them that they started to bring them to Mass. Must've been distracting—barks at the Sanctus, meows during the Benediction.'' He smiled wickedly. ''So it was put to a stop. Hard on some of the nuns, though. Many of them were little more than girls and, no doubt, terribly lonely.''

She hoped she didn't look lonely. ''But during the Middle Ages many girls were more or less given to the Church by their families,'' she said. ''They didn't have real vocations. Of course, some did choose the convents and abbeys because they were attracted to a life of learning. And in some instances they had as many rights in a convent as they would have had in a marriage.'' She stroked the dog's ear. ''What's this one's name?''

''Belle. Because she's so pretty.''

The dog was a mixed breed of friendly disposition but not particularly pretty. And she'd expected a more literary name—Clarissa, perhaps, or Ophelia. She looked him straight in the eye. ''It's kind of you to say nice things about my paper, but, as you said the other day, it isn't possible to be a Catholic and an intellectual.''

''I am sometimes clever at the expense of truth. What I meant was that accepted belief often destroys curiosity. It puts the mind into a defensive posture. A truly open mind can't be defensive. It's better to discover than to prove.''

She smiled, but knowingly, for hadn't she heard him prove his own theories and beliefs in class? But his criticism was apt. From now on she would discipline herself to approach all subjects with a more open mind. She finished her sherry, thanked him for his time and got up. Belle followed her to the door. ''You should be flattered,'' he told her. ''Belle is an excellent judge of character. She won't come out from under the desk for just anybody.''

She knew it was common for pupils to be attracted to teachers (look at all the girls who'd developed adolescent crushes on her), but what she felt for Professor Ferzaco, for James, was more than that. During the past year he'd become her friend, the first male friend of her adult life. She could talk to him about anything. They shared a similar sense of humor. Sometimes he told her about theater parties or faculty dinners in such detail that she had the vicarious pleasure of being there. She wondered who he took on these outings. She knew he'd been divorced for several years and had grown children. But it was their discussion of books and ideas that she relished most. She loved his mind— could there be anything wrong in loving a man's mind?—and because she loved his mind, she'd stopped thinking of him as ugly. She'd come to crave his presence as she might crave the sun after a long winter. And yesterday, when he'd given her the book, he'd placed his hand on her shoulder. His touch was like his jokes, light but authoritative. It would have been as natural as taking the next breath to have let him take her into his arms. As she'd hurried from his office, mentally rearranging her schedule so that she could get to the book, she'd had a full-blown fantasy: after she'd finished her dissertation, she'd seek a faculty position at the university. That way they would be true colleagues—and she could see him every day. When she got to the parking lot she realized that if Michele, a younger nun whom she had persuaded to take classes, had not been waiting for her, she would have driven straight to the beach.

"Have you left us entirely, Sister?" Sister Bruno wanted to know.

Joan blinked, realizing that she'd closed her eyes. "No, I was just . . ." From the practice room she heard another skirmish of notes, a hesitant retreat, then a vicious new attack on the unyielding keyboard.

"Joan was just closing her eyes," Sister Ursula said. "She probably wishes she could close her ears, too. I know I do." Sister Ursula's head bobbed up and down, insisting on a regular rhythm, then wobbled from side to side in disgust. "That must be little—what's her name? Joyce Kirby? Why is it that the least talented . . ."

"Yes." Sister Bruno pounced on the subject of Megan Hanlon again. "An uncle who was an atheist, a mother who ran off, *and* an American father who was an actor, so . . ."

". . . the least talented girls invariably have parents who insist they take music lessons? And why . . ."

". . . my guess is that Megan Hanlon long ago fell away from the Church and . . ."

". . . is it that we teach Chopin but we can't sing Bach or Handel at Mass? Even though they were Protestants, they were men of God. Their music tells you that.'' It was the great sorrow of Sister Ursula's life that she had never conducted *Messiah*. She pulled on her single chin whisker. ''That Joyce Kirby shouldn't be allowed to touch anything more delicate than a hockey stick.''

''Joyce is an obedient and pious little girl,'' Sister Bruno said. ''We must pray that the Lord will grant her talent.''

''Joyce Kirby can't pray for talent any more than Megan Hanlon could've chosen what sort of family she'd be born into,'' Joan said testily.

''The quiet heart is open to God,'' Sister Ursula replied, reminding them of the Order's rule against unnecessary or argumentative conversation. She handed her glass to Joan and looked up through the branches of the jacaranda. Sister Bruno finished the last scone and took up her rosary beads.

''I'm sorry I burned the scones,'' Joan apologized.

''Sure, it's hard to read and cook at the same time,'' was Sister Bruno's reply.

Sister Ursula gave Sister Bruno a warning then supplicating glance, but Bruno was busy with her beads, appearing not to notice. ''The barley water was so refreshing, Joan,'' she said, but Joan, too, was preoccupied, her head resting on the back of the wicker chair, her grey eyes mere slits as she gazed over the convent wall, her arms wrapped around her bosom as though she was comforting herself. Joan did not look like a potential Mother Superior. She hardly looked like a religious, but Sister Bernadette, the current superior, was scheduled to retire in a scant six months and, to Ursula's mind, Joan was the only one qualified to replace her. Ursula had already been lobbying the other nuns, hoping to insure Joan a unanimous vote. ''In a way,'' Sister Ursula said, trying to strike a positive note, ''I believe we give girls like Megan Hanlon the best sort of preparation for the world. Discipline doesn't hurt the strong ones, you know. They come up against it, and when they kick over the traces they do it with a certain conviction. And many, many return to the Church. Yes. There are worse preparations for life than being a St. Brigid's girl.'' She patted the newspaper. ''You must give this to Michele, Joan. Tell her to put it on the bulletin board.''

Sister Bruno rose and drew on her gardening gloves. Her

expression suggested that she might be having one of her attacks of acute indigestion.

"Yes," Sister Ursula went on, "our girls should know that suffering through their Latin, learning penmanship and embroidery and singing Our Lord's praises in our lovely choir will not prevent them from getting to Hollywood."

Joan patted Sister Ursula's hand. Latin had been dropped two decades ago, ditto embroidery and penmanship, and the choir had never been more than third rate since Sister Ursula's retirement. In her more lucid moments, Ursula was aware of this as well as of the deeper problems facing the school. Enrollment had hit an all-time low, and so few girls were drawn to the religious life that they'd been importing nuns from Ireland and the Philippines. Even so, they were considering hiring lay teachers. The problem was finding the money to pay them. St. Brigid's was barely self-supporting. Sometimes Joan felt that her vocation, indeed her entire life, was a foolish anachronism. She existed in this marshy tributary, away from the tides and tempests of the larger world, watching the girls come and go. Many returned to show wedding photos, or to talk about their first jobs or their travel experiences. A smaller number came to show off their babies, though as the demands of motherhood increased, their visits fell off. There were exceptions, of course. Greta Papandreou, now Burke, visited regularly, bringing flowers or home-baked bread and pastries. But Greta, Joan suspected, came more out of loneliness than loyalty. Her children were almost grown, she was estranged from her own family (who wouldn't be estranged from a sister like Loukia?) and her husband, Tasman Burke, was a famous surgeon who—Joan deduced more from Greta's omissions than her complaints—spent little time at home. It was hard to imagine how a woman so shy and socially ill at ease had managed to attract a famous man, though they had married young. Most likely Greta had never guessed that she would be cast as a celebrity's spouse. It was not an enviable role. Greta's eyes had told her as much.

The few St. Brigid's girls who had made a name for themselves rarely came back, not only because they were occupied with their careers but because, almost to a woman, they had left the Church and had a derisive, often resentful attitude toward the nuns. Joan tried not to take it personally, though some of the more sentimental nuns who thought of their pupils as surrogate daughters were hurt by it. They'd never come to grips with the fact that, the structure of the Church being what it was, they could never outgrow their own position as children. Just last week Father Celebrizzi, he of the psychology books, the earnest smile and cheeks that had only recently become acquainted with a razor, had called her "my daughter." She'd said, with almost flirtatious indignation, "But I'm old enough to be your mother." Since then he'd treated her with curt pomposity, which had made him seem even more immature. James had laughed when she'd told him and said she'd have to watch her step or her bid for the position of Mother Superior might suffer. Then they'd had a discussion about the nature of patriarchy and James had said . . .

"Joan, dear, will you please wheel me back to my room?" Sister Ursula asked. "Listening to Joyce Kirby practice is more penance than I can bear."

Negotiating the wheelchair over the grass, Joan thought again of Megan Hanlon. How she would love to see her and find out how she'd turned out. Perhaps she could write Megan a note in care of the film festival, though it was presumptuous to suppose that Megan would remember her. Or she might explain the situation to James and ask him to go see Megan's film *Chappy*. He could tell her about it, and that would be almost as good as being there herself. Almost.

"Still," Sister Ursula mused as Joan stopped the chair and went to open the door, "there must be great temptations in Hollywood." She raised her voice. "We must remember Megan in our prayers, Sister." She tried to remember—Holy Mother of God, what had happened to her memory?—a disquieting incident involving Megan Hanlon and herself. It was almost within her grasp, then was gone, as though she were a child creeping up on a bird that suddenly flew away. She must pursue it, because she felt as though she'd committed some misdeed and should attain forgiveness, though for the life of her she couldn't imagine what it had been. "And be sure you tape the article securely to the bulletin board." No more needed to be said. They both knew that Sister Bruno, on the excuse of keeping the board neat, removed articles that were not to her liking. "Yes," she muttered again, as Joan held open the door and took hold of the handles of her wheelchair, "there must be great temptations in Hollywood."

"There are temptations everywhere, Sister," Joan said.

It was a stock response, uncharacteristic of Joan, and therefore seemed to hold a deeper meaning. Sister Ursula tried to turn her head to see Joan's expression, but her neck was too stiff. "Upsy-daisy," Joan said as she bounced the wheelchair over the threshold. She laughed. It was a strange laugh, easy and open, but somehow holding a secret. Sister Ursula decided to remember Joan in her prayers, too.

CHAPTER
TWO

TASMAN BURKE LEANED AGAINST THE DOOR FRAME OF the farmhouse bedroom. His wife, Greta, had called him in. She was going through her closet. The blinds had been drawn against the heat and the room was stuffy, smelling of Vicks (their daughter, Chrissie, had a cold) and the bags of dried lavender that Greta put among her underclothes. The whir of the electric fan on the dresser made him feel drowsy. "Well, sit down, won't you," she said over her shoulder. He looked at the bed, rubbed his hands on the seat of his jeans to indicate that he didn't want to get the spread dirty, and crossed to the rocking chair near the window. He disliked the very idea of rocking chairs and had a particular antipathy for this one, since Greta had a habit of sitting in it for long periods of time, her hands in her lap, swaying backwards and forwards while staring out the window. He sat on the very edge of it, stopping its motion, his long legs apart, his elbows on his knees. Greta held up a dress. "What do you think?" He didn't think anything. "Tas?" She held up another dress, "Is this one all right?" Though only dimly aware of how women put themselves together, he knew that neither of the dresses was fashionable. How was it that Greta had never managed to learn such things? She subscribed to all those women's magazines that told you how to make yourself over, and it wasn't as though she couldn't learn new things—she'd mastered keeping the accounts for the farm and he was as likely to find an Indonesian rijstafel on the table as a lamb roast—but when it came to anything having to do with her person . . . "Wear anything you like," he said. "It's only a cocktail party."

"But what do you think they . . . I don't know what they'll be wearing."

The ever-present "they," from a woman who rarely saw anyone but the handyman.

"I wouldn't want to be out of place," she muttered.

Greta's fear of being out of place was so great that she manufactured the most paltry excuses for staying on the farm; her nails were a fright, one of the animals was sick. "Bugger 'em," he said. "They might be wearing rings in their noses for all I care."

"But Mrs. Tishman . . ."

"She won't even know you're there." He tried to stretch his understanding to encompass her anxiety. She wanted to look right, not just for herself, but because of him. "Mrs. Tishman gives these parties," he added more gently, "because she's bloody useless and she wants to see her name in the paper. Now, show us what else you've got."

She carefully replaced the two rejects and pulled out an orange-colored dress she'd bought ages ago, for some christening or wedding. Holding it to her, she moved to the mirror above the dressing table, already shaking her head. He came up behind her, narrowing his field of vision to concentrate on the dress. "I see a lot of women wearing these things with shoulder pads now," he said. But no, that wouldn't be right for Greta. She'd look like an American football player in something like that. He touched her shoulder, pressed harder, seeking the bone. She was not a fleshy woman, but there was a density to her, something he couldn't penetrate, though he supposed that was only because of his inability to get through to her emotionally. Penetration was, he mused, as much emotional as physical, though he'd been too callow to consider that in his younger days. She moved ever so slightly under his touch, turning her head to smile up at him, so that the moment threatened to become tender. That was the last thing he wanted. He stepped back. "Why don't you buy yourself something new?"

"But the party's tonight. I wouldn't have time. I can't get into town before the party."

"Ask for a solution, then tell me why it's impossible!"

She stood dumbly, feeling the power of his exasperation but waiting him out. She was good at waiting him out. She'd waited him out through desertion, infidelity and pleas for divorce. "All right then," he said. "In the future. Go into the city and . . ."

"I dunno. There's always something. And you said that if we're going to hire Edgar full-time we should watch the money."

"Greta." She was stuck in a time warp, proving her devotion through sacrifice. Not that he hadn't been grateful years ago when the money was short, but how could he get it through her head that making do wasn't how he wanted to live anymore? He took her by the elbow and steered her back to the closet with the same concerned impartiality with which he might guide an aged patient into an examining room. "There must be something in there for you to wear. If there isn't, then I don't know what I can do about it. I'm not your parent. I can't dress you."

"Tas, please. I only asked for a minute of your time."

He turned. "I'm going to the stables."

"But Tas . . ."

He turned back. Her face looked as though it were about to come apart. She might have exploded, smashed the mirror, thrown things at him. In a way he wished he could goad her into some fearsome burst of anger. That would have made his own more acceptable. But she only repeated his name, then said, "Don't you want me to come to the party?" as though she was twelve years old.

"Greta. You got the invitation. You accepted it. I said at the time that I'd rather not go. I'd just as soon forget the whole thing." Look me in the face, he commanded her mentally; but her brown eyes were downcast, which produced in him such a combination of annoyance and guilt that he seized upon a practical suggestion. "Why don't you dress up in the best you have and we'll leave here early. We'll stop by the apartment and . . ."

She looked up. She had only been to his apartment in the city a handful of times. It was entirely his domain. Loukia said she was crazy to let him have it (as if it were up to her to *let* Tas have anything). Besides, it was a necessity, close to the hospital while the farm was over two hours away. "But we're supposed to stop and visit your parents on the way in."

"We'll do that some other time." It would be a bonus if he could put off that visit. "You can drop me off. I'll shower and dress while you go shopping. Righto?" He was so accustomed, professionally, to having his suggestions taken as orders that he was out the door before she could agree.

She lowered herself into the rocking chair, holding tight to its arms. If she stayed calm and counted her breaths she would not go over the edge and hyperventilate. Tas said hyperventilating was psychosomatic, his word for crazy. But what did he know? He didn't have nerves; only reflexes. Thank God she wasn't his patient, though he often treated her like one. Slow, easy breaths, like she'd learned in the Lamaze class when Chrissie, her last child, had been born. Easy breaths and keep your mind on something else.

The orange dress lay in a heap on the bed. She might call Loukia and ask to borrow the wine-colored dress Loukia had worn to their parents' anniversary party. Loukia would be only too glad to lend it to her, but through sly questioning Loukia would ferret out information and exaggerate it. Though Greta never confided in her, Loukia was the only one who understood what was going on. Besides, Tas would balk at stopping by Loukia's.

Getting up, she went to the dresser, opened the bottom drawer and found her inhaler, hidden as carefully as a teenager would hide his stash of dope, under her winter nightdresses. She sprayed it into her mouth, holding on to the side of the dresser and looking at the photo of her parents, standing in front of their fish-and-chips shop, proud as though they had been at the door of a mansion. Theirs had been an arranged marriage, her mother selected by relatives in Greece, then shipped over to Australia. As a girl she'd thought it remarkably lucky that they had come to love each other. It was as though they'd bought a ticket in a lottery and, against all odds, had won. But now she understood that the odds had not really been against them. They had built on the foundation of family honor, an unbreakable contract and clearly defined roles. Their love was a mutual compliment for having followed the rules. They had worked hard—her mother in the home, her father in the shop—they had produced children, they had prospered. She had rarely seen them touch, though her father, in a good mood, might give her mother's arm a pinch that bordered on hurtful. Her mother regarded sex as a generally acceptable obligation, rather like fixing a meal because it was dinnertime, not because you, personally, were hungry. Their conversation was confined to the mundane: budgets, food, the gossip of the Greek community. And yet there was love. At nineteen she had not imagined that her own life would be appreciably different, except that she was already passionately in love with Tas and had chosen him of her own free will.

Her parents had carried on something awful when she'd told them she was going to marry Tas. Her mother had wept buckets; her father had hit her. They had already decided that she was to marry her second cousin, Alex, who'd just bought a greengrocer's shop. Alex was squat, good-natured and, on those rare occasions when they embraced, handled Greta with the same caution he used when packing bruisable fruit. He clipped the hair in his nose and conjured future intimacies by telling her that once they were married, she could help him do it. She could never love Alex. "Don't talk to me about love!" her father had roared, backing her into the sideboard and knocking over her mother's best wineglasses. "The truth is you in the family way. In the family way with this Australian university boy you meet in a park. A boy can't support you! You disgrace this house. You get out and don't come back!" But she wasn't pregnant because Tas had given her the pill. She'd stopped taking it as soon as they were married, partly because she thought of contraception as necessary only in an affair, partly because she was miserable in her estrangement from her family and guessed that the appearance of a grandchild would bring her back into the fold. Since a respectable interval of eleven months had elapsed between her marriage and the birth, and since the family had restored their honor and fulfilled their obligations by marrying Loukia to cousin Alex, eventually she was welcomed back.

As Tas started to climb higher in his profession, indeed become famous—something she had never figured in her plans— it seemed that she was justified in going against her parents' wishes. By the time Tas had gone abroad for his research work, her family had not only come to accept him but were puffed with pride, telling her not to complain that she'd been left alone with their two infant sons. A husband going abroad to further the family fortunes was something they understood. They didn't see, would never see, that anything was wrong as long as he paid the bills and the marriage was legally intact. It was only Loukia, compliant but sharp-eyed Loukia, who had been forced to accept Greta's leftover fiancé and had, for years, viewed her with envy, who intuited what was going on. Now, when Greta turned up alone to family gatherings, Loukia smiled with a self-satisfied compassion that said, "For all of it you ended up at home with the kids just like me, but worse off, because none of the men in the family can pull your famous husband into line."

Her head jerked up. Chrissie was standing at the door. Chrissie had been conceived just after Tas had come back from New York, when he'd first asked for a divorce. Tas held her responsible, saying she'd deliberately planned the pregnancy. The truth was that she'd stopped taking the pill during his absence and, being so miserably confused upon his return, had skipped a few days. Or perhaps—this thought had grown during the introspection of the following years, when she'd added psychology books to prayer—she had unconsciously planned it, hoping, with the help of another child, to reweave the fabric of their married life. They had both changed, Tas had insisted. But that wasn't true. Only Tas had changed. He'd come to think that a marriage should be broken if it didn't further an individual's pursuit of happiness. But how could one seek a future that was likely to prove illusory, to give up an intimacy, however flawed, that had taken years to develop? And so she'd held on, accepting his absences, knowing that at least because of the children he would always come back. She had achieved, by act of will, a certain blindness. And the days and nights had added up, hundreds into thousands. That in itself strengthened her belief that the marriage would survive. But recently she'd sensed his renewed restlessness, watched him wipe his hand across his eyes and sigh his shuddering sigh, felt him awake while she feigned sleep. It didn't occur to her that her own misery was reason enough to get a divorce. She'd been shocked when Chrissie had said recently that if she were married to a man like her father she would leave him. Their sons were almost men and had grown up used to Tas being gone. If they noticed the silences, the tensions when he was around, they didn't mention it. Oddly enough, it was Chrissie who was Tas's favorite, perhaps because she so stubbornly rejected his affections. Greta had made every effort to bring the girl up to be independent and speak her mind, but perhaps, having seen what she had seen, Chrissie would always be resistant to a man's affection. Greta couldn't decide if that was a blessing or a curse.

"Mum? Having one of your attacks?"

"I . . ." Greta inhaled deeply, head down.

"You should be setting your hair," Chrissie scolded. "Don't tell me you're not going to go. It's a party, Mum. All those famous people will be there. You'll never get a chance to meet them otherwise. Don't tell me you're not going to the Tishmans'."

"No. I . . ."

"And you can't go with your hair like that. If you sit down I'll roll up the back for you." This from a child who until last year had needed help to get her part straight. Greta pulled Chrissie to her, passed her hand over her hair and, like a monkey mother, picked out a bit of fluff. She'd read a study about how female monkeys who had less status in the group used their offspring as playmates, thereby making the offspring less adaptive. She held Chrissie at arm's length. "I'm all right, luv. You go back to whatever you were doing."

"Don't tell me you're not going."

"No, I . . ." It seemed she must always function at someone else's behest. Now she would put herself through a night of misery rather than show her nine-year-old that she was a coward. "No, Chrissie. I'm going."

Tasman drove along the country road, one hand on the steering wheel of his red Porsche convertible. He liked to drive long distances at high speeds. It gave him a certain balance, freeing his mind for reflection but requiring enough concentration to stop his demons from poking at his conscience. But Greta didn't like the convertible and high speeds made her nervous, so he eased up on the accelerator. Greta sat, hands folded in her lap, looking straight ahead. The pretense that they were both intent on listening to the Debussy she'd put on the tape deck relieved them of the obligation to talk. He was not indifferent to the beauty of the countryside, the fields of sheep, the flocks of Twenty-eights and Rosellas flying overhead, but the pungent smell of bushlands baking in the late-afternoon sun made him feel drowsy. He'd had less than his usual five hours of sleep the night before. Insomniac by nature, and not wanting to go to bed at the same time as Greta, he'd stayed up long after she and the children had gone to bed, reading until after one. But she was still awake when he'd slid in next to her. He knew she was awake though she made no sound and, once his eyes had adjusted to the darkness, he could see that her eyes were closed. Finally he'd dropped off, only to come awake a few hours later. He didn't have to check the clock: he knew that it would be around four-thirty, the hour of the wolf. He'd watched lots of patients give up the fight at that hour, when light began its first struggle against the darkness.

By sunup he was in the stables, mucking out the horses. He'd ridden while Greta and Chrissie had gone off to Mass. His sons, Colin and David, had also ducked that obligation on the excuse that they wanted to help him finish putting up the fencing in the far paddock. His partner, Dr. Herbert Tishman, had gone white around the mouth when he'd found out that Tas did rough work around the farm. "For God's sake, Tasman, drop this country-boy pose," Tishman had fumed. "How can you be crazy enough to engage in that sort of dangerous manual labor? One slip of the buzz saw and there goes the career of one of the most brilliant surgeons in the country." The praise, Tas knew, was a sop to his vanity. Tishman's only concern was with his investment. Tishman had abandoned the practice of medicine for the more lucrative and, to him, more challenging opportunities of entrepreneurship even before he'd left his native South Africa, and was now more comfortable at cocktail parties and in lawyers' offices than he was in an operating room. "He'd probably puke if he saw a used hanky," Tasman thought. Yet the partnership served its purpose. Tishman was the administrator, the fund-raiser, the wheeler-dealer, freeing the rest of the team, with Tasman at the helm, for research. If Tasman had to respect the skill or ethics of his fellow physicians he would have left the profession long ago.

Up ahead, he saw the bright red blossoms of the bottlebrush tree near the petrol station that marked the turnoff to his parents' house. Greta gave him a sidelong glance of what he took to be disapproval. "Right," he said. "I'll give them a call from the city." Greta couldn't possibly guess how visits to his parents' unhinged him. No question that he owed his mum a debt that his gifts of a new lounge suite or a color TV couldn't begin to repay. If it hadn't been for her unshakable belief that he was marked to "make something" of himself, he'd be grinding out a paycheck at the paper mill like his father and grandfather before him, spending his off-hours grousing about the bosses and dreaming of the dubious utopia of a socialist state. Yet the very education his mother had pushed him to get was now an insuperable barrier. His most casual remarks—correcting a piece of misinformation or even stating a preference—were blocked with a defensive "Well, you'd know. *You've* got the education." His father, who since retirement rarely bothered to shave and was never out of his slippers, would be silent in front of the TV. His mother, by way of conversation, would ask his advice about swollen glands, chilblains, dropped wombs, or other problems that beset her neighbors. When he'd tell her that he couldn't diagnose patients without seeing them, Mum would become respectfully silent. Then her silence would turn reproachful. To block his escape she'd put on the kettle and while saying, over and over, "You can't complain," she'd proceed to do just that.

If he was really out of luck one of his brothers or his sister would drop by. They treated him with an uncomfortable combination of awe and mistrust. Though they were all younger than he, they all looked much older. They'd had the usual working-class flare-up of youthful sexiness and then, without any appreciable adult life in between, had passed directly into ashen middle age. Over cups of brackish tea (sausages and onions already on the fry "in case you change your mind about staying"), Mum would talk about his brother Alf, unmarried and now a pulp washer at the mill; his brother Roger, whose wife was now pregnant for the sixth time; his sister, Muriel, divorced for the second time and working as a barmaid; Muriel's son, Jimmy, who had shamed them all by going on the dole and, it was suspected, was on drugs. At the mention of Jimmy, his father would rouse himself from his torpor and state that socialism was never intended to support layabouts, at which point Mum would come, feebly but indignantly, to Jimmy's defense. He couldn't discuss politics, disaffected youth or drug abuse with his parents, and so he would fall into silence, his knee bouncing with caged irritation, and Mum would fret that he was "a case of nerves" and say he worked too hard, not understanding that were it not for his work, he would go entirely bonkers.

One of the few objects that had excited his childhood imagination in that house jammed with bric-a-brac, doilies, crochet work and kitsch, had been a reproduction of a sentimental, turn-of-the-century painting depicting an exhausted doctor sitting by the lamplit bedside of a sick child. His mother, who'd had two miscarriages before she'd brought him to term, would look at the picture, misty-eyed, and say, "If it weren't for Dr. Davis, you wouldn't be alive today." Even before he'd grown up he'd suspected that Dr. Davis's expertise consisted of little more than firm and mildly flirtatious orders that his mother keep off her feet and avoid lifting heavy objects. But the vision had implanted itself: "There is no finer calling for a man than to be a country doctor." Which is what he'd set out to be.

After receiving his degree, he'd been offered a residency in Edinburgh. He'd accepted, but because of his work load and the meagre stipend, Greta and their two baby boys had stayed behind. It was his first time out of Western Australia, and he'd felt like a raw-boned colonial. Colonial or no, he'd proved himself enough to be offered a plum: a research grant at Sloan-Kettering in New York. Fearful of living in a fast-paced, expensive and dangerous city, Greta had again stayed behind in Australia. Had that been the fateful crossroads in the marriage? But how could he have settled for treating earaches and flu once he'd been told by men with international reputations that he had the talent to be world-class? In New York, even while his advisers told him to expand his horizons to fit his talents (while putting their names at the top of his research papers) and when his contemporaries took off for the really big money in Houston or Atlanta, he'd still thought of himself as a working-class Aussie preparing to minister to the needs of his own. It wasn't until he'd come back that he'd realized that they weren't his own anymore. Meeting with old friends had made him feel lonely and separate. Nothing they said related to life as he had come to know it. The alienation was most severe with his family. And with Greta. He still felt a deep love for the bushlands of his boyhood—indeed, the land

itself was the only thing with which he still felt a connection—
so they'd bought the farm. A hundred acres. Small by Australian
standards, but still large for his income. He'd set up a practice
in Perth. Now, after a decade of struggle, the money was rolling
in. He had his Porsche, he was starting to raise racehorses on
the farm, both his practice and his research were going well.
His personal life, as the saying went, "didn't bear thinking
about." And surely he'd done enough thinking, especially on
these long drives. Soon he would have to make a decisive move.
A move that . . .

"Shall I change the tape, Tas?"

He hadn't even noticed that it had finished. He grunted assent.
They crested a hill and came into the valley, seeing the miles of
vineyards and the bottling plant of Golden West Cellars belong-
ing to the Mastroiani family. A dilapidated house, where old
Mrs. Mastroiani (always referred to as "that Dago woman" by
his relatives) still dispensed free glasses of wine, was all that
remained of his boyhood. They came into the country town. Its
streets were as deserted as the scene that precedes the gunfight
in a cowboy movie. But there would be no fights here, unless
you counted the domestic violence. Most of the men would be
off, getting into a dirty big booze-up before the work week
started again. The wives who could assert themselves enough to
get out of the house would be with their women friends at the
meeting hall/movie house, watching Meryl Streep or Robert
Redford. Young lovers would be sealing their fate in the back-
seats of cars. He realized that he'd skipped lunch and was hungry. But this was a union town. Nothing would be open now,
except the Chinaman's. The Wong family had been there for as
long as he could remember, but had not assimilated to the point
where local rules and customs applied. Young Jimmy Wong now
operated a chain of carry-outs in the city, but the elder Wongs
still sold a concoction of overcooked vegetables and stringy beef,
served—with a nod to local tastes—with chips. As a boy, any
restaurant had been special, a place for toffs. But he had tasted
the cuisine of several continents. He would rather go without if
he couldn't have what he wanted—an attitude that, much to his
surprise, also applied to sex. He hadn't touched Greta for

months. That, too, she'd pretended not to notice. She must see . . .

The first traffic light, a pub of high Victorian design the only relic of the past amid auto dealerships, American fast-food transplants, convenience stores, then mile after mile of uniform brick houses, each with its requisite garage and rose bush. Another clot of shops. They were into it now—the suburban sprawl. Bloody hell, all Australia was turning into a soulless, middle-class suburb. It was a relief to crest the hill and see the Perth skyline.

"It always surprises me," Greta said, and he nodded, knowing what she meant. The rapid growth of the city amazed him as much as the developments in his own life. In a mere twenty years it had thrust upward, sprawled outward, gained freeways, a stadium, a Japanese-owned twenty-four-hour casino, an art museum, international restaurants. It had millionaires, entrepreneurs, real estate moguls and tourists. The first high-rise hotel had gone up on North Beach, albeit after some feeble protests from the locals. A streak of cynical conformity had developed in the national character during the convict days. Aussies weren't much good at protest.

He was well and truly tired when they reached his apartment in Nedlands. He pulled up to the curb, handed Greta the keys, and, knowing how much she feared driving the Porsche, gave her shoulder a reassuring pat. "Spend as much as you like; take as long as you like," he told her. If they got to the party late, so much the better. He watched her drive off, then took the elevator to his flat on the fifth floor.

He took off his shoes, listened to his answering machine and called the hospital. The refrigerator held some Camembert, a half-dozen eggs, wilted lettuce and several bottles of wine. He poured a glass, bit into the Camembert, and walked to the enclosed balcony. It was glass from floor to ceiling, empty except for a scattering of books on the beige carpet. Through the glass he could see the Swan River. People below could also see him. He retreated, reminding himself to speak to his secretary about ordering draperies. But in truth he liked the couch, bed, bookcases and single Steinberg drawing of the Manhattan skyline. This was the student/bachelor apartment he'd never had, its spareness a relaxing contrast to the clutter of his parents' home or the farmhouse. Greta couldn't bring herself to throw anything out. Just this morning, rummaging through the back room, he'd come across a baby crib. He shook his head, downed the wine and went into the bathroom.

Toweling himself after the shower, he noticed a few more grey hairs on his chest. Naomi always teased him about the grey hairs. He wanted to call her now, but that was out of the question. With something akin to disgust (because he always said that tranquilizers were for neurotic housewives), he tipped two Valiums into his palm. He stretched out on the couch, waiting for the pills to take effect, glancing at the pile of unread newspapers. The headline proclaimed, ''City ready for first major film festival.'' He could imagine Mrs. Tishman, who'd gotten herself up in nautical gear for the America's Cup, preening her culture-vulture feathers and getting ready to swoop on her celebrity prey. He assumed the film crowd at the party would be the same self-serving, posturing windbags he'd met some ten years ago in New York, when Megan Hanlon had dragged him to previews and parties. He wondered if Megan had prospered. There was no doubt that she'd survived. Strange, he hadn't thought of her in ages, and yet only a few days ago . . .

He'd been about to leave the ward when a young nurse had called, ''Doctor Burke!'' as though issuing a challenge. She'd appeared Amazonian as she'd strode toward him, but as she'd reached his side he'd seen that she barely came up to his shoulder. He'd braced himself, thinking she was about to reprimand him, however subtly, for not spending more time with a dying patient's relatives. He couldn't and wouldn't explain that he was simply no good at that sort of thing. He did what he did and did it well, but his attempts at sympathy were always bungling and could, in the long run, make the family feel worse. Christ, how he hated to lose a patient! He'd put on his cool but impatient face, but, as it turned out, the nurse had only wanted to ask a question about medication. Then, she had whispered that she was sorry about the patient, though, of course he'd done everything he could do. Yet it was the initial challenge in her voice, and his misperception of her size that had reminded him of Megan. Once, at a party, a man had referred to Megan as petite, and Tas had laughed out loud. Megan might be five foot two, but she could never be thought of as petite. As he closed his eyes, he was amazed at the number of things he remembered about her.

He had met her at Sloan-Kettering a few months after he'd set up his research lab. Arriving at the hospital one morning, he'd been informed that a fund-raising commercial was to be shot on his floor. He'd watched from his lab door as the film crew had swarmed into the corridor. There were so many of them that he had trouble figuring out who was doing what. Long periods of seeming chaos were followed by even longer periods of boredom as lights were set, tape was put on the floor, cameras were positioned and a hairdresser and makeup man fussed around an actor in a lab coat. Tas's attention was caught by the redhead in dungarees who walked about whispering to people. He went back to work. Coming out of his lab hours later, he found coils of cable obstructing his door. A man asked what the hell he was doing on the set and he explained that "the set" was next to his lab and that they'd blocked his door. The redhead swung around, told the man to shift the cable and said, "You sound like an Aussie. Where from?" He said Western Australia. "I am, too. Sort of." She'd extended her hand, smiled and said, "I'd like to talk later—but just now, try to stay out of the way, will you, luv?" As she walked off, the man rolling up the cable said, none too happily, "You'd better do what she says. She's the director." At wrap-up he'd invited her into his lab.

If his profession was titillating to most women and, in America, such a status symbol that it insured something close to adoration, Megan was not impressed. She asked intelligent questions, listened intently, but simply shook her head and said, "Poor damned dogs," when he told her about the animal experiments. She suggested a Szechwan restaurant in the neighborhood, a place he'd walked by daily without noticing. She told him the best things to order and asked more questions about Australia: What was happening there politically? Had he seen the wonderful new films that were coming out of Australia? He said he didn't have time for politics or movies, and asked about her work. Her goal was feature films, but now she was directing anything that came her way. She was trying to raise money for a documentary about midwives. Did he know that midwives had been driven from the medical profession around the turn of the century when the male establishment had decided to tighten its control? He must've looked a bit bored, because she asked what he was thinking. "Work," he'd replied, and she laughed. "Not to worry. My mind's always wandering back to the project at hand. When I'm working I'm rarely one-hundred-percent attentive to anybody." It put him at ease to hear that. One of the reasons it was a relief to be away from Greta was that she took it personally when his mind wandered. "I suppose," Megan said, dipping her finger into the hot sauce and applying it thoughtfully to her tongue, "that surgeons have to be obsessive and full of ego. How else could you cut?" No one had ever said anything like that to him before. He wanted to tell her to bugger off; instead, he asked to see her the following Sunday.

It was a blustery, threatening-to-snow day. They met outside the Plaza, had an outrageously expensive drink in the Oak Room and started off walking through Central Park. Megan was bundled in stylish but shape-disguising clothes. She wore a scarlet scarf around her throat. The tip of her nose was red and cold, her hair so thick and springy that the wind barely ruffled it. From certain angles her face was too sharp to be pretty, but its range of expression made it attractive. She swore a lot. He had never liked to hear a woman swear. She even whistled when she walked, reminding him of his father's rhyme, "A whistling woman and a crowing hen, is not fit for God or men." But her eyes were green and when she laughed, often at him, the word "infectious" took on a positive meaning.

She was eager to show him her adopted city and he felt New York open to him. They stopped to listen to some street musicians near the Fifth Avenue entrance, paused again near the pond to hear a lone bagpiper, his chafed knees sticking out from his kilt; and near the Central Park West entrance they sat on a bench to hear a black jazz combo, too zonked to feel the cold, sending remarkable spirals of sound into the chilly air. The sun broke. Megan, shedding her coat, said, "I wonder if there are any hyacinths out yet? You know the Russian saying, 'If I have two kopeks, with one I will buy bread for my body; with the other I will buy hyacinths for my soul.' " But it was too early for hyacinths. Instead, Megan bought a book of Rubens nudes from a peddler who had lined the pavement with his wares. "All that flesh," she said with enthusiasm, showing him a reproduction of a recumbent beauty. He didn't bother to say that his tastes lay elsewhere, that the blue veins in Megan's wrists made him imagine the larger veins of her inner thigh. She then bought a homemade potholder (he couldn't imagine she had any use for a potholder) from a woman who looked like a bag lady, engaging the old woman in a long conversation. He marveled, and was even a bit envious, of her ease in talking to strangers. She suggested hot dogs. He said he wasn't hungry. But by the time she walked back from the cart and presented him with the steaming sauerkraut, mustard and sausage, he was salivating.

They stopped for Irish coffee at a book-lined bar called the Library. A string quartet provided an artsy atmosphere for melancholy afternoon drinkers. Megan gave her opinions about everything from the prospects for peace in the Middle East to where he might buy the best bagels. He half listened and felt extremely happy. His life had been spent going from laboratory to apartment and back again, and now this leprechaun, this silkie, had lifted the shades. She mentioned that she was divorced. He said that he was separated and with only a flicker of guilt, let her assume that he meant the dissolution of his marriage rather than merely a geographical separation.

They ended up at St. John the Divine, a must, Megan said, in any architectural tour of Manhattan. The choir was rehearsing, so they sat in the back of the church to listen. Her features softened, becoming contemplative and sad. He had never seen a woman so desirable.

As they were leaving the church, Megan fumbled with her collapsible umbrella. He reached around her to help. The smell of wet wool and almond shampoo hit his nostrils. His mouth sought the nape of her neck and lingered. She stayed absolutely still, so that it was impossible for him to read her response. Then she turned, slowly, the whiteness of her neck in sharp contrast to her scarlet scarf, her eyes both appraising and promising. "You know," she said offhandedly, "I've never had one of my countrymen."

His own voice came out casual but hoarse. "Shall we give it a go?"

She nodded once, gravely, then laughed to herself, pushed open the heavy door and started down the steps without bothering with the umbrella.

He couldn't remember the cab ride to her SoHo loft, but he could still picture her, undoing the three locks on the door, moving ahead of him, already taking off her jacket, pulling her sweater over her head, unzipping her skirt and stepping out of it without seeming to lose the stride that took her to the big, unmade bed. "Good, the bastard landlord turned on the heat," she said. The radiator hissed a tropical warmth. He could feel himself sweating as he struggled out of pants and shoes, but outside the window the snow fell against a darkening sky, like the flickering on a TV screen before the show starts. Her breasts were so small that they didn't move as she bent forward to unzip her boots, but there was nothing girlish about her hips and thighs, or the glitter in her eye as she swept back her hair to look up at him. He took hold of her and they came together with a fierce sweetness—she still with one boot on.

Afterward, as they lay panting in the heat, he was stunned at the ease of it all. He had not had to cajole, promise or seduce—not that he had the experience or disposition to do any of those things. She had simply made love with him because she'd made up her mind to do so. Marvelous. Extraordinary. It had only lately occurred to him that such things did happen in real life, and that they might happen to him. He hadn't realized until recently that women found him sexy, and he'd attributed that, at least in part, to his profession. A sad commentary when you thought about it—something to do with women not believing that they had power over their own bodies, so a poke and a probe from an examining doctor made them pliant, almost pathetic in their trust. But Megan wasn't like that. She'd opened of her own free will. "You look a bit dazed," she teased, smoothing his hair back, nibbling on his shoulder. He was. But she felt so small and slick and pungently inviting that his desire renewed itself. He took her again, more slowly, more acutely tuned to her rhythms. They slid off the bed and onto the floor. As he subsided, she smiled down at him, her eyes liquid with satisfaction, and picked a bit of carpet fluff from his hair. "I'm not much of a housekeeper. Can't eat off these floors. Shouldn't even be lying on them. Chinese? Japanese? Italian?" He was so foggy with contentment, so besotted, that he didn't take her meaning until she explained, "We'll have something delivered. Aren't you starving? I am." He was, but as she lifted herself from him, stretched and started to move away, he seized her ankle, pulling her back down.

"Sore," she muttered later, when they'd regained the bed. She rolled away from him, curling up with the pillow between her legs. He wasn't sure if this was a tribute to his virility or a clue that she didn't do this sort of thing often. Both, he hoped, as he dropped into a deep and dreamless sleep.

He woke as the first light came through the window, her hair tickling his chin. She turned, gave him a drowsy and friendly "Hello, you," then slipped from his arms, threw off the covers, stood for the briefest moment, shivering and cursing the lack of heat. She said, "I'm first in the shower," and disappeared with the swiftness of an apparition. In a state of confused arousal, he pulled on his shorts and shirt and found the kitchen. Damn it, it was cold. As he searched for the kettle in the wintry light, the weight of his infidelity hit him. Pure lust, sexual exercise, understandable physical release, he told himself. Nothing emotional about it. But there *was* something emotional in giving and getting so freely, so completely. Passion without illusions or promises. But no. He heard the pelting water from the shower. He would not join her under the spray or wait till she emerged, dewy and tempting. He stirred the boiling water into the instant coffee—damn sure she wasn't going to fix breakfast—then left the cups standing. As he dressed he took in the chaos of the apartment. No, she certainly wasn't any housekeeper. He wouldn't call her again and, bold as she was, he knew she wouldn't call him. And yet . . .

They had given it a go for almost a year. He'd confessed early on that he planned to return to his wife. Megan said fine; she had no long-term designs on him or any other man. The best that could be said of her was that she was never boring. He tried to remember who had said good-bye and how. The why had always been a foregone conclusion.

* * *

He started up at the ringing of the apartment buzzer. Wrapping the bath towel more tightly, he went to the door. Greta stood before him. "Sorry," he said. "I must've dropped off." There were no packages in her arms and she was still wearing the orange dress. "You didn't . . ."

"No. I couldn't find a thing," she lied. In truth she'd only driven to Queen's Park, where she'd sat on a bench and watched the swans until the light had faded.

"Right. I'll be ready in a tick."

CHAPTER
THREE

"I CAN'T BELIEVE I'M HERE," MEGAN SAID, NOT FOR THE first time, as the taxi neared downtown Perth. "The light—isn't the quality of light different?"

Toni, Megan's assistant, stifled a yawn. "Yeah, I guess it is." New York, L.A., Sydney and now Perth. Her brain was as numb as her backside and she could barely keep her eyes open, let alone perceive a difference in the quality of light. "It kinda reminds me of what southern California was like twenty-five years ago."

"Why do Americans filter everything through their own experience?" Megan demanded. "It's not southern California, it's Perth!"

"I meant the quiet and the greenery and the clean streets. And the heat." She shifted the bundle of sweaters and coats they'd discarded on the trip, and loosened the collar of her blouse. "This kinda heat, in April."

"Mmmm. I remember having picnics at the beach at Christmas and . . . oh, there's the Swan River." Megan rolled the window down farther, took a deep breath, then turned, anxiety forming a crease between her brows. "The screenplay. Are the extra copies in your suitcase or in mine?"

"One in your suitcase, one in mind and"—Toni patted a carry-on bag—"one in here in case the luggage got lost." Megan was to attend screenings, socialize and meet with money people, most notably Dennis Danher, while Toni investigated the nuts and bolts of overseas production, talked with union reps, a tax man and a lawyer.

"I'll bet Danher hasn't even read it."

"So what? You have a meeting set up with him. You'll talk it to him. You'll wow him."

"And if I don't? You wanna work without a paycheck like you did two years ago?"

Toni sighed. When they'd first met she'd thought that Megan, like the goddess Athena, had sprung full-grown from the head of Zeus, but over the years she'd learned that Megan's spurts of high energy often preceded a slide into depression and doubt. "Hey, you remember the old Mae West joke?"

"No, but I think I'm about to hear it."

"Well, Mae runs into an old friend and the friend sees that Mae is looking pretty fancy, so she says, 'Did you meet a man with a million dollars?' and Mae says, 'No, but I met a million men with a dollar.' "

Megan laughed. Toni was the perfect woman to deliver a Mae West joke. She was heavy-breasted, wide-hipped and had a gravelly voice. Earthy was the word, though Megan wouldn't have used it because Toni was self-conscious about her weight. As a young woman Toni must've been the quintessential Italian bombshell. Even now she was handsome, her olive skin virtually unlined and moist-looking around the eyes, her cropped hair streaked with grey. Toni's easygoing manner belied the fact that she had an elephantine memory and could figure a production budget down to the penny. Megan, quite literally, couldn't imagine how she'd ever functioned without her. But Toni lacked confidence, let alone vanity. She didn't think of herself as attractive, consequently few others did; whereas Megan had learned years ago that if you projected confidence it passed for glamour, which in turn could pass for beauty. "This is it," she said as the taxi pulled up to the hotel.

The lobby had already been taken over by the film crowd. It looked like a party where everyone knew one another (which they didn't) and loved one another (which they most certainly didn't). Megan was greeted and kissed by a writer friend from L.A. almost as soon as they entered. Toni skirted them and made for the registration desk, looking back to see Megan listening and nodding intently. The ability to give undivided attention to anyone she was listening to, and to draw them out, was one of the things that made Megan such a fine director. People told her their secrets, then ended up telling them to the camera.

Toni was signing the registration forms when Megan came and whispered, "Sorry, I got waylaid."

"Aren't you Megan Hanlon?" a man asked. Megan flashed a smile and offered her hand as he introduced himself as a host from the festival. Toni collected their keys.

"Where's Megan Hanlon?" Toni turned to stare at a woman who was all teeth, space-age jewelry and hair that could only be described as maroon.

"I don't know. She was here just a second ago . . ." Toni craned her neck, but Megan had been sucked into the crowd. "Could I help you? I'm Toni Massari, Ms. Hanlon's assistant."

"And I'm Merle Jaunders," the woman said with a miffed egoism that implied Toni should have known that already. "I'm a feature writer for *Lulu* magazine." She handed Toni her card while scanning the crowd. "I also have a daily column in—"

"Ah, yes." Toni faked recognition. You couldn't afford to let any media fish get out of the net. It was a game played with mirrors: if you acted enthusiastic and said your movie was going to happen, then you generated excitement, which, in turn, might generate money. "Well, I'm sure Megan would love to talk to you. She's not just here to screen *Chappy* . . . wonderful movie . . . the latest feature she's written and directed . . ." (Actually the first feature she'd written and directed.) ". . . she's also here to scout locations for her next."

"What's it about?" Jaunders asked, her attention momentarily galvanized by a new arrival.

Toni talked fast. "A love story set in the 1790s and based on fact. A lieutenant who came over with the First Fleet, thought all convict women were trash, and ended up falling in love with one of them. Their affair is the core of the film, but Megan wants to open it up, to show the experience of convict women, how they were doubly damned because they were treated like whores, the fact that they were out-numbered by the men seven to one."

Merle leered. "I wouldn't mind that ratio."

"But they were practically sold off the ships." She sounded almost as impassioned as Megan did when she talked about it. "They were flogged and—"

"Oh, a little S&M, too?"

Okay. This bimbo's taste was probably confined to porno flicks. Toni shifted gears. "Now that Megan's up for an Oscar for Best Documentary—"

"Ah, yes. What's it called?"

"*On the Streets*. It's—"

"Yes. I'm sure it's marvelous. But tell me a little something about Miss Hanlon's personal life. Is she married?"

"Divorced." Megan's youthful marriage was a subject about which she rarely spoke, even to Toni, though she could have gotten a lot of mileage out of it. Her ex, Victor Taub, was now one of the most powerful producers in Hollywood, but Megan had nothing but contempt for him. He'd made his reputation in horror/sleaze movies (*Gory Saturdays*, *Teen Coven I* and *II*) and his most recent film, *Deadly Desire*, was both a box-office and—to Megan's disgust—even a critical success. "It isn't easy for a woman director, even one with a track record, to get major financing," Toni rushed on, "but her new screenplay is really fine, and she has meetings scheduled with Dennis Danher and—"

Merle stopped rubbernecking and looked at her for the first time. "And Danher's interested? The project sounds a little too artsy for Mr. Danher."

Toni smiled mysteriously. "A high-quality script may be just the thing he's looking to put his name on. He's been criticized a lot lately." Toni opened her hands to the host of things Danher had been criticized for: union busting, shady takeovers, playing to the lowest common denominator in his publications.

Merle played with her jewelry and gave Toni a condescending look. "Dennis Danher's my boss. In fact, I know him personally." She made it sound as though she were still damp from taking a shower with him.

Strikeout. Big smile. "Well, I have your card, Miss Jaunders, and I'm sure that Megan will want to meet you. But we've just come off a very long flight, so if you'll excuse . . ." But Merle, frantically waving, had already plunged into the crowd.

Toni finished registering, got the keys and a stack of mail that had been left for Megan, and turned to see her. "Sorry again,"

Megan said. "Hey, come on up to my room while we wait for the luggage."

Megan unlocked the door to her hotel room, already pulling out her blouse, unzipping her jeans and ducking into the bathroom while Toni trailed after her. "That fellow who's the host from the festival is very pleasant," she called out. She and Toni had reached the degree of intimacy that allowed them to have conversations through partially opened bathroom doors. "He was telling me that . . ."

Toni started to the window but stopped, noticing a bouquet of long-stemmed roses on the dresser. "Hey, wait'll you see this. A beautiful bunch of roses." She reached into them and took the card. " 'Welcome home. With fond memories . . .' " She put the card on the dresser. "Sorry, I think this is personal."

"No. Go on. Read it." Megan came out and sat on the bed, unzipping her boots.

" 'With fond memories.' And it's signed 'your constant admirer.' I wonder who . . . ?"

Megan took the card. The handwriting looked strangely familiar. "I can't imagine. There's only one possibility . . ." Her smile was sardonic.

"The Aussie doctor?" Toni tracked Megan's affairs as only a long-married woman would. "I'll bet it's from him. He must've read about you in the papers. Do you suppose he finally got a divorce?"

"I couldn't guess. But roses and 'constant admirer' wouldn't be his style."

"People change."

"Not men. Not in my experience. Ah, Tas. Tasman Burke." She was absolutely still for a moment, then she drew in a breath, shrugged and picked up her pile of messages. Toni couldn't tell if she really didn't care or was feigning indifference. After all these years with Megan it was still hard to tell.

"But men do change," Toni persisted, laughing. "Joe used to send me flowers and now he doesn't. Oh, Megan, you should've seen his face when he drove me to the airport. You would've thought I was leaving him alone in the emergency ward."

"Yeah, well . . ." Megan said no more. In her opinion Toni's husband, Joe, was a jerk, but she'd learned that it was best not to agree too readily with criticisms of lovers, husbands or relatives. She sprawled in a chair and began reading. "Here's a schedule change from the film festival . . ." She folded it into an airplane and sailed it across the room. "And a note reminding me that I'm a panelist at a seminar . . ." She placed it on the floor and tore open an envelope. "And an embossed invitation: 'Dr. and Mrs. Herbert Tishman request the honor of your presence at a buffet reception . . .' Let's see, that's tonight. I don't suppose . . ."

"Are you crazy? My feet have swollen to a size twelve. I don't know what day it is. It's a hot bath and ten hours' sleepy-bye for me. And for you, too, if you have any sense. Which you don't. Besides, you don't have to accept just any old invitation anymore. You're a celebrity."

Megan snorted and stuffed the invitation into her jacket pocket. "Big deal. Anyone can be a celebrity for a few months nowadays. Crooked TV evangelists, politicians' discarded mistresses, mass murderers—they're all celebrities."

"Do you know how many people envy you? You're up for an Oscar, for God's sake."

"Tell me, darling." Megan affected the smarmy but harsh voice one could hear at any preview or soirée. "Who won the Oscar for Best Documentary last year?" And when Toni was stuck for the answer, "I think I've made my point, sister."

"But you've got *Chappy* coming out."

"And if it's not successful? I'll have about as much chance of raising ten million bucks as a panhandler in Times Square. Half the people who know me will forget my name." She headed for the little refrigerator. "Hey, I'm going to fix us a drink."

Here we go, Toni thought. The slippery slide into self-doubt. Next, Megan would deny her talent and obliterate all her years of struggle and attribute her success to "luck," a sentiment with which the envious would all too readily agree. Over the last year she'd watched them come out of the woodwork—the opportunists and hangers-on who hoped Megan would provide them with a job, an introduction, or at least the chance to drop her name, and Megan, fiercely egalitarian, afraid to appear the snob, was an easy mark despite her tough exterior. "But what about this?" Toni dug into the carry-on bag and pulled out a handful of clippings. "This article says you're *the* young woman director to watch."

Megan dropped ice into the glasses. "*Young* director? Ah, yeah. That was the writer who said I was thirty-two."

"A confusion, if memory serves, that you abetted."

"You bet. Beats the one that says I'm aggressive and demanding."

"Sloppy choice of words. I'm sure he meant to say you were assertive and professional." They laughed as they clinked glasses.

"My fav," Megan said, taking a sip of her Scotch, "was the one that said I was from a family of wealthy sheep ranchers. Shit, no one can talk about Australia without mentioning sheep, koala bears or surfing. And my family rich!"

"It's good copy. Must have something to do with declining values. People would rather think you were born with it than that you earned it."

"Naw, the best, the very best," Megan said derisively, stuffing the clippings back into the bag, "is the one that says I'm pursued by a cavalry of rich and important men."

"Now that's based on fact," Toni said with mock seriousness, " 'cause didn't you tell me that Sam Alhauser tried to grab your tit in his limo once?" Sam was the seventy-four-year-old producer of *On the Streets*.

"That he did." Megan rolled her eyes. "That he did. He knew there should be something to grab around the area of my ribcage. But given the size of the goods and Sam's having had three glasses of champagne, he ended up in my armpit."

"But darlink," Toni imitated Sam's Yiddish accent, "didn't I call the next day to apologize and say I thought of you as a daughter?"

"Actually, he was still so hung over that he said he thought of me as a son."

As Toni began to laugh, her mouth stretched into a yawn so wide her hand couldn't cover it. "Hey, if the world wants to believe that you're a swinger who's financed by rich men, what's the harm? We know the truth." The truth was that though Megan made the most of her female charms and wore what she called her Joan Crawford follow-me high heels to money meetings, she had never, so far as Toni knew, traded sex for favors. She was far too moral and too independent for that. Successful men did, occasionally, pursue her, but Megan said (probably because she'd been married to one of them) that powerful men threw an already unequal sexual equation further off balance. For boyfriends Megan preferred working-class men or, until recently—when she'd been in a position to hire them—actors.

"We know the truth," Toni said again.

"Hey, my own mother doesn't know the truth."

"Mothers aren't supposed to." Toni guessed that Megan's mother, Irene, would have preferred to see Megan married to a well-to-do lawyer, instead of fighting her way to the top of her profession. Megan couldn't understand the innate conservatism of mothers. Watching her prowl the room and knock back her drink, Toni understood, with the lucidity of hindsight, that Megan's downslide had started maybe a day ago, when they'd met Irene and Megan's stepfather, George, at the Los Angeles stopover. George was a soft-spoken man in a polyester suit who didn't appear to be in the best of health. Megan seemed to be very fond of him. Irene, more stylishly groomed, a henna rinse trying to assert the glory of hair that had once been the color of Megan's, had lines of disappointment around her mouth and an air of controlled nervousness. She questioned, one might even say nagged, Megan throughout the visit, even reaching across the restaurant table to pick a stray thread from Megan's fringed leather jacket and telling her she looked like a ranch hand.

"Well, I'm the daughter of a ranch hand," Megan had said, and if looks could kill . . . But both mother and daughter had broken down in a flood of tears when the flight was announced.

"You know, your mother—" Toni began.

Megan was peremptory. "Fix us another drink, will you? I'm going to call Uncle Mick and Auntie Vi."

Toni got up and went to the refrigerator. Her feet felt as though they were the shape and consistency of Pop-Tarts. What was she doing pouring a second drink when the sun hadn't yet gone down? And eavesdropping on Megan's excited phone conversation.

Megan hung up and sighed. "It was just like when I call them from the States," she said dejectedly. "We all talk too loud, as though sheer volume will bring us closer together, then we ask about each other's health, then Mick says, 'This must be costing you a fortune' and we hang up. I asked them if they'd come in to see *Chappy* but Mick said he can't stand the crowds in the city. Imagine how they'd feel about New York." She shook her head and clinked her glass to Toni's. "Well, here's to 'em. You know, I'm almost afraid to see them again. It's been so long, and they're all so wonderful in my mind. What if I find out it's just nostalgia?"

"No. It'll be good when you see them again," Toni comforted. She brought her glass to her lips. Its faint fusel fragrance made her feel sick. Her face tightened into a controlling grimace. It was her nature to cry freely, at weddings and funerals, when moved by an old movie or a favorite aria, but these sudden, seemingly unmotivated fits of weeping were something new.

"Toni, whatever's the matter?" Megan put her arm around her.

"Just tired, I guess. That and my falling hormone level." Or maybe it was thinking about families.

"I didn't know you were going through the change, though I guess I could've figured it out."

"Yep, I'm getting old."

"Shit, you're what? Forty-seven? Forty-eight? That's not old."

"Say that again when you get here."

"Go," Megan ordered, knowing that Toni would be loyal enough to stay up with her if she thought she needed company. "Take a bath. Go to bed."

"You won't get depressed? You won't get drunk and stay up all night—or day—or whatever it is?"

"No. Go." As she opened the door a good-looking bellhop appeared with their luggage. Toni ran her hand through her hair and dropped into her Mae West imitation. "Maybe I'll sashay around the halls and see if some young buck is willing to tuck me in."

"You'd scream for the police if any man except Joe laid a hand on you. Now, go fall into bed!"

Megan closed the door and went to the window. The brilliant sun made her eyes smart. Perth. But not as she remembered it, though she had never seen it from high up. Only the Swan River was recognizable. She must get some sleep, try to reconcile her body's rhythms with real time. But she was too wound up. She replayed the tense meeting with her mother. Well, she would never please Irene. She had become the repository of Irene's dreams and hopes, but those dreams and hopes were too vague and conflicting to be fulfilled. Years of therapy had not convinced her that Irene's capacity for disappointment might not be inherited, for wasn't she herself filled with wild imaginings, vain hopes, inexplicable longings and regrets? She closed the draperies, took off her clothes and sat on the bed. Fishing out an ice cube, she crunched it, then fished out another, felt it drip down her wrist and remembered her childhood fascination with ice.

There'd been no refrigerator in the old bush house they'd visited on weekends. The iceman had come with great blocks of the precious stuff, capturing it with pincers, hoisting it into the "safe," that wire-screened cupboard with the pan underneath to catch the drippings. She and her cousins had chipped off the ice, sucked it, rubbed it onto sunburned faces, slipped it down the back of each other's clothes. There'd been no indoor toilet, either. As the oldest child she'd been responsible for emptying the chamber pots, though except in rainy weather they'd all crept into the moonlit backyard. All except infant cousin Jeremy and Great-grandmother Kathleen, who was frail. Every morning Megan had walked to the dunny, holding the chamber pot at arm's length and averting her face. Which is why she'd once tripped, arse over elbow, and smashed Kathleen's favorite pot, the one with the hand-painted roses and lilies around the rim, the one Kathleen had said was a work of art. When she'd broken that, Mick had laughed so hard she hadn't spoken to him for a whole day; and Kathleen hadn't spoken to her for two, and then only out of necessity, to tell her that the reserve chamber pot, that World War II relic with the likeness of the Emperor Hirohito in the bowl, had been full. "And pray the fate of the Republic will never be in hands such as yours," Kathleen had scolded as

Megan had knelt on the bumpy linoleum and retrieved it, gagging, careful not to spill.

She looked through the bathroom door at the gleaming tile and mirrors. "Ah, Kathleen, Katy, I wish you were with me now. Wouldn't I sit you on that sterilized, shiny throne and wouldn't we laugh when you flushed it? Wouldn't we just know we'd arrived?" She put her glass on the carpet and lay back. She shouldn't have sounded so bitchy about the press clippings. Gossip and misrepresentation were part of the game and she had no patience with people who sought the limelight, then complained about its glare. If it was lonely at the top—or near the top—how much lonelier was it when you were down there, looking up? The myth that successful people were more unhappy than others was comforting only to nonachievers. If it was sometimes a pain in the ass to be recognized, to have your social mask always close at hand, how much more wretched was anonymity? She would never forget the years of scrounging, wheedling her way into assignments, convincing idiots that she deserved their confidence. Though an outward show of forgetfulness and magnanimity was the best offense, she'd always kept strict accounts. She recalled who'd helped and who'd hindered as vividly as Great-grandmother Kathleen recalled British injustices. The Irish were a generous but not a forgiving lot.

Fatigue washed over her, wave after wave, like a time-lapse movie of an incoming tide. In her mind's eye she saw the opening scene from her new screenplay. CLOSE UP: Sarah's feet, horribly grubby, chained at the ankles, a jailer unlocking the chains. CUT TO: Lieutenant Clarke's face, his eyes narrowing as he sees the pale band of flesh beneath the leg irons . . . Christ, she had to get the money to do it. She couldn't imagine life if she didn't. She reminded herself to ask Toni about checking costume collections. Because of the bicentennial, there must be enough ready-mades to dress the extras. She pulled her feet up to her chest and, since the air-conditioning was going full blast, groped for the bedspread. Wouldn't it have been nice if she'd been able to afford to bring Irene with her? No. Nothing could have been worse. Without intending to, Irene would reinforce her every insecurity. Don't rise above your station/prepare yourself for disappointment/you're only a woman. Another picture floated into her head, she could see it in minute detail: a gold-rimmed cardboard chocolate box decorated with a battered rose.

"You were conceived in love," Irene often told her. She would gather little Megan onto her lap, open the chocolate box with the artificial rose on top and take out the photos. The wedding picture came first. It was brown and white but Irene colored it with her words: the bridesmaids' dresses were baby blue, Daddy's uniform was khaki, the bouquets were pink and white. Sometimes Irene would go on to tell more about what had happened that wonderful day—how the car that was to bring the musicians to the reception had broken down, so Bluey Hughes, already the worse for drink, had taken up his fiddle and squeaked through "When the Lights Go On Again All Over the World" and everyone had linked arms and sung. How Tom's buddies had pulled contraband tins of pineapple and fruit cocktail from their uniforms to add to the tables of sandwiches and homemade, eggless cakes. How the musicians had finally arrived and Tom, wildly happy and full of champagne, had stopped their first waltz together as a married couple, whipped off her veil, put a cowboy hat on her head and told the band to play "Deep in the Heart of Texas." Young Megan, searching for her likeness in the photos, would ask, "Where am I?" and Irene would laugh and say, "You were only a gleam in your father's eye." And Megan would hold the picture close, seeing that her father's eyes were indeed gleaming, as were her mother's.

Decades later, when she was about to make her move to New York, Megan had gone through the storage closet in Irene's Garden Grove tract house. She'd found carefully mended clothes, piles of letters, satin spike heels as well as orthopedic oxfords, Mother's Day cards, tarnished costume jewelry, report cards and certificates of merit . . . and the chocolate box. Its edges were bent and the artificial rose was missing. The wedding photo had been ripped in half, but carefully glued back together. The seam barely showed, except where it cut through Irene's face, so that while one of her eyes continued to gleam, the other already seemed sad.

CHAPTER
FOUR

IRENE CORCORAN AND THOMAS SHELBY HANLON WERE joined in marriage in St. John's Church on an overcast August afternoon in 1944. The bride's dress was made of parachute silk and had been fashioned by her own hand. Her brother Mick, the only one of three brothers to survive the war, gave her away. Despite a postmalarial pallor and a suit now too big for him, Mick was in high spirits, as were most of the guests. Grandmother Kathleen was the exception. Kathleen didn't trust any man who traveled too far from his home base. The fact that the U.S. Marine command had ordered Thomas Shelby to do so did not soften her suspicions. Thomas Shelby Hanlon had no close relatives. This touched Irene's heart, but Kathleen took it as a further sign of his instability. The marriage was, to Kathleen's mind, far too risky. But the family secretly referred to Kathleen as "Pickle-Puss" and her grim glances were generally ignored in the merrymaking. Victory was at hand. There would be no more ration cards, no more casualty lists, no more air raids, drills, sandbags in schoolyards or blackout curtains on the windows. The bride was beautiful, the groom bore a startling resemblance to John Garfield—indeed, they seemed the very symbol of hope. If tears were shed it was in the fullness of emotion and the knowledge that once Tom had cut through the red tape, Irene would be joining him in the States.

Irene, who'd never been farther from home than a visit to a cousin in Adelaide (and counted herself experienced for that), was dizzy with her good fortune and anticipation. Tom had warned her that he didn't have any real profession (he'd been what he called a roustabout, which she supposed was something like a cowboy, before he'd joined up), but she was sure that a man who had won the Purple Heart, was respected by his buddies, and could charm the birds out of the trees wouldn't have any trouble finding work. She would never have to chop wood and wash clothes in a copper as her mother had done. It might be tough at first, but as a country girl who'd gone through a war, it wouldn't have occurred to her that anything could be accomplished without sacrifice. Soon they would have a lovely home in which to bring up the children she already imagined. She could rely on Thomas Shelby Hanlon. As he'd told her when first courting her, the Shelby in his name was after Rebel general Joe Shelby, who, rather than surrender to the Yankees, had wrapped the bloody Confederate flag around a rock and sunk it in the Rio Grande before leading his troops into exile in Mexico.

Thomas Shelby Hanlon had never consciously deceived his wife about his prospects, though having fallen in love with a pretty foreign girl with high moral standards, it was only natural that he put himself and his future in the best possible light. He had been reared in foster homes and had little education. His fondest memories of the small Texas town he'd come from were of his victories on the football field and his appearances in high school plays. He had no notion that he, like many of the men of his generation, would never recover from the war. He had no physical injury save a long, puckered scar near the small of his back, inflicted by a Japanese soldier who'd paid with his life. His psychological wounds seemed common enough: a tendency to hit the ground when he heard a loud noise, the occasional combat nightmare. Nevertheless, he was a lost soul. Never again would he feel the joy of purpose, the surge of courage and loyalty, the sense of community that the war had given him. And he would spend the rest of his life trying to recapture them.

His buddies confessed to a certain restlessness after being mustered out, but Tom did not guess the depth of his problem until his young wife arrived in his hometown of Lubbock, Texas. Never before had he felt clumsy embracing a woman, but as he came toward her he found himself blocked by diaper bag, purse and baby, and the suitcases he carried from the train station seemed heavy with responsibility. The fact that he had already quit one job was passed over in the excitement of kisses, questions and an examination of his baby girl, but seeing the dilapidated house he'd managed to rent on the outskirts of town, he felt an inward shudder of inadequacy. "I wish there was a tree around," was all Irene said. "We'll grow a whole forest of trees," he assured her, lifting her off her feet. And that night, holding her close, baby Megan having been put to bed in an empty suitcase, it had been easy, once again, to believe in a limitless future.

He found a job in an auto parts store, but the manager, who'd sat out the war, was always on his back and after a few months Tom told him to "put it where the sun don't shine." He took another job as a trucker. It meant that he was on the road much of the time, something he really didn't mind, though he kept that a secret from Irene. But it was a dead-end job and he knew it. Irene began to come up with irritatingly naïve suggestions about all the things he might do and he mentioned, casually at first, that he'd heard there were more opportunities in California. Still convinced that he could do anything he put his mind to and sure that the public would be as smitten with his good looks as she, Irene encouraged his desire to become an actor. Mired in loneliness, worn down by the unending struggle to keep things clean in the perpetually dusty winds of the Panhandle, seeing that the few beers Tom took in the evening to unwind were now augmented by a few in the morning to get him going, she would have encouraged almost anything. So they loaded two-year-old Megan and their few belongings into the Ford and set out for Los Angeles.

For the next few years, while Tom tried to get a foothold in the movie business, he had various jobs and they moved from one apartment to another. He landed a few parts and might have succeeded in becoming an actor had he not hated taking direction. Anything or anyone who sought to control his behavior made him angry. Even coming home to a freshly bathed wife who already had dinner ready threatened him by seeming to claim his gratitude. Gradually, he found his métier in stunt work. He had an athlete's reflexes and he was willing, even eager, to take risks, because, for those few moments—leaping from a speeding car, jumping from a cliff, bailing out of a burning plane—he felt the exhilaration of putting his life on the line.

The money was good when he worked, but he couldn't manage money, so he often had to come to Irene for the cash she'd squirreled away out of her housekeeping allowance in hopes of buying a washing machine or saving for a trip back home. And there were long periods of unemployment. At first these were treated as holidays. Tom would gas up the car and spontaneously suggest a picnic at the beach, a drive down to a Long Beach amusement park called the Pike, or into the Santa Monica Canyon where they might be lucky enough to spot some horses. They even went for drives at night, Megan bundled in blankets in the backseat while Tom zoomed down the Pacific Coast Highway. Once, at Irene's suggestion, they went to see the Academy Awards at Grauman's Chinese. Irene didn't mind standing on tiptoe and being jostled behind police barricades to get a glimpse of limousines and stars in glittering gowns, but the sight of a high life in which he had no part made Tom embarrassed and resentful. "I can't stand here with a bunch of sappy women," he told Irene. He put Megan on his shoulders and shoved his way out of the crowd.

When he wasn't working, he would sit around the apartment, careful to space his drinks and avoid spilling ashes on the furniture. He tried to read. He played his harmonica. He entertained Megan. But then his restlessness would overwhelm him and he would go out drinking with the boys, paying, so Irene accused, for their rounds as well as his own. Sometimes, in an excess of frustrated energy, he would lash out. Never, at this point, at his wife. He loved her. He loved his child. In violent moods he was more likely to hurt himself—a fist through a window, an aluminum kitchen cabinet dented as he banged his head against it. Mornings after these outbursts, finding Irene asleep in Megan's bed, he would feel a groggy remorse, wanting to apologize and promise better behavior but unable to humble himself. It was usually Irene who made peace. Seeing him miserable, his body slackened as though all will had drained from him, she would blame herself for having been too hard on him. A touch, a look would cause her to give way to the inarticulate reunion of weeping or lovemaking. By nightfall harmony would be restored and Tom, relieved, but not wanting to risk conversation, would take Irene and Megan to the movies.

As a young woman, sitting in a film history class at UCLA

or at a marathon retrospective, Megan would feel almost constant *déjà vu*. She was able to project entire scenes before realizing that she'd seen the movies before, when she was too young to remember them consciously. "You were always a good kid at the movies," Irene told her. "Even in the scary parts you never cried." And why should she have cried? What hurricane could sweep her away, what vampire could fix his teeth to her throat when she was close in the dark, her head on her mother's breast, smelling her father's hair tonic and nicotine? In the flickering light, their faces, so often drawn with anxiety or twisted in anger, were rapt and happy. She was always safe at the movies.

By the time Megan was almost school age they were living in a one-bedroom apartment in Panorama City. The name elicited a good-natured though occasionally rueful laugh from Irene since the only view, through the kitchen window, was of an oil-stained parking lot and, beyond that, a Laundromat, gas station and Bud's Quick Stop Liquors. Irene struggled to expand this horizon, hoping that after Megan was enrolled in school, she would overcome Tom's objections and get a job. She had no idea what she might do. She only knew that she had to come up with more than the occasional ten dollars she earned by posting her phone number on the bulletin board at the supermarket and making a dress for a neighbor. She had not been brought up to believe that girls needed more than a minimal education, enough to allow them to take jobs as sales or office girls until they married; but the circumstances of her own life convinced her that Megan, whom she had already taught to read and write, should have "something to fall back on." In more fanciful moments she groped toward a future for her daughter that would be entirely unlike her own, though how such independence could be achieved she could only dimly imagine. She had never, personally, known a woman who had a career, who wore smart clothes and commanded respect; she had only seen them in the movies. During the day she made the beds and made do, obliterating thought by cooking, sewing, playing with and teaching Megan, upholstering secondhand furniture, putting wallpaper up, steaming wallpaper off, always muttering, "Housework is such a dumb job." At night, while Tom was in the shower, she knelt by the side of their bed and said her Hail Marys. On nights when he didn't come home, she got into the bed alone and prayed more fervently, if less formally. After asking for blessings on all of her loved ones, she always ended with "And please, Holy Mother, help my husband to find some peace. And help me to get enough money for a trip back home."

She had salted away what she thought of as "her" money: payments for her dressmaking and a hundred or so she'd managed to pare off her housekeeping allowance. Tom had been working steadily for several months, doing stunt work for the star playing the Indian chief Cochise, so they even had some money in savings, though she wouldn't have asked him for that. She knew it might be years before she could save the rest, so what happened on that sweltering July afternoon seemed to have the quality of a miracle.

She was standing at the kitchen sink, scrubbing the makeup off the collar of Tom's shirt and listening to a radio quiz show when the announcer asked, "In what year of the Civil War did the city of Richmond fall, and to what general?" The fact that she knew the answers was remarkable in itself. The only books in the apartment were novels she checked out of the library, an encyclopedia she'd bought from a door-to-door salesman and was still paying off, Megan's storybooks and a few volumes about the Civil War that Tom had picked up at a secondhand shop. She'd read about the fall of Richmond only nights before, restlessly waiting for Tom to come home. She made a dive for the phone, knocking over a cup of tea and watching it drip onto the floor while she'd dialed the station and stammered out the answer. She won a washer, a dryer and a stove.

Tom was as jubilant as she and with his usual spontaneity suggested that if she traded in the appliances (which wouldn't have fit into the apartment anyway) they could pool the money with the savings and she and Megan could go back for a trip to Australia. He encouraged this even though he knew it might mean a permanent rupture. Irene was pining for her family. Grandmother Kathleen was ill. It was only right that he should let her go. And if she chose to stay, who could blame her? He vowed that he wouldn't ask her to come back until he'd established himself. And what were the chances of that? A script girl with whom he often flirted had told him that certain directors considered his risk-taking too eager to be professional. "A man like you can scare people," she'd said, adding with a go-ahead smile, "though personally I can't understand why."

Eight weeks after Irene and Megan left, Tom woke up in the script girl's apartment, feeling beached and no longer young. He watched as she scrounged through slovenly kept drawers and found a sweater to pull over the see-through nightdress he no longer wanted to see through. Shamed that he'd broken his vows to his wife, he declined the sexual favors she offered in lieu of breakfast, drove to Bud's Quick Stop for a hair-of-the-dog bottle and went back to his apartment. After slugging back two quick ones to numb his shame, he made enough phone calls to make sure he could get his hands on some cash. He poured the rest of the bottle down the sink and rummaged through drawers until he found some of Irene's stationery. The look of his heavy hand on the flowered paper made his heart sink. He knew he would never be able to buy her the pretty things she craved, that she would always be caught in pathetic attempts to bring beauty into their lives, like this dime-store stationery. He got up and looked into the trash can at the empty bottle, sat back down and began, "My darling wife . . ."

Receiving the letter saying how much he needed her and asking her to come back, Irene swung into a wild happiness. She put the letter in her apron pocket and read it at least a dozen times throughout the day, but that night, lying in the dark, her hand still touching the letter she'd put under her pillow, a knot of mistrust formed in the region of her stomach. She was protected and content with her family. Megan, with that amazing childhood resilience, had settled in. Much as she wanted things to change, much as she believed Tom's desire to make them change, she knew that they just might not.

But the decision to return was made for her when she discovered she was pregnant with their second child. She knew she must have conceived the afternoon before they'd left, when she'd cooked all morning, trying to assuage her guilt by making sure Tom had a refrigerator full of food. She was so distracted that she'd burned the roast. Then the cake had flopped. She'd pulled off her apron and gone into the bedroom and he'd followed, shutting the door behind him. "Don't worry about the cake," he said. "I never had a sweet tooth for anything but you." He lifted her up, slowly and deliberately, lowering her onto the bed. The open suitcase jabbed into her shoulder but she clutched at his back, bringing him down. They had not made love in the afternoon for years. She saw the sunlight pick up the grey at his temples and glance off his teeth. Her rebel lover, her wild Texas boy. She did not remind him to reach into the nightstand where he kept the rubbers, thinking only, "This may be the last time."

To Irene's surprise it was her grandmother Kathleen, wizened, and glassy-eyed as a china doll, who first noticed her condition and, to her even greater amazement, suggested that Mrs. Cassidy down the road might be able to help her out. But Mrs. Cassidy said if she was more than eight weeks gone she couldn't risk it. Irene discussed the situation with Mick and Vi. They decided that it was best, at least until she and Tom found a real home and she was sure he had mended his ways, for Megan to remain in the care of the family. Irene left, buoyed up with renewed expectations and a love so strong that it took another seven years to destroy it.

When she made the final break, Tom left Los Angeles and did not contest the divorce. Six months later she quit her job in the yardage store, married a man she'd met while standing in line at the bank, and sent for Megan.

George bought Irene her first real home, a tract house in the suburbs. It was Model Number Two of three possible models, the uniformity of which Irene attempted to conceal in every possible way. She had made unavoidable compromises, but she was not resigned. Her home would be better kept, more originally decorated than any of the others, just as her children would be better mannered, better dressed and better educated. Having found a haven in the constricting middle of the middle class, she reached out for something better for the daughter she had, to her mind, so cruelly abandoned. One of her chief considerations in accepting George's proposal was that it provided her with the means to have Megan with her again, and she stretched her budget for piano lessons Megan didn't want to take, and braces she didn't want to wear. On Sundays, when Megan and her little brother Michael went off to Mass, Irene, forever cast out from

Holy Mother Church because she'd sinned against the sacrament of marriage, did penance by digging in her garden. It bloomed with wattle, Geralton wax, boronia, even kangaroo paws, which she had brought, against customs regulations, from her homeland. George, glad to be given direction in his free time, burrowed along beside her like a contented mole. He was, as she never tired of pointing out, a good man. He had taken on a woman with two children; he provided what Thomas Shelby could not or did not care to provide.

Megan could see that her stepfather was a good man, though cautiousness and reliability, along with a receding hairline, were not qualities that impressed a girl of her age and imagination. She might have allowed herself to feel appreciative had Irene not reminded her that this was what she *should* feel and had she not believed that it would constitute a betrayal of her father, whom she remembered indistinctly, but loved with a fierce loyalty. Hadn't Irene already betrayed them both? Megan's painful early memories had been overlaid with visions of glamorous, warring couples—Tracy and Hepburn, Gable and Lombard, Myrna Loy and William Powell. And her dumb, unadventurous mother had deserted the Silver Screen for the flickerings of TV's "Leave It to Beaver." Nothing had turned out as she'd prayed it would. She'd wanted to be with her real father, in Hollywood, to escape the iron grip of the nuns, to be a bona fide teenager (a state of grace only Americans seemed to acknowledge). Instead, she had been dragged from the freedom of the bush to end up in a tract house in Garden Grove (an appalling misnomer since all natural vegetation had been razed by developers). Here she lived with a strange, meek man she was told to call "Daddy" but who said, " 'Scuse me" when he bumped into her in the hall. Her high school was a zoo of leering boys (she kept her elbows at her sides to hide the bumps on her chest), and girls who painted their faces, had "love bites" on their necks, and asked her stupid questions. Where did she learn to speak English? Did they wear shoes in Australia? None of them could imagine that any country but America—"God's country" they called it, as though the Almighty had geographical pets—was fit to live in. She missed Mick and Vi and the cousins. She even missed St. Brigid's. God had abandoned her.

Whenever she pressed Irene for information about Thomas Shelby, Irene gave the same answer she gave when asked too closely about sex: ''When you're older you'll understand.'' She'd tried to pry something more substantive from her mother by practicing emotional withdrawal and once, after she'd feigned indifference to Irene's affections for days, it seemed as though she'd succeeded in nudging Irene into a revelation. ''Love . . . ,'' Irene said, and Megan waited, impatient with the struggle reflected on her mother's face, ''Love can . . . just wear out.'' Megan turned away in disgust. It was such a fatuous remark, so typical of the defeat that passed for adult wisdom. She knew Irene didn't really believe that love was something that could wear out, like a chair or a pair of shoes. She'd watched her, dancing alone to the record player with *that* look on her face. She'd seen her stop, paring knife in mid-motion, faucet streaming, while she gazed out the kitchen window, eyes full of longing. ''George might be her husband,'' Megan convinced herself, ''but Thomas Shelby is the one she really loves.''

And she got the proof of it when Tom finally came to visit. Irene was against it, but Tom, who had a way with men as well as women, prevailed upon George, who always wanted to do the right thing. ''The children, especially Megan, have a right to know what their father is really like,'' George said, and Megan heard the self-righteousness in his voice. But if George hoped to redeem himself by comparison he was mistaken.

Tom rolled up in an almost new, unwashed convertible. The reckoning that Irene had expected, even hoped for, was a mirage. If there had been any justice, George, who ate the right things, bowled regularly and did the heavy work in the garden, should have been the better physical specimen. But he was not. Tom's step was springy, his body tough, his smile irresistibly charming. He looked at Megan for a long time. She was conscious of her flaming cheeks and hair, which despite dabs of Lustre-Creme and controlling barrettes, frizzed out in ugly clumps. Tom shook her hand first, which made her feel very adult, then pulled her to him, making her feel very much a child. But he recovered, passing his hand over his eyes, and called her ''mate'' and teased her about her Aussie accent. He asked her questions about school, what she wanted to do with her life, if she had any boyfriends. Desperately wanting to show how intelligent she was, she stammered her replies, her tongue cleaved to the roof of her mouth. She wasn't much better after Irene and George left, ostensibly to do some grocery shopping. She sat on the back porch, watching Tom roughhouse with Michael, already critical and a little bit jealous of their inarticulate male physicality.

George and Irene were back in no time. Irene unpacked the groceries, while George rattled on about bargains on cans of Spam and Tom stared down Irene's censorious looks with a we've-got-a-secret smile. The adults retired to the den, and after intense negotiations, only some of which Megan could hear by lingering in the hall, it was decided that Tom could visit every two months.

Tom showed up with military punctuality. He took Michael for outings, some of which were so babyish—softball games, county fairs—that Megan declined to go along. Megan he took mostly to the movies.

After his visits they were all thrown off balance for days: Michael wild, Megan closeting herself in her room to write in her diary, George staying up long after Irene had gone to bed, falling asleep in front of the test pattern.

"Didn't he look nice?" Megan ventured as Irene busied herself with the housecleaning that always followed Tom's visits, and Irene, usually expressive, could only mutter, "Handsome is as handsome does," as though she were a schoolgirl drone from St. Brigid's.

Tom's visits became less frequent when he took a job managing a rodeo that toured the Southwest. They had neither seen nor heard from him for several months when he turned up one Christmas Eve, long after they'd opened their presents and gone to bed. He was wearing cowboy gear. His hair needed a wash and he was wildly drunk. He dumped an armful of unwrapped gifts on the living room floor, said he'd driven all the way from Tucson and demanded to see his children. George, rumpled and foolish-looking in the Santa Claus pajamas Michael had bought him for Christmas, was shoved aside as Tom staggered into the hallway. Irene met him there, holding the front of her ruffled nightdress closed. Megan blocked the door to her brother's room, seeing a look of such rage and contempt on Irene's face that she saw her mother as ugly for the first time in her life. She was amazed at the flood of curses that Irene spewed, confronting him. She hadn't known her mother had even heard such words. George forced himself between them, knocking askew a sconce Irene had made in her ceramics class, begging for reason. Michael started to cry and ran to clutch Irene's legs. In a drunkenly abrupt change of mood, Tom uncurled his fist, offered his hand, palm up, to Irene and winked. He said, so quietly that it was both threat and promise, "I'll be back. I'll be back for you and the kids." George pressed himself against the wall as Tom swaggered out. He roared off in the beat-up Chevy, singing at the top of his lungs; lights came on in the neighbors' bedrooms.

But Thomas Shelby Hanlon never came to the house in the suburbs again. Postcards arrived, showing Indians, mountains, bucking broncos. One, addressed only to Megan, was of desert flowers. The postmarks read Reno, Flagstaff, San Antonio, Phoenix. The messages promised, "One day I'll show you . . ." the Grand Canyon, Pyramid Lake, the ranges at sunrise, the big gambling casinos. Then even the postcards stopped.

When she was about to graduate from UCLA, Megan decided that she had to see her father. She got an old address from the stuntmen's union and, after a series of letters and phone calls, managed to track him to an East Los Angeles address. She asked her boyfriend to drive her there. It was a pink stucco apartment building called the Chateau Pierre. A sign said "Vacancies— No pets," though a bitch with swollen teats and three puppies was sunning herself on the overgrown patio. A Mexican woman answered the door. Tom came up behind her, in undershirt and jeans. The physical reckoning he'd magically delayed was apparent now: his face was bloated, his belly soft, though he still had a full head of hair and his arms were muscular enough to put Megan's boyfriend's to shame. He sent the woman out for a six-pack and welcomed them into the kitchen, taking on some of his old charm as he teased Megan, calling her "the college girl" and asking about Michael. By his fourth beer he was eyeing her boyfriend's shoulder-length hair and STOP THE WAR button. Tom could not believe that America was losing a war. The press was lying when it reported that soldiers were smoking dope, fragging officers, shooting civilians. And as for the draft dodgers, "No son of mine . . ." he began; and Megan interrupted to say that he was right about that: Michael, over Irene's tearful entreaties and Megan's angry reasoning, had enlisted and was on his way to Saigon. "Damned straight," Tom toasted him and told the woman to cook up some tacos.

Megan sipped her beer and kicked her boyfriend under the table when he persisted in informing Tom about the historical causes of the Vietnam War. The smell of onions, greasy meat and cumin was making her sick. As Tom pounded the sink and slurred, "My country, right or wrong!" she got up to leave, apologizing to the woman for not eating her tacos. She tried to kiss Tom good-bye, but he waved her aside and, as they left the apartment, he yelled after them, "You and your lousy generation! You're soft. You're all soft. You should be lined up against the wall and shot."

As they approached the car her boyfriend said, "Hey, wow. At least my old man hired me a draft attorney. Your old man's a dinosaur."

She put out her hand for the keys. "I'll drive." She never wanted to see him or her father again.

Michael came back from Vietnam with three medals, a stuffed koala he'd bought while on leave in Sydney, and a rare strain of VD called Saigon Rose. Megan was the only one he told about the VD, though he brushed aside her other questions with "You promise not to ask me about my war experiences, I'll promise not to ask you about your periods." He dragged an old TV set and a cot into Irene and George's garage and settled in, watching whatever came on the screen and washing down his medication with prodigious amounts of beer. Whenever he sobered up, he cleaned up and went to Mass.

On Megan's increasingly infrequent visits to the house, she found Irene preoccupied, bitter and defeated. Though Thomas Shelby Hanlon was never mentioned by name but occasionally referred to as "him," his presence remained palpable. Irene seemed to believe that, despite her efforts, he had triumphed. Her children had followed in their father's footsteps, Michael with his drinking, preoccupation with war and his aimless wanderings. But it was Megan who seemed to disappoint her most. She didn't approve of the way her daughter thought, dressed or spoke. She questioned her about her virginity and cried when Megan told her it was long since gone. She bought what Megan called "lady dresses" and insisted that Megan wear them instead of "those hippie weeds." When Megan seemed too happy, Irene wondered aloud if she was on drugs. And Megan's announcement that she planned to go to New York and become a film director was greeted with a stony expression that predicted the failure Irene had experienced in her own life.

"You know," Megan said, on what was to be her last visit to the house in the suburbs, "you remind me of that old rhyme 'May I go swimming, mother dear? Yes, my darling daughter. Hang your clothes on a mulberry bush, but don't go near the water.' You've always encouraged me and now, just when I'm setting off on something wonderful, something that means my entire future, you look at me as though I'm committing a crime."

Irene, furiously scrubbing a pot, wanted to say, "I want the world for you, but I'll miss you. I'm afraid for you." Instead she muttered, "Grand ambitions. Pipe dreams. And nothing to back you up."

"I'll back me up," Megan insisted, throwing the dish towel aside. "Didn't I get through college on scholarships?"

"But New York? And a film school? I've never heard of a woman being a director. You'll be broke all your life, Megan. I know it."

"Mom, just come and sit down. Sit down and talk to me."

"And the pots and pans will finish themselves, I suppose. What are you going to do for money?"

"I'll get a job. Haven't I had jobs since I was sixteen? Haven't I always paid my way?"

"And where will you live?"

"Victor, Victor Taub—you know I've told you all about him— he's going to NYU film school, too, and he already has this big apartment and I can stay there until—"

"Stay with him? You mean sleep with him."

"Mom, it's not like that," Megan lied. In fact she was besotted with sexual love. Compared to Victor Taub, the two boys she'd had affairs with seemed just that—boys. Victor was an enormously talented Jewish intellectual; he had opened up a whole new world of taste and culture, not to mention pleasure, to her.

"If this Victor's so fond of you, why hasn't he come out to meet us?"

"He's busy packing and saying good-bye to his parents." In fact she had asked him to come with her but he'd said, "A two-hour drive to the suburbs? After what you've told me about your family?"

And she was just as glad he hadn't come. She knew what he'd think of Irene in her apron, George in front of the TV, discount coupons tacked to the bulletin board, the fake wood paneling, mashed potatoes and gravy, the picture of St. Patrick driving the snakes out of Ireland that Irene had shipped all the way from Grandmother Kathleen's house in the bush. Not to mention her crazy brother Michael sitting in his hootch in the garage, reading his missal and getting sloshed. Victor's family was third-generation Hollywood elite. His grandfather, Sol Taubinski, had come from Astoria to keep Louis B. Mayer's books; his father had become fabulously wealthy as a film distributor; his mother, Sylvia, was still beautiful in a lacquered sort of way (certainly no one could think of Sylvia in an apron). Sylvia was purported to have given up a career as a concert pianist to become a wife and mother, or, more accurately, a hostess and shopper. The Taubs had a house in Beverly Hills. They had cocktail hour, a pool, a grand piano, a Mexican housekeeper Sylvia insisted was Spanish and a Japanese gardener who cultivated orchids, an original Matisse . . . None of this impressed Victor, who had learned at Brandeis that the East Coast was where it was at. Hollywood was vulgar and passé, Victor informed her. The best young filmmakers were serving their apprenticeship on the gritty streets of New York. That's where they were going, to pursue their individual careers (though she knew Victor was far more talented than she) . . . to pursue their individual careers. Together.

"You don't have to meet him yet, Mom. It's not as though we're getting married."

"And why shouldn't you want to get married?" Irene asked, scouring the sink, eyes intent on any speck of dirt, voice rising.

"Why wouldn't I want to get married? Well . . ." Sarcastic, wanting to bait her. ". . . just guess."

Irene turned off the faucet, wiped her hands on her apron and stared out the kitchen window. "What if you get pregnant?"

"We're talking about my career! We're talking about my going to New York," Megan yelled, angry, refusing to mention the birth-control pills she took more religiously than she'd ever said her morning prayers. "If I get pregnant I'll have an abortion."

"What a thing to say to your mother. You're just like *him*. Selfish and irresponsible. Full of grandiose ideas with nothing to back them up. Wandering all over the place, never settling down, not caring who you . . ."

"At least I won't be in front of a sink full of dishes for my entire life. At least I won't be dumb enough to put all my hopes in some man and then expect my children to do all the things I never did and then try to stop them when they try."

"Miss High and Mighty, you'll see . . . you'll . . ." The words trailed off. Megan had scored a direct hit. The anger drained from Irene's face, leaving only hurt and bewilderment.

"Don't cry!" Megan ordered, stiffening herself. "For Chrissake, don't cry!" She half hoped that George would have heard the ruckus and come in to smooth things over, take Irene in his arms so that she could effect a less painful exit. But it would take a bomb blast to bestir George from the Rams game. And even if he came in, what help could he be? He had never been able to give Irene any comforts except material ones and, in light of Megan's growing knowledge of the world, a very inferior brand of the material at that. In the presence of Irene's tears—the worst kind of tears, the silent kind, not even punctuated by a sob—George would be more impotent than she. She felt, perhaps fully for the first time, just how disappointed and alone her mother was. The knowledge filled her not with compassion but with a guilt that was quickly swallowed up by fear. "I will never allow myself to be like that," she silently vowed. Perhaps three thousand miles was not enough to put between her and all this misery. "Look, I'll write," she said at the door.

Irene, tears streaming but ignored, asked, "When are you leaving?"

"I don't know. Sometime next week."

Irene moved to the refrigerator. "Would you like to take some lemon cake with you?"

"To New York?"

"No." Irene shook her head and smiled. "Silly bugger," she muttered, and Megan didn't know to which of them she was referring. Irene looked at her for a long time, her body yearned forward, and again Megan stiffened, warding off the embrace that might unhinge her.

"You are so much like him," Irene said, resignation mingling with regret.

"Mom, I have to go." A few decisive steps, a quick hug. "Say good-bye to George and Michael. I'll call before I leave. Hey, you'll see me in the movies." And she was out the door, OUT, leaving her past behind her.

CHAPTER
FIVE

MEGAN WOKE AROUND SUNSET, SITTING BOLT UPRIGHT, afraid that she'd missed a plane. She sank back, shivering and ravenously hungry. The king-size bed made her feel small. She didn't think of herself as a lonely woman but sometimes, particularly in hotel rooms, loneliness seized her by the throat. She got up, splashed her face with cold water and looked at the clock. She didn't want to disturb Toni, but room service, alone, in front of a TV might turn her blue meanies into black weejams. If she could force herself to dress, get downstairs, and find a little corner table, she might stave off the worst of her funk . . . She pulled on blouse, jeans, boots and her fringed leather jacket.

As she stood at the entrance to the restaurant waiting for the hostess to seat her, she noticed a scrawny teenage girl in a candlelit back booth. The girl's hair was long and twisted into a knot on one side, shorn almost to the scalp and exposing a rhinestone earring that almost touched her shoulder on the other. Her tight silver leotard was covered with a man's oversize black coat that might have been found in a trashcan but had probably cost a couple of hundred bucks in a boutique. Her face was heavily painted but Megan could tell by her neck that she was very young, about sixteen. She felt an inward shudder of distaste—a sure sign she was getting old if she was so quick to scorn youth's fads and fashions. But the jeans, tie-dyed cottons and homemade jewelry of her youth had been popular because they were cheap, and even adults who'd made fun of the braless, unmade-up girls or called the long-haired boys effeminate, had known that the kids were sexy. By contrast, this punk look was pathetic, its hooker-tight leotard, heavy makeup and glitzy jewelry at war with the convict haircut and baggy man's coat. These poor young girls, she thought. They'd come of age in a time of apathy, crack, pornography and bus stop advertisements about AIDS. No wonder they were hopelessly confused.

The girl stared ahead with vacuous self-absorption as two men came from the bar and slid into the booth beside her. One of them paused and, feeling Megan's eyes on the girl, turned. Megan looked away. Her head snapped back in a double-take. It was her ex-husband, Victor Taub.

Panic. The impulse to pretend she hadn't seen him and leave. But he was walking toward her, his expression more pleased than surprised. Her own expression had melted into a slack-jawed, moronic stare as she juggled memories of how he used to look and fantasies of how he would look after all this time, against the reality. She'd pictured him as tan, pridefully slim, with dark glasses, a chestful of gold jewelry and a blow-dried hair style arranged to cover a bald spot. In a word, Hollywood vulgar. But he wore his success with an understated nonchalance. He was trim, though the slump of his shoulders spoiled the line of his body. His clothes were expensive but almost tweedy, and he wore no jewelry save a Rolex. He still had a full head of hair and it needed a cut. His brown eyes, bedroom eyes, looking out from behind tortoiseshell-framed glasses, seemed more weary than vain.

"Megan." They made tentative movements—she to offer her hand, he to kiss her cheek—but stopped and stepped back. "Megan." He captured her hand and held it tight. "You look wonderful."

Liar, she wanted to say. Just her luck to run into him when she looked like warmed-up stew. "So do you. What . . ."

"We always said we'd come to Australia and here we are."

"So it seems." Was this really happening? "You're here for the festival I guess."

"It seemed like a good time to come. I'm not showing anything. More or less here on vacation. And other business. Won't you join us?"

And sit with a punk who's young enough to be your daughter? "No. Sorry. I really can't. I just came down to get a quick cup of coffee."

The hostess came up. "Madam? You wanted a table for one?"

"No," Victor answered for her, "the lady will be joining us."

"Victor, I really can't. I . . ."

Another couple had come up behind her. The hostess looked from Megan to Victor, urging them to make up their minds. "The lady will be joining us," he repeated, taking Megan by the elbow. "I know you just got in this afternoon."

"How did you . . . ?"

"I checked with the festival people. Did you get my roses?" So they were from Victor. "Thank you. They're lovely."

"I should've signed my name. Who did you think sent them? I guess you have a list to pick from."

She ignored this. They reached the table. The other man got to his feet and was introduced as Les Something-or-Other. "And this," Victor said, "is my daughter, Deirdre." Deirdre looked up and mumbled "Hi." Megan mentally kicked herself for her evil thought of a moment ago: not "young enough to be" but actually his daughter, the product, she assumed, of the marriage he'd contracted soon after their divorce. She'd heard he'd been divorced and married again since then but, no surprise, he was not wearing a ring.

The waiter came to take their drink order. Megan knew Deirdre wasn't old enough to be asking for a vodka stinger but Victor didn't bat an eye. "Just coffee," Megan said, "and if you could, I'd like it in rather a hurry. I have an appointment." She turned to Les. He was a real estate developer and he and Victor were discussing the possibility of building a resort complex down near Cape Leuwin. Megan kept the questions coming, barely able to take in the answers, wanting only to study Victor but determined not to be obvious.

The drinks were set down in the middle of the chitchat. Victor made a toast to the success of Megan's film *Chappy* and said he was eager to see it. He sounded genuine. Deirdre played with the silverware and Les asked Megan politely what *Chappy* was about.

"I suppose you'd say—or the PR people would say—that it's a coming-of-age movie. About a girl whose father is a rodeo rider. She travels with her father and mother through all these seedy, dying cowboy towns. It was great fun shooting in Arizona and New Mexico, but the heat . . ." She rattled on, sounding like a press release, knowing she should say something about the films Victor had produced, most particularly about his last, *Deadly Desire*, but she couldn't bring herself to mention it.

She'd seen it over a year ago while she was filming *On the Streets*. Restless after the shoot, she'd wandered into an all-night Cineplex in Times Square. The place reeked of popcorn and disinfectant. Those members of the audience who weren't drunk, drugged or sleeping it off had yelped like hyenas at the gore on the screen, though she'd imagined she would have felt an even deeper disgust had she been in some clean suburban theater. She'd had to admit that from a technical point of view the movie was artful. It delivered shocks with the force of electric current, leaving her dazed and sick to her stomach. She'd left just as the protagonist was about to get her comeuppance in the form of several stabs to the chest. And she'd walked home through drizzly, refuse-choked streets, feeling both superior and sad, having dark thoughts about society in general and current movies in particular.

"And so you're originally from Australia?" Les asked, pulling her back to the present.

"Yes." She burned her tongue on the coffee. She poured in more cream so she could gulp the rest and hit the conversational ball back into Les's court by asking where he was from. Deirdre pulled on her straw as though sucking a milkshake. Victor shot Deirdre a look of annoyance and when she stared back at him from wide-spaced, disinterested eyes, his features tightened and went slack, so subtly that only an ex-wife would have noticed. Oh, God, Megan thought, he loves the kid but he's ashamed of her. She could understand that anguish; she used to feel it about him. The waiter was back, ready to take their dinner order.

"Won't you change your mind and join us?" Les asked. "I've really been enjoying . . ."

"Sorry, I really can't. I have an engagement . . ."

Victor reached for her hand. She pulled it away, stuffing it into her jacket pocket. "You mean you can't spare another hour?" He was persistent, but that was Victor. He could never believe that anything or anyone could come before his wishes. "You aren't really going anywhere now, are you?"

Her hand found an envelope. She brought it into the circle of candlelight. Saved. She pulled out the invitation. "I'm going to this party," she lied, quickly glancing at the invitation. "At Dr. and Mrs. Herbert Tishman's place."

"I know the Tishmans," Les smiled. "They live only a few streets from me. On Jutland Parade, isn't it?" Another glance at the invitation confirmed it. "I'd be happy to give you a lift."

"I wouldn't think of imposing." She clutched for an excuse and came up empty-handed.

"No imposition."

"But I have to get ready."

"Go ahead," Victor urged. "We'll have dinner and wait for you in the lobby."

"Ah . . ." Trapped. "Righto."

In her room she tore through a suitcase, pulling out a draped blouse, harem pants and big-sleeved coat in soft turquoise silk. It needed to be pressed. Wasn't it the Italians who preferred unpressed silk? So tonight she'd look as though she'd just flown in from Rome. Moving into the bathroom she glanced over her shoulder at the roses. What did Victor want? Producers didn't give you anything—not even a bunch of roses—unless they wanted something. She'd been half hoping they were from Tasman Burke. "Son of a bitch," she said over and over, but applied her makeup with a steady hand.

What could be worse than running into an ex when you looked like a bag of rags tied in a hurry? But the lights had been low in the restaurant and sometimes, in dim light, without makeup, because she was slim and small-boned and her hair was springy, she looked much younger. That was a trick she couldn't turn much longer, she thought as she patted moisturizer on the shallow wrinkles that engraved the corners of her eyes. "Son of a bitch!" Why had she lied? She remembered all those childhood injunctions against it. Lying set a trap, but only for the liar. When you told a lie you got a black mark on your tongue as well as on your soul. She'd been about six before she'd realized that her tongue didn't develop black spots; it was only her refusal to show it that gave her away. The notion of a besmirched soul had stayed much longer, was vivid even now. She could imagine her soul—luminescent ectoplasm somewhere around the region of

her heart—spotted with hairy black dots like the mold on de-
caying fruit. She was, and always would be, a lousy liar. Oh,
the nuns had done some job on her.

She took a tissue and wiped off blush from her cheek. Too
much blusher was always a sign of desperation. Perhaps, as her
more metaphysically inclined friends would say, she was *meant*
to go to the Tishmans' damned party. At any rate, she was
now too wired to stay in her hotel room. She clipped on the
jade-and-silver jewelry that completed the ensemble and went
downstairs.

The three of them were sitting on a lobby couch, Victor staring into the mid-distance. It had taken her years to figure out
that his faraway looks were more a sign of impatience than deep
thoughts. Deirdre was playing with her rhinestone earring, her
feet drawn up onto the couch; Les was looking at his watch.
Victor got up.

"You look terrific!" That gave her only a frisson of satisfaction. She knew she looked terrific. One of the many advantages
of the single state was that she did not rely on a particular man
to tell her so.

"Yeah. That's a neat outfit," Deirdre muttered. "You buy it
here? Maybe we could go shopping sometime."

"Megan hates shopping," Victor said. "It's something that
always endeared her to me."

Deirdre looked from one to the other, sensing a connection.

"A designer friend made it for me," Megan said. Her friend
Clifford, who'd taken her in hand a couple of years ago, said
she'd have to shed the jeans and sweatshirts until she was really
famous, and had created for her, at cost, a few outfits that were
individual, artsy and stylish.

"Sure you won't change your mind and come along, Victor?"
Les asked. "I know you got an invitation."

"Naw. Deirdre needs her beauty sleep."

"What's that supposed to mean?" Deirdre bristled.

"We'll see Megan again, won't we, Megan?" He brought his
lips to her cheek and whispered, "I'll call you first thing in the
morning. We have a lot of catching up to do." His cheek was
rough. His hair, which took a curl when it was humid, snaked

around his ear. She wanted to bite the lobe of that ear off and use it for the belly of a little voodoo doll.

The trouble with celebrity parties, Megan decided as she stood waiting in the Tishmans' entrance hall, was that since everyone was "someone" and expected to be recognized as such, the hostess had to possess not only unflagging enthusiasm but an impeccable memory of her guests' accomplishments. Mrs. Tishman, a fragile-looking woman in a shiny gold dress, had plenty of enthusiasm. "*So* happy you could join us," she gushed to the bearded man who'd preceded Megan through the large front doors, but then her memory failed and her eyes went wide as her mouth sought in vain to form itself into a name.

"Fred Waterman," the bearded man supplied.

"Of course! Mr. Waterman," Mrs. Tishman rallied, then stalled again. "You're . . . ?"

"From the Australian Film Board."

"From the Australian Film Board," she repeated in an accent Megan had trouble placing, then, turning to her right, "Herbert, this is Mr. Waterman. You know him, don't you?"

Her husband was not inclined to help her out. "Can't say as I do." Dr. Tishman was as corpulent and self-possessed as his wife was thin and nervous. The sort of man, Megan thought, who was used to giving orders and would describe a woman in terms of her breast size. His hand, held casually but protectively close to his genitals, extended itself and he smiled broadly, so that a line formed from jowls to chin, as though he were wearing a mask. "*I'm* Dr. Herbert Tishman," he announced, subtly shifting the emphasis, so that it appeared that the guest was at fault for not knowing him.

A wave of laughter from the step-down living room covered Mrs. Tishman's lapse and her guest's bruised ego. Megan saw that there were well over a hundred guests and, further witness to Mrs. Tishman's inexperience as a society hostess, they were not a happy mix. She had tried to blend her husband's associates with the film crowd, but the well-dressed, well-heeled businessmen and professionals had herded themselves to one side of the room and eyed the noisier, more colorful movie people with suspicious longing. Abandoned wives sat here and there, like kids at a new school who couldn't find anyone to play with. A few intrepid souls had tried to bridge the gap—a dark-haired woman in a shapeless orange dress was listening to a would-be impresario, her too-frequent nodding exposing her fundamental inattention; an elderly couple were chatting up a miniskirted actress. Only the waiters circulated freely, bearing trays of drinks and canapés. She imagined her mother being here, thinking how impressed and simultaneously ill at ease Irene would be. Megan was merely tired. And angry. First at Victor, but mostly at herself. A raucous burst of laughter came from the back of the room, where a group of men clustered around what she supposed was the bar. Well, the Aussie tradition of boozy mateship hadn't changed. She studied the collection of African masks on the wall and gave the Tishmans (or more likely their decorator) marks for good taste.

She felt a draught of air as the door opened behind her, and turned to see a couple—all leather, metal and Technicolor hair—who looked as though they'd just come off a *Mad Max* set. Mrs. Tishman repeated, ''*So* glad you could come!'' and she realized it was her turn. ''I'm Megan Hanlon,'' she said, and to save her hostess more embarrassment, added, ''I'm a director from the States.''

''I know who you are.'' The recognition came from a young blonde in a beautifully tailored mauve cocktail dress. Her features suggested Mrs. Tishman's bygone beauty, but she had her father's more aggressive stance. ''I'm Naomi Tishman. I saw *On the Streets* at the New Directors' Forum in New York and I thought it was terrific.'' Despite her thin-strapped high heels, dozen bracelets and cap of platinum curls, her eyes were by no means unintelligent. ''Daddy''—she touched Tishman's arm—''here's someone you really should meet. Miss Hanlon's been nominated for an Academy Award.''

''Directing a documentary,'' Megan put in, not to be oversold. ''I plan to do a feature here in Australia.''

''Oh, a woman director.'' Dr. Tishman put on his masklike smile. His eyes dropped to her breasts. Such an embarrassing habit, Megan thought. Like picking your nose in public. She wished could control it, though, she guessed, Herbert Tishman wasn't in the habit of controlling many of his impulses.

"Yes," Naomi said. "There are two other women directors here. Maybe we can put them in a triptych and donate them to a museum." Her eyes met Megan's with a look that sought to establish intimacy. Mrs. Tishman was dithering through the next introductions and Dr. Tishman's glance had already slid over to the more impressive cleavage of the girl in the *Mad Max* sheath. "What I really enjoyed about your film," Naomi went on, so self-confident that she was more amused than embarrassed by her parents, "was the way you managed to get those kids to forget about the camera. How did you do that?"

"I hung around with them for a long time before I even introduced the camera. And some of them were so drugged out that they wouldn't have noticed an oncoming truck."

"But they talked to you as though they were confiding in their best friend."

"They're desperate to trust someone. That's the heartbreak of it. I was always afraid that I was exploiting them, but the priest who runs that shelter on Forty-third Street told me that after the film was released the contributions started coming in, so that eased my conscience a bit."

Naomi took her by the elbow and they moved to the steps leading down into the living room. "There are plenty of movie people here," she said. "You probably know some of them. Or they'll know of you, which is even better. That redheaded fellow"—she nodded in the direction of a man who, legs bent, arms extended, was entertaining a semicircle of guests by imitating falling off a surfboard—"he was the cinematographer on that series about the Great Barrier Reef. Good thing we've got a heavy carpet. He's full as a goog . . . and there, by the mantelpiece . . . the woman in the satin pantsuit, she's Nita Narinto. I don't think she's big stuff in the States, but she's a marvelous actress."

"Yes. I've seen her work in a couple of Aussie films. She *is* marvelous."

"I heard they offered her a Hollywood contract on the condition that she get her mouth totally redone and she told them to bugger off. You can always spot the Aussie and Brit actors, can't you? They didn't know that dentistry would be the cornerstone of a successful career." Naomi smiled, exposing a set of teeth that, by nature or investment, were toothpaste-ad perfect. "And that woman with the dark glasses," she went on, "that's Merle Jaunders. She's a gossip columnist. Don't suppose you want to meet her?"

"I don't want to meet anyone until I've had a quick pee."

"Right." Naomi's eyes, still on the guests, narrowed slightly. "Mummy couldn't resist asking everyone she knows, so the room's full of—what's the line?—successful men and the women they married when they were young." She turned quickly, flashing the perfect smile again. "Right. The loo. Come on back to my room."

It was a princess room, pale and lacy, probably more reflective of Mrs. Tishman's tastes than her daughter's. Megan went into the adjoining bathroom, and when she came out found Naomi had thrown a raincoat over her cocktail dress and was furiously brushing her hair. "Another date?" Megan asked.

"No. I'm just going out for a drive."

"Is the party that bad?"

"It's not my party, is it? Daddy didn't think Mummy could handle the introductions without help, that's why I stayed. But now it's in full swing . . ." She put down the brush. "Do you think of Australia as an island or a continent?"

"A continent," Megan answered, not quite following.

"Yes, it is, but after you've traveled it seems like an island. A vast island with nothing in the middle."

"There's Ayers Rock," Megan said dryly. "How long have you been back?"

"About six months. Though it isn't accurate to say back. Back for me would be Jo'burg."

"Ah, you're from South Africa. I was trying to place your parents' accents."

"Mmmm. We're poor bloody immigrants. Daddy made the chickie run over six years ago." Responding to Megan's quizzical look, she added, "Haven't you heard that expression? Daddy literally made the chickie run: he had packets of diamonds smuggled across the border into Zimbabwe in a truckload of chickens so he had a nest egg to start up his clinic here. Mummy was the one who pushed to get out. She didn't want my older brother to have to go into the army. Personally, I think it would've done him some good. Anyhow, as soon as they got here they sent me off to England to school and after I finished they gave me the grand tour of Europe and America. Now I suppose I shall have to find something to do.''

"What sort of work are you interested in?''

"I haven't a clue. I do so envy people like yourself.''

Megan looked away. She was not sympathetic to the inertia of privileged youth, yet she supposed Naomi was more to be pitied than blamed. Despite her own continuing scramble, she knew she was blessed. She loved her work. Men might come and go, but the work was always there.

"It just seems so dead here, after London and New York, I mean,'' Naomi went on.

"Then why not go back to London or New York?'' Megan asked, surprised at the degree to which her Aussie pride had been offended. "Unless . . . ah, I know . . . you've got a boy-friend here.''

"You might say that.''

"And you're nicking off to see him. Then you'll probably have a better time than anyone at the party.''

Naomi shook her head. She seemed on the verge of some romantic disclosure but blurted out, "Sometimes I miss South Africa. I miss seeing black people. I walk the streets here and get the feeling something is missing. Of course, *they're* missing, which is the reason my parents came here. And I miss Alice. She was our housekeeper. Daddy was going to try to get her a visa, but I know she'd never come.''

"It's hard to be brought up in one place and then live in another. I think it fosters a chronic discontent.''

"Not that I'm sorry my parents got out.'' Naomi continued, "I was only sixteen but that was old enough to be scared. That's the thing of it, almost everyone's scared. It takes so much energy to pretend you're not. To sit around talking about the beautiful weather and the garden and sipping gin and pretending that everything's ticketty-boo. You always think it's going to explode, but at the same time you can't really believe that anything's going to happen. I suppose that's true of any rotten situation. Rather like a bad marriage,'' she said with unexpected vehemence. "You keep expecting divorce; on the other hand you think, 'It's gone on forever, what's to say it will ever split apart.' '' Her sigh was so deep and heartfelt that Megan invented Naomi's childhood: bullying, seductive father; neurotic mother; material overindulgence coupled with emotional neglect.

"It's tough being the child of warring parents."

"I didn't mean my parents." Naomi broke off with a little laugh. "I'm not so narrow as to think that a rotten marriage is the same as South Africa."

"In microcosm I suppose it could be."

"No. South Africa will blow up. The only question is when. A rotten marriage . . ."—again the sigh—". . . can really be till death do us part."

Megan smiled. "That's what it says in the contract." Perhaps Naomi was a young divorcée. Or was she seeing a married man?

"Well, I'd never put up with it," she said with convincing finality.

"It was the only contract I've ever broken," Megan admitted. The need to talk about Victor was almost compulsive; but not with a stranger, years younger than she. To her relief, Naomi appeared not to have heard her. She took a set of keys from her dressing table, put them in her raincoat pocket and offered her hand. "It has been a pleasure to meet you. And I trust we'll meet again. I've got tickets to the festival. Your new film will be showing this week, won't it?"

"Yes. And no one will be more eager to see it than I."

"But you must've seen it lots of times."

"Sure. But not the final cut. The producer has the final cut. Only a very few directors—like Woody Allen—have the power of final cut. The rest of us . . ."—she lowered her head in a parody of submission—"are at the mercy of the producers."

"I suppose," Naomi reasoned, "if they put up the money . . ." She was her father's daughter.

"Yeah. That's what Louis B. Mayer said when he was still doing business in Germany in 1941: 'I am responsible to my stockholders.' Or"—she thought of an even better producer story—"as the writer Herman Mankiewicz said when he heard that Harry Cohn claimed he could predict the success of a movie if it made his rear end tremble, 'Imagine! The whole world wired to Harry Cohn's ass!' ''

Naomi laughed, but it was obvious that she was eager to leave.

"I think I can find my way back to the party," Megan said, opening the door. "Nice to meet you. And do come to see *Chappy*. I'd pay you if you'd laugh in the right places and cry at the end." They nodded and she stood back while Naomi made a quick check that the hallway was empty, smiled absently and said good-bye. Megan strolled back to the living room.

The decibel level had increased and the liquor had served to blur the division among the guests. Fortifying herself with a quick glass of champagne, she wandered over to where the actress Nita Narinto stood discussing a revival of *Hedda Gabler* in which she was about to open. After brief but friendly introductions by a man she took to be Nita's boyfriend, she listened to more rehearsal chitchat, studying Nita's face. Those large but haggard eyes. Those crooked teeth. Perfect for a convict woman in the eighteenth century. Megan said she'd try to come to a performance of the play and drifted off to meet a husband-and-wife team who'd made a documentary about aborigines. After discussing possible U.S. distributors—they were savvy enough not to be too hopeful—she was introduced to a burly, soft-spoken director whose film about Anzac forces in World War I she had seen and admired. They fell into conversation about the number of Australian films that were based on historical fact. "Funny, i'n't it," the man observed, "that despite the Americans' overweening and often overbearing sense of national pride, they haven't produced any first-rate films about American history."

"Americans aren't interested in history," said a sharp-eyed, chain-smoking woman who'd introduced herself as a costume designer.

"And think of the great characters," the man went on, "Jefferson, Jackson, Robert E. Lee, Davy Crockett. There's the Revolution, the Civil War, the Alamo."

"My father is a Texan," Megan said, almost to herself. "He was always telling me stories about the Alamo and the Civil War. Of course Southerners are generally more interested in history."

"Americans aren't interested in history," the chain-smoker insisted again.

"Not unless it's told by John Wayne or Rambo," the director observed, which brought a round of laughter.

"Americans think they know who they are. We Aussies . . ." The woman waved the cigarette around. ". . . we have a permanent identity crisis. It's as though we had a snooty older sister—that's England—and a bully-boy older brother—that's America—and we're always wondering which one to imitate."

"Too right," a middle-aged man with a craggy face agreed. "When I was growing up they didn't even teach our history. It was all kings and queens and the bloody Empire. We had to stand up for 'God Save the Queen' when . . ."

Megan couldn't hear the rest of what he was saying because two men standing directly behind her had raised their voices in a boozy argument about football scores. The Aussie director stepped closer, asking her about her next project. She shook her head to indicate that she couldn't hear him. He took his card out and, leaning even closer, asked for one of hers. She realized she'd left them at the hotel, or since Toni hadn't been there to help her pack, perhaps she'd neglected to bring them. She brought her face close to his, caught a whiff of Russian Leather, and gave him the name of her hotel. He said he'd call and wandered off.

"He's got his eye on you." The smoker winked.

"No. He's just . . ."

"He was flirting with you. But Aussie men haven't mastered the art. It's all shy, dig-the-toe-in-the-dirt until they make a grab, then it's whoosh! like a possum up a gum tree." The woman took a final drag on her cigarette, looked around to see where she might deposit the remains, and noticed a general movement in the direction of another room. "Time to put on the tucker bag. We'd best get a move on, otherwise there won't be anything left. You know how show people are when it comes to free food. Free anything. Last year at Cannes I was almost knocked to the ground when some greaseball started handing out free sunglasses."

Megan realized she hadn't eaten in perhaps eighteen hours. "Damn, I'd love a meat pie."

The woman raised her eyebrows in mock horror. "No meat pies here, ducks. It's prawns and undercooked veggies. This is a posh affair. Oh, look there's . . ." She waved. "C'mon. I'll introduce you."

But Megan begged off and said she was going to get another drink. She didn't really want another, but the bar was in the opposite direction from the general crush and through the glass doors behind it she glimpsed a deserted veranda. If she could steal ten minutes of fresh air and solitude she'd revive herself, then go and eat.

"It's a great concept," she heard someone say. "A cross between *Crocodile Dundee* and *Platoon*." And what might *that* be like, she wondered, though she was used to hearing people pitch projects by saying they were a hybrid of former hits. She noticed a grey-haired woman staring at her and realized that she'd laughed out loud. She really must be tired. Crossing the room, eyes down, she heard a medley of accents in snatches of familiar conversations:

". . . you can't maximize potential unless you have a target audience *and* high concept . . ."

"Eighteen! I'd hate to be hanging since she was eighteen. Twenty-five if she's a day. The script requires a young girl."

"The script?"

"All right. *I* require a young girl."

". . . five hits in a row, then the asshole decides to take himself seriously and makes a flop!"

"The grosses in South America were shit. Weintraub knows fuck-all about distribution."

She had almost reached the doors when she heard "Megan Hanlon!" A woman, all shoulder pads, mouth and dark glasses, was bearing down on her as though she wanted to take her into custody. Megan's impulse was to keep moving but she nodded, extending her hand. "I'm Merle Jaunders," the woman pronounced. "I talked with your—well, whatever she is—at the hotel this afternoon."

"My assistant? Toni. You met Toni? Sorry, she didn't mention it, but we'd only just . . ."

"Wonderful party, isn't it?' She pumped Megan's hand once, repeated "Wonderful party" in an even higher pitch, then lowered her voice to say, "Perhaps you've heard of my column. Let's sit down and have a chat."

"Well, I was just . . ."

"Looking for more champagne. Here." She picked up one of a line of full glasses from the bar.

"No. Thank you. I . . ."

She plunked the glass back down, not noticing that she'd splashed it onto the bartender's hand. "What are your impressions of the festival?" she asked, pushing her glasses onto her head.

"It hasn't really started yet, has it?" She was tempted to tell Merle Jaunders that she had a mascara smudge under her left eye, and then tell her to bugger off.

"I meant," Merle said with emphasis, as though Megan were retarded, "your feelings about attending, having your film exhibited. Hoping it will generate some interest in your next?"

"I'm pleased, of course. And nervous." She tried an apologetic smile but felt so insincere that she let it fade before it had formed. "I am sorry, but I just got in yesterday. I mean today. Perhaps we could set up a more appropriate . . ."

"What do you perceive as being the particular problems of the woman director?"

"All directors have problems. As someone once said, a poet needs a pen, a painter needs a brush and a film director needs an army."

"But are you prepared to be a general? Will the sexists stop you? What particular disadvantages do you feel women have?"

Megan shrugged. "Cramps?" she suggested.

This was greeted not with laughter but with a too-serious nod.

"I was jok—" But she was cut off again as Jaunders bulldozed on.

"At *Lulu* we try to do features on the balanced woman, you know, husband and kiddies as well as career. You were married at one time, weren't you?"

"I—"

"Having been born in Australia you must . . ."

Megan didn't hear the rest. By her count, she'd now been interrupted five times. Being interrupted was one of her pet peeves, especially when she'd been asked a question. She gave politeness one last try. "Let's set up an appointment to talk. I'm really very—"

"But you must have some impressions of Australia," Jaunders insisted.

"My impression"—she was frosty—"is that people here are just as pushy as they are in New York. And now, if you'll excuse me." She exited to the veranda and kept walking down the steps and out onto the lawn, her pleasure in squelching Merle Jaunders's rudeness already diminishing. In social situations one must be social. It was self-destructive not to be. Especially with the press. But what the hell, she excused herself, the woman had asked for it.

She'd come to the edge of the promontory. The air was sweet, eucalyptus-scented; the moon was bright, shining on the river. She sat on a bench that had been placed to take advantage of the view and threw back her head. The heavens glittered with long-forgotten constellations. There, there, there and there. The brilliant points of the Southern Cross. As a child, she and the cousins had slept on the veranda at the bush house and looked through Mick's rusty telescope, pushing each other and giggling until Mick had threatened to "come out and bash the lot a ya!" Now she was surrounded by people who thought they were stars. But how seriously could anyone, including herself, take their ambitions when looking up at this glorious canopy? Living in the city, she rarely saw the sky. Perhaps that was one of the reasons ambitious people rushed to the cities: Nature was not in evidence enough to humble them.

Someone was crossing the lawn. She felt intruded upon, as if she'd staked out a site on a deserted beach only to be invaded by another camper.

"Oh, excuse me," the interloper said, sounding genuinely distressed. She was breathing as heavily as if she'd just run a race. "I didn't notice that . . ."

"There's plenty of room. Sit down if you like." She'd noticed this woman when she'd first come into the party, noted her unflattering dress, her obvious discomfort and, she now realized, how much she reminded her of Toni. They were not much alike in appearance—this woman was younger, taller and slimmer—but they shared a similar lack of confidence that made them appear ungainly. Their natural good looks would be noticed, if at all, by other women.

"It's so hot inside," the woman said, sitting down.

"Yes," Megan agreed, though the air-conditioning had been going full blast and it was noticeably warmer outside. "The gum trees smell so lovely," she continued, aware of the woman's labored breathing. "I have some eucalyptus bath oil, but when it comes out of the bottle it smells antiseptic. Some smells—like gardenia—just can't be reproduced."

"I know. We have gum trees around our farmhouse and I always leave the windows open, even when the weather's not the best."

"Air-conditioning can make you sick."

"Perhaps it can. Yes, it does."

"I felt as though I was on the subway in there."

"I've never been on a subway. Are you from New York?"

"From Australia originally, but now I'm a New Yorker."

They fell silent, tacitly acknowledging that they were coconspirators in escaping the crowd, though Greta, casting a sidelong glance, couldn't imagine why this woman had needed to escape. She'd watched her in action—laughing, flirting, chattering. At first she'd thought she recognized her, but decided she must have seen her photo somewhere. Then she'd just studied her, wondering how someone who looked as though she never combed her hair and wore a costume that needed to be pressed managed to look elegant instead of slatternly. "I'm Greta . . . ," she began, but found herself out of breath.

Megan offered her hand, ready to introduce herself, but felt she couldn't interrupt Greta's wheezing struggle. To make their silence seem more natural, Megan rolled her head from side to side and slipped off her sandals. A laugh escaped her. "Don't mind me. I'm not drunk. I'm just so tired I'm at the giggly stage, know what I mean?"

Greta's breathing evened but she still held herself stiffly, back straight, hands folded in her lap. "Oh, yes. When my kiddies were little, sometimes, after I'd gotten them all bathed and put to bed I'd be so tired I'd find myself like that."

"We got in this afternoon. I took a nap. I didn't feel tired until I hit this party. My partner had better sense. Sacked out at the hotel.''

"You came without your husband?'' Greta asked, as though this was something of an accomplishment.

"I don't have a husband. My associate. My friend. Toni,'' she explained, wishing Toni were there.

"My husband lost me, or I lost him, almost as soon as we arrived.''

"Is he in film?''

"Excuse me?''

"I meant, since the party is for the film festival . . . ,'' Megan began.

"Oh, no. He's a doctor.''

"Like our host.''

"I never think of Dr. Tishman as a doctor. Of course he is, but my husband is a real doctor,'' she said with pride.

"You mean he still makes house calls?''

The joke was lost on Greta. "No. He doesn't make house calls, but he cares about his patients, he cares about medicine. He's an associate of Dr. Tishman. They've invited us several times before but we live rather far out, so . . .'' She was short of breath again. She thought to explain her deep inhalations by mentioning the night air, but "Excuse me. I always get short of breath when I'm nervous'' popped out.

"I usually break out in hives.''

"That must be miserable.''

"It is, but it's easier to cover up.''

Encouraged by this exchange of confidences, Greta rushed on. "I almost didn't come to the party. My youngest, Christine—we call her Chrissie—has been sick. Not really sick. Just a cold. Still I don't like to leave her when she's not feeling well.'' She was aware that now the children were grown and really needed her less, she tended to magnify her responsibility. "Chrissie was the one who insisted I come. She's at that age, almost ten now, where she's terribly worried about her old mum having a good time. She's filled with all sorts of notions about how much fun a party like this should be. She insisted on fixing my hair the way she'd seen it in some magazine. I had to brush it out in the car. And she instructed me that if I met any film stars I was *not* to ask for their autographs because that would make me look like a deadhead.'' Greta gave a little laugh. "Chrissie's very good at sizing people and situations up. She's like her father in that. And she's also like him in that she's very intelligent. I know all mothers say that, but it's true. She takes after me in that she's a bit shy. But my oldest boy, Colin, is just the opposite. He . . .''

From the corner of her eye she saw Megan stifle a yawn. And no wonder. She was doing it again: talking about her children, making the same blunder that had caused her to leave the party. Tas had no more than introduced her to the Tishmans before he'd had to leave to go to the hospital and there she was, out of place as a wren in a pride of peacocks. The film people were quite beyond her. Their eyes left her even before introductions were completed. She had been equally ill at ease with the professional wives. They'd chatted about clubs and shopping, travel and Liberal Party politics with a power-behind-the-throne assurance. She'd been dumb as a post. When the man standing next to her at the buffet table had drawn her out, she'd started talking about her children. Realizing her mistake, she'd shifted to the most obvious topic at hand: food. As she'd tasted the pâté, she'd compared it to her own recipe. The man had smiled with such condescension that she'd wished for the honesty of an outright yawn. And now she'd got one. "I'm sorry,'' she said.

"Whatever for?'' Megan studied her face. It might have been pretty if not so strained with anxiety.

"For going on about my children.''

"I'm the one who should apologize for yawning, but as I said, I'm terribly tired.'' Greta covered her mouth, unable to suppress another yawn. Greta felt her own jaws open and they laughed simultaneously.

"I wonder why it's catching?'' Megan said. Pulling her feet up onto the bench and clasping her arms around her knees, Megan went on. "I don't mind your talking about your kids. It's a bit of a relief after all the self-promoting ballyhoo inside. Matter of fact, while you were talking I was trying to remember this Marge Piercy poem I like. There's a line about 'Now I get coarse when the abstract nouns start flashing. I go out to the kitchen to chat about cabbages and habits.' ''

Greta was pleased. "I like Marge Piercy, too."

"But I don't suppose we could go out to the kitchen here."

"No." Greta put her index finger under the wire in her bra and pulled it away from her pinched flesh, then slipped off the high heel that had been punishing her left instep. She couldn't think of anything to say about Marge Piercy except that she liked her. "Do you have any children?"

"Uh-uh. Always thought I would, but it appears that's not in the cards. The last man I was seeing—no, the one before him— he kept giving me articles about my biological time clock and I was almost ready to say okay and go for it, until he started listing his conditions, chief among which was that I give up my next film. So that ended that. Anyhow, I can't exactly see myself on location in a maternity smock."

"What do you do?"

"I'm a writer and director."

"Oh, that must be . . ." Interesting was too bland a word. "Did you love the man?" Greta asked, and realizing that the question was too prying, added, "I'm sorry."

Damn, Megan thought, I wish this woman would stop apologizing. She does it so much it's like a form of self-expression. Still, Greta's apologies were preferable to the onslaught of someone like Merle Jaunders. Indeed, in the circles in which she now moved the only question that was *verboten* was "How much money do you make?" Queries about your sex life were more the rule than the exception. "Can't say as I did," she answered.

"I don't think I could have a child with a man I didn't love."

"Yeah. That's what they taught us. Though if love was the prerequisite I don't suppose we'd have a population problem. It's strange," she went on dreamily. "I only wanted to be pregnant twice in my life. First with my ex-husband and then with a man I had an affair with, oh, over ten years ago. Both times I imagined the child as a little replica of the man. It's only recently that I've thought about a child as being like me. Isn't that ironic? By the time I get around to thinking that maybe *I'm* worth reproducing, it seems unlikely that I will."

"I don't think I could even go to bed with a man I didn't love," Greta said. She realized that sounded terribly naïve, but her truths often did.

"I know one thing; if you're not willing to put in a lot of time on a kid, not just money, but time, then you shouldn't have one." That, Megan realized, sounded very opinionated, and if there was one thing you shouldn't express an opinion about if you were childless it was having children. A sixteen-year-old unwed mother will pull rank on you. Whatever you knew, she *knew*. "I made a documentary about runaway kids," she explained. "Not that I'm blaming the parents in all cases, but . . ."

Now they were off to the races, one topic easing into the next. They talked about the lack of decent movies for kids, their favorite actors and old movies. Greta wanted to know about Megan's next film and Megan, with the same compulsion that always brought Greta back to talking about her children, obliged. Behind them the sounds of the party rose and fell. The moon drifted behind the clouds.

"But"—Megan yawned again—"between you and me and the lamppost, I still have to get the financing. That's the real reason I'm here. That, and to see my family."

"I wouldn't know where to begin," Greta said, awed by Megan's formidable vision and the seeming impossibility of her task. "I have trouble enough keeping the accounts for our farm."

"Hey, I know producers who couldn't manage a farm without three accountants and two lawyers. But I'll get the money somehow."

Greta was impressed and a little chilled by the determination in Megan's voice. "I expect you will," she said encouragingly, though raising and spending millions of dollars was more outrageous than contemplating a pregnancy with a man you didn't love.

Megan ran her hands through her hair. "Yes. As Sister Mary Magdalene used to say, it's all a matter of faith."

"Did you have a Sister Mary Magdalene, too? So did I. When I was a girl at St. Brigid's there was a nun called Sister Mary Magdalene."

"You didn't go to St. Brigid's, did you?"

Greta nodded.

"Not the St. Brigid's near the old hospital up on Shaftsbury Road?"

Greta nodded again.

"I don't believe it! I just don't . . . And your Sister Mary Magdalene, was she tall, with beautiful grey eyes and a mole high up on her cheek, right next to her hair, I mean her wimple? And she taught history . . . ?"

". . . terribly strict . . ."

"Oh, not if you did the work. She was the youngest one there. She . . ."

". . . she taught history. But she's called Joan now."

"What?"

"Yes. After Vatican II, the Order was liberalized and Sister Mary Magdalene threw off her habit . . ." Greta laughed and gestured, as though throwing off a great weight. "And now she drives a car and goes to the university and she's called Joan."

"I simply don't believe it," Megan exclaimed again. Then, shaking her head, "So her real name was Joan. She would never tell me. I . . ."

"You're . . . ?"

"I'm Megan Hanlon."

Greta hit her forehead with the palm of her hand. "You're Megan Hanlon!"

"Right."

"How stupid of me. When I saw you in at the party I thought I recognized you but I thought it was because I'd seen your photo in magazines. How stupid of me!"

"Well, I don't look much like I did at twelve. At least I hope I don't. But did we ever know each other? I don't seem to remember . . ."

"No. Not really. I was two years behind you in class and you left St. Brigid's about two weeks after I arrived. But everyone talked about you for ages after you'd gone. All the wicked things you'd done at school and that you'd gone to Hollywood and become a child star."

"Not hardly. And you're . . . ?"

"I was Greta Papandreou. My family was Greek Orthodox but my father didn't want us going to school with boys so he enrolled my sister, Loukia, and me at St. Brigid's. The girls were always teasing that I wasn't a proper Catholic. One day after school they held me down and baptized me all over again."

Megan grabbed her hand. "Are you still in touch with anyone there? Do you ever see them? The nuns, I mean."

"Oh, yes. As a matter of fact I'm going to visit next Saturday. It's Sister Bruno's feast day."

"Bruno! Old Bogface? She can't still be alive. And why in the world would you want to see Bruno?"

"She was always very kind to me. I don't suppose you'd have time to come along?"

"Oh, God, I'd love to. What day did you say?"

"Saturday. I could drive to town and fetch you. I'd much prefer to have someone to go with. And what a treat it would be for the nuns."

"I wouldn't be too sure of that. Now let's see. I don't think there's anything I desperately want to see that's screening on Saturday. If I could get back into town by the evening . . ."

"My husband will be coming back in. We could visit the convent and then perhaps drive out to our farm for lunch." She took Megan's hand and squeezed it. They might have been thirteen years old. "Oh, say you'll come."

"I promise. I wouldn't miss it for the world. Goddamn! I don't believe this. Now tell me: you wouldn't happen to know anything about Aileen Ingpen, would you? She was my best friend."

"Aileen. No. We didn't know each other well." The beautiful Aileen wouldn't have given her the time of day. "But Mona Gallagher might know something about her."

"Mona Gallagher!" Megan yelped. "I'd forgotten all about Mona Gallagher. Don't tell me, she must be a nun."

"No, she isn't. She's a bank manager. She comes round to the convent quite often, so she may be there when we visit. She never married, you know."

"That wouldn't surprise me. Mona Gallagher. Christ."

Greta hoped that Megan would clean up her language when they visited the nuns. "Mona's not a bad sort."

"And Sister Ursula. Is she still alive?"

"Yes, she is, though not in the best of health."

"She must be eighty if she's a day. And Sister Claire?"

They nattered away, questions tumbling over answers, laughing when Megan recalled the boys from the state school who'd hidden in the bushes, calling out to the girls to let them see their panties and to trade religious insults.

"I never shouted back at them," Greta said. "I'd always pull my hat down and pretend I didn't hear."

"Not me. I once pelted a boy with an apple. Hit him right in the eye, too. Not because he'd said the Catholic thing, but because he was chanting . . ." Megan shook with laughter, controlling herself enough to singsong: " 'Boys are strong, like King Kong; Girls are—' "

" 'Girls are weak; chuck 'em in the creek.' " Greta let go of Megan's hand, clutched the edge of the bench and doubled over with laughter.

"That's it! That's it!" She swayed so that her head was almost touching Greta's shoulder, so convulsed that she was only dimly aware that Greta had turned toward the house and that her laughter was subsiding. Pulling herself up, Megan saw a man, hands stuffed in his pockets, taking the final steps to join them. It was the actress Nita Narinto's boyfriend. "Glad I found you," he said. "Nita's got to get back because of that early rehearsal tomorrow, and since you said you were tuckered out, we thought we'd offer you a lift."

"Great idea. Thanks. I'll go with you. Can I sneak up the side of the house without having to say my good-byes?"

"Sure. Meet you at the car. It's a white Toyota." He turned and walked off.

"Now, Greta, don't let me down," Megan ordered. "You'll call me at the Palmyra Hotel, right? And we'll go off to St. Brigid's, then I'll come visit your farm."

"Don't think I won't. I'll call later this week. It's been such a pleasure to meet you, Megan. Such a pleasure. I can't wait to tell my husband that you're coming."

CHAPTER
SIX

TONI LAY BACK IN THE TUB AND LOOKED DOWN AT HER breasts, belly and thighs. They were buoyant in the water, a smoothly plump horizon of flesh. Had she lived at the turn of the century, she would have been the ideal; nowadays, the well-upholstered look was out of vogue. If she said she didn't mind being overweight, people, even her husband, Joe, assumed she was rationalizing or being an eccentric defeatist. Being a size fourteen and not minding was as socially unacceptable as saying you didn't give a damn about nuclear fallout, so when diets were discussed (far more often than nuclear fallout) she joined in with the same willing conformity with which she'd made her first confession at age seven or read Dr. Spock when her children were little. It was only when she was alone that she could accept and enjoy her body.

She let in more hot water and lolled back, watching her feet turn pink. Just looking at the hotel's complimentary bottles of shampoo, bath oil and lotion made her feel pampered. She rinsed off in a cold shower and patted herself dry. Had she been at home she would have reached for a bathrobe so as not to invite comparison to the girlie magazines Joe kept in his desk drawer, but now she walked happily naked into the other room. It was decorated in muted blues and greys, and apart from the paintings of outback scenes, had no character but tasteful comfort. She sighed with satisfaction. No one would call her; she wasn't responsible for the functioning of a single appliance; she couldn't fix a meal even if she'd wanted to. She crossed to the window, enjoying the feel of her bare feet on carpet she'd never have to vacuum, and stared down to the street below, realizing, with just a shadow of guilt, how relieved she was to be away from her family.

There was no doubt that she loved them dearly, but she wasn't sure that she liked them anymore. Her daughter, Giovanna, was an acquisitive snob, her son, Mario, lacked any achievable ambition, and Joe was suffering from a middle-age malaise that she was powerless to help. He seemed dissatisfied with everything about his life, including her. It was good to be alone, for almost the first time in her life.

Until she left her parents' house she'd always shared a room with her sister. As a young woman, back in the days when they'd air-brushed the crotches of *Playboy* centerfolds and Doris Day had been her idea of a liberated woman, she'd become an airline stewardess. It was the only way a girl of her limited means and education could see the world and maybe meet a rich man. Her parents had heard the "Coffee, tea or me?" jokes and worried about her morals. They needn't have. She was a good Italian girl. To save money, she always shared rooms with other girls and she never let her dates, even the rich ones, get beyond the clutch-and-grab stage. Then she'd met Joe at a cousin's wedding. Joe wasn't rich. In those days he was barely solvent, having just started his own construction business. But he was high-spirited, generous and good-looking in a rugged sort of way. And he was crazy about her. Airline stewardesses weren't supposed to be married, so they'd tied the knot in secret and she kept on working, adding to their nest egg, until she got pregnant and failed the airline's periodic weight check.

They'd lived in a cramped one-bedroom in lower Manhattan until Giovanna was almost two, then, finding she was pregnant again, and too strapped for money to get a larger apartment in the city, they'd moved to the suburbs. She'd missed Manhattan, but there was no other choice. As their fortunes improved they'd moved into larger houses, but mere space had never given her a sense of privacy. She was always occupied with the yard, the kids, the neighbors and the neighbors' kids. Then, the great financial leap forward—the summer place in Vermont, and finally, their present home in Alpine: three bedrooms and a view of the Palisades. In all those years she'd rarely been alone except in the shower, and sometimes not even there. The children, when they were little, would climb in with her, or a younger, more amorous Joe would join her under the spray. She'd looked ahead: the children would leave home, perhaps she would use one of the bedrooms for her "workroom." It didn't turn out that way.

When Giovanna left for college, Joe appropriated Giovanna's bedroom as his office. Mario's grades weren't good enough to go anywhere but a local college. He stayed at home until he dropped out in his sophomore year and went to seek his fortune as a musician. Then Giovanna moved back in. She had a job in the city, but was willing to exchange the freedom of her own apartment for the money she could save (or rather spend on a car and expensive clothes) by living at home. No sooner had Giovanna found "Mr. Right"—who, to Toni's mind, was entirely wrong—married and moved to a Manhattan co-op when, just a month ago, Mario and Mary Lou, his wife of two months, moved back in. Mario and Mary Lou said they were "between gigs," though to Toni's knowledge their USO tour to entertain the troops in Iceland was the only paying job they'd ever had, if you didn't count the beer bars in Mary Lou's native Tennessee. It was hard to understand how Mario, a boy of Italian descent raised in the affluent suburbs of New Jersey, believed he was destined to become a country-and-western star. But Mario had never had much of a grasp on reality. Toni had known from the boy's infancy that he was never going to be the leader of men Joe wanted him to be, so she'd undertaken a delicate balancing act: on the one hand nudging, cajoling and encouraging Mario to try a little harder; on the other reasoning, hinting and urging Joe to lower his sights for the boy. As a result, Mario thought she was a nag while Joe accused her of coddling.

Ever since Mario and Mary Lou had moved in, Joe had been in a foul mood. He wouldn't confront Mario directly, so he complained to Toni. Caught up in preparations for her trip, and virtually certain that Mario didn't have any plans for the future, she told Joe that she didn't really mind Mario and Mary Lou being there. In truth, she dreaded coming home to find them plopped in the den like a couple of couch potatoes, watching TV and munching snacks. It was worse when they roused themselves to rehearse. The electric guitar and their yowling about cheatin' hearts and failed crops made the entire house throb. Things weren't much better after hours. Shrieks and giggles escaped from Mario's bedroom well into the night, which may have explained why Mary Lou had trouble getting up in the morning. Toni had never known a human being who slept so much. The girl was bearlike, in a constant state of hibernation. When Mary Lou wasn't sleeping or watching TV she was in the bathroom washing her hair—another mystery, since it never looked quite clean.

The night before she'd left for Australia, after she'd misplaced her passport and last-minute jitters started to creep in, Toni had turned to Joe in bed, too preoccupied to feel real desire, but craving the snuggles and hugs that, over the last years, had served as a substitute for lovemaking. Joe patted her hand and told her to take a Valium. She'd smiled to herself in the darkness of the familiar bedroom, knowing Joe wasn't even aware that he was trying to punish her.

He hadn't objected when, years before, she'd reentered the job market. The children were grown, she'd done more than her share of volunteer work, and the extra money would come in handy. They would save for the European honeymoon they'd never had. She'd worked first for a producer at CBS, then become a production coordinator for public television. They'd had a few knock-down drag-outs about sharing household responsibilities and, as usual, she'd capitulated. Though she'd argued otherwise, deep down she still felt the house was her responsibility. Out of her salary, she'd hired a gardener and a once-a-week cleaning lady. (Women's lib or no, she knew she'd never see a man clean a toilet in her lifetime.)

It was after she'd begun to work with Megan that the real trouble had started. To the general public the business of moviemaking looked like fun, and though Joe had seen her struggle in after a shoot, weighed down with bags and fatigue, he chose to think of her work as glamorous. She'd changed, he complained, she'd turned into a careerist with a big head, she was neglecting their friends, she was neglecting him. It was true that she'd changed. For the first time, work was something more than a paycheck. It excited her. She didn't mind putting in the extra hours or taking on more responsibility. She had no desire to be a mover and shaker (more lucrative offers from other film companies surprised but didn't tempt her), but she was glad that Megan, who always praised and encouraged her, was becoming one. Joe, who'd never worked for anything but money, resented her enthusiasm and her autonomy. When she tried to talk it out with him, things only got worse. Her trip to Australia was the capper. Joe became surly. The cleaning lady developed a back problem and quit. The gardener was on vacation. Even inanimate objects began to fall apart: the refrigerator started to freeze everything, the microwave began to send out warning beeps, the dishwasher piddled water on the floor. "I'm sorry the repairman can't come till Saturday," she'd said to his back. He'd grunted, fumbled for her hip and patted it. She'd debated about getting up for the Valium. When she had almost fallen asleep, he'd turned and they'd shared drowsy sex.

The next morning on the way to the airport, her mother in the backseat alternating reports of recent airline crashes with prayers to St. Joseph, patron of travelers, Joe had said, over and over, what a great idea the trip was. His voice had all the sincerity of a White House spokesman telling the public not to worry about the budget deficit. She didn't expect that Joe would run wild with wild women, but she was sure he'd take advantage of her two-week absence to gamble in Atlantic City and she'd come home to a scrambled checkbook as well as spoiled food, a piddling dishwasher, and Mario and Mary Lou lounging on the couch in the same position in which she'd left them. When Joe kissed her good-bye, he'd had the about-to-be-abandoned expression she remembered on Mario's face when she'd left him on his first day of nursery school. It both infuriated and touched her. "Have a good time," Joe said in parting. Tuned to every nuance of his voice, she knew he was hoping for the opposite.

Toni pulled the draperies, slipped into her robe and picked up the room service menu. Medallions of veal, lamb with mint sauce, crayfish salad. And she wanted . . . a hamburger. A big juicy hamburger. With fries. She felt so rejuvenated that nothing else would do.

She was sitting at the desk, dipping French fries in catsup, or tomato sauce as the waiter called it, and reading about the mating habits of the platypus, when there was a knock on the door.

She looked around, trying to locate her travel clock, reckoning that it must be after midnight.

"Who is it?" But who could it be.

"Me."

Megan's face was as smilingly composed as a graduation photo but her skin was mottled, a sure sign of distress.

"How come you're all dressed up?" Toni asked. "Don't tell me you went to that party after all."

Megan moved into the room.

"Did you take an upper? Megan? You must've taken an upper."

"No. But I feel as though I'm hallucinating. Do you know that old story, *Appointment in Samarra*?" Toni shook her head. "A man," Megan explained, "is warned of his impending confrontation with Death, so he flees the city and goes to Samarra. And there he meets Death, who says, 'How did you know that this is where we were supposed to meet?'"

Toni raised her hands and eyebrows. "Sorry, I don't get it."

"Victor," Megan hissed. "I saw Victor."

"Your Victor?"

"He's not my Victor. He was never my Victor."

"But Victor. Your ex. You met him at this party?"

"No. I met him downstairs in a restaurant. After all these years. Did I run into him in Hollywood or New York? No. At a restaurant in Perth. And I looked like something the cat dragged in. So I lied and said I was going to the party, so then I had to go."

"Wait. Slow down. You ran into Victor and . . ."

"And his daughter. Did I say I met his daughter? At first I thought she was his date. Her name—" Megan paused for significance, then spat it out—"is Deirdre. Deirdre," she repeated, and when Toni didn't register the appropriate response, "That's what we were going to call our kid if it was a girl."

"Maybe he just liked the name." Wrong response. "Or maybe he was still thinking of you." Even worse. "I didn't know you and Victor planned to have kids."

"Oh, yes. Oh, yes." Megan paced, pulling off her bracelets. "We were going to do it all. The whole megillah. We used to fantasize the perfect genetic combination: his eyes, my nose, etc. Well, she got his eyes *and* his nose. I'm surprised Sylvia hasn't made her get it bobbed. I've told you about my ex-mother-in-law, haven't I?'' Toni nodded uncertainly, but Megan rushed on. ''Sly old Sylvia. Boy, did she ever intimidate me. She used to go on about how she'd given up her career as a concert pianist—like she was on her way to Carnegie Hall but she got waylaid at Saks. I only heard her play once and she could barely get through 'Stardust.' It was one of those little lies that grew into a big lie. Victor thought I was being a bitch when I pointed it out. When we got married Sylvia told me how wonderful it was that I was determined to have a career. I didn't find out until we were getting the divorce that she'd warned Victor that he was buying trouble by marrying a woman who wouldn't put him first. I'll never forget when he told me that. We were already separated. He'd just come back from California. We were at Ratner's—you know, the kosher restaurant on the Lower East Side where they have bowls of pickles on the tables—and Victor was into cocaine at the time, so you can imagine how much sense he was making. I started yelling and crying. Got so out of control I knocked over a bowl of pickles. God, I hate people who make scenes in public.'' She tossed the bracelets onto the nightstand and attacked her earrings. ''I knocked over a bowl of pickles and the manager asked us to leave. Victor stormed out and we argued some more on the street. Then he bounced off and there I was, sitting in the gutter at the corner of Rivington and Delancey, reeking of pickle juice and licking my tears. Not exactly Tristan and Isolde, huh? I didn't even have taxi fare to get home.'' She half grunted, half laughed and sat on the bed. ''Well, I was the one who refused to take alimony.''

''In God's name why?''

''Feminist principles?'' she suggested, and when Toni looked dubious, ''Aw, because I didn't want him to think he could buy me off. Treat me like shit and then tip me. Because . . .''—she kicked off her sandals—''I didn't think I deserved it. But it was the right decision. The state I was in then, if I'd had even a pittance coming in I would've rolled up on the couch and watched soap operas for the next ten years. You know there was a time, right after my divorce . . . shit, I didn't wash my hair for three weeks. And I wasn't even the one who'd wanted to get married. Victor talked me into it. I didn't want to be anyone's wife. Like my mother said, you follow a man somewhere, you end up nowhere.'' Memory and fatigue unfocused her eyes and made her shoulders sag. Toni offered a cup of cold coffee, but was ignored. ''Isn't it awful,'' Megan went on, ''the way our minds revert to clichés when we hold a grudge? I'd pictured him all gold chains, hairspray and swagger, a sort of Hollywood pimp. Of course he isn't like that. He was never like that. He looks . . .''

''Don't tell me he looks unhappy,'' Toni warned. ''Don't say that.'' She'd been around enough to know that the seeming misery of an ex-husband could act as a powerful aphrodisiac. ''He's not exactly the orphan of the storm. He's got millions.''

''I know. I know. He was taking meetings with studio execs when I was busting my ass for a crew assignment on local TV.''

''So what do you care if he's unhappy?''

''I don't.'' But she looked contrite. ''I used to be envious of him. Envious of his connections and his confidence and his ability to walk away from things. Isn't that shameful?''

''I'd say it was right on.''

''I used to have these strong revenge fantasies. Y'know? I'd be rich and famous and have two lovely children and a box-office hit and he'd be . . .'' Megan shrugged. ''I wanted to punish him. When he kissed my cheek tonight, I wanted to bite off his earlobe.''

Toni laughed. ''Well, that's just normal.''

Megan chuckled weakly, then shook her head, once and slowly. ''Toni, if you'd only known him when we first met. He was the one with the talent. He was so sharp. What an eye he had. When we were students and I made my first twenty-minute film—a really ghastly little thing about a woman cracking up on a subway platform . . .'' She snorted at the memory. ''. . . he was the one who told me how to cut it, how to make it work. I was sure he was going to be the next Kurosawa, the next Fellini or Truffaut.''

''Yeah, well, he won't be the first one to drive the money-lenders out of the temple at twenty and end up behind the cash register at forty. And *you* didn't stand a chance of being the next famous woman director because there weren't any, so don't get all soft and runny about Victor.'' Toni had heard about Megan's marriage before. Heard it as horror story and farce, but never as love story. Now Megan had gone from anger to self-castigation to tenderness in the space of fifteen minutes. Most assuredly a love story, and like all good love stories, a messy one. "So, did you go to the party with Victor?"

"Uh-uh." Her eyes felt full of grit and she jerked her head up as though she'd heard a loud noise. "All during the party I was totally disoriented. I kept thinking, 'I'm finally back in Oz'—it seemed that unreal. Oh, and I met a woman named Greta. It turned out we went to St. Brigid's around the same time. Can you imagine that coincidence?"

"Is she in the business?"

"Hardly. She's afraid of her own shadow. She's just some guy's wife. But can you imagine the coincidence?"

"Sure. There are only fifty people in the world and we keep running into them. I remember once when I was a stewardess I was making small talk with this old man and it turned out he was not only from Castrovillari, the village my grandmother had come from, but that they'd played together as children. Life is full of coincidences you wouldn't dare put in a screenplay."

"I told her I'd visit the convent with her and then go out to her farm."

"How the hell are you going to fit all that in?"

"I'll juggle it. I can't miss seeing the nuns." She wobbled to her feet and rolled her head around. "Christ, I'm beyond tired. Sorry I interrupted your supper."

"That's okay." Toni glanced longingly at the remaining French fries. But even she wouldn't eat cold French fries. "I was finished anyway. Just enjoying the time alone. But let's go to bed now."

Megan bent to retrieve her sandals and scooped up her discarded jewelry. She moved to the door, then turned. "By the way, it was Victor who sent the roses."

"Since he's being so nice, for reasons I can't understand"— she had never met a producer with a conscience, let alone a guilty one—"why not show him your script? He's got plenty of gelt and even if he doesn't want to invest himself he knows the people who can."

Megan's face lost its muzzy, ready-for-sleep softness. "You must be crazy."

"Don't be so Irish," Toni cautioned. She understood vendetta, she understood revenge, but there was this flinty unforgiving thing in the Irish she would never understand. Only the Irish would send a child to bed without any supper. Surely "cut off your nose to spite your face" must have come from them.

Megan had been leaning against the door frame but now drew herself up grandly. "I wouldn't take a dime from Victor if I was a bag lady in a snow storm."

We'll see about that, Toni thought as she said good night and closed the door.

The moon had gone behind the clouds. It was humid and windy, threatening rain. Greta glanced at the speedometer, knotted her scarf more tightly under her chin and resisted the impulse to tell Tas to slow down. Up ahead she saw the little store and petrol station illuminated by a single overhead light. It would be another forty-five minutes before they reached the farm. The rushing wind and the roar of the motor made conversation impossible and she could tell from his expression that Tas was in no mood for a postmortem of the party, but her desire to communicate her good feelings was so persistent that she raised her voice above the noise. "I can't wait to tell Chrissie that I met Nita Narinto."

"Right. She'll be pleased to hear that."

"And that film director I told you about. What a surprise that was. To think we both went to . . ." But it was hopeless trying to be heard, and Tas was concentrating on the road, as well he might at seventy miles an hour. She locked her hands in her lap and replayed the party in her mind, skipping over her initial discomfort and focusing on her meeting with Megan. It was just like those articles about overcoming shyness advised: if you opened up, people responded. You could make friends even though you had little in common. That a woman like Megan Hanlon, whom she didn't understand, didn't quite approve of, but greatly admired, should talk and laugh with her, even make a date with her! The encounter had blown away the smell of social failure and sent her back into the party with new confidence.

The film crowd, judging from the noise, had taken over the dining room. Mrs. Tishman was on the landing, bidding good night to parting guests. Greta had looked around the living room at the stragglers who sat, or rather sprawled, on the many couches, thinking that Tas must be back from the hospital. She'd spotted him in the alcove near the bar, with Tishman and a group of men. Tishman put his arm around her waist, introduced her as Dr. Burke's lovely wife (she knew he'd forgotten her name), then proceeded to ignore her as he continued a story about Tas's performance during a complicated operation. Tas turned away, one arm resting on the bar, and began to talk about sailing with one of the men. Hospital stories, especially those lauding his skill, embarrassed him. Tishman noticed that Tas's glass was empty, took it and, with a wink to his audience, leaned over and whispered to the bartender. The bartender poured the glass so full that the liquid belled up around the rim and would spill at the slightest touch. "Your drink, Tas." Tishman tapped his shoulder and Tas, still talking, half turned, picked it up and brought it to his mouth without spilling a drop. "See what I mean!" Tishman boomed like a salesman. "Burke's hand wouldn't shake if he was getting electric shocks in a blizzard." The men laughed and one woman who was on the periphery of the crowd applauded. "Bugger off, Tishman," Tas said, with such good-natured gruffness that Greta was sure she was the only one who'd detected the underlying belligerence.

"I can understand why you don't like Tishman." She raised her voice over the roar of the motor. "He turns everyone into performing . . ."

"He has his good points," Tas yelled back.

"I can't say as I much like any of the Tishmans." As they were pulling out of the driveway at the party, Naomi Tishman had driven up. Greta thought it strange the Naomi had left the party, even stranger that she leaned out from her BMW to say how much she'd enjoyed meeting her. Surely Naomi couldn't be genuine. They'd barely exchanged words upon being introduced and she'd felt an uncomfortable current between them, as though Naomi was sizing her up. But that was ridiculous. Why would

Naomi Tishman want to size her up? How could she ever hope to socialize if she was always on the defensive, always comparing herself to younger, prettier women? She glanced across at Tas. His face, dimly illuminated by the dashboard lights, had the expression it took on when he'd lost a patient, a sadness sharpened by frustration. She raised her voice again. "But overall," she added, hoping to improve his spirits, "I think it was a good evening, don't you?"

"Christ, no." He eased up on the accelerator and stared ahead. Why had he made the mistake of going to the party? To please Greta, yes; but also because Naomi had promised that she wouldn't be there. He suspected that she'd gone back on her word not, as she'd whispered upon greeting him, because her mother couldn't handle the guests alone but because she couldn't resist the chance to get a look at Greta. Naomi had a Pandora-like compulsion to get into things. He'd noticed that the first time he'd met her, months ago when she'd just come back to Australia and her mother had brought her to the offices to show her around. Naomi had wanted to know about the staff, the state-of-the-art medical equipment. And about him. She'd heard that he'd done research abroad. How could he possibly stand the dullness of being back in Australia? Her restlessness and outspoken dissatisfaction had made him acutely aware of the difference in their ages. "Just call me Tas," he'd insisted, conscious that in her eyes he was almost her father's contemporary. But he had nothing in common with Tishman. All the vices of middle age had congealed in Tishman. He was corpulent, greedy, self-satisfied, whereas he, Tas, was fit, striving, still dedicated. He noticed Naomi's smooth neck, her fine, pale gold hair. Mrs. Tishman grew restive and Naomi said that she would come back alone, probably the next day around quitting time. Could he show her around? Her dismissal of her mother and her confident flirtatiousness had reversed their ages, making him feel younger than she.

She hadn't come the next day or the day after that. He'd almost forgotten about her, shifting his anticipation to the lesser pleasures of a swim after work or some good Italian food at Marintello's. Then, just as he was about to leave the office, young Dr. Wright had come in wanting his opinion on some test results. Tas looked at them and confirmed the worst. How much, Dr. Wright asked him, should he tell the patient?

"Let me get a look at him," Tas said. They'd stepped into the corridor and Dr. Wright had pointed out the man. He was not much older than Tas himself. "You're going to die, poor blighter," Tas thought. There was something about the man, a certain dejected caution that suggested that he'd never really lived.

"Order him to take a holiday," Tas said. "Tell him to enjoy himself." Suddenly he felt very tired. And then Naomi had appeared, coming toward him with a slow smile, slow walk. She was wearing a Chinese-style dress, a combination of demureness and exposure. It was high to the neck and loose-fitting, but her arms were bare and, as she moved, the slits in the skirt showed her thighs. She was worn out from shopping, she said. But after Bergdorf's and Bloomingdale's, what was there here that she'd want to buy? Would he like to go for a stroll?

The boats on the river had never looked so graceful, nor the sunlight on the bare arms and legs of office girls so innocently entrancing. Even a near collision as a Toyota fought a Hillman for a parking place had seemed amusing. If only every workday could end like this, strolling on the riverbank, listening to a pretty woman talk about frivolous things. He looked down at the part in her hair. Her very scalp seemed enticing. He imagined her bald and smiled at himself that he should find that erotic. He had no intention of going any further than this ego-stroking flirtation; indeed, he found himself talking about his children, even talking about Greta and the farm. So he was surprised when, approaching his car, he asked, "Can I take you somewhere?" and she moved a step closer, so that they were almost touching, closed her eyes to show lids brushed with mauve shadow and said, "You can take me anywhere you like."

That had been the beginning of what was now a full-blown affair. More than an affair. They loved each other. Naomi fantasized their escape: they would go back to America together; he would accept a position in Houston or New York. To his surprise, she even talked about wanting children. It would be a second chance for him in every way. His own children were completely alienated from him. It was natural enough for the boys since he'd seen so little of them during their childhoods and they were now almost men, filled with their own concerns. It was his daughter Chrissie's palpable disapproval that really hurt, the most stinging rejection he'd ever experienced. Here again, he felt that Greta had killed him with kindness. She was always ready to make excuses for his absences and his black moods. She did not nag, she never lost her temper, but the undercurrent of reproach, mingled with the suffering nobly born, had turned Chrissie against him. Chrissie would never forgive him if he got a divorce. But Chrissie was already lost to him.

He cursed himself for not having made the break years before. He, to whom others in the world deferred, was a hypocrite in his own house. God knew he had tried—first, when he'd returned from America, and afterward, before any particular woman was involved. But whenever he pressed for a divorce, Greta seemed to take leave of her senses. She didn't do it in the usual way—she didn't rant and rave, cry or get hysterical. She literally took leave of her senses: expression drained from her face, her eyes became sightless, she cocked her head to the side as though her hearing were impaired, she lost the power of speech. To Greta, marriage was more than a vow or a contract. It was a sacrament. "The bond of Christian marriage cannot be broken except by death." As a boy at the Marist Brothers school, he, too, had parroted that. But it was crazy to think that anyone could go through twenty years without questioning, without change. But Greta still held that belief. It supported her intransigence, her inability to exercise her will. But she would never see it that way. He didn't want her to think that he was leaving her because of Naomi. Fidelity was not, and never had been, the issue—or so he'd convinced himself. He had no desire to wound her; if anything, he still felt an obligation to protect her fragile ego, so it was crucial that she not find out about his affair with Naomi. That would muddy the issue. This time he would just have to insist on divorce, and if she resisted he would have the courage to desert—such a brutal word—not desert, but *leave*. Because it was hopeless. Impossible. Like talking to a patient with lung cancer who refused to give up smoking. He glanced over at her. Something she'd just said had jarred his attention, some name.

". . . and really very nice. You wouldn't think that someone so famous would be so nice, though I suppose that since we both went to St. Brigid's . . . I'd love to see her new film but I suppose the tickets are already sold out."

What was she talking about? He'd have to admit that he hadn't been listening. "Who?"

"Megan Hanlon. I've been telling you how . . ."

"What?"

"Megan Hanlon," she shouted. "She's coming out to the farm after we visit the nuns. She's staying at the Palmyra Hotel and I'm going in to pick her up, but I thought you could drive her back to—"

The car swerved sharply to the left, wheels crunching onto the gravel shoulder, headlights flashing on a wall of trees. "Tas!" He righted the car, clicked the headlights onto high, then low, eased up on the accelerator. "Righto. I'm all right. You were saying?"

Her heart thudded. "Would you like me to drive?"

"No. It's all right. You were saying?"

"Megan Hanlon. The film director. She has masses of red hair and she was wearing this aqua-colored silky outfit. I'm surprised you didn't notice her. Oh, I suppose she'd left while you were still at the hospital. Was your patient all right? I didn't think to ask."

"He'll pull through. You invited her out to the farm?"

"Yes. I just told you. I said . . ."

"Sorry, Bakie. Really, sorry."

She wasn't sure if he was apologizing for swerving off the road or for not listening to her, but he hadn't called her Bakie in years. It was a pet name from their early days, a derivative from baklava, the honey-sweet Greek pastry. And his voice had been so serious, as though he were still a Marist Brothers boy in confession, striking his breast and saying, *"Mea culpa."* She touched his leg. "I thought I might make a quiche when she comes to visit. What do you think? Chrissie will be so excited. I think . . ." But she had lost him again. He floored the accelerator and gripped the steering wheel with both hands, and they hurtled on into the darkness.

CHAPTER
SEVEN

THE WAKE-UP CALL JARRED MEGAN OUT OF A FEVERISH sleep. She put the receiver back in its cradle and lay, staring wide-eyed at the ceiling, trying to recapture her dream. In it she'd been riding in an open car—was that her father driving?— then the car had turned into a bus. A very crowded bus. The other passengers were dressed in tuxedos and fancy gowns, so they must be going somewhere important. She was dressed in her navy blue St. Brigid's uniform. The skirt came up to her crotch and she kept trying to pull it down. The landscape became dense and junglelike. Branches scraped the windows. "Fasten the seat belts," she warned. But there weren't any, and the other passengers were all asleep, or drugged, slumped against one another, arms pinioned, heads lolling. The bus went faster and faster. She began to climb over the passengers, frantic to get to the wheel. If she could get to the wheel and take control . . . The rest was lost. She hated to lose a dream. Losing a dream could leave her with an unbalanced feeling that lasted the whole day.

A shaft of hot sunlight sliced into the room where the draperies didn't meet. She threw off the sheet and went to the window, grounding herself in reality, muttering, "Perth. Morning." She called Toni to say she was up, ordered their breakfast and rummaged through her suitcase, hearing Irene's voice say, "Hang up your clothes." Later. She put on white slacks, an aqua linen shirt, and cinched them with a silver-and-turquoise belt. She was applying mascara when Toni came in. "I guess you think you're going to run into Victor, huh?"

"No. Why would you think . . . ?"

"Because you don't usually bother with makeup to go to screenings."

It hadn't occurred to her why she was taking the trouble, though of course Toni was right. They ate their steak and eggs and drank too many cups of coffee. Megan slipped on huaraches, put on her cattleman's hat and took a taxi to the theater.

The first film was French, a love triangle of seemingly blasé sophisticates that nevertheless ended in a grizzly crime of passion. The next film, also French, was set during the German occupation. She nodded off while the hero was losing his virginity and jerked awake as a train was being blown up. Afterward, she went out into the lobby. Except for the fact that people were kissing and exchanging business cards, it was like a subway platform at rush hour. She ran into a New York screenwriter and her girlfriend and they dodged across the street to a pub, had trouble getting served, lingered too long over beer and meat pies. She dashed back to the theater just as the doors were about to close, flashed her pass to the doorman and went into the auditorium. It was so crowded she thought she'd best stand near the back. Then she saw Victor, down near the front, motioning for her to join him. "I thought you'd be at this one," he said as she crawled over those already seated and slid in next to him.

"I'm surprised you are," she said. The movie was a documentary about El Salvador, made on the cheap.

"I never miss anything Haskel Wexler photographs. Hey, lady, take off your hat." He grinned, reaching for it. She took off the hat, asking where Deirdre was. He started to answer as the lights dimmed. In their old days together the dimming of the lights had been the signal for a kiss, a nuzzle of the neck. He'd take her hand and pull it into his crotch; she'd hiss that he should pay attention. As though sharing the same thought, he now whispered, "Pay attention." She straightened, trying to concentrate on the titles. He scrunched down into his habitual viewing posture, knees pushed against the seat in front of him, one arm draped over the back of her seat. "Didn't your mother teach you to sit up straight?" she'd always teased him. During their marriage, they'd spent as much time in movie theaters as they had in their apartment. Grand old mausoleums like Loews with its velvet curtains and bare-breasted statues; grungy revival houses—the Thalia, St. Mark's, the Regency—two features for a dollar, the air thick with cigarette smoke, latrine disinfectant and popcorn, the audiences so vocal they would literally hiss a loser off the screen. Those movie houses, the grand and the raunchy, were gone now. Nowadays it was seven dollars at the Cineplex V, squeezed into odd-shaped auditoriums, sound seeping in from the movie next door, commercials on the screen and signs warning you not to talk, smoke, break the law.

Victor shifted his weight. His arm grazed her shoulder. She wanted him to let it rest there, to feel the weight of it. After all these years she could still feel that tension between them, like a mild electric current. It made her hair stand up on her arms, made her neck tingle. Strange that she should have such a reaction. The first clue that she was getting over an infatuation was when she began to notice the man's physical faults—this one's ears were too large, that one's eyes were too closely set, another's hands began to look blockish. Her dissatisfaction with the man's character was never far behind. But none of that seemed to apply to Victor. Her eyes slid sideways. Victor looked better than ever. She reminded herself that this was the theater in which *Chappy* would be screened and, listening to the sound levels, decided that they were off. She'd best get into the booth and check them before her showing. Then she was riveted to the screen—a wonderful aerial view of the jungle, a series of cuts coming closer to the ground, marvelous editing . . .

They came out into the warm glow of a setting sun. It was still in the nineties. "Your hair looks like it's on fire," Victor said. She put her hat back on. Victor was buttonholed by a thickset man who pumped his hand and reminded him of a meeting in Cannes. She stepped to the curb, motioning for a taxi. Victor stepped up behind her. "Share a cab? Have a drink back at the hotel lounge?" She couldn't say no because she'd arranged to meet Toni there. To her annoyance, the cabby who'd been ignoring her pulled up when Victor hailed him.

The hotel bar was crowded, hot and noisy. She spotted Toni in a back booth. She and Victor worked their way over, stopping for greetings, handshakes, hugs. Toni's face stayed so pleasantly bland as Megan introduced her to Victor that as soon as he went to fetch their drinks Megan said, "You missed your calling. You ought to be in the foreign service."

"It must be hard to stay mad at a man who's that good-looking."

"Handsome is as handsome does." She might have been a ventriloquist's dummy sitting on Irene's lap.

Victor shouldered his way back with Emile Gallimard, the French director of the crime-of-passion film she'd seen that morning, in tow. More introductions. More small talk. The din made real conversation impossible. She downed her Scotch fast, and as it hit her the noise seemed farther away. Toni leaned into her. "I called Dennis Danher's office. His secretary said he hasn't read the script yet."

"How come I'm starting to hate him when I haven't even met him? We sent him the script over two months ago."

"I got talking to the secretary. Turns out she has a sister living in New Jersey. She said she'd read it."

"Does she have ten million to invest?"

"She'll like it. She'll give it to him. I'll call her up again in a coupla days. Relax. Even if he hasn't read it, your appointment with him is still on. Producers don't like to read, you know that. You'll pitch it to him. That might be even better."

She listened to Toni's encouragement with half an ear, the other one turned to Emile and Victor's conversation. Emile, egg-headed, a small man with nervous gestures, was telling Victor how much he liked his films. Well, there was no accounting for Gallic taste: they loved the macabre; they thought Jerry Lewis was a genius. Emile smiled and said he liked her hat. She smiled back. "How about I take you ladies to dinner?" Victor suggested. Megan gave Toni's knee a warning nudge under the table.

"Love to but can't, Victor," Toni said. "I met with a union rep today, trying to untangle some red tape, and I've got to fill Megan in. You know she plans to shoot a movie here next year, don't you?"

"Megan hasn't told me anything about her plans. We've hardly had a chance to talk." He looked straight at Megan but she offered no apologies.

"It's a terrific screenplay," Toni said, ignoring another nudge.

"The best she's ever written. And the biggest." She wasn't going to miss a chance to talk it up with Victor Taub no matter how much Megan complained later.

"So? No dinner?" Victor asked again.

"But you will certainly all see each other at my party," Emile put in. "But of course you are coming."

"But of course," Megan assented. Being at a film festival was like being on an ocean liner: there was no escape. Gossip ran through the crowd like a new strain of a virus. Everyone knew what everyone else was up to. That was the point of being here. "But right now I'm going up to my room to shower."

Victor rose with her. "Sounds like a good idea."

"You scrub my back, I'll scrub yours?" Emile suggested.

"It's scratch," Toni told him. "*Scratch* my back."

"You also want your back scratched?" Emile asked, and as Toni shook her head in protest, he winked and said, "I know the difference between scrub and scratch. I did graduate work in America."

"I'll bet you knew it even before that," Toni said in her gravelly voice.

"Believe me, madam, I did. Stroke, scrub, scratch, smooth, soothe, snuggle, smooch . . ."

"We'll finish the 's' words at your party," Toni assured him, gathering up her things.

They had almost reached the exit when Merle Jaunders, followed by a photographer, bore down on them. "Aren't you Victor Taub? *The* Victor Taub?" she cawed like one of the parrots on her jungle-print dress.

"*The* Victor Taub stayed at home. I'm his clone."

Merle laughed. "I'll even talk to his clone. Your movies! They've given me more shivers than a month of cold showers. Not since Alfred Hitchcock . . ." She gushed like an open fire hydrant. "By the way, I'm Merle Jaunders. I have a daily column and I also write for *Lulu* magazine."

"Pleased to meet you, Miss Jaunders, but—"

"Call me Merle."

". . . but Merle, I'm just part of the audience at the festival. I'm not showing anything."

"I know that. Word has it that you're here to build a new

resort complex. Down near Augusta, isn't it? We could talk about that, too.''

Megan made a move to leave but Victor snaked his arm around her. ''This is the person you should be talking to. She's the rising star.'' Megan couldn't tell if he was using her as a decoy or giving her a well-intentioned push into the spotlight.

Merle, who had hitherto ignored Megan, insisted, ''But I *do* want to interview Miss Hanlon. I told her so last night but she was busy.''

Toni took charge. ''No time like the present. I'm Toni Massari. We met yesterday. Why don't we do a short interview in the lobby right now?''

''That's a good idea,'' Victor said. ''I have to be going. Pleased to meet you, Merle.'' He pointed to Megan, then touched his finger to his nose. ''She's the one to watch. And Toni, if you run into any hassles with that union rep let me know. I know a guy high up. Be glad to give him a call.'' He nodded and walked off to the elevators.

Merle looked after him with the glazed fascination of a voyeur watching someone undress. ''Have you worked with Mr. Taub?'' she asked Megan.

''We knew each other in film school.''

''How lucky. Did you know back then that he was going to be famous?''

''I never had any doubt,'' Megan replied with a coolness that Merle mistook for envy.

''What was he like back then? Was he shy? He seems so shy.''

''Victor was never shy.''

''Were all the girls wild for him?''

''I know one who was,'' Toni said, then, ''Ah, there's a place to sit down.'' She gestured to a couch that had just been vacated. ''Shall we?''

Merle dashed over to claim the space. ''Five minutes with this piranha,'' Megan whispered to Toni as they followed and seated themselves.

''Fred? Where's Fred? I've lost Fred.'' Merle swung around, almost hitting the photographer in the chest. ''Ah, Fred, there you are. You don't mind if Fred clicks away while we talk, do you? I always think candid shots are the best.''

"Fine," Megan said. Greta Garbo in her heyday could look bad in a candid shot. She was sure she'd pick up the paper and see herself, eyes closed and mouth open, looking either dim-witted or drunk.

"Now. Tell me how you felt when you learned you'd been nominated for an Academy Award. And it's only three weeks away! Do you think you'll win? And about this new project of yours . . . set in Australia, isn't it? And you're hoping to be bankrolled by Dennis Danher?"

Megan reeled off answers she'd refined in previous inter-views, and Toni followed up, like a street sweeper after a pa-rade, getting it tidy, making sure Merle got information they wanted to see in print. Megan looked around the lobby. The place was alive with people glad-handing, flirting, making deals. She saw the husband-and-wife team who'd made the movie about the aborigines and waved, then saw a tall man moving through the crowd. He was clearly a civilian since he went to the desk with purpose, neither stopping nor being stopped. His walk was . . . "Tas!" Megan was on her feet, going to him, muttering, "Excuse me" over her shoulder.

Tas was leaning on the desk, questioning the clerk. Megan tapped him on the shoulder and stood back, eager to see his surprised expression. But when he turned, his face was as im-mobile as hers was excited.

"Tasman Burke! Whatever are you doing here?" She stood on tiptoe, threw her arms around his neck and leaned back, staring into his face.

"I came to see you." He smiled in spite of himself.

"To see me? I didn't think you were enough of a film buff to even know this thing was going on."

"This isn't New York. Even the dustman knows about the festival."

"I can't believe it! After all this time. Let me look at you." Since he was standing so stiffly she let her arms drop. "Not a grey hair yet. Are you taking monkey glands?"

"They're mostly on my chest." He was conscious of being looked at and swiveled his head to see a camera aimed in their direction.

"I'm doing this interview with a newspaper columnist," Megan said, following his glance. "But here . . ." She reached into her slacks pocket for her room key. "Go on up to my room. I'll be there in two shakes of a lamb's tail." She hugged him again. He loped off to the elevator.

"Sorry," she said, resuming her seat. "An old friend." She opened her eyes wide and looked at Toni significantly. "Tasman Burke."

"Dr. Tasman Burke?" Merle inquired.

"Right. That's him. Now, where were we?" She did her best to continue with the interview but couldn't hide her impatience. Toni, seeing Merle was miffed, took out her appointment calendar.

"Sorry I suggested talking in a public place. There are just too many distractions. Why don't we arrange for you to come up to Megan's suite? Say, day after tomorrow, around seven in the evening? Would that be convenient?" Merle gave a toothy smile but played hard to get. "Let's see . . ." She had trouble finding her appointment book, opened it slowly, had more trouble finding the date, then couldn't decipher her own writing. "Let's see . . ." Her eyes narrowed with trancelike concentration. "Let's see . . . day after . . ." Megan bounced on the edge of her seat. "Day after . . ."

"If you don't mind, I'll leave the details to you ladies. Thanks for your time, Merle. See you later." Megan was gone.

Toni apologized. "He's a friend of Megan's from New York."

"Oh, I know who he is. He's one of the best-known surgeons in the country."

"A very old friend."

"And a very good one from the looks of it." Merle made it sound lewd.

"They met in New York," Toni explained. "You know how expatriates are—always seeking each other out. And Megan's never lost her attachment to Australia. She's really looking forward to filming here next . . ." But Merle had already directed her attention elsewhere. "Fred. Fred, that's Oliver Stone coming out of the elevator. Quick. Quick!"

Tas stood at the window, jiggling the keys in his pocket while Megan went to the room refrigerator and fixed them drinks.

"You could have knocked me down with a feather when I saw you," she said. "What a surprise! Though life's been full of surprises ever since I arrived. Now tell me how it's going. Have you discovered the secret of eternal life yet? It was valves, wasn't it? Something about blood flow through heart valves."

He'd taken her to his lab once, after hours, when there was no one about but janitors and security men. She'd felt as though they were kids playing doctor when he'd hooked her up to some machine that gave a computer readout of the rhythm of the heart. Then he'd hooked himself up, watching the terminal with cold-eyed objectivity, saying he could already see the signs of stress-related dysfunction and that he'd probably die before she did, though women like her, who "lived in a man's world," ran increasing risks of cardiovascular disease. It must've been the talk of death that had turned them lustful. He'd locked the door and turned out the lights and they'd made love on the floor. She could still remember the icy linoleum and the whir of the electric floor polisher in the corridor outside.

"You look good," she said, handing him his drink, though on closer inspection, she could see that grey hairs now blended with the sandy ones and sun exposure had creased his forehead, deepened the lines from nose to mouth and given him a ruddy complexion that intensified the blue of his eyes. But his eyes had a wintry look, as though he were scanning some internal horizon hoping for a change in the weather.

"You look good yourself," he said, which was as much of a compliment as any woman would get out of Tasman Burke. "Not too frazzled by your success, are you?"

"It's still uphill. I'm trying to round up the money for my next. Oh, I want to make this movie, Tas. I want it more than I've ever wanted anything in my life."

He nodded. Her next project had always been the thing she wanted most in her life.

She handed him his glass and clinked hers to it with the old Irish blessing, "May the wind be always at your back," then sat down near the window, motioning him to the opposite chair. It was too low to accommodate his six-foot-three frame, and he stretched out his legs and leaned back, still tense, looking out the window.

"You don't happen to have a coupla spare million lying about, do you?" she asked.

"If I did, I'd know how to use it. I can't exactly do my research in the back shed, so I've hooked up to a partnership I don't much like." As she questioned him about the research he answered haltingly, his face impassive, but, she remembered, his face never gave too much away. Even during sex it showed little more than the strain of exertion until it broke with the intensity of orgasmic pleasure. So different from Victor. Victor could melt you with a look and enjoyed verbal seduction, but that was the difference between a mid-European Jew, albeit third generation, and a sixth-generation, tight-lipped Australian male. "They can do everything but talk," an Aussie woman had said about their male counterparts. Of course there were Australian men who were articulate, but Tas's nature and profession made him fit the stereotype.

"I'm so glad you came to see me," she said, sensing his unease. "It had crossed my mind to contact you but . . ."

"You're busy. More or less here on business, right?"

"Right. And . . . ten years is a long time." Should she ask about his marriage? His children?"

"I don't suppose I would have contacted you," he went on, "even if I'd known you were at the festival. Except—" A full stop.

"Except?" There was a flicker of flirtation in her smile.

"You met my wife at a party last night?"

She was dumbfounded. "I did?"

"Yes. You met Greta."

She tried to shape a sentence but couldn't. If he'd ever mentioned his wife's name, she'd forgotten it. His wife had been a world away and since she'd had no expectations of a future with him, if she'd thought about her at all it had been with vague concern and some pity, never as a rival. Once, sitting on a bench in Washington Square, they'd seen a woman changing a baby and he'd mentioned that he'd never changed a diaper. When she'd said that was selfish, he'd countered that since she was a feminist she should give women credit for making their own choices: some women wanted to be wives and mothers. She expected most did, she'd said, but keeping a home together while the man was off enjoying his freedom and making a name for himself was too high a price to pay. "I had no idea," she got out at last.

"Yes. On the way home last night she told me all about meeting you."

She would never have guessed that Tas would be married to someone like Greta. But guessing who was married to whom was harder than guessing someone's income or political persuasion. No matter how sharp you were (and she prided herself on being very sharp), you could never guess the hidden needs and secret ties. She knew Tas had been married while still a university student, barely out of his teens. It was beyond imagination to consider the men who'd attracted her when she was eighteen—football heroes, motorcycle enthusiasts, good dancers. If she'd hooked up with one of them and gotten pregnant she might be living in a trailer park in Tarzana, working in a car wash. "I don't know how you and I could have been at the same party and not seen each other," she said, as though that technicality were the issue at hand.

"I'd ducked out to go to the hospital. I didn't get back to the party until after you'd left."

She tried to re-create her conversation with Greta. What had she said? Surely she couldn't have given away anything about Tas because he hadn't been on her mind. "Oh, this is awful. We—Greta and I—went to the same school," she said lamely. "We were going to visit the nuns at St. Brigid's together, then come out to your farm. 'Course I didn't know it was your farm. Though you always used to talk about having a farm—breeding horses, wasn't that your dream?"

"Yes. We've got a stud farm. Or the beginnings of one."

She sucked in her cheeks and rolled her eyes upward. "A stud farm. Oh, Tas, gimme a break." She couldn't help laughing, but he looked so serious, she looked down at the carpet. "If I'd known Greta . . . I mean, I liked her, so . . . well, I'll just have to call her up and cancel."

"I wish you wouldn't."

She looked up. "You do? Why in God's name?"

"Your coming out is important to her." Another pause. "She doesn't make friends easily."

"I could see that."

He took a swallow of his drink. Who would have thought that Megan would like Greta? He would never understand women. "She's already up to her neck in preparations." When he'd left that morning she'd been at the dining room table poring over some gourmet cookbook, wondering if she would have time to have her hair done, saying again how kind and friendly Megan had been. And Chrissie sat next to her, chattering away, saying how great it was that Greta was going to have a guest, and a famous guest at that. "And she's already called those damned nuns to say you're coming and they're treating it like a major event." He wiped his face, put the drink on the windowsill and put his head in his hand to hide the twitch in his left eye. "We . . . Greta and I . . . it isn't a good marriage," he got out at last.

"You implied that ten years ago." She hoped that didn't sound sarcastic. She could see that he was in a bad way.

"It's worse now." He wanted to confide in her, to spill it all out. The urge to talk intimately had, over the past month, taken on a physical manifestation—a recurrent headache that made the muscle in his eye jump. It was the first time in his life he'd ever had a symptom with a clearly emotional origin. It humbled and disturbed him, made him realize how important his reputation for cool detachment had become. It also made him realize that there was no one in whom he could confide. When faced with the possibility of discussing emotional problems, the men he called friends suddenly became what they were—not friends but colleagues and acquaintances. He'd even thought of going to a psychiatrist, but that had seemed such a humiliating experience, and one in which he had no faith. He'd tried to talk to Naomi, but any mention of Greta sent her into a rage or a pout. Only natural, he supposed. How could he expect his mistress to understand how responsible he felt toward his wife, even though he was desperate to leave her? An older and more experienced woman might understand that a man's need to confide could be as great as his need for sex, and Megan had been, possibly still could be, his friend. The only woman friend he'd ever had. Taking his head out of his hands, he looked at her. She had an intent, worried expression but was clearly willing to listen. It occurred to him that he'd come not just to warn her about Greta but because he wanted her understanding.

"I know I can't twist your arm about going through with this meeting with Greta, but . . ."

"You can't twist my arm about anything." Now it was her turn to stare out the window. She understood intuitively that, apart from protecting Greta's feelings, he wanted her to keep the date and come out to the farm so that she would witness his side of the story. Perhaps it would be better to follow through with it. Even on brief acquaintance she could see that Greta was the sort of woman who'd go to a lot of trouble for her and, if she begged off, Greta would feel hurt. And it wasn't as though she and Tas had been lovers in the romantic sense. They'd never, as she and Victor had, shared stories about the past or dreams of the future. She'd never told him about her family. She hadn't known how he'd gotten the little scar under his chin. They had just been friendly, sometimes argumentative bedmates. Consenting adults, attracted and lonely, who happened to be in the same place at the same time. And it had been ten years ago. So perhaps the best way around this messy situation was simply to go *through* it. For one afternoon. And Greta would never guess. And, she admitted, she was curious about Tas's life. "I suppose I could," she said slowly.

"It's only for a couple of hours. And I'd like you to meet my kids. We'll drive back to the city together, isn't that the plan? We can talk then." He got up. "I have to be getting back to the hospital."

"Don't you ever take time off?"

"Do you?"

"Uh-uh. Not even in my dreams."

He didn't know if he should shake her hand or kiss her, so he did neither. The heavy feeling in his head had gone, replaced by a lump of gratitude in his throat. "You're all right, Megan Hanlon."

"Damned straight. So are you, Tasman Burke." She closed the door after him and leaned against it, wondering if she'd done the right thing. The phone rang. "Bugger it all!" She had to shower and meet with Toni, then go to Emile's party. As she strode across the room it occurred to her that she had not been completely honest. She and Tas had been more than "consenting adults"—that euphemism for noninvolvement—but they had shared a tacit understanding: their relationship could only continue if their affection was not articulated. Naturally, he'd been more comfortable with that than she. Tas had never been, as the saying goes, "in touch with his feelings." If he hadn't been married . . .

"I'm coming. I'm coming," she muttered as the phone rang for the fifth time. Just now she didn't have time to be in touch with her feelings either.

CHAPTER
EIGHT

JOAN SAT AT THE WINDOW OF PROFESSOR JAMES FER-zaco's office, a pile of uncorrected papers on her lap. The setting sun burnished the buildings and deepened the greens of the shrubbery. The peacocks who roamed the lawn near the humanities offices were still strutting around. A young man crossed the lawn, blinking, rolling his head to relieve the tension in his neck, glancing at a couple in a semiprone position. Joan looked at them, too. They were reading from the same book, the boy's hand making a gentle circular motion on the girl's shoulder, as though he were buffing a piece of fine wood. A quarter to six. No doubt James had been held up at that faculty meeting, but if he didn't come soon she would have to leave. She inhaled deeply, taking in the smell of books and tobacco. As though sensing her restlessness, Belle came out from under James's desk and nuzzled her foot. She scratched Belle's head and moved to the bookshelves, taking down a heavy volume of the *Oxford English Dictionary* to lift out the box of dog biscuits behind it. "Now don't tell him I've been spoiling you," she said, squatting down to offer the biscuit and watching Belle chomp. She got up and moved around the room, looking at the familiar objects—James's framed degrees, a first edition of *Bleak House* protected by a plastic cover, the print of Sir Thomas More, the little statue of the goddess Kali, which she'd found so frightening (until James had convinced her that a mother goddess might well be naked and wear a necklace of skulls), the mask of Dionysus (somewhat like James himself, with its full lips and sly look), the humidor containing James's cigar. A tray with a sherry decanter and two waiting glasses was on his desk, along with piles of correspondence, a monograph, books and two photos. One photo showed

James with his arms around his children. They were both gone now, the daughter to Oxford; the son, who had no academic interests (''Thank God,'' James had said), was bumming around Malaysia looking for a journalism job. ''Really looking for trouble,'' James said tolerantly, ''which is not only his choice but his right at his age.'' The other photo was of James in swimming trunks, lolling on a little balcony, pots of bright geraniums on either side, the blue Aegean off to the side. She often wondered who'd taken that photo because his eyes, though squinting, had an undeniably fond expression. She capped the tortoiseshell pen on the desk—he did have a habit of leaving things about, one could only wonder (and she often had) at the state of his house. She sat back down, cupping her chin in her hands. She had no sense of interfering because she'd touched his things—he'd invite any visiting student to do the same—and she was as at home here as she would have been at her room at the convent. Rather more so, since his collection of treasures reflected her own tastes. And to think how intimidated she'd been the first time she was in here, how defensive and disparaging, because she couldn't believe that anyone who went around his office in shirtsleeves and stocking feet, swatting flies with an old whisk that had come from Egypt, wasn't a poseur. But now she understood that James was as rare as a creature in a medieval bestiary—if people thought he had three eyes and a serpent's tail he didn't care. He was above the fray, beyond convention, comfortable in his eccentricities.

Five minutes to six. She straightened the uncorrected papers and started to put them into her briefcase. She would have to go without seeing him today. She was bending over his desk writing him a note when he came in. His suit was rumpled and he was eating an apple.

'' 'Shall I compare thee to a summer's day?' '' he asked. ''Will you, too, make me crotchety and uncomfortable?'' He took off his dented Panama hat, removed his jacket and hoisted his waistband over a stomach that was by no means gross but usually won the battle with his belt. ''Sorry I'm late. Faculty meeting.'' He sat at his desk and began to pull off his shoes. ''Ah, academic life. The smaller the stakes the more vehement the infighting.''

Initially she'd assumed that academics were above the pettiness she'd witnessed at the convent, but he'd disabused her of that notion. Munching on the apple, he told her about that afternoon's ruckus, impersonating his colleagues like so many characters out of Dickens. She laughed, and he playfully offered her the apple core. "Take it back, Eve. I've had my tucker on the knowledge of good and evil and it's turned to mush." He dropped the core into an overflowing wastebasket. "Have a sherry?"

"I can't. It's time to meet Michele."

"If she can find her way from the classroom to the library steps without a map."

"And I have this bundle of papers to correct." She pulled them from her briefcase. "Do you know what Joyce Kirby wrote about the Black Plague?"

"I wouldn't venture a guess."

"She wrote . . ." She leafed through and found the paper. " 'The Black Plague was a social disease that *desiccated* midevil—that's m-i-d-e-v-i-l—Europe.' I wrote, 'Hope you're looking forward to a career in sports' in the margin, in ink. I should always write in pencil so I can erase it after I've conquered my incredulity."

James laughed. "Not to worry. Joyce won't get it."

"Poor Joyce. It's not as though she doesn't try. I should be more charitable with the ones who genuinely try."

"And poor you. Agonizing about being charitable or truthful. What's the matter?" He was quick to pick up on her moods. "You look disgruntled and restless, and surely not because of Joyce Kirby."

"No. One of my former students, Megan Hanlon, is in town. And we had a call this morning from another former student saying that she and Megan will be coming to visit. Megan was one of my favorites. She's become quite famous. She's a film director from the States."

"That's quite a distance from St. Brigid's."

"Yes. Her father was an American. She left here when she was still a girl. Thinking about her . . ." She wrapped her hands around her knees and raised her feet off the floor. "I can remember almost verbatim the discussions I used to have with her. She was an intense, rather self-dramatizing girl. She used to talk about her 'crisis of faith' and badger me with all sorts of questions. I didn't know the answers, only then I used to fake it, give her the party line. And this morning I found myself thinking about her accomplishments and . . . yes . . . I am in a restless mood. And I started the day listening to Sister Bruno reading the obituaries at the breakfast table.''

"Somehow I knew Sister Bruno would turn to the obits first." Joan had created such a picture of convent life that he felt he actually knew, and shuddered at, Sister Bruno.

"So listening to the obituaries while eating my cornflakes, I started the day as morose as a first-year philosophy student. You know, the 'What does it all mean and have I wasted my life?' mood you're usually in when you come from a faculty meeting.'' She grinned and filled his glass. It hadn't been the listing of dead people's accomplishments that had upset her while listening to the obituaries, but ". . . survived by three children . . ." or ". . . beloved wife of . . ."

"Yes. I know the feeling. Every day I look into faces that are bored with the notion of cause and effect unless in relation to a football game, students who'll never understand the first thing about their own lives and times, let alone what happened in the Renaissance.'' He sipped and smiled. "Though admittedly, understanding one's own life is more of a challenge. But you mustn't be downhearted, Joan. You can publish next year."

"And then continue to correct papers like Joyce Kirby's?"

"Not if you don't want to. It's up to you."

She straightened her spine and bit her lip, impatient with this old argument. "I saw a brochure for the film festival on the faculty bulletin board. You don't have any plans to go, do you? Megan has a film showing.''

"I haven't liked a movie in the last ten years."

"That's not true. You told me you enjoyed *The Last Emperor*.''

"But I don't suppose your Megan has done anything on that scale.''

"No, but she wants to make a historical film in Australia. She did have a unique imagination about history—the kind of student who can imagine an entire world. Oh, you would have liked her.

It's probably too late to get tickets, but if you could, if you aren't going to be busy . . .''

"If I can lay my hands on a pair, would you be able to come with me?"

She said no too quickly and too emphatically. She had left the convent for a few evening lectures given by important guests, but going off to a movie with him . . . that sounded too much like a date. And he'd sounded too expectant when he'd asked her.

"I didn't really expect you would go," he said, leaning back in his chair. "Ah, Joan, Joan, Joan. When will you . . ."

She got up, holding her books and briefcase protectively to her chest. "I really do have to be going."

"I'll see about getting that ticket."

"Then you could tell me about it."

"Then I could tell you about it," he repeated, following her to the door.

"I would appreciate it."

"I know you would."

"I've almost finished the book you gave me for my birthday— I especially enjoyed the chapter on George Eliot and Henry Lewes." Had she liked that chapter best because Eliot, the minister's daughter, the brilliant, ugly-duckling spinster, had found her mentor and grand passion late in her life and defied convention to live with him? "I really do have to rush."

"Yes. We can talk about the book tomorrow." He placed a hand on her shoulder and bent toward her as though to kiss her good-bye, then continued the motion and bent even lower to fondle Belle's ear.

"Yes. Tomorrow."

She hurried out of the building and cut across the lawn to the library. Michele was nowhere to be seen, so she sat on the steps, folding her skirt around her legs. The young couple she'd been watching earlier closed their book and got up. This time it was the girl who used the excuse of brushing grass from the boy's shirt to touch him. They walked off hand in hand. How lovely it must be to touch so casually and so often. She felt a slight annoyance at James. He could have been more insistent, and more subtle, about asking her to go to the movie with him. If he'd really pressed her, she might . . . but that was ridiculous. James would never try to pressure her into anything. That would be against his principles, if not his nature. Each time there had been a growth in their intimacy, the cue had come from her. She would have to indicate willingness if it was to go any further, and she had already felt herself doing so involuntarily. Her eyes must give her away every time they met. She was aware that they both used Belle as a surrogate for their affection, patting and stroking her, petting her simultaneously sometimes. Now, having left him, she felt like a child sent from the table without her supper. The natural course of things would have been for them to continue to talk, to take a walk perhaps, to have dinner together. Wasn't that what married couples who loved each other did at the end of the day? Take each other's emotional temperature, ask how it had gone, have a meal and a laugh, and then "pillow talk"? How lovely it must be to lie snuggled in each other's arms, whispering, getting drowsy. It was ridiculous to believe that you had to remain celibate in order to love and serve God. Why should your love of an individual diminish your love of the Creator? Surely it would nourish it, make it more likely that you could share a warmer love, not just the bloodless, theoretical sort, with your fellow humans. James often said . . .

"Oh, there you are." Michele was in front of her. "Wherever have you been?" The question came as intrusion and challenge, but she knew Michele didn't mean it as such. Michele craved constant companionship and the question came from wanting company, not a fear that they would be late getting back to the convent. "I walked by here once, but I couldn't see you, so I thought . . ."

"I was talking to Professor Ferzaco."

"Oh" was all Michele said. Conversation with a professor held no attraction for her. She was only at the university because of Joan's push to upgrade the teaching level at St. Brigid's. Studying was an uphill slog for Michele, but she kept at it, wanting to prove herself a good girl. And a good girl she was. A worker bee. Would there were more like her in the Order, Joan thought, getting up and brushing off her skirt. She must remember to give Michele more encouragement and to help her with her papers. If only Michele would curb her need to chatter. Inconsequential conversation was so annoying. Real conversations, the sort of exchanges she had with James, were stimulating, entertaining, proof of humanity. But this incessant yapping about the weather or what was to be eaten for dinner or what had been eaten the night before or some silly television show! Why couldn't everyone with an IQ under 140 just take a vow of silence?

"What are you thinking about?" Michele asked as they walked to the parking lot. Joan was hugging her briefcase to her breast and looking up at the sky, sure signs that she was in one of her moods. She knew Joan wouldn't say boo all the way back, and if she turned on the radio Joan would want the classical music or the news, which wasn't fair because Joan wouldn't really listen any more than she was listening now. She was surprised when Joan said, "I was thinking about the beach. I've been wanting to go all summer."

"We *are* going! Didn't Bernadette tell you? The McCarthys are giving us their place at Bunbury two weeks from now. They're such good people . . . ," and, always uncertain about her judgment, she added, "Don't you think?"

"If Mr. McCarthy had lived prior to the Reformation he'd be doing a swift business selling indulgences from a roadside stand." What else could you say about a man who every Easter sent kangaroo-skin slippers from his shoe factory to the convent, leaving the retail price on the boxes and enclosing an unctuous note asking the nuns to pray for his immortal soul?

"What do you mean?"

"You know, Michele, before the Reformation there was a business of selling indulgences. You paid your pennies and hoped it would take time off your sentence in purgatory. It was one of the abuses Martin Luther objected to. At the time the Church was very corrupt and—"

"So was Martin Luther," Michele put in, her face aflame. "After all, he married a nun. He . . ."

"No matter what they taught you at St. Anne's, the Reformation wasn't just a case of a lascivious monk, though there were plenty of those around." She sought an example that Michele might understand. "The buying and selling of indulgences was a great corruption, rather like plea-bargaining—what those

American lawyers were doing on that show you were watching last night. You know, make a deal so you don't have to take the rap."

Michele quickened her pace. Joan knew so much about history, especially derogatory things about the Church. She hoped Joan was wrong, but she knew she didn't have the knowledge to refute her. "I'm sure Mr. McCarthy means well."

"We all mean well," Joan said impatiently. "We can start from the premise that most people *mean* well." She softened her tone. "Yes, I'm sure the McCarthys' cottage will be nice." Another planned holiday, with no privacy at all. She remembered the yellow bathing suit she'd had as a girl and how she'd loved swimming or running along the beach. Her first intimations of a love of God were rooted in her love of His physical universe—the robin's-egg-blue skies, flowered bushlands, sudden rainbows and wide beaches of Western Australia. How she longed to stride through the bush again, or feel her naked arms and legs cutting through the surf.

"We'd best hurry," Michele warned. "You know they'll wait if we're late." Turning the other sisters into "they" would show Joan that even if she didn't understand what was on her mind, she was on her side. "Remember last week when you had to go over those papers with Professor Ferzaco and we got back just as the soup was cooling and Sister Bruno couldn't eat it because she said she could see the grease forming on the top?"

"She's always had a weak stomach."

"And isn't that ironic for someone who likes food so much?" She was not sure of the meaning of "ironic" but Joan used the word a lot. "Do you want to drive or shall I?"

"I will." Michele had a tendency to ride the clutch in traffic.

"But you seem preoccupied."

"If I stopped activity every time I was preoccupied I'd be a catatonic," Joan assured her, slipping into the driver's seat. Michele switched on the "easy listening" station that, to Joan, was the most difficult listening of all. But it was just as well she was with Michele. If she weren't, she knew that she'd turn the car in the direction of the beach, and when she got there she'd take off her shoes and run, yes, run along the water's edge. And while she was running she would pray.

CHAPTER
NINE

SHE'D HAVE TO STOP COMING TO PARTIES ONLY TO escape from them, Megan told herself as she closed the sliding-glass doors to Emile Gallimard's suite and stepped onto the balcony. She looked back at the tightly packed bodies in the fug of cigarette smoke, took a breath and strolled to the railing. She'd tried to signal Toni that it was time to go, but Toni had been backed into a corner by some big-boned guy with curly grey hair. In the process, Megan had caught Victor's eye. He was standing in the middle of the room, looking very *GQ* in a white suit and no tie, being chatted up by a brunette with melon-sized breasts. He'd nodded at her, then turned back to the brunette, politely bored. Or maybe he was disguising his interest in the brunette because Deirdre, still in her street-urchin outfit, was at his side. Then again, perhaps he was jaded. Maybe he'd had his fill of female adoration. Fat chance.

In the old days she'd watched him visibly expand at any woman's attention, especially if the woman had big breasts. What greater proof of his love for her, he'd joked, than that he—a chest man—had married a girl who had trouble filling an A cup. And what anguished insecurity she'd felt at the slightest hint of his interest in another woman. Thank God she would never be jealous again. It was such a shameful and depleting emotion. She'd gotten physically sick imagining him in bed with other women, hated those women without knowing a thing about them. "It didn't mean anything," he'd said when she'd discovered his first extramarital affair. "Then why the hell did you do it?" she'd cried, wanting to die. No affair could be casual; not if Victor was having it, though before they were married they'd agreed, at least in theory, that no one should be anyone else's sexual property. In that, as in so many other things, she had not been on to herself.

She swatted a mosquito, her hand lingering on a shoulder left bare by the sarong that always made her feel sexy. Admiring glances at the party had confirmed that she was. She had felt so unattractive, so downright ugly after their divorce. Never again would she anchor her sense of self to any one man's judgment. She had never intended to, even with Victor. They were not going to fox-trot through life, him playing Pop to her Mom. They were going to be different, to dance with no one leading, in the free-form gyrations of their own superior generation. They would model themselves on Alfred Stieglitz and Georgia O'Keefe, Jean-Paul Sartre and Simone de Beauvoir. But she'd known, right after the wedding ceremony, that that was a myth. She'd stood in the judge's chambers, unaccountably upset, though they'd both decided to forgo the hoopla. She was in street clothes. There were no flowers. Her mother wasn't there. The judge, seeing her distress, had bent forward, kissed her cheek (he'd had terrible halitosis) and said, "Congratulations, Mrs. Taub." She and Victor had spoken simultaneously: he'd laughed, "Mrs. Taub? That's what my mother's called," and she'd blurted, "My name is Megan Hanlon." It was not an auspicious beginning.

She leaned against the railing, twisting the loop of her earring, an adult substitute for smoothing down her hair. The noise from the party rose and fell as though someone were playing with the volume on a radio dial. She turned and saw Victor closing the sliding-glass door. She was suddenly aware of the river breeze, the scent of her shampoo and his cigarette, her naked shoulders. A man and a woman on a moonlit balcony. The heartbeat before a kiss. Christ, she'd seen too many old movies. But such moments did exist in life. And wasn't everything in between a long waiting? Wasn't that why people needed movies? To capture the turning points, be they ecstatic or painful.

"I like your dress, stranger."

"I keep it up with Scotch tape," she said, intentionally shattering the mood.

He put his elbows on the railing and leaned back, turning his head to her. The silence between them seemed more acute because of the noise from the party. "We always said we'd come here together, remember?"

"To a hotel balcony overlooking the Swan River?"

"To Australia."

"I haven't seen Australia yet."

"I guess you will when you go out to visit Uncle Mick and Auntie Vi."

She was surprised that he'd remembered their names. "Yes. I'm going out to stay with them after the festival."

"I always wanted to meet them."

Surely he couldn't be angling for an invitation. "I don't think Mick would be too happy about your plans to build that resort complex. He'd say, 'Bloody Yank taking over Australia.' "

"Yeah. From what you've told me, I guess he would. I always imagined their place in the country—the brush all around, that veranda you used to sleep on. You said the kangaroos came up to it at night . . ."

"It's probably nothing like that anymore," she said, blocking entrance to a shared past.

"And the nuns. Toni told me you're going to visit the nuns."

"Mmmm."

"Sister Mary Magdalene. Wasn't she the one you always talked about?"

"You used to laugh at them."

"As I recall, you laughed at them yourself."

As though executing a dance step, they simultaneously shifted positions, he turning to look out at the river, she to stare through the glass doors at the party. He took a drag on his cigarette. "So, sweetheart, wanna tell me about your next caper?" He was always lousy at imitations; this one was supposed to be Bogart but slid into John Wayne. She smiled in spite of herself. "What's it gonna be?" he went on. "Some dame and some guy who have the hots for each other but nothin' turns out right?"

"Yeah. My screenplay's based on diaries of an English lieutenant's affair with a convict woman. And no, it didn't turn out right."

"If you're gonna be a dream merchant you gotta come up with a happy ending."

"Thanks for the advice, Sammy Glick."

"So you don't want to talk about it. Superstitious? You're gonna have to talk about it to Dennis Danher and a few other lords of creation. Toni tells me you're going for a big budget."

"Seems Toni's told you a lot of things."

"Yeah. You lucked out with her. She's a one-man band. So, c'mon . . ." His voice was mock seductive. "You show me yours and I'll show you mine."

"Why this sudden interest?"

"Maybe I can help."

Maybe you could've helped by caring about me eighteen years ago, she thought.

"If you've got a winner I might want to invest." He tossed away his cigarette. "God, you're stiff-necked. I'd forgotten how stiff-necked you are."

"And hardheaded."

"I voted for *On the Streets* for the Academy Awards."

"That's one vote," she said laconically.

"No. You have a good chance at winning. It was good. It's hard to get a fresh slant on the runaway thing. All those kids wasting away, shivering on the streets of New York. Must've been a bitch shooting in winter."

"It was. It wasn't my plan to shoot during that snowstorm, but the money was running out and I had a great crew, so we did. Serendipity."

"I took Deirdre to see it. Scared the shit out of her. Scared the shit out of me, too. I don't think she'll run away from home again."

"She's run away from home?"

"Not from my home. I've only had her for about six months. But from her mother. Frances. I knew the kid was miserable. I've been going through a custody battle for years. Frances didn't really care about Deirdre. She let her get away with murder—overnight visits from boys and ignoring the dope in the kid's bedroom. It's tough trying to pull Deirdre into line now. She wants controls but she resents the hell out of them. Frances just figured she could get more money out of me if she had custody. Once I got it she moved to Rome. Doesn't even write the kid. I wish you'd talk to Deirdre."

"Talk to her about what?"

"About anything. Just talk to her. She needs a smart woman to talk to."

Deirdre would be a hard nut to crack. Victor, so sharp about so many things, was naïve about that. Or more likely just desperate. And it was too rich that he wanted to call her into service as a surrogate mother. "I saw your last movie," she said. She'd seen all his movies.

"Did you? I wouldn't have thought it would interest you."

"I keep up."

She knew it cost him to ask, "So what did you think?"

"Technically it's brilliant."

"But you didn't like it."

"I expect you made mega-bucks." She'd read the grosses in *Variety*.

"Yeah. So don't tell me you're not interested in making money."

"I am. They won't let me make movies unless I make money. But making money isn't all I'm interested in."

"Me either."

"You coulda fooled me."

"So what didn't you like about it?"

She straightened, looking him full in the face. "Let's say I don't like the woman-as-victim genre. And I guess I didn't like the fact that it was so effective, so artful. Sucked me right in."

"So?"

"And all the blood and guts at the end. The audience was really drooling for the kill. They really wanted to see that crazy woman punished. You made her so evil."

"And you don't believe there are evil women? You should meet my ex-wife."

"I am your ex-wife."

"The other one. One of the other ones."

"I don't like shock-and-sock movies. I don't think it's right to see people dismembered and want to cheer about it."

"No violence in movies, huh."

"Don't be stupid. There's violence in life, so there has to be violence in the movies. But if it's only there to shock and manipulate, that's brutalization. And I noticed your director hardly ever did a full body shot—it was always close-ups of a breast, a thigh . . .''

"His background is in rock videos."

"His background is in shit. I felt as though I were in some Roman arena and the mob was rooting for the lions." She was on a roll now. "And I don't like graphic sex. Graphic sex in movies embarrasses me."

"I didn't think anything sexual could embarrass you," he said.

"Well, it does. It destroys the sense of character, turns the audience into voyeurs."

"Sex isn't about characters. It's primal. It's a man and a woman getting it on."

"And that, if you don't see them as individuals, is boring."

"A possible difference in the male and female point of view."

"You think everything is determined by gender?"

"Don't you?"

"Only up to a point. Only on my bad days do I think all men are alike, but then I haven't gotten married three times." She shook her head. "I'll never understand how you can say 'I do' and promise a lifetime again and again."

"Hey, you've slipped your conversational gears. We were talking about movies. How'd you get onto marriage? Why can't women stick to the subject?"

"Why can't men follow the shifts or grasp the subtext?"

"Testosterone poisoning?" he suggested with a grin, then shrugged. "Why did I get married time after time? I dunno. The triumph of hope over experience. A very human failing, Megan, though not one you're prone to. You'd never give anyone a second chance. You're much less romantic than I am."

"Bullshit."

"You were the one who asked for the divorce."

"One of my better ideas."

"I've thought a lot about us lately, about why we broke up. If you just could've held on and ridden it out we would've been okay. You knew I loved you."

"Oh, I see. Your role was to test, my role was to hold on. What was I supposed to be? Your mother?"

"Not *my* mother. Not Sylvia. She would've guilt-tripped me

and busted my ass for alimony. I don't think you ever understood the pressures that were on me then. I felt rotten that I wasn't making any money, that we were living in that crummy walk-up. I wasn't some mean-streets artiste from the Lower East Side; I was just pretending to be. It would've been stupid for me to stay in New York. Hollywood's a family town and I had the family. You never understood the pressures on me to make it big and make it fast because I was a Taub.''

"Oh, God, let me weep for the little prince who's always finding an excuse to feel sorry for himself even when things are going well. Correction: *especially* when things are going well.''

"You've always thought of me as Golden Boy.''

"Well, weren't you? Aren't you? And for what? For more money, more sex, more cocaine?''

"I went through hell kicking that habit, Megan. You don't even want to try to imagine it, do you? You can make millions of people cry because you have compassion for some teenage druggies in some Times Square alleyway, but *me* you can't imagine. Your compassion doesn't extend itself to—''

"The privileged and powerful? No. It doesn't stretch that far. But you have your consolations, massive self-concern not being the least of them.''

"You never got over the fact that I came from money, did you? That my father had made it while crazy Thomas Shelby was rootin' around looking for his next paycheck and his next bottle.''

"My daddy worked for his money, schmuck. He has the scars to prove it, and you, who had every advantage, every opportunity, you sold yourself cheap.''

"That's not what my accountant tells me. And money is what this business is about. That's just about all it's about. You know that, don't you?''

"I'm glad you're not writing scripts anymore. All these tough-guy clichés.''

"I'm glad I'm not writing scripts anymore, too. You're the one with the talent. I knew it before you did, only in those days it made me envious. That's part of the reason I fucked around. Hey, don't give me that concrete expression. I spent a lot of time on the couch to realize this stuff. Now I'm a big boy. A real responsible adult who's glad he was married to a classy lady like you and wouldn't mind doing her a few favors. Show me your screenplay. And after *Chappy* is screened, let me help you celebrate by taking you to a party on Dennis Danher's yacht. Couldn't hurt to meet him socially first and have me there saying how great you are, now could it? That look again! You know, Megan, it's easy to tell you're Irish—you're like the IRA: you'd rather fight than win.'' When this didn't raise a smile he said, more gently, his hand hovering above her shoulder but not touching it, ''Hey, even a Jew can do penance. You taught me all about penance. And grace.''

''You never understood the concept of grace. To you it was just like luck.''

''Okay. So if you can't give me a little grace . . .''

''A person can't bestow grace. Grace comes from . . .''

''So how about a little luck?''

''You've had plenty of luck.'' She felt her throat tighten, as though she was about to cry. ''You could have been a world-class director.''

''Megan. Megan. Sweetheart. What's this 'Ya coulda been a contender' shit?''

''You had an amazing talent. You knew when to get the shot, you knew how to edit so it moved. You . . .''

''No, sweetheart.''

''Stop calling me sweetheart.''

''But you are. You are my own dear . . . first wife.'' A humorless chuckle. ''Since we're into a summing-up, let me do some truth-telling: I impressed you because, as you've so rightly said, I had a lot of advantages. I'd been around the business all my life. My grandfather bought me my own film equipment when I was eleven, and Dore Schary and Elia Kazan and John Houston and a lot of the boys ate my mother's—or rather our cook's—dinners, and we had a screening room where other people had a library. And I understood gross and net before I cut my teeth. And I'd gone to the best schools money could buy. That gave me a leg up. But that was it. That was all. It didn't make me a genius. You saw an amazing talent because you were in love with me and you wanted to be married to an exceptional man, wanted all that fellow-artist crap. But unlike you, I never had any vision, any message I had to give to the world.''

"I don't have any message to give to the world. I . . ."

"But you always have an opinion. Or at least a way of looking at things. You want your audience to come out laughing or thinking or uplifted.'' She shook her head violently. "Hey, sweetheart, I believe you do. I believe you can. But for me to aspire to that would be phony. I've known phony all my life and I don't like it. I'm a businessman. I'm in the movie business. I had to score big. And I have. I make no apologies to you, and you seem to be the only one who wants them. You think my movies are shit, but I'll tell you something, sweetheart, that audience has free choice and if it wants to slap down the moola to be scared out of what little wits it has, I'm their man.''

"You were immensely talented. You taught me so—''

"No." The word was like a stone dropping to the bottom of a well.

Their voices had taken on the harsh whispering tones of parents who are afraid they'll be heard by the child in the next room and, feeling such a presence, they turned to see Deirdre.

"Shall I get you that drink?" Victor asked, and was already halfway to the doors before Megan answered. "Yes. Something nonalcoholic, please.'' A Scotch would tip her right over the brink. Her heart was pounding. And she had to make small talk with this kid in clown makeup.

Deirdre lowered herself into a deck chair, studied Megan and finally said, "You hung out with those kids while you were making that movie, huh?''

"Yes. For several months.''

"Awesome," Deirdre said tiredly, then, looking up at the sky, "You were like married to him, right?''

" 'Like' married? Yes, I guess that's an accurate description.''

"When we say your movie he just said you'd gone to film school together, but last night when you saw each other I knew you were both freakin' out, so I like asked him if he'd had a thing with you, because you don't look like his type, and he, you know, told me. So. You were married to each other.''

Megan sat down. This was going to be as taxing as explaining death to a six-year-old. "Yes. It was a long time ago."

"You weren't much older than I am."

"A little older. In our early twenties."

"And he's always saying he's against young marriages."

"I guess he has reason to be."

"And he told me that my name was something you'd liked, you know? From some play. Unhappy Deirdre or somethin'."

"No. *Deirdre of the Sorrows*. It's a beautiful play. By Yeats."

"Who?"

"William Butler Yeats. Ever heard of him?"

Deirdre shook her head. "I don't go to plays much."

"Where do you go to school?"

"This snob factory called Westlake since I moved in with him." After a pause she hissed, "I hate it."

"Why? Apart from the fact that kids your age are supposed to hate school."

"Didn't you hate school?"

"Let's say I was anxious to get out. But I had some great teachers. Don't you have some good teachers?"

"They're like, you know, wage slaves. They hate us because we're rich."

"I see. Well, maybe you'll like college more. I liked college."

"I don't want to go to college."

"What do you want to do?"

This was ignored and Deirdre went on, "My grades are so bad I'm not going to be able to get into any good college. I'll have to go to some place like Westlake, you know? Where they'll let you stay even if you're an air-head because your parents pay a shitload tuition."

"And you think you're an air-head? You seem pretty sharp to me."

"I do?"

"Under the veneer. And that's quite a veneer. Why do you wear so much makeup?"

"I just do. I hate that preppy, scrubbed-up look, you know?"

"I don't like that look much myself. But you could develop your own look."

"With a nose like this, I already have."

Megan laughed, pleased to see the girl had a sense of humor. "You'll grow into your nose, Deirdre. I grew into my hair."

"Yeah. You have so much of it I guess you had to."

"I hated it when I was a kid. Even hated it when I was your age. The faster you can learn to like the cards you were dealt, the better off you'll be. A lot of women go through their entire lives trying to change the way they look. And I don't dislike your makeup just because it's punk but because you're missing something."

"Like what?"

"You're seventeen, right?"

"Just turned."

"You're only young once, it's a shame to cover it up." She was afraid that she'd alienated the girl but Deirdre's face had lost its bored look. She was leaning closer. Even criticism implied interest. But Megan was feeling the backlash of her fight with Victor and didn't hear the girl's next question. "I'm sorry, what did you say?" she asked. Deirdre's face was sullen again. Boy, is this kid narcissistic and demanding, Megan thought. Just like her father. "Do you have many friends at school?" she asked, knowing the question was a mistake. She'd learned during *On the Streets* that the fastest way to dry up a conversation with a kid was to ask too many questions.

"A few bimbos like me."

"You shouldn't call yourself a bimbo. That's like a black calling himself a nigger."

"Wow. Dad told me you were a libber." Deirdre yawned. "It's just an expression, you know?"

"And while we're at it, I wish you'd stop saying 'like' and 'you know.' "

"Why?"

"Because it's a verbal tic."

"A what?"

"A tic. A nervous habit. Like an uncontrollable blinking of the eyes or a twitch around the mouth."

"So?"

"Ending every sentence with 'you know' is a lazy demand

for understanding. You can't expect people to understand just because you tag 'you know' at the end of every sentence.''

"People don't understand each other anyway."

"But we've got to keep trying. You can't cut through a log with a blunt saw. Words are like tools, so—"

"There. You said it. You said 'like.' ''

"That was a simile. You know what a simile is, don't you?''

Deirdre ran her tongue around her lips. "I'm not sure."

"Where have you been going to school?"

"I already told you that."

"It was a rhetorical question. That means I didn't really expect an answer, though rhetorical used to mean something entirely different. Excuse me, I'm sounding like a teacher."

"You sure are," Deirdre said, glad for the concession. "You know . . . oops, I said it again . . . the way my father was talking to you, quiet and angry, like? I thought I was the only one he talked to in that uptight way. With everyone else he's real mellow."

"Even with your mother?" Megan asked, and could have bit her tongue.

"With her . . . naw, they don't fight. When she tries to talk to him he just . . ." Deirdre giggled. "He just gives her what you said I've been doing. A verbal tic. He just says, 'Sure, Frances, sure.' But mostly they don't talk unless there's a lawyer there."

"That must be more fun than a barrel of monkeys."

"For sure. Hey, do you think I could get that play you told me about here? The one I'm named after?"

"This is Australia, Deirdre. It's not a rain forest in the Amazon. Of course you can get it. Maybe tomorrow, before I go to the screenings, we could walk by a bookshop." What had she let herself in for?

"Did you get along with your mother and father?"

Where *was* Victor? "My parents got a divorce, too."

"How old were you?"

"Around twelve. But they didn't tell me they were getting a divorce."

"I know. They never tell you anything. Like they assume you're a retard. Did you live with your mother?"

"Yes."

"And your father just came to visit, right? And bought you things."

"He once bought me a cowboy hat."

"Where does he live now?"

"I don't know." She'd been more comfortable asking the questions. "I haven't seen him since I was about your age."

"What a drag. Do you still think about him?"

"Sometimes."

"My shrink says if you don't work it out with your father you'll always be hung up about men."

"Is that so." Megan accepted this bit of psychological wisdom with raised eyebrows. "And are you working it out with your father?"

Deirdre rolled her eyes. "Are you kiddin'? You don't know what he's like. But hey . . ." The thought struck her. "Maybe you do. Did you want the divorce or did he?"

There was a blast of sound from the party, rescuing Megan from a reply, as Victor opened the doors. Deirdre slumped back in her chair, affecting disinterest. Victor looked from one to the other, then offered Megan a glass. "It's ginger ale. Is that okay? Sorry I took so long but . . ."

"That's all right." Megan got up. "I have to be going anyway. Perhaps Deirdre would like it."

"No. I want a real drink," Deirdre insisted.

"What were you two talking about?" Victor asked.

"*Like*," Deirdre said, "she was teaching me what a simile is. We're gonna go to a bookstore tomorrow and get that play I'm named after. What time, Megan?"

"Say ten. In the lobby. Then I'll have to go to some screenings."

"I have an appointment at ten," Victor said.

"That's all right," Megan said, relieved.

"Sure. That's all right," Deirdre echoed. "She wants to go with *me*."

"Good night, Deirdre." Megan nodded. "And Victor."

"Stay loose," Deirdre called after her. Victor raised the ginger ale and said, "Sleep tight, sweetheart."

The crowd had thinned enough for her to get to Toni's side

after just two handshakes and a hug, and Toni introduced her to the man with the curly grey hair. They said their good-byes and made their way to the door. Three handshakes, two kisses and another introduction, and they were in the hall. "You were on the balcony with Victor for a long time," Toni said. "I saw him make a beeline for you as soon as you went out there."

"Mmmm."

"I'm sure everything you've said is true, but he doesn't strike me as such a bad guy."

"His charm is obvious upon first meeting. It takes a little longer to pick up on the rest."

"Know what I found out? One of the reasons he's here is because he plans to bring a program of restored films to next year's festival. You know, all those oldies that are crumbling because they're on nitrate-based stock? Victor's a real force in having them transferred onto safety stock. He's put in a lot of time and money."

"Isn't that noble. He's probably already working on his acceptance speech in anticipation of the special award he'll get ten years from now."

"Boy, you're really sour. I figured someone who loved movies as much as you would think he was bringing back the Holy Grail."

"He's a regular saint. I'm sure we can wangle a ticket to his canonization if we promise to worship at his shrine."

"Well, it does seem like a worthwhile thing to do."

"What are you, his press agent?" Megan punched the elevator button. "Sorry. I'm tired. And I've heard enough about Victor Taub for one day."

"He asked me to dinner," Toni said after a while.

"Victor?"

"No. Matthew White. The man I was talking to for so long. I just introduced you."

"Mmmm."

"He's an assistant director and his movie's going to be screening tomorrow afternoon. Boy, did he have some stories. They filmed up near a place called Darwin and the entire second unit came down with a virus in the middle of a heat wave. It was a hundred and three and no shade and . . ."

"Uh-huh."

"I said Matthew asked me to dinner," Toni repeated. "Night after next."

"So?"

"I'm trying to figure out what he wants. Maybe he figures there's a job in it when we shoot here next year."

"Now who's being cynical?" But Megan smiled, because Toni always said *when* we shoot, not *if*. "Maybe what's his name . . . Matthew . . . just wants your company."

"No one, I mean no man, has asked me to dinner since . . . was it the Kennedy inauguration? I remember I was wearing a pillbox hat."

"So go if you like him."

"I like him fine. But why would he ask me when there were so many cute young things standing around? I'm so out of practice that at first I didn't even realize he was coming on to me. Why is he looking at me like that? I wondered. Do I have spinach stuck between my teeth? Do I remind him of his mother?"

"Bloody hell, where is this elevator! Did it occur to you that perhaps he found you attractive?"

"That was the one thing that didn't cross my mind," Toni said, leaning against the wall, liking the idea now that it had crossed her mind. "But what would Joe say?"

"Sharing a lamb chop isn't adultery. Go with him. I'm going to be visiting the nuns and going out to Tas's farm, so I probably won't be back for dinner. Where is this elevator!"

"Y'know, Megan, maybe I shouldn't say this, but now you know about this situation with Tas . . ."

"I'm going to find the stairs and walk down if this elevator hasn't come in sixty seconds."

". . . it seems as though you could get yourself into hot water. I just think it's a bad idea, his wife and all . . . if I were you . . ."

"I hate sentences that begin with 'If I were you.' "

"I know. But you're even worse at faking things than I am, so . . ."

"I said I'd go and I'm going. At least I won't be around people in the business for a day. Dear Lord, I'm sick of people in the business." She shook her head and tugged at the front of her dress. "Victor's asked me to go to a party on Dennis Danher's yacht after *Chappy* screens."

"Great. Don't tell me you're not going. Don't tell me that, Megan."

"I don't know what I'm going to do."

Their conversation was cut short as a trio of men from the party, two propping up the white-faced third, reeled down the hall singing, " '. . . millions of hearts have been broken, just because those words were spoken . . .' " The elevator arrived. "Hold it, will you, luv?" one of the men called. Megan stepped in, prepared to ignore them, but Toni held the door. " 'Be sure it's true when you say I love you . . .' " the one who was the worse for drink warbled as his buddies guided him into the elevator and propped him against the wall. "You ladies want to come down to the lounge and finish off the evening?" one of the men inquired, straight-arming the drunk against the wall. "We'll have to drop off our mate here first. He's about to have a Technicolor yawn."

"A what?" Toni asked.

The man opened his mouth, clutched his gut and bent forward, pantomiming vomiting.

"Oh," Toni said with a stiff smile. "That's a colorful expression."

"How 'bout it? You game to come with us?"

"No," Megan said sharply, punching the button, "we've had enough for one night."

"All right. All right. Don't spit your dummy."

"A dummy," Megan said in answer to Toni's look, "is a pacifier. He means don't have a temper tantrum."

"Very colorful," Toni said again.

The elevator started to descend. The drunk got out the last wavering words to the song, " '. . . so be sure it's true, when you say I love you; it's a sin to tell a lie . . .' " while sliding to the floor. As Megan and Toni got out, he put his head between his knees and sobbed.

CHAPTER
TEN

BECAUSE OF HER DESIRE TO KEEP THE CONVERSATION going, Megan didn't realize that they were in familiar territory until Greta pointed out a row of shops. "See that chemist's? That's where the public school boys used to hide in the bushes. And that health food store? That's where Corcoran's used to be. Remember Corcoran's?"

"How could anyone forget Corcoran's?" A dark and dusty little shop, schoolchildren its exclusive clientele. Mrs. Corcoran like the witch in "Hansel and Gretel," smarmy when she took their pennies, flying into a rage if they smudged the counter glass; and Mrs. Corcoran's familiar: a one-eyed, pure-white cat named Smudge, who hissed and piddled on the floor and slept amid the toffees, barley sugar, Violet Crumbles and licorice whips. They'd joked about contracting spotted fever as they'd picked Smudge's hairs from their purchases. And now Corcoran's had been transformed into a pristine health food store.

"And there's the church." Greta nodded up ahead. Its once impressive spire seemed diminished by new buildings and the overhead tangle of telephone wires. "I suppose you must feel like Alice in Wonderland. Everything must seem so much smaller."

"Not so much smaller as . . ." It was the same, but irreparably changed, like looking into a mirror and trying to imagine your face as it had been twenty years ago. The open paddock, once her shortcut to school, was now a parking lot. Next to it, where the canopy of trees had led to the railway station, stood a bank. A lone pepper tree, now surrounded by asphalt, had been allowed to survive.

"Father Coffin sold off the paddock just before he died. He

had a verbal agreement with the bank allowing the parishioners to use the parking lot, but now the bank's expanding, so they want to renege on the agreement. Father Cellebrizzi, the new priest, is always fighting with the bank. He's a wonderful priest. You can really talk to him. As a child, I was afraid to talk to priests. And they never talked to me.''

"The only thing I can remember Father Coffin saying to me was 'Go child, and sin no more; that'll be three decades of the rosary.' ''

"Yes. Three decades of the rosary. That's the penance he always gave me, too. I suppose it would have been the same if you'd fibbed to your mum or committed an ax murder.''

"When I first started going to confession, he was so silent that I thought my sins had shocked him. It took me a while to realize that he'd fallen asleep, was taking his little afternoon z's while I knelt there with my bowels in a knot. I used to wonder if absolution was valid if the priest didn't really hear your sins, but I knew a good thing when I saw it, so I always went to him.''

"Father Cellebrizzi really listens. And he's had special training in marriage counseling." Or so she had heard. She hadn't the courage to find out. She'd mentioned Father Cellebrizzi to Tas and he'd said that talking to a priest about marriage was like asking someone who was afraid of blood to perform an operation. Tas didn't need to confide in anyone, whereas she . . . she wondered if Megan, so wise in the ways of the world, might not be the confidante she craved. With Megan she would be safe from gossip, Megan was only passing through. She gave her a sidelong glance, but couldn't stammer anything more personal than "Father Cellebrizzi has taken a very courageous stand on birth control.''

Megan snorted. "Margaret Sanger took a courageous stand on birth control. In fact she coined the phrase. But that was in 1915. It's hardly a hot issue now." She knew it was still a hot issue for more than half the world; but not for her. A few months ago she'd come out of Saks Fifth Avenue thinking she'd walk across the street and sit in St. Patrick's. She wasn't clear about when she'd started going into churches again. During her late teens and early twenties she'd given them a wide berth. But then she'd found herself drawn back, reasoning that you didn't have to be a believer to find solace in the warm stained-glass windows, the triumph of stone made fluid, the vaulting arches and domes. She'd taken Victor to St. Patrick's once and tried to explain her feelings to him, but he'd only said the place gave him the creeps and teased her about "once a Catholic, always a Catholic." But she felt a connection to the long-dead Marys and Eileens who, so legend had it, had contributed their hard-earned wages to the building fund so that they might have a place of beauty in their hard lives. She could ignore the scuffling of tourists, the souvenir gift shop near the entrance, and dip her fingers into the cool holy-water font and kneel in a pew, removing herself from the noisy shove and bustle of Fifth Avenue. Sometimes she even performed the comforting ritual of lighting a candle. On this particular day she had seen a group of women on the cathedral steps. They were holding placards about reproductive rights, conducting a silent vigil. The cardinal, O'Connor, often called in the police to remove gay rights activists, but apparently these women, some nuns among them, were not sufficiently troublesome to deserve police intervention. For a moment, her purchases of underwear and cosmetics dangling from her arm, she'd thought of joining them, had wondered yet again at those who stayed Catholic, who sought to change the institution from within. Did they possess a faithfulness and belief that was beyond her, or were they simply prisoners of upbringing, souls too tepid to go it alone? In any case, she was not one of them. Silent protest was not her thing.

Greta asked, "Did you leave the Church because of birth control?"

"Hell, no. I stopped going around the time I was sixteen. Somewhere between 'French kissing is a mortal sin' and the infallibility of the pope they lost me. And I suppose I had a grudge against them. My mother wasn't allowed to receive the sacraments because she was divorced. That caused her a lot of misery and it seemed terribly unfair to me. But she never really cut the cord. When I stopped going to church, she was the one who pushed me to see a priest. But I left anyway." Irene's recriminations had hung about the house like smoke, choking them both. Megan shrugged. "And another reason I left was because there were books I wanted to read and movies I wanted to see that were on the forbidden list. I thought, 'Nobody tells me what to read, what to see.' ''

''So you liberated yourself.''

''Not entirely. Not right away. I was afraid of hell for a while, even though, rationally, I didn't believe in it. Then I let men I went out with give me lists of their favorite books and take me to their favorite movies, and instruct me in their political views. I guess making up your own mind is a lifetime proposition.''

''There's the school,'' Greta said as they approached a box-like, two-story building. The architect had tried to disguise its institutional aspect by adding a circular drive and many large windows, which glinted in the sun.

''Is the old school entirely gone?''

''No. It's behind this. They're going to tear it down next year. This driveway is where our playground used to be, remember?''

Again, trees were Megan's best point of reference. She recognized the stand of gum and wattle at the end of the drive, where the dunnies and wooden lunch tables had once been.

''Chrissie goes here,'' Greta explained. ''It's a terribly long drive from the farm but I trade off with two other mothers who live out near us.''

''I don't have such happy memories that I'd send my kid here.''

''Truth to tell, I didn't want to. I thought she'd be better off in a coed school. It was Tas who thought she should go here, and he's not really a believer. But he says boys and girls don't study properly when they're together. He does take an interest in the children's education.'' By specifying something he took an interest in, she feared she'd exposed his general neglect. Embarrassed, she turned the conversation from the personal to the general. ''Do you think girls make a better adjustment to the opposite sex if they're around them at school?''

''Shit, I haven't a clue as to how one makes adjustments to the opposite sex. Maybe we'd be better off if we had a society modeled on ancient Crete. You know, the women run things, but a couple of times a year we invite the boys in for competitive games, then we have a dirty big booze-up, create the next generation and pack the men off to the woods until the next orgy.''

Greta raised her brows and smiled as she turned off the motor. "Are you going to suggest that to Sister Bruno?"

"Not a chance. I'm a good St. Brigid's girl. A model of deportment. I wouldn't have come to visit if I'd planned to make them uncomfortable. Besides, I don't think Bruno has much acquaintance with ancient civilizations—unless we count County Mayo. And I'll have my hands full answering the really important questions." She squinted her eyes and imitated Sister Bruno's Irish brogue. " 'And are y' a practicing Catholic, Megan? And did y' ever marry?' I'll tell her I'm a Hare Krishna and I married a Jew in a civil ceremony and divorced him two years later."

Greta checked her reflection in the rearview mirror and reached into her purse for comb and lipstick. "No one would believe that."

"But it's true. At least the second part."

Greta tidied her hair, blotted her lipstick and did up the top button of her dress. Getting out of the car, she smoothed the vertical wrinkles in her skirt and straightened her shoulders. She felt proud of herself. Driving, except in the country, made her nervous, but she'd negotiated city traffic without any trouble, probably because Megan was such easy company. "Oops. Forgot the chocolates. Get them out of the backseat, will you please?"

They walked around the side of the new school building, an odd couple: Greta with her easy-to-care-for haircut, seersucker shirtwaist and low-heeled shoes, all of which proclaimed Wife and Mother as much as if she'd been wearing a sign on her chest; Megan in her elaborately tooled cowboy boots, tight jeans, blue silk shirt, and sunglasses pushed onto her nimbus of wild hair. "Hey, this does look smaller." Megan stopped as they rounded the building. "And it looks positively Dickensian." Here was the old school, its brick worn and grimy, the scrollwork above the entrance weather-pitted. She felt the same queasy anxiety she felt on the first morning of a shoot, or when one of her films was shown for the first time, but that was a pale shadow of the fear she'd experienced behind these walls. No adult undertaking could end in the total failure, the swift, certain and inexorable punishment that had been meted out here. Million-dollar budgets down the drain could never be as devastating as misplaced homework, a poor mark on an exam, a prediction that she would come to no good. Greta touched her elbow, said, "Come on," and led the way to the path, now covered with a shiny aluminum awning, which separated the nuns' living quarters from the old school. The garden was so quiet that the crunch of their shoes on gravel sounded like an invasion. The statue of the Virgin, face placid, arms held out in languid supplication, was ringed with a new planting of red, pink and purple petunias. Greta smoothed her hair again and pressed the button to the convent door. Megan turned back to the garden. "Remember our kids' joke? Why did Miss Petunia blush? Because she was put in the same bed with Sweet William. Didn't we think that was naughty?"

The door opened immediately, as though the round-faced young woman with the Dutch-boy haircut had been lurking behind it in anticipation. "Good morning, Mrs. Burke." She might have been anywhere from eighteen to thirty. She was wearing a pale blue jogging outfit, but Megan felt she would have instantly recognized her as a nun. Perhaps it was the jogging outfit itself. On her Sunday walks in Central Park she often thought how nunlike the young women joggers were. They were possessed of the same innocent but grim rigor, dedicated not to Holy Orders but to career and self-improvement. Their bodies were to be disciplined. Excess calories, smoking or alcohol all had the weight of sin. They woke to clock radios instead of bells but their days were just as ordered. At work they wore shape-disguising suits and running shoes, carrying their high heels in their briefcases "in case." But because of hectic work schedules, lack of eligible men, fear of disease or being taken advantage of, there were few opportunities for romance. She knew many of them were celibate. Holidays found them homesick and lonely. On birthdays they celebrated with the girls.

"Megan, this is Michele," Greta said. "Michele is one of Chrissie's teachers. Michele, this is Megan Hanlon. Miss Hanlon is . . ."

"Oh, I know who she is." Michele colored at her interruption. "Pleased to meet you, Miss Hanlon. They're waiting for you in the parlor."

The vestibule was dim, cool and odorless. Two straight-backed chairs, never used, were placed on either side of a long table beneath a portrait of a bald, ramrod-backed man, his eyes glinting with the achieved ambition of a politician or a chief executive officer, his scarlet robes proclaiming him a prince of the Church. Patriarchy rules, Megan thought, though, ironically, it had been at St. Brigid's that she'd first seen women running their own show. The nuns were deferential toward the youngest of priests, but many of them viewed the male hierarchy the way citizens of a small southern town viewed the federal government: its power was distant, it rarely affected their daily lives, it could be circumvented if never outright ignored.

Michele led the way to the parlor, her rubber-soled shoes squeaking on the fanatically polished floor, and opened the door on a scene as still and composed as a painting. Two figures in black sat on either side of a fireplace. One was stoutly packed into an armchair, the other sunk into a wheelchair. Despite the warmth of the day, a single log smoldered on the hearth. The only source of light and air was a tall window overlooking the garden, beside which a younger woman stood, her back turned, her hands thrust into the loose sleeves of a russet-colored dress that was almost the same color as her hair.

"Ah, here you are." Sister Bruno eased herself from the armchair, reaching for Greta's hand with the awkward movement of habitually repressed emotion.

"You remember Megan Hanlon, don't you?" Greta asked.

"How could I forget Megan?" Sister Bruno's tone suggested it was not an altogether pleasant memory.

Megan smiled and said what a pleasure it was to see Sister Bruno, but her attention was drawn to the window.

"And Sister Ursula . . ." Greta directed her toward the wheelchair. Sister Ursula's hands came up in a graceful movement, reminiscent of her conducting days, before arthritis seized them and dropped them into her lap. Megan bent and took the hands, finding them icy cold, and looked into a face so bony that its smallish nose looked beaklike. "Ah, Megan. Megan Hanlon." The old woman's gaze lasted so long that it seemed to lose focus, as though she strained to look beyond Megan's

face and capture some elusive memory. "Do you still sing?"
she inquired at last.

"Only in the shower."

"But you have such a lovely voice," Sister Ursula admonished. "We must use our talents or they will grow rusty."

The woman in the russet dress could contain herself no longer. She took a step forward, commanding attention.

"And is it Sister Mary Magdalene?" Megan asked, moving to her.

"The same. But call me Joan." Her smile was wry, acknowledging that she had finally answered the question asked so many years ago.

"Then Joan."

They folded each other in an embrace, laying the double kiss of welcome on both cheeks, then drew back, arms loosely draped, studying each other.

"You haven't changed at all," Megan said. There was a deep vertical crease in Joan's forehead and an etching of fine lines around her penetrating grey eyes, but time had blurred the sharpness of her chin and her hair, freed from wimple and veil, had a softening effect. It was such a joy to look into her face again that Megan was reminded of one of their conversations about the nature of heaven and hell. Heaven, Joan had told her, was not a place with pink clouds and gauze-draped cherubs, any more than hell was a devilish barbecue with damned souls skewered like so many sausages. Those were comic-book notions. Heaven was a state of bliss, like being in the presence of a person you truly loved, and hell was the desolation of knowing you'd never see that face again. When she'd first been married to Victor, she'd felt that waking up to see his face was as close to heaven as she could hope to come.

"Oh, but I have changed," Joan said. "And so have you. Most certainly, so have you." Megan had flowered in just the way Joan had hoped she would. She was a bit wild-looking, yes, but she was vibrant, colorful, a presence.

Michele, who had lingered at the door, asked if she might serve tea. Joan and Megan drew apart, simultaneously aware of an intimacy that excluded the others. "That would be nice,

Michele,'' Joan said, still holding Megan's hand and leading her back to the group.

"We've brought you some chocolates, Sister Bruno," Greta said, settling onto the couch. Megan handed over the chocolates, thinking how generous it was of Greta to include her as gift-giver, while Sister Bruno muttered the obligatory "You shouldn't have." All seated, the conversation settled into the polite ritual in which they'd all been trained. Had the drive been pleasant? How was Megan's flight? And Greta's children? Did they think it would rain? Even while answering questions, Megan kept looking across at Joan, knowing Joan had as little tolerance for small talk as she. She longed to talk with her alone, but saw little hope of that.

Michele came in balancing a large tray of tea, lemon, a Toby jug of milk, plates of arrowroot biscuits and meat-paste sandwiches cut into triangles, garnished with shredded lettuce. Sister Ursula, who had mostly absented herself from the conversation, came to. "So you live in Hollywood?" she asked, gingerly placing cup on saucer.

"Mostly I live in New York."

How could you live somewhere "mostly"? Sister Ursula wondered. She pulled on her single chin whisker. "And how did you come to be mostly in New York," she asked in wonderment, as though Megan had just said she'd been abducted onto a space ship.

"I moved there right out of college about a hundred years ago."

A hundred years? But no. This Megan Hanlon had always been an exaggerator. Sister Ursula smiled at her. "I thought all films were made in Hollywood."

"Not anymore. Mostly I shoot on location."

Sister Ursula said, "I see," but didn't.

"So, you live in New York," Sister Bruno said, as though she were cross-examining a witness. "New York must be . . ."

"Yes." Gotham. Equidistant from Sodom and Gomorrah.

"And your mother and father? Where do they live?"

"And is your father still in the films?" Ursula wanted to know. "I remember that photo of him you used to carry. All done up with his chest bare and feathers in his hair."

Megan nodded. How she had treasured that photo! Thomas
Shelby as Flaming Arrow, or Geronimo or Son of Cochise.
She'd tracked down some of those B-grade shoot-'em-ups and
watched them on her VCR. Because he did stunt work, doubling
for the lead actor, his name did not appear in the titles. He had
never had a close-up, but she could freeze the frame and study
him riding into battle, leaping to his death, being knifed by a
cavalry officer. Even when he worked, Thomas Shelby was
always on the losing side. "I don't see my father much. He
lives . . ." God only knew where. ". . . in another state.
My mother . . ."

Sister Bruno's eyes swam behind her thick lenses, her broad
nostrils flared with the scent of divorce. "So your parents
are—"

"And your Australian relatives, how are they?" Joan came
to the rescue.

"I haven't had a chance to see them yet. I've been tied up
with the festival."

"And you came to Australia alone?" Sister Bruno asked. Her
eyes traveled to Megan's hands. Rings aplenty, but on the wrong
fingers. "And you're . . ."

"No. I'm not married. I'm traveling with my assistant, Toni
Massari."

"I met Toni this morning," Greta put in, realizing that the
name could belong to either a man or a woman. "She's a lovely
woman."

"And your brother?" Sister Bruno inquired after taking a sip
of tea. "Didn't your mother have another child when you were
with us? And wasn't it a boy?"

"Yes. I have a brother. Michael." Computers of totalitarian
governments couldn't have gathered and stored so much information. "Michael's a priest."

"Ahhh." A sigh of satisfaction whistled from Sister Ursula.

"Well, that must make your mother very proud," Bruno said.

Megan nodded. No point in saying that both she and Irene
had been shocked when Michael had entered the seminary, that
he was still more comfortable in jeans than a cassock, that Irene
would have preferred him to marry and produce a grandchild.

"It's quite stuffy in here. Shall I open the window?" Joan asked.

"Do open it. It's my fault that it's stuffy," Sister Ursula explained, pulling up the afghan to show fleece-lined slippers. "My circulation is appalling." She began to natter about the inconveniences of old age. Sister Bruno shifted in her chair and cleared her throat, a signal to bring Sister Ursula back to the topic at hand. "So you write and direct films," Sister Ursula said, again shaking her head in wonderment. "I've never heard of a woman doing that."

"There are quite a few," Joan explained. "Quite a few Aussies. Do tell us more about your work, Megan. I understand you're up for an Academy Award."

"Which I probably won't get," Megan answered, taking a biscuit.

"Oh, you will get it," Greta encouraged. "Imagine a St. Brigid's girl getting an Academy Award."

"Do tell us how you two girls happened to run into each other," Sister Ursula said.

Greta put her sandwich beside her teacup. "Tas and I went to a party given by Dr. and Mrs. Tishman. They entertain a lot, but I usually don't have the time to go to their dos. But this time Tas insisted. It was such a lovely party. So many famous people there and . . ." She drew in her breath.

"Go on." Sister Ursula leaned forward, eager for gossip.

"When I first saw Megan I thought I recognized her, but only from newspaper photos, but then we started chatting and before long we were going like a house on fire, talking about the old days here at the convent. My husband, Tas, was so surprised when I told him I'd met an old school chum. And when he found out she was a famous director . . ."

"What did they serve at the party?" Sister Bruno wanted to know.

"Oh, you tell about it, Megan," Greta offered.

"No. You tell." Megan bit into a biscuit but couldn't produce enough saliva to swallow. She winced inwardly with every mention of Tas's name. The two older women tutted at the happy coincidence of the meeting and Greta, enthusiasm overcoming shyness, provided them with details: "Mrs. Tishman served

pâté, which is a sort of fancy meatloaf, and prawns and . . ."
She looked both pleased and vulnerable. Megan wouldn't betray
her for the world. Except she already had.

"I shall write to Eleanor Pujoli and tell her all about this,"
Sister Ursula said when Greta came to her breathless conclusion.
"It takes me a long time to write a letter these days." She lifted
her arthritic hands in evidence. "But I shall definitely write to
her. You remember Eleanor, don't you, Megan?"

Megan nodded. Eleanor Pujoli had been a chubby, slatternly
girl, her uniform always spotted and her shoes scuffed. Sister
Bruno had always said Eleanor looked like a bale of hay tied in
a hurry. Her family had been large, paint-licking poor, and had
lived in a council house. Eleanor had once taken coins from the
poor box to buy the other girls ice cream and when Aileen Ingpen had found out about it, she'd replaced the money with her
own allowance. Aileen, Megan and Eleanor had cut their thumbs
with the razor Megan used to sharpen colored pencils and had
sworn never to tell.

"Eleanor is one of us," Sister Bruno said. "She joined the
Order almost fifteen years ago."

"Well I'll be damned!" Megan exclaimed before she could
censor herself.

Sister Ursula bobbed her head, ignoring Megan's lapse. "I
was very surprised myself."

"She's at our convent in Darwin," Joan said. Her tea, un-
touched, cooled in front of her. Her hands were folded in her
lap, her legs crossed at the ankles. Only her eyes betrayed her
intensity. "Eleanor doesn't teach. She runs a program for battered women. Officially, we're still a teaching order, though
there is some awareness of meeting other community needs."
Sister Bruno shifted her bulk and began to finger her rosary
beads. Ministering to the victims of domestic violence was, to
her mind, a dubious proposition. "Eleanor set up the program
herself," Joan went on. "She's quite tireless. Still her rough-
and-ready self, which is a blessing under the circumstances."

"And you'll remember Mona Gallagher," Sister Bruno said,
eager to put one of her favorite alumnae in the limelight. "Mona
has a career in banking. Her father was a banker and since he
had no son to carry on . . . Mona's been asked to move to the

Sydney office, but her mother's an invalid, you know, and Mona would never think of putting her in a home. Mona's coming by this morning. She should be here any minute."

Megan dislodged the last of the masticated biscuit from the roof of her mouth and swallowed it with the help of a sip of tea. "It's Aileen Ingpen I wanted to hear about. Do you hear anything of Aileen?"

This question created a silence so deep that the ticking of the clock on the mantel was audible for the first time. "Aileen died," Joan said. "In an automobile accident. In her first year of university." Megan had a sense that Joan wanted to say more but couldn't.

"Oh, no."

"Yes," Sister Ursula confirmed. "Such a tragedy."

"We used to write to each other," Megan said dumbly. It had been a typical adolescent correspondence, full of exclamation marks, descriptions of boys and clothes, complaints about parents and teachers. They'd signed their letters "your friend for life" or "yours till hell freezes over" and sworn to be bridesmaids at each other's weddings. Aileen had sent Megan Aussie care packages: tins of passion fruit, a calendar of bush flowers, a kangaroo-skin wallet and a jar of Vegemite (obviously an acquired taste since Megan's American friends said it smelled and looked like axle grease). The correspondence had come to an end around Megan's final year of high school when she'd written that seeing Fellini's *La Strada* had changed her life, that she had no desire to marry and thought she might be an anarchist. Who was this Fellini? Aileen wrote back. He sounded like a Dago. And was Megan really going to be a spinster? And if she was against the government, did that mean she was against the Church, too? The questions were so naïve they didn't warrant a reply. In the intervening years, as Megan hacked through the underbrush of nonconformity, she imagined Aileen, with a small mind and large bank account, tripping along the sunny path of normalcy. Aileen would have a nice husband and two lovely children. She would be docile in everything except her tennis game. But Aileen had been twenty years in the ground.

"Mr. Ingpen spared no expense at the funeral," Sister Bruno said by way of consolation. "The church was packed with flowers and dignitaries. The bishop himself said the Requiem Mass. Of course, the Ingpens have always been pillars of the Church.''

''But it's always a tragedy when the young die,'' Sister Ursula said, her head wobbling on its stem like a flower in a breeze.

''She died with her soul unspotted and she's in a far better place than we are, I'm sure,'' Sister Bruno said.

''A far better place . . .'' Megan stopped the words but continued the thought; a far better place would be the balcony of the Miranda Hotel in Santa Barbara, watching the sun on the water and sipping a piña colada. It was not so much Sister Bruno's beliefs that made her bristle as the smug certainty with which they were expressed.

Joan got up. ''Perhaps I could show you the new school building, Megan. That is, if you have the time.''

Greta, always relieved when confrontation was averted, encouraged them to go and leaned forward to replenish Sister Ursula's teacup. As Megan followed Joan out of the room, a discussion about the effect of tannic acid on the stomach lining was already in progress. In the hallway they ran into Michele, hurrying along with another kettle of boiling water. ''Miss Hanlon, if it's all right, I'd like to get your autograph before you go. Not for me. For one of the students.''

''Yes. Surely. And please call me Megan.''

''Do you like being a celebrity?'' Joan asked as they moved on.

''I don't think St. Brigid's gave me the proper training for it. The homilies about humility must've made an impression. I'm afraid people will think I'm full of myself, so I end up letting myself in for things I don't really want to do. I'm not assertive enough.''

''You young women are all so concerned with being assertive.'' Joan gave her a wry smile. ''You seem quite assertive enough to me.''

''The requirements vary with the location. I may seem like . . .'' She censored ''ball buster.'' ''. . . like gangbusters here, but in New York I'm considered a pussy cat.'' As they turned into another corridor she caught the faint smell of stewing vegetables and realized they were going deeper into the convent itself. ''Aren't we going the wrong way?''

"I didn't think you'd really want to see the new school. It's an improvement, I suppose, though it has no real character. It's just cleaner and larger. Too large, in fact. Our enrollment has dropped off over the years, sad to say. There's even some talk of merging with the Marist Brothers, making it coeducational."

"Oh, no," Megan heard herself say with unexpected vehemence.

"I'm opposed to it myself, but tradition may be overwhelmed by financial considerations. It wouldn't be the first time the bishop has heard the word of God through his financial adviser. Still, we will have some say in it. So let's skip the new school. I'd like to show you the chapel, and then we could sit in my room. That way we won't be disturbed." Joan moved ahead, a lifetime of custom causing her to keep her eyes on the floor and her hands hidden in her sleeves. She paused at the chapel door. "I remember Sister Bernadette sending you into the nuns' chapel once. You'd done something naughty and she told you to come in here and listen to the voice of God. Presumably He'd tell you to be more obedient. When you came out you said that you hadn't heard anything but Sister Cecilia humming to herself as she dusted the pews."

"I was courting disaster."

"Perhaps Sister Bernadette was courting disaster. It's risky business to expect a divine voice to back up your directives. Were I the superior—and there's some talk that I might be considered, though I certainly don't want the job—I should simply have to rely on that personal assertiveness I was teasing you about a moment ago." Before Megan could respond to any of this news, Joan pushed open the door to the chapel. "Remember how the pews used to be arranged?" She lowered her voice. "All facing front toward the altar?" The altar had been replaced with a simple Jarrah-wood table in the center of the room. The pews were ranged around it. "I like the idea of forming a circle to worship," Joan went on. "It gives more of a sense of community. And Michele plays the guitar, and we exchange the kiss of peace. Small changes, to be sure, or at least they must seem so to you. But no institution changes quickly."

The pride with which Joan referred to the innovations made Megan suspect that she must have had some hand in them. She could imagine the resistance with which they had been met. How could Joan, who said institution instead of Mother Church, who had such a sharp analytical eye and such a strong personality, have subjected herself to the confinement of these walls?

They sat for a moment of silence, then Joan crossed herself and got up.

"Now . . ." Joan closed the door on the chapel and turned to her. "I don't suppose we'll be missed for fifteen or twenty minutes." She led the way down another corridor with a series of doors on either side. Through one that was partially opened, Megan glimpsed a single bed, a crucifix. To her surprise the wall was painted a lolly pink. "I always imagined your rooms would be white."

"They used to be. Now we're allowed to paint them any color we like. Mr. Johnston who has the paint store donates the paint. We even have a TV room, though only the younger women watch with any regularity. I suppose watching TV is a generational difference that even the Church doesn't want to buck. Not all of these rooms are occupied. We don't seem to be able to recruit on home ground anymore. We have a new sister from Ireland and one who's Vietnamese, but Michele is our only Aussie." She opened a door. "And this is my room." A wardrobe, a narrow bed, a cluttered desk, piles of books stacked on the floor, on the windowsill a bud vase with a single rose in such full bloom that it had already dropped petals. A crucifix on the white wall had tilted so that its right arm seemed to be reaching toward the window. Joan swept up papers from the chair and motioned for Megan to take it, then seated herself on the edge of the bed, suddenly self-conscious. In all her years at the convent no one except other sisters had been in this room.

"Thanks for bailing me out of that scene in the parlor. I was getting a bit claustrophobic."

"Sister Bruno does have a way of playing the Grand Inquisitor. I'm sure she means no harm. I was sorry to be the one to tell you about Aileen."

"I had the feeling that there was more to it than you let on."

"I don't know the truth of it all. There were a lot of rumors at the time. She was engaged, and then the engagement was broken off and her young man went off to study in England. She was alone at the time of the accident and it was on a deserted road, so some people thought that it might have been . . ." She sought the right word. ". . . purposeful. The last time I saw her was when she came to the convent to show us her engagement ring."

Megan circled her head with her arm and looked out the window. "She was going to have a magnolia satin wedding dress with a long train and I was going to be her bridesmaid. I was the one who stopped writing to her." She stared into Joan's face. Joan's lips were slightly parted, her gaze calm but intent enough to crease the vertical line between her brows. Joan had always been a good listener. "I meant it when I said you hadn't changed. Though it was a shock to see you out of the habit."

"It was a shock to me at first." Joan looked down at her sensible shoes and caught a glimpse of Megan's fancy boots. "When I started graduate classes at the university I was at pains to disguise myself, but I'm sure anyone could have spotted me as a nun."

"No. I'd cast you as an academic. The dean of women at some establishment East Coast college in the States."

"All sense and no frivolity," Joan asked.

"Those habits must've been miserable, especially in the summer, but they did have a certain . . ."

"Drama?"

"Yes, the drama appealed to me."

"And to me when I was younger, though I didn't think of it that way at the time. But I remember the anticipation with which I took the veil, the importance of cutting my hair, accepting the ring. I shall always cherish that. The modern world has so few rituals to mark important events."

"The bride of Christ," Megan said. She thought of the ordinary suit she'd worn for her own wedding and the strange superstition she'd felt at the last moment: that her marriage would fail because she and Victor had not given sufficient importance to the ritual. "It must've been difficult to give up the habit."

"I felt quite exposed at first, but it was mavelously freeing once I got used to it. Of course change becomes more difficult as we get older. Most of the older nuns found civvies impossible."

"In a strange way I miss it, though that's silly for me to say. I'm not . . ."

"Not a practicing Catholic?"

"You guessed."

"I would have been surprised if you had been."

Megan thanked this understanding with a quick smile. "And my parents were divorced by the time I got back to the States. And I'm divorced, too."

Joan nodded. "Was it painful?"

"Very. My ex-husband is here at the festival. Seeing him again has thrown me into a cocked hat." She was tempted to confess the added complication of her meeting with Tasman, but decided against it. "You know, we girls used to speculate about why you had entered the convent. Blighted love affairs and all that. Though even as a kid I didn't really believe that was why you entered."

"No. No blighted love affairs. When I entered, my idea of a love affair was *Pride and Prejudice*. I'd gone to a few local dances and I'd been kissed by a few local lads, but none of them fired my imagination enough for me to envision a life with them." Her eyes twinkled as she added, "Perhaps they weren't very good kissers."

Megan laughed. This was a different Joan, worldly enough to make a joke about kissing, willing, even eager to talk about herself. "Were your parents very religious?"

"They would have said yes, but no, not really. Religion was something in the general scheme of things, never questioned and never more than part of the routine. They weren't particularly pleased when I told them I had a vocation. The notion of a vocation—of being called to something—seemed self-dramatizing to them. The decision to enter the Order was entirely mine and in retrospect, I suppose there was something rebellious about it." Joan's tongue swept her upper lip and she stared out the window. "I suppose it was because of the sheep." Megan's eyebrows lifted in inquiry. "We had a sheep station," Joan went on. "We were quite well-to-do by local standards but except for holidays in town our lives revolved around the sheep. Have you ever listened to sheep for very long? That constant bleating can drive you crazy. It's no accident that stupid people are referred to as sheep. And our daily routine, it seemed to me to be only slightly above that of the sheep. Also our dinner-table conversation. With all the arrogance of youth I felt I was the cygnet amid the ducks. I was always sneaking off to read. I read till my eyes smarted, till my mother threatened to take the books away. If I was in love with anyone it was Mr. Hickey. He ran the local library. And he was old enough to be my grandfather. He'd traveled all over the world, been a soldier and a merchant marine, and it was only after he'd contracted TB that he'd started to read. He had a wonderful mind, absolutely eclectic, daring. We'd sit on the running boards of his truck after the library closed, and talk about books, about the meaning of life, in those philosophical conversations unique to the queer young and the lonely old. And then I read the life of St. Teresa of Avila and I thought, 'That's for me.' I wanted to give myself to something bigger than myself. And I loved God.'' She sighed. ''I had such grandiose and silly ideas about what convent life would be like. I imagined it as a place of blissful quiet and meditation, as far from bleating sheep—the two- and four-footed variety—as I could get. Had I known about academic life I might have chosen that, but I didn't at the time.''

''And now you're at the university?''

''Yes. I'm about to get my Ph.D. It's taken me years, what with my obligations here.'' She drew in a deep breath and straightened her spine. ''I shall never forget my first day at the university. It was sunny, brilliantly sunny, the sort of day when you can see for miles. And blustery. I was going up the main steps, the wind whipping my skirts. I was very conscious of my exposed legs. And a piece of notebook paper blew up and wrapped itself around my ankle. It was some student's notes on the topography of ancient Carthage. It's difficult to describe the excitement I felt—the topography of ancient Carthage not being a subject that speeds most hearts—but I had such a feeling of coming home. I loved the look and feel of the place, the students lounging on the lawns, the musty smell of the library, the arguments and debates in the coffeeshop. I hadn't felt such a combination of anticipation and anxiety since . . . well, since I'd taken my vows. All those years I hadn't allowed myself to realize how deprived I felt, how hungry for real conversation.''

"Yes, you can be hungry for real conversation in a worse way than you can be hungry for food. I'm awfully glad they let you go to the university. It's made you blossom."

"Blossoming out of season—when you're middle-aged and think you've grown as much as you ever will—can be quite a surprise. But you," Joan said admiringly. "I always had faith that you'd succeed, and succeed brilliantly."

"That remains to be seen."

"Do you mean you're worried about this nomination for the Academy Award?"

"Getting it would help, though I'm more concerned with raising money for my next film."

"I feel sure you'll win. I'll be praying for you."

"But you were the one who convinced me that we shouldn't pray to God as though He were a parent we could petition for favors," Megan teased.

Joan's laugh exposed irregular teeth. "A figure of speech. I only meant I wish you well. But on the night of the Awards I shall go to the TV room and pull seniority and insist on watching. The Awards are transmitted by satellite, aren't they?"

"I have no idea."

"I'd love to see the new film you'll be showing at the festival. James will probably go, so he'll tell me about it."

Megan leaned forward. Sometimes the mere pronunciation of a name revealed intimacy. "Who's James?"

"Professor Ferzaco. He's my adviser. Now that I'm within striking distance of my Ph.D. he says we're colleagues"—her voice caressed the word—"so he insists on my calling him by his first name. We're . . ."

"Good friends?" Megan supplied, sensing Joan's embarrassment.

"Yes. Good friends." Joan relieved her palpable tension by getting up and moving to the window. "James thinks there'll be an opening for an assistant professor's position in the history department next year. So if I play my cards right . . ." Her hands moved as though shuffling cards, then folded. "I have no patience with students on the level of St. Brigid's anymore. Not that I've ever had much patience." She considered her shortcomings. "I push them too hard. I'm not charitable in my criticism. I've tried to improve, I've prayed, but . . . Agnes was ill a few weeks ago and I took her religious instruction class. I found myself equivocating when answering the girls' questions. Finally I said, 'I don't know.' ''

"But children always respond to honesty."

"Ah, yes," Joan smiled, "but the Church, understandably, finds certainty more appropriate in the early-learning stages." After the class, she had gone to the chapel to meditate, but she had come away feeling desolate. God's love and guidance were elusive; whereas the affection of a particular, burly, rather egotistical man was with her during all her waking hours.

"Would the Order allow you to teach at the university?"

"The trouble, as I've told you, is that we're short of help here. There will have to be major changes if we're to revitalize St. Brigid's. We'll elect a new Mother Superior soon, and I . . . I don't know what I'll do." With the outward calm with which she sought to quell inner turmoil, Joan gripped the sill and studied a fly resting on it. The fly suddenly came to life, furiously buzzing against the window. Megan wanted to ask if Joan loved this professor, but that would be going too far. "Have you spoken to anyone else about all this?" she asked, as Joan threw up the window and shooed out the fly.

"No. I didn't even know I was going to talk to you about it."

"Sometimes, when you talk to someone you trust . . ."

"Yes, it can help to clarify one's thoughts. James has been my only confidant and even he . . ."

There was a tap on the door. "It's me. Michele."

Joan and Megan started like children who've been caught in a forbidden game. Joan said, "Yes?"

Michele's head came around the doorjamb. "Sorry to disturb. I didn't know where you'd gotten to, but . . ."

Joan nodded, urging Michele to get out what she'd come to say.

"Miss Gallagher has arrived and she's in a bit of a rush and she wants to see Miss Hanlon."

"We'll be around directly," Joan assured her, but Michele, unable to conquer her curiosity, lingered. "Directly," Joan said more sharply than she'd intended. The door closed. "The gossip from this afternoon will keep Michele going for months. We lead such narrow lives.''

''Mona Gallagher is the last person I want to see. We never liked each other. She was always such a goody-goody, always ratting on us.''

'' 'A new commandment I give to you, that you love one another.' ''

''Easier said than done when it comes to the likes of Mona Gallagher.''

''That's why it's a commandment instead of a suggestion.'' Joan squeezed Megan's hand, released it and went to the door.

Mona Gallagher got up from the couch as they entered. She had changed, at least insofar as will and cosmetics would allow. Her once pallid, horsey little face was deeply tanned, her high forehead disguised with a sweep of brightened hair. A carefully drawn lipline improved her long upper lip and her cerise suit fairly shouted gaiety. ''Megan Hanlon!'' she gushed. ''How wonderful to see you. I always knew you'd do great things.''

If memory serves, Megan thought, you always predicted that I'd end up in the gutter. She responded to Mona's greeting and took her place on the couch. The conversation was a replay of the ''who's married, who's dead, what's the price of soap flakes'' chatter. Megan was on automatic pilot, smiling, answering questions, careful not to look at Joan. Sister Bruno offered her chocolates. Mona went on about her diet, then launched into a description of her recent trip to Singapore, all the while surreptitiously checking her watch. She was like a sleek car whose idle has been set too high. Michele appeared with a sheet of paper and asked Megan to autograph it. As Megan reached into her purse for a pen, Sister Bruno noted its untidy contents and reminded them all that Megan had failed penmanship. Sensing that another round of criticism was about to begin, Greta got up. Mona followed her lead, explaining that she had another appointment and hoping she'd be forgiven for just popping in. ''It was so good of you all to remember us,'' Sister Ursula said, dabbing at her rheumy eyes. She motioned for Megan to come to her, reached up and took Megan's chin in her hand and again stared into her face as though seeking the answer to some puzzling question. ''Forgive us our sins and pray for us. Will you do that, Megan? I shall pray for you and for your intentions. Such a lovely voice you had. I shall never forget . . ." She shook her head. "A silly thing to say because I forget things all the time. But do you remember . . ." Sister Ursula began to hum, found the right key and croaked,

> *Hail Queen of Heaven, the Ocean Star,*
> *Guide to the wanderer here below,*
> *Thrown on life's surge, we claim thy care,*
> *Save us from peril and . . .*

"The girls have to go now," Sister Bruno reprimanded her.

" '. . . and from woe.' So kind of you to remember us." For Sister Ursula the visit had finished. She stared into the fireplace while the women gathered up their purses and moved to the door. Sister Bruno eased her bulk from the chair and trailed after them, offering prayers and chocolates.

"Megan," Joan said solemnly, "I hope to see you again."

"And Mona, dear," Sister Bruno called when they'd almost made their escape, "do remember to speak with your superiors at the bank about the parishioners being able to use the parking lot. A little word from you . . ."

"Yes. Yes, of course. Good-bye. God bless you."

"God bless *you*."

All three were silent as they walked though the garden, but as they approached the driveway, Mona burst out, "Talk to my superiors at the bank about the parishioners using the parking lot! Next she'll be asking me to take up a collection at the office." She opened the door to a tan Toyota and turned back, squinting against the sunlight. "You girls wouldn't have time for a quick drink, would you?"

Megan and Greta exchanged a look, each offering the other the decision.

"Oh, come on." Mona's prefect voice still urged obedience.

"I think we'd better not," Megan said, but seeing the slight pursing of Mona's lips and fearing she'd be thought a snob, she glanced at Greta again. Greta, who always had trouble saying no, acquiesced. "Just for a bit."

"Good. The pub."

The Harp of Erin was so locally famous that it was just referred to as "the pub." It was a fake two-story Tudor with heavy doors and windows frosted with an elegant scroll inelegantly promising BEER. A defunct gas lamp dangled over the entrance, but the building itself, the town's closest thing to a historic landmark, had been given a new coat of pea-green paint. It was the den of iniquity of their childhood, man's province (though women of irredeemable reputation, not permitted in the bar itself, were known to sit in the lounge, and on payday, children sent to fetch their fathers had loitered around the doors). In the adjoining alleyway, men had played two-up or handed over their wages to the bookie, hoping for a rocket to riches that would buy the old lady a new dress or a set of dishes. The alleyway was now a Kentucky Fried Chicken joint.

Mona pushed open the pub doors and the fog of stale liquor and cigarettes assaulted them. In the sudden gloom, Megan made out the age-spotted mirror behind the bar, the photos of rugby teams, winning horses, leaders of the Irish Republican Army put to death after the 1916 insurrection. Two old men propping up the bar turned to look at them and, either with disinterest or disgust, turned back to stare into their beers. Mona led the way to a Formica-topped table. "All right, girls . . ." She put hands on hips, affecting the growl of a harried barmaid. "What'll it be?"

They both asked for a beer, exchanging silly smiles while Mona swaggered off, returning with two draughts of Swan Lager and a double shot of whiskey. Megan took out her wallet. "Put it away," Mona said expansively. "It's my shout. Now what shall we toast?"

"The nuns?" Megan ventured.

"No. To Megan," Greta said.

"How about to the conversion of Australia?" Mona raised her glass, and began to intone, " 'O God, who hast appointed Mary, Help of Christians, and St. Joseph . . .' "

"No." Greta laughed. "It was St. Francis Xavier."

"Saint whoever . . . 'Grant that through their intercession our brethren outside the Church may receive the light of faith so that Australia may become . . .' " They clinked glasses, laughing.

"Do you think they still say that prayer?" Megan asked.

"No. Now the Japanese pray that Buddhism will take root." Mona tilted back her head, downing half the whiskey. "God, how I hate those visits to the convent. It's like being walled up in a tomb, isn't it?"

Megan was about to ask why Mona bothered to visit if she found it so distasteful, but Greta said. "I find it peaceful. I like to visit them."

"You probably don't mind going to the dentist either," Mona said, shuddering as she took another swallow. "No, the toast should be to Megan. Megan got out. Out of the convent and out of Australia." She unbuttoned her suit jacket and sat back. The right side of her mouth creased upward. "I'll never forget the time Ursula caned you and you flounced out of the church. You didn't come back for ages—we all thought you'd run away—and when you did come back you wouldn't talk to anyone, just stood there and looked 'em in the eye, daring them to punish you again. They had us all bamboozled. All except you."

"I don't remember that at all. I thought Sister Bruno was the only one who ever caned me."

"No. Ursula did, too. I'll never forget it."

"How old do you suppose she is?" Megan asked.

"Eighty if she's a day."

"It makes me so sad to see her all crippled up," Greta said. "The way she used to conduct that choir . . . And Sister Bruno doesn't look well either."

"Sister Bruno never looked well." Megan took a sip of the cold beer. "Ill humor is the only privilege Sister Bruno's taken in life."

Mona hooted and downed more whiskey. "And what about Mary Magdalene? Hasn't she come out of the cocoon? I expect the next time I walk in there I'll see her in fishnet stockings and dangle earrings."

"It doesn't matter what they wear," Greta said. "That's just superficial. What matters is that they're still devout. Even Tas says—and Tas isn't a believer—that he likes working at the Catholic hospitals. The nuns aren't just serving for a paycheck. They have genuine compassion for the patients. How can you be around suffering all the time if you don't have a faith to sustain you?"

"Greta, you were always a softie. Those nuns walled us up, they blighted our lives. When you think of all the nonsense they stuffed into our heads." Mona ran her hands through her hair and shook her head.

"I enjoyed seeing them again," Megan said.

"Yeah. For you it's a once-in-a-lifetime stroll down Memory Lane. I still live here. And will. At least till my mother . . ." She gripped the glass and Megan noticed that her fingernails were bitten to the quick.

"How is your mother?" Greta asked.

"The same. Always the same." Mona drained the glass. "Now Megan, tell us all about yourself. Do you have a battalion of lovers?"

"Not even a company."

"A successful woman like you?"

"Women chase men because they're successful; it doesn't work the other way around. Success is an aphrodisiac only men wear."

"Oh, come on, you're holding out on us. You're sounding like St. Maria Goretti. Remember how she was held up to us as the ideal? A girl who chose death rather than submit to sex . . . but we didn't call it sex . . . what did we call it?"

"Sin." Megan grinned and Mona hooted.

"Yes. We called it sin. I was thirty years old before I lost my virginity. I waited so long for my ship to come in . . ." Mona put her arms under her breasts and gave them a little hoist. ". . . that my pier was collapsing." One of the men at the bar turned around at their laughter. Greta took a long swallow of her beer. The sooner they finished, the sooner they could leave. Mona got up. "Hey, how 'bout another?"

"No, thanks," Greta said. "We really should be getting on."

"But you haven't finished. I'll just get a quick one while you do." As Mona went to the bar, Megan and Greta exchanged glances over their raised mugs. "I've never seen anyone get drunk so quickly," Greta whispered, then, as Mona approached, "We really must be going. Tas is waiting for us."

"Aren't you the dutiful little wife?" Mona said, a wide smile masking her belligerence. "Keep the spuds on the boil, keep your pennies in the jam jar and pray the old man comes home.

Ah, we're all good girls in our own ways, God love us.'' Mona's carefully drawn lipline was gone, her hair disheveled, and the pale face of the little girl who'd been so cowed she'd always chosen conformity showed through her tan. "And speaking of St. Maria Goretti, did you know that her attacker and her mother went together to her beatification or whatever it was? Now that's what I call complicity. That's what I call a sin. The rapist survives to get credit for repentance and takes Holy Orders, and the victim becomes a model for an entire generation of girls." Megan was having trouble following Mona's ranting, but Mona's next words brought her up short. "It's just like poor Aileen Ingpen."

Megan leaned forward. "What about Aileen?"

"Oh, her funeral was the event of the season. What her wedding was supposed to be. But her boyfriend jilted her. Her only choices were all sinful—unwed motherhood, abortion—I suppose it was easier to commit the final, big sin and do herself in."

"How do you know that?" Megan demanded.

"She told Eleanor Pujoli she was pregnant. That car wreck couldn't have been an accident."

Megan pushed her unfinished beer aside, feeling sick. "I see."

"Even if that story's true," Greta said, "you can't blame it on the nuns."

"Ah, no. They're all dear, sweet souls," Mona said sarcastically. "Considering they don't lead a normal life."

"I don't think they're all sweet souls," Megan countered. "They're just human. And as for leading a normal life . . ." She shrugged. "My notion of a normal life has pretty wide parameters."

"Living in Hollywood I suppose it would," Mona said.

"I don't live in . . ." Megan began, but knew it was useless. Greta was right. She had never seen anyone get drunk as fast as Mona had. It was the desperate abandonment of a woman who'd spent her life internalizing controls. "Sister Bruno said you were doing so well at your bank job that you might get a promotion to the Sydney office."

"How can I move to Sydney and leave m' mum alone?" Mona

asked her drink. "But when Mum goes I can promise you that I won't be slaving at the bank and visiting the nuns."

"What will you do?" Greta asked.

"I'll do what all Aussies do when they're young and venturesome, I'll go on walkabout, see the world. Put on m' backpack and . . ." She interrupted herself long enough to take another slurp. "I s'pose I'm a bit long in the tooth for backpacking. Maybe I'll move to Singapore and see if m' boyfriend means it when he says he wants more than a once-a-year shag."

"You have a boyfriend in Singapore?"

"Mmmm." Mona winked. "But on the QT. He manages a hotel. I met him when I went there on holiday 'bout seven years ago, and every year . . . But he's a Pom. And he's married." She sighed. "I do get myself into some messes, don't I?"

"I hope . . ." Megan began. But what were the chances that Mona could create a new life for herself? More than likely she would continue to be the dutiful child, get up morning after morning, curry and comb herself into a facsimile of chic, go to the job, take care of her mum . . . carry on. And every so often she'd cut loose, knock back the whiskey and wail against life, then feel so full of shame that she'd redouble her efforts as a dutiful child.

Greta stood up. "Sorry, Mona, but we really must go. Will you be all right to . . . ?"

"I'll just finish this one off, then I'll toddle along myself."

Anxious about leaving Mona, Greta looked about. Her eyes met the bartender's. He nodded, accepting responsibility.

Mona pulled herself up to lean on the table. "It's been great to see you, Megan. I'm sorry I was such a shit to you when we were kids."

"I expect I was a shit to you, too," Megan said, touching Mona's hand.

"Good to see you, too, Greta," Mona called out as they moved away. "Best of luck."

Walking into the early-afternoon glare, Megan felt as though she'd just been to a matinee of a poignant but depressing play.

"Who would have thought that Mona Gallagher would get herself involved with a married man?" Greta said, and when

Megan made no reply, "I met her mother years ago. She's been an invalid since Mona was a girl."

"Those early invalids always last the longest."

"That does seem to be the case."

"The tyranny of the weak." She got into the airless car, her bottom uncomfortable on the hot upholstery, and buckled up her seat belt. She had started the trip to Australia in full sail, buoyant and full of expectation. Now she felt sucked into the backwaters of the past. "Mind if I turn on the radio?" She found a rock-and-roll station. The Pet Shop Boys were singing "What Have I Done to Deserve This?"

"We're late," Greta said, pulling onto the road. "I hope Tas won't be annoyed."

"To hell with Tas," Megan said lightly, her feet and shoulders moving to the beat. "Something about being in a car with rock and roll going . . . makes me feel like the young and desperate. I want to step on the gas and drive to the nearest border."

"The nearest border is pretty far away," Greta said, but she did step on the gas and as the music took her, she laughed and repeated, "To hell with Tas," then added, "We'll be home in forty minutes."

Megan threw back her head and closed her eyes.

CHAPTER
ELEVEN

THEY DROVE UP THE GRAVEL ROAD, PAST FIELDS AND outbuildings, to the house. It was a single-story structure sheltered by gum trees, a man-made pond and a wide front veranda, so picturesquely bucolic against the cerulean sky that it might have graced a calendar. Tas's red Porsche seemed strangely out of place here. Beside it was a late-model Ford. Seeing it, Greta said, none too happily, "It seems my sister, Loukia, is here."

She should have known better than to mention Megan's visit to Loukia. Loukia was a stickybeak, always ready to poke her nose into other people's affairs, passing off her insatiable appetite for meddling as concern. She was *concerned* about her neighbor's miscarriages ("probably abortions"), their finances ("they live right up to the penny, they'll be bankrupt soon"). She was concerned about Liz Taylor's latest diet and Princess Di's alleged affairs. She was particularly concerned about the marital problems Greta did her best to hide. Greta was ashamed of the fact that she didn't like her sister, partly because she held herself responsible for Loukia's fate. When Greta had broken off her engagement to their second cousin, Alex, he'd accepted Loukia as a substitute as readily as a man hungry for an apple would take a Granny Smith instead of a Delicious. He'd retained old-country attitudes when he'd immigrated to Australia: an apple was an apple and a wife was a wife. He loved Loukia after his fashion, rewarding her with jewelry after the birth of each of their four sons. With her help his greengrocer's business had prospered. They now owned a string of juice bars—"Loukia's Luscious Health Drinks" painted on the blue-and-white awnings—and Loukia still helped out behind the counter, wearing good dresses, high heels and jewelry so as not to be confused with the help. She would brag about her happy marriage and growing prosperity to anyone who would listen, but she crammed the carrots and celery into the juicers with a vehemence that betrayed her lifelong resentment at having accepted a hand-me-down husband.

"Loukia's an ear basher," Greta whispered as they pulled around to the back of the house. "I hope she has the manners to leave before lunch." Greta got out of the car, wondering what excuse Loukia would give for her presence. "Don't try to crawl through that mess." She gestured to the bicycles, seedlings in tins and a pile of boots on the back porch. "Come around to the front."

As they mounted the veranda steps the screen door opened and Loukia came out. It was easy to see that she and Greta were sisters, though Loukia was darker and built closer to the ground. Wearing a green pantsuit, her hair piled high and sprayed into place, her bracelets, earrings and rings glinting, she gave the appearance of a squat and overdecorated Christmas tree. "I didn't know you were having anyone over," she exclaimed. "I just dropped by to return that punch bowl you loaned me."

"This is Megan Hanlon. Remember Megan?" Greta said.

Loukia brought her hands to her mouth in surprise, as her eyes narrowed, sizing Megan up. "Megan Hanlon! I don't believe it. What luck to see you again. I've been hearing all about you. I don't suppose you remember me?"

Megan said something imprecise but polite. Loukia settled herself into one of the wicker chairs, saying she was dying for a cup of tea before she took to the road again. "Where's Tas?" Greta asked, reaching for the screen door.

"Out in the stables. Where he usually is." Loukia smiled at Megan. "Tas is so busy with his practice he rarely gets home. And when he's here he's so busy he only comes in the house to eat."

Greta let the screen door slam behind her. "Chrissie," she called, passing the dining room table and seeing that it had been set. "I'm home."

Chrissie came out of her bedroom, one arm behind her back, clasping the elbow of the other. "Is she here?" she whispered.

"Yes." Greta stroked the top of Chrissie's head. "Thanks for setting the table. But you only set it for four."

"Don't tell me Auntie Loukia's staying. She's been here for ages. I caught her snooping in the cupboards."

"I wouldn't be surprised. No, I'm not going to ask her to stay. But what about the boys?"

"Colin's playing footie. And Dad let David take the truck into town, so he won't be back. Not if he has the truck." She tiptoed over to the front window and peeked out. "She's beautiful," she said, returning to Greta's side.

"Yes, she is, isn't she? And she's terribly nice. You'll like her."

"And you're friends." Her mother was always telling her about the importance of friends even though she didn't really have any herself. "Colin tried to get into the quiche but I stopped him."

"Good." Greta went to the sideboard and took out the soup spoons. She was disappointed that the boys had nicked off. She thought she'd made the lunch sound important enough to secure their company, but she couldn't expect her enthusiasms to be shared. The days when they'd begged her to come see their tree house, lain beside her doing jigsaw puzzles, pleaded for her jam and kisses, asked her why and how and may I please, were long gone. Even with Chrissie they were going, going . . . "You might have put on a dress."

"*She's* not wearing a dress. Did she go to the convent like that?"

Greta smiled. "Yes. I s'pose she didn't know she'd be visiting the nuns when she packed."

"I love her hair."

"I suppose by next week you'll be asking for a frizzy permanent and fancy cowboy boots." The speed with which Chrissie was willing to accept Megan as a model caused her a twinge of jealousy. "Go out and introduce yourself."

Chrissie shook her head at this preposterous suggestion, rolling her eyes.

"All right. I'll introduce you in a minute. Come into the kitchen and we'll put the kettle on. A quick cup of tea for Auntie, then we'll pack her off. We're late already. Your father must be waiting for his lunch."

"Bugger him," Chrissie said under her breath, moving back to the window.

Megan stood at the railing, her back to Loukia, her hair bright in the sun. "No, I don't actually know Robert Redford," she was saying, "though I met him once at Sundance Institute. He was very low-key."

"I heard he was getting a divorce."

"You probably know more about his personal life than I do. Though I wouldn't believe most of what I read."

"Well, I did read that . . ."

Megan leaned forward, staring up through a hanging plant, thinking of an article she'd read called "I Want a Wife." It was a comic piece written by a woman, talking about the advantages of coming home to a lovingly cared-for nest with clean laundry, good food and inquiries about how things were going in the larger world. She wondered if Tas had any idea of how lucky he was. Then again, she knew she wouldn't want a house-husband. A man who'd exist only to serve her needs, who'd live in her shadow, had no appeal. She straightened, ready to dip her conversational oar into Loukia's torrent of questions, when Tas came around the side of the house.

He was in work clothes, his hat pulled down over his face, his sleeves rolled up, making his arms seem unnaturally long. Her impulse was to smile in recognition. Their eyes met. She saw the sequence of quick, contradictory impulses cross his face. "Howd'y' do." He grinned. She nodded. "Megan, isn't it?" Loukia introduced them. Tas wiped his hands on the seat of his jeans and slowly removed his hat.

"Take a seat, Tas," Loukia said. "Greta's bringing out some tea."

"I don't want tea. It's almost two o'clock. I want to put on the tucker bag." He was consciously rude, hoping to dislodge his sister-in-law. He'd been on to her for a long time. Her "concern" for Greta always took the form of subtle humiliation, but whenever he pointed this out, Greta came to her defense.

Loukia formed her mouth into an O, brought her little finger to its corner and wiped away some caked lipstick, her eyes narrowing. Tas was such an arrogant bastard. If he had any bedside manner he only used it in beds away from home. But poor Greta was blind to that.

"We were held up," Megan explained. "We met an old school friend at the convent and stopped at the pub for a quick drink."

"Who was that?" Loukia wanted to know.

"Mona Gallagher."

"If you went into a pub with Mona Gallagher, it couldn't have been a quick drink," Loukia said.

"Been hanging about the pub checking out the other customers, have you, Loukia?" Tas asked.

"Everyone knows . . ." Loukia began.

"And if they don't, you'll be the first to tell them, right?"

Greta came out with the tray, pushing open the door with her hip. "Oh, Tas. You're here. Megan, this is my husband, Tas. Tas, this is Megan Hanlon."

"We've met." Megan couldn't look anybody in the eye on that one.

"And this is our daughter, Chrissie," Greta said as Chrissie came out carrying the teapot.

"I'm pleased to meet you, Miss Hanlon."

Genetic probability suggested that Greta's dark hair and eyes would dominate, but the girl was the spitting image of her father. She had his blue eyes, long limbs and sandy hair. She even had a measure of his confidence, a definite lift of her chin that belied her apparent shyness.

"Call me Megan."

Greta put down the tray and draped her arm around Tas's shoulder. It was a lovingly possessive touch of which Tas seemed entirely unaware. "Would you like some tea, Tas?"

"No tea, thanks. I'll take a beer. Fetch your old man a beer, will you, Chrissie?"

The girl didn't move. Annoyance flickered over Tas's face. "So you've been visiting the penguins, have you?" He looked up at Greta.

"Don't call them penguins, Dad," Chrissie said. "Most of them don't even dress like that anymore."

"Tas doesn't believe in anything," Loukia said. "He's always slinging off at the Church."

"Let's say we believe different things," Tas said, then, giving Chrissie the authoritative and winning grin that sent nurses scurrying, "Get a move on and fetch your old man a beer. I've been working all morning."

"Everyone works around here. Especially Mum," Chrissie said with a cheekiness that made Greta want to slap her.

Loukia looked from mother to daughter with a glance that said no child of hers would dare to answer like that. She crossed her legs and smiled at Megan. "I suppose you've traveled a lot, Megan?"

"Some."

"My husband and I are going to Athens next year. Stopping off in London."

"The only thing you can get in London that you can't get here is a cold," Tas said.

Loukia ignored this. "Have you ever been to London, Megan?"

"Yes. Right after I made a documentary about the history of midwifery." She'd been trying to raise the money for that when she'd first met Tas. It had been the first of her films to get foreign distribution. She'd literally jumped up and down when she'd heard that it would be shown on the BBC some years later. "I was supposed to do a lot of interviews, but the little prince was born just as I arrived so I was shoved off the media circuit and spent most of my time at a friend's house in Surrey. All that ballyhoo—'It's a boy! It's a boy!' Strange, when you consider that the two most famous British monarchs were women."

"Elizabeth the First and . . ." Chrissie began, eager to show her knowledge.

"I suppose everyone still wants a boy," Loukia said. "I have four myself. In China they still practice infanticide if it's a girl."

". . . and Queen Victoria," Chrissie finished.

"You know what Grandmother and Grandfather say," Loukia cautioned. " 'Children should be seen and not heard.' "

"They don't say it as much as you do," Chrissie answered back.

"Come to think of it, I'd prefer a beer to tea," Megan said.

"I'll get it," Chrissie volunteered. She stopped at the door. "I'm going to get beer. So you won't have to see me *or* hear me, Aunt Loukia.'' With a child's instinct that she'd pushed it to the limit, she made a quick exit.

Loukia shook her head. "Don't they always do it to you in front of visitors? Sometimes I think children are more trouble than they're worth."

"Chrissie's usually very polite," Greta said quickly.

Loukia leaned into Megan. "Greta's always reading these psychology books. She's even taken some classes on child development in this accelerated program they have for older students. Personally, I think a good whack on the backside is the best way to deal with kids. But Chrissie's not used to having people around. Greta's always been a hermit, haven't you, Greta?"

Tas got up. "I'm going in to shower. I ought to leave for the city soon. I'm to drive you back, right, Megan?"

"Yes. If you wouldn't mind."

"I suppose I'd best get on shank's pony," Loukia said, but made no attempt to move.

As Tas went to the door, Chrissie came out with two bottles of beer. "And thank you, Queen Elizabeth," he said, pulling a face. He reached to ruffle her hair; she moved away from him.

Greta felt a tightening in her chest. Not now, she warned herself, please not now. Just breathe normally, get into the bedroom and get some inhalant. "Perhaps you could show Megan around, Chrissie. Show her your chooks."

Chrissie sighed at the stupidity of the suggestion. "She wouldn't be interested in chooks, Mum."

"Yes, I would," Megan said. She could hear Greta's breathing. She got up. "Nice to see you, Loukia." Still, Loukia didn't budge.

"Would you like to come into the kitchen and give me a hand, Loukia?" Greta suggested.

"No. I'm off. See you in the papers, Megan," she called as Chrissie and Megan descended the steps. "You having one of your attacks?" she demanded of Greta. She stared after Megan. "You'd think she'd get herself up better than that, wouldn't you? She must have plenty of cash. She looks like a scrubber. Still, attractive in a wild sort of way. I can tell you I wouldn't be bringing a woman like that around to my house or sending her off for a long ride with my husband.''

''Tas hardly noticed her.''

''That,'' Loukia said pointedly, ''is just what I mean.''

Megan walked, bottle in hand, breathing in the potpourri of farm smells—grass, manure, flowers. A dusty Irish setter came from behind the house and trailed after them, tail wagging. ''I take care of the chooks,'' Chrissie said, not sure if this was a source of pride or embarrassment. At their approach the chickens bustled and clucked. ''Want to meet Hilda? She's the best layer.'' She looked at Megan's boots. ''But you'd get your boots dirty.''

''I don't mind.''

The chickens scattered as they went into the yard. Megan had to duck her head to follow Chrissie into the henhouse. It was dark, hot and fecund-smelling. Chrissie squatted, stroking the head of a hen sitting in one of the hay boxes. ''Hilda never goes out even when it's hot. She just lays eggs all the time. She's our champion.'' She slid her hand under the hen's bottom and brought out an egg. ''See?'' Megan took it, felt its warmth and the specks of cockadoodle.

''Sometimes we have too many eggs, because Dad won't eat them because of cholesterol. My brothers are supposed to help with the chickens but they won't anymore. Since footie practice started, Mum has to nag them to do anything.''

''Yeah. When you're a kid you get stuck with the chores nobody else wants. I used to have to empty the chamber pots.''

''You didn't have a real lav?''

''No.''

''And *you* emptied the chamber pots?'' Chrissie was incredulous that someone of Megan's stature had been forced into such an odious task.

''Mmmm. I couldn't wait to grow up. I knew that when I grew up I would do what I wanted to do.''

''Hardly anyone gets to do what they want to do all the time.''

Here, Megan was sure, was Greta's echo. ''And how about you? Do you know what you want to do?''

''I might be a journalist and travel all over the world. Or

maybe I'll stay home and keep Mum company. Be a veterinarian.''

"Not a doctor?''

"My brother David's going to be a doctor. I like animals better. Animals are easier than people, don't you think?''

"I guess so." Megan straightened from an uncomfortable crouch. "Want to show me some more of the farm?''

They walked to the fields, past the stables, the barn, the horses' exercise yard. Four mares, docile, with lake eyes, grazed in one paddock. In another a stallion galloped furiously after a mare, trying to corner her. Megan, then Chrissie, fell silent, galvanized by the chase, the great heavy bodies, the flying manes. The stallion mounted, girding the mare's middle with his hoofs. The mare reared and escaped long enough for another wild run. Mounted again, and successfully, she stood still as a statue.

The sound of a car made them turn back toward the house. "That's Edgar. He's coming around looking for a job. Mum thinks we should hire him. C'mon." Shyly, Chrissie slipped her hand into Megan's. Megan forced her glance away from the horses and followed. Approaching the house, she saw Tas and a pleasant-looking man sitting on the veranda. "We'd best go in the back way," Chrissie said, picking her way through the clutter of the back porch and pushing open the door. "Hey, Mum, isn't lunch . . .''

Greta was crouched on the floor, vainly trying to put dirt back into a smashed pot plant. Pots and pans littered every countertop, a scorched dish towel floated in the sink. She started and flushed, reaching for a broom. Dear God, she had botched it. She'd been close to tears by the time she'd gotten Loukia off, then, just as she was correcting the spices in the soup and beginning to breathe normally, there'd been a knock at the door. Running to answer it, she'd left the dish towel too close to the gas ring and it had caught fire. Flinging it into the sink, she'd spun around and knocked over the geranium. She had wanted to spare Megan the behind-the-scenes preparation and serve an elegant little lunch, but even this seemed to be too much for her. She was afraid she was going to cry.

"What's that delicious curry smell?" Megan asked casually, seeing the anguished look on her face.

"Mulligatawny." Greta took a deep breath. "I don't think I'm ever going to get this dinner on. I knocked over . . ." She made an ineffectual motion with the broom.

"I'll sweep that up," Megan offered.

"No. I'll just . . ." The plant would probably die. She moved to the sink to wash her hands.

So as to appear less the honored guest, Megan picked up a bread crust. "Mind?"

"No. No. Take what you like. I'm sorry for all these delays, but a local chap who needs some work . . . Edgar . . . he's done odd jobs for us before, but . . . I think we need him full-time."

"Don't you want to be there while Tas talks to him?" Had she said Tas's name with too much familiarity? "I don't mind waiting on lunch." How could Greta be so passive? She was the one who actually ran the farm, yet she was allowing Tas to make the decision.

"I'm . . ." Greta wiped her hands and leaned against the sink. Sweat beaded her hairline. She struggled for breath. "I told you the other night . . . I get these . . . can't . . . hyperventilate."

Megan put her hand on Greta's shoulder. Chrissie, concerned and embarrassed, reached for the broom. "Get me the inhaler, will you, Chrissie? You know where . . ." Mutely, Chrissie left the room. Greta slumped into a chair. "I hate anyone to . . . see . . . me . . ."

"I don't mind. Really I don't. I mean, I mind that you're going through it, but . . ."

Greta's lips were drawn back, exposing her lower teeth. Megan looked away as Greta fought her panic, then continued to speak, through wheezing breaths. "One of the things Tas admired about me . . . was my good health. He . . . used to joke about my peasant . . . stock. I went through all my pregnancies without . . . complications." She stared down at the linoleum. "A healthy body is something he greatly admires. You might say . . ."

"Being a doctor, it's probably his highest aesthetic."

"Any illness connected with emotion . . . migraines, allergies, asthma . . . he thinks they're put on . . . manipulative . . ." She swallowed. "Sometimes I think so myself."

"Have you ever thought of seeing a psychiatrist?"

"I did, but he just prescribed tranquilizers. I didn't want to . . ."

"No. I can see why you wouldn't. But if you're this miserable . . ."

"I suppose so. You're being very . . . understanding about this. I'm sorry . . ."

Megan wanted to say, This is part of your problem: you apologize for your entire life. "Don't apologize. And don't say thanks. Really, there's no need."

The sounds of voices raised in farewell and a motor starting up made Greta raise her head. She passed her hands through her hair, her nostrils dilating. "The quiche! Oh, God, I've burned the quiche!"

"That doesn't matter. Here, let me help you get things on the table."

"No. No. You're the guest. Go on into the other room and talk to Tas."

"I'd rather help you." If she talked to Tas, she'd probably call him a son of a bitch.

Chrissie opened the door. "Edgar's gone and Dad's waiting for lunch." She held the inhaler close to her side, then slipped it to Greta as though it were contraband. Greta took it, moving to the sink, grasping the edge and turning away as she put the inhaler into her mouth. Megan and Chrissie exchanged a glance. Chrissie suddenly looked like a shrunken adult, her eyes betraying a burden of understanding. "All right." Greta straightened. "Let's get this show on the road." She followed her own directive with slow, concentrated movements, turning off the stove, picking up dish towels, bending to take out the quiche. Megan looked away, her eyes lighting on a painting above the kitchen cupboards. At first she was struck by the sense of color, the simplicity of composition, then she realized it was the view from the veranda. "Who did that?" she asked.

"Oh," Greta said, barely glancing up. "I did."

"It's really good. I didn't know you painted."

"I was going to go to art school before I got married."

"It's good," she repeated. She'd heard so many women say

"before I got married," as though marriage were equivalent to the parting of the Red Sea.

"And once the children were in school I took a few classes. Painting, child psychology—the usual housewife's dabbling. And gourmet cooking, though"—she stared at the quiche with disgust—"you'd never know it. Chrissie, will you get down the soup tureen? The one that used to belong to Grandma. And Megan, there's a bottle of wine in the fridge. Perhaps you can take it in and Tas will open it. I hope it's the right kind."

Megan got out the bottle and pushed open the kitchen door. The living and dining rooms reminded her of her mother's house, chockablock full of furniture, doilies starched and ironed, knick-knacks laboriously dusted, photographs that pulled one back to memories of seemingly happier days. And more of Greta's paintings. One in particular caught her eye: it was almost abstract, a sky, a threatening storm. It conveyed such a sense of incipient upheaval that it seemed out of place. Greta was no mere dabbler, though Megan knew that Greta would never take her talent seriously or think of putting her work on the market. She looked for the corkscrew, her eyes sweeping over the linen tablecloth embroidered with swallows and nosegays, then moved to the sideboard to continue her search. She felt Tas's presence and turned. He stood silhouetted at the front door. The low ceiling gave him a caged look. "I need a corkscrew." He moved to her side. "Watch out, it'll bite you," he said, picking up a corkscrew that was directly in front of her. He reached for the bottle. "No," she said. "I can manage."

"Suit yourself." He sat at the table, his long legs stretched out to the side. She attacked the cork, angry at Greta, angry at Tas, at this picture-postcard house that caged the one and suffocated the other. Pushing down too forcefully, she split the cork. Tas raised an eyebrow and grinned. "What the hell, just push it in. A few bits of cork won't kill us." He held out a glass. She filled it. He offered it to her and she filled another. "To your next film." Before he could ask her about it, she asked about the wine. They began a discussion of Australian wineries, their voices consciously level. Chrissie came in with the soup tureen, Greta followed with the salad and bread. "Would you say grace, Chrissie?" Greta asked, taking her seat. They bowed their heads while Chrissie intoned the blessing. Then, crossing herself, her eyes mischievous, Chrissie said, "Rolly, rolly round the table, fill your belly while you're able," and everyone laughed.

The food was excellent but the tension made it impossible for Megan to relish it. Greta apologized for the burned quiche and said she hadn't put enough turmeric in the mulligatawny. Tas refilled the wineglasses. His hand touched Megan's as he handed Chrissie her thimbleful. They said "Sorry" simultaneously, without looking at each other.

"I told Edgar he could start full-time beginning next Monday," Tas said.

"He's a good worker, Tas, but I worry about the money."

"Don't," he said peremptorily. He stared at the ceiling, his tongue probing his teeth. "And since we're making improvements around here, why don't you get yourself that dishwasher?"

"I've managed the washing up all these years. I don't really . . ."

"Get it, Mum. Please, get it. Colin and David never help. They're just rainbows. That means they only come around after the water's been turned off," she explained to Megan.

"You said he was a good worker," Tas said with a touch of impatience.

"He is, but . . ." It wasn't just the expense. Though Edgar was hard-working and easygoing, his presence sometimes made her nervous. He deferred to her, praised her cooking, noticed when she was tired. Once he'd suggested that he rub her back. She'd wanted to let him.

"It's on, Greta. He'll be around Monday. Not to rush you, Megan, but I ought to be getting back." He pushed his plate aside.

"Yes. Okay. Just let me help with—"

"I wouldn't think of it. Chrissie and I will do it."

"I'll just get my things." Tas got up so quickly that he had to right his chair, and left the room.

"I can't tell you how nice it's been having you come out to visit," Greta said.

"The lunch was lovely." Megan felt sick to her stomach.

"And visiting the nuns." She had trouble looking Greta in the eye. "And I enjoyed meeting you, Chrissie." The girl beamed. "I'm sure you're going to do great things when you grow up."

"Are you sorry you don't have any children?" Chrissie asked.

"Chrissie," Greta admonished, "that's a very rude question."

"When I see one as good as you, I guess I am," Megan said.

"It's different for someone like Megan," Greta explained. "Her movies are her children."

Chrissie's eyes twinkled. "Then I hope you'll be like the old woman in the shoe and you'll have so many you won't know what to do."

Megan smiled. "I do, too. Thanks."

Mother and daughter stood on the veranda, arms around each other's waists, as Tas and Megan got into the car. Tas turned on the motor. Greta, hating to see them go, began to call out questions: Was Megan sure she didn't want to borrow a scarf? Has Tas taken the jar of homemade chutney she'd put out? Would he be coming home again on Friday night? Tas revved the motor and shouted that he'd give her a call. It reminded Megan of getaways from her mother's house. Irene's last-minute pleas for affection always muddied the good-byes, turning leave-taking into guilty escape. Tas turned the car toward the road. Megan waved. Chrissie ran down the steps. "Good-bye, Megan! I'm going to see all your movies. Good-bye! Come and see us again!"

CHAPTER
TWELVE

AS IF BY MUTUAL CONSENT, THEY RODE AWAY IN SI-
lence. The sun was warm through the windshield. Megan rested
her head on the back of her seat and turned it to the side, holding
her hair back from her face and looking at the coollabah, bottlebrush and wattle trees. "This country is so beautiful. There's
nothing like it in the world, is there?"

"I don't want it to change but I know it will. All of this used
to be bush when I was a kid."

"I know." She continued in the same casually friendly vein,
as though they were strangers seated next to each other on a
train. "I can't wait for the festival to be over so that I can get
out to my aunt and uncle's place. We only went there on weekends when I lived with them, but once their kids had finished
school they moved out to the bush for good."

"You should have been here in October, when the wildflowers
were coming out. This hill was purple with Patterson's Curse."

"Yeah. I remember how pretty that is. Only Aussies would
call such a plant a curse."

"It's not good for the cattle. You're not a farmer."

"But you are. A gentleman farmer anyway. You got your
wish."

"Right. I'm a real ocher. The sort my father always hated."

"But you remember your roots and vote Labour, right? When
you remember to vote."

"It's mandatory here, remember? First country in the world
to give women the vote and we've been going downhill ever
since."

"Give it a rest, will you, Tas?" Ten years ago she would have

204

risen to the bait. She was less sure of herself then, and she was sleeping with him, so his taunts had had some sting.

They were out of sight of the house now and he relaxed visibly, humming under his breath until they approached a little stream. "This is the end of my property. Right here." He nodded toward the stream.

"Pull over, will you? I want to get a branch of silver gum to take back to the hotel."

"Bloody tourist," he grinned. "I'll bet you're going to buy wallets made out of kangaroo skin and little koala bears. No, you're too upscale for that. You'll raid the galleries for aboriginal art."

She'd been thinking of doing just that. "Just pull over, don't give me any of your lip."

They got out and walked to a silver gum. "Don't even try. You're too short," he said, taking a pocket knife out of his back pocket. As he reached up she took in the long line of his body, and his face, upturned, squinting against the sunlight, so that the creases near his eyes deepened. Affection and remembered pleasure rippled through her. "Here." He handed the branch to her. Their eyes met and held; there could be no more small talk now. He said, "It went off all right."

"I felt awful."

"It didn't show."

"I'm not sure that's entirely to my credit."

"It was better this way. She was happy you came. If you hadn't she would have felt rejected."

Her shoulders came up in what was meant to be a shrug, but didn't relax down. He put his hands on them, his eyes warm with remembered intimacy, then shook his head and stepped back, glancing over his shoulder. "Yep, this is the property line." His voice was melancholy, as though he were leaving, never to return.

"It's a beautiful setting."

"But for what? You can see . . ."

She nodded. Of course she could see. Fewer things were plainer than a rotten marriage.

"You probably won't believe me, but I have tried."

Perhaps he had. Yes, surely he had.

"It should've ended years ago, when I came back from America. But Greta was an immovable object. She seems passive, but she has incredible determination. I've got to get a divorce whether she wants to or not. This time I've got to get a divorce."

The words "this time" loomed like a neon sign on a deserted midnight highway. She knew that over the last ten years there must have been other women. He was good-looking, highly sexed and unhappy—and infidelity was charged with enough fundamental recklessness to absorb thought and dissipate anxiety. But "this time"? There must be a particular woman who'd brought his simmering dissatisfactions to the boil. "What's she like?" she asked.

"Who?"

"Don't play the innocent with me. Your girlfriend."

His eyes slid away, ready to deny.

"Skip pretty," she said. "Also skip young. And intelligent. *Please* skip intelligent. If you believed men you'd think they found mistresses by looking at IQ scores instead of behinds."

He laughed. "Megan, I'd forgotten how you are." What a relief that he wouldn't have to pull any punches with her.

"So? Cut to the chase."

"How did you know?"

And now she reached up and put her arms on his shoulders. The branch of silver gum tickled his back, made him squirm. "I don't live in Grover's Corners, Tas. Half the people I know make infidelity a vocation, most of the others cultivate it as a hobby. You were already in the hobby category when I met you."

"That's not true. It knocked me for a loop when we . . . you were the one who treated it like a hobby."

She didn't want to hear his version of their affair. If he had taken it seriously, he'd never let on. And it was all too long ago. There was this other woman now. She was annoyed that she hadn't guessed it before. The knowledge seemed to drag her into a larger conspiracy of which she wanted no part. "So tell me, what's your girlfriend like?"

"She's a lot like you. Not physically—she's younger and blond, but she *is* intelligent. She's worldly. She walks into a room, people notice. She knows what she wants."

"And what does she want? Other than you, I mean."

This seemed to stump him. He stepped back and squatted, picking up a twig and raking the ground with it. Finally he snapped it. "I'm in love with her."

The words sounded strange coming from him, as though he were a proud man who'd been forced to make a public apology. But of course, Megan thought. Being in love is the only remaining high after a string of affairs. For a man at least. Experienced women generally became less romantic. "Is she a nurse?"

"I didn't expect a cliché out of you. Do you sleep with men in your crew?"

She shook her head. A man might consolidate his position by having an affair with an "underling," but it was too much of a risk for a woman; it destabilized her authority.

"Would I sleep with a nurse?" Though, in the past, he had.

"What does she do?" When he didn't respond, she tried, "Where did you meet her?"

"She's my partner's daughter."

"You mean . . ." She searched for the name.

"Naomi. You met her at the Tishmans' party. She told me you'd met."

And I'll bet you didn't tell her about us, she thought. Quite a little circus we have going here. "Naomi Tishman. Yes, we did meet." And what stuck in her memory, apart from Naomi's beautifully tailored lavender dress and helmet of cornsilk hair, was the way Naomi had surveyed the crowd and said something about the room being full of successful men and the women they'd married when they were young. And Naomi's nicking off. The pieces began to fit. "Does Greta know?"

"Not yet."

Why had she bothered to ask? "So, Tishman's daughter. You do like to complicate your life. I can't believe he'll be too happy about that."

"Tishman's an asshole."

"That was my impression." Also that Naomi was her daddy's girl.

"I have to get a divorce now. Naomi says she'll leave me if I don't."

"And you think she will?"

"Yes. She wants to have a child."

She had not perceived Naomi as a girl desperate for the responsibilities of motherhood. "And you want to?"

He got up. "You can see for yourself what a botch I've made of it the first time around. I was hardly ever with my kids. Greta took care of all that. All right, I was a chauvinist pig. I let her. But that was what she wanted to do as well. You're going to say it worked to my advantage, and it did. But twenty years ago neither of us questioned that. I had my career. I had to study. I had to accept opportunities to go overseas. I made the only choices I could make, and they were the right choices professionally. I didn't want to end up in a semidetached house, planting spuds and treating sinus infections. I don't regret it. Regret is only grumbling hindsight."

"So now you have all this." She made a sweeping gesture, meaning the entire impossible situation, but he took her to mean the farm.

"It's going to hurt to give it up. I love it." He said so with a pride and tenderness that had not been apparent when he spoke of Naomi. "And I've worked damned hard for it."

"So's Greta."

"I'm not denying that. I don't begrudge her. It's just that it's only been in the last year or so that it's all come together. I was planning to race my three-year-old in the Cup next year. Now we'll have to sell off the horses. But Greta will keep the farm—that's the least I can do."

The division of the spoils. She remembered telling Victor to take everything in their apartment because everything they'd shared was tainted, and her bitterness when the moving men came to collect his "half"—which, at the time, had looked much more than that. "But Greta wouldn't want to stay on out here alone. She couldn't manage."

"Don't underestimate her. She's a real bushie. She thrives on isolation."

"Surely because she's waiting for someone to come home."

"What can I do about that?" he demanded, slamming his hand into the tree trunk. "Do you know what it's like to have someone perpetually waiting, making you feel like shit even when there's a legitimate excuse? I tried to get her to go back to school on one of those accelerated programs, but she wouldn't. Everything frightens her. She just wants to sit in that goddamn rocking chair and wait. She waits for me. She waits for her period. She waits for the kids to come home, which the boys do less and less.'' His hand throbbed. He rubbed it against the bark with a slow, caressing movement. ''It's leaving Chrissie that will hurt. She already thinks I'm a right bastard.''

''She's a lovely kid.''

''A bit too cheeky, though you wouldn't mind that. Yes, she is a lovely kid, but she can't stand me. The boys, they're mainly indifferent. They never got to know me very well and at their ages I suppose they're just looking forward to being out of it. They don't say much. Chrissie takes it all in, so what's the use of my staying?'' He sucked in air and surveyed the countryside like some general who has lost a battle and sees corpses littering the field. ''This time . . .'' he vowed.

She turned and started back to the car. ''This time you may have to change a diaper.''

''I know I'll have to be different.''

She believed he would try. Also believed that he would fail miserably. She yanked open the car door. ''This time you'll be able to hire a nanny. In fact, I imagine Naomi will insist on it.''

He got in on the driver's side, noticing the drops of rain that had begun to spatter the windshield. ''Don't sound so bitter about it.''

''I'm not. Then again''—she shifted to face him—''maybe I am. Women don't have the option of doing it all again, of marrying someone twenty years their junior . . .''

''You wouldn't marry a younger man? You're much more conservative than you used to be.''

''I might have an affair with someone twenty years my junior, but marry him? That would be like hiring an assistant manager. I still believe that marriage should be between equals.''

''Very democratic. And who would you accept as your equal, Megan?'' He turned on the ignition. ''Shall I put up the top?''

''I wouldn't want to be sixty with a forty-year-old mate.''

''I've thought of that. I've thought of everything. I've thought for ten years. And I'm not sixty. And I'm tired of living a half life.''

"And even if an older woman does marry . . ." The sky had darkened quickly and a few raindrops landed on her face. ". . . she won't have the second family . . ."

"And because I'm a man I'll never collect alimony or have someone send me roses."

"She won't have that option."

"Options. Options. You sound like a Yank. We've all of us got limited options, from the moment we're born, from before we're born, when sperm meets ovum. Sure you don't want the top up?"

She shook her head like a two-year-old refusing to have her coat put on.

"You've got it, babe. I don't mind getting wet," he said.

The rain turned to a fine mist, dampening her neck and shoulders, matting her hair. The discomfort seemed apt punishment, as guilt sharpened her memory of Greta's face. It was one thing to choose a new life, but Greta would simply have one thrust upon her. What if she couldn't make the leap? If she just sat there in her rocking chair gasping for breath? Such things did happen. "My sympathies—" she asserted over the roar of the motor.

"Are with the woman," Tas finished it for her. He'd anticipated her response, even found it strangely comforting. Naomi didn't give a damn about sisterhood, but he knew Megan would carry the banner, even for housewives like Greta who, though they might admire her, felt they had nothing in common with her and viewed her with mistrust.

"Are with Greta," she corrected him.

"You couldn't live with someone like Greta for six months," he yelled.

"I didn't marry her," she yelled back.

"The voice of St. Brigid's, via New York and Hollywood." He reached over to ruffle her hair. She pulled away. He negotiated a hairpin turn so swiftly that she lunged to clutch the dashboard. But Tas was in control, at least of the car. If he thought that she and Naomi Tishman had anything in common except a sense of fashion and the ability to work a crowd, he didn't have control of much else. She watched the rain discolor the shoulders of his shirt and drip from his hair onto his collar. Sheep stood dumbly in nearby paddocks, their wool soaking up the wet. "You don't have sense enough to get out of the rain," Uncle Mick had often teased her. She shivered, wanting to ask Tas to put up the top, but since she'd been the one who'd insisted it stay down, it seemed a point of honor to tough it out. "Look," he said after a time, "there's a local winery up ahead. I'm pulling over. I'm buying a couple of bottles to take back to town. And I'm putting up the top."

She nodded once, grudgingly.

A large stucco building with a sign "Golden West Cellars—Winner of the 1987 Bordeaux Award" stood next to a dilapidated little house with a faded, hand-lettered sign, "Mastroiani's Wines," hammered above the door. There was a light on in the house. "Go on in," Tas directed as he put up the top and reached into the glove compartment for a rag to wipe off the seats. Megan made a dash for it.

Inside, bottles lined the walls of what had once been a living room. A table, knife-nicked and scored with circles and half moons left by glasses, held a plate of cheese and crackers and a card ordering "Sit down! Taste! Enjoy!" An old woman with dark eyes and a puckered face sat watching a TV without any sound. She was wearing a black, high-necked dress and shawl. Her head bobbed in greeting. "Come in. Get outta the rain." She jerked her head in the direction of the other building. "Good you don't go next door," she warned. Taking up a bottle and a tea towel, she hobbled to the table. "Dry off your hair," she smiled, handing the towel to Megan. Tas came in, muttered hello and began to inspect the bottles. "You sit and taste while your husband look," she said, and despite Megan's negative gesture, poured two glasses of wine.

"He's not—" Megan blurted.

"You from America? What part America you from?"

"New York." Her tooled boots and Tas's Porsche must have marked them as outsiders.

"My brother go to Philadelphia. He go there the same day we come here. Nineteen-seventeen. No Aussies drink the wine then. Only beer. Now they grow up, drink the wine. You know Philadelphia?"

"I've been there once or twice."

Tas selected a couple of bottles and put them on the table.

"Sit. Sit," the woman insisted. "Let your wife dry your hair." Megan and Tas exchanged an amused look and she began to towel his head. He caught her hand, took the towel from her and began to do it himself.

"He's impatient," the old woman observed. "Impatient to go, get you back to the hotel. You movie stars, huh? This your second honeymoon?" Megan laughed. Tas took some bills out of his wallet. The woman shuffled to the cash register, then came back, laboriously counting the change into Tas's palm. "Men!" Her head shook even more. "So impatient. He be on time for everything but his own funeral."

Megan thanked her and they started to the door. "Such a beautiful couple! Movie stars," the woman insisted, touching her finger to the side of her nose to indicate that their secret was safe with her.

The shower had finished and as they took to the road a rainbow began to appear on the horizon. "Movie stars," Tas said. "She should know who I am. I've been in there a couple of hundred times. Old Mrs. Mastroiani has senile dementia. She gets very irate about Golden West Cellars being next door. Doesn't seem to realize that it's her sons' bottling company."

"She's something," Megan said. The encounter had eased the tension between them. As she looked at the rainbow, she could sniff, along with the smell of gasoline and gum leaves, an unpleasant whiff of her own self-righteousness. Hadn't she gotten a divorce, and after only two years? And was her annoyance about Naomi all based on sympathy for Greta, or had the news dented her own ego? She and Tas had both kept their eyes on the prize and, as a consequence, neither had a placid or loving home life. They were more successful than they could have imagined when they'd played in these bushlands as children, but not successful enough, never, in their own eyes, successful enough. She might not wholly approve of Tasman Burke, but she had to admit that she understood him. "I shouldn't have gotten on your case," she said. "I've never wanted to change diapers myself."

He eased up on the accelerator. "I'm not really in a hurry. I want to go to the hospital and check on a patient when I get back, but if you don't mind waiting we could go back to my apartment and try a bottle of this wine before I take you back to the hotel.''

''That'd be fine.'' With tomorrow night's screening of *Chappy* lurking in the back of her mind, she'd be as relaxed in Tas's company as she was likely to be. ''Goddamn, that rainbow's pretty.''

''Shall I put the top down again?''

''Please. Then drive on, Macduff.''

When he came out of the hospital there was a lightness to his step and a satisfied expression on his face. ''Patient's doing fine. Fourteen-year-old boy with a busted heart valve. Didn't think he'd make it through. Makes me remember why I'm in this business.''

''Do you ever think of practicing in the States?''

Naomi had suggested the same thing and didn't like it much when he'd said no. ''I'd like to do research there. They've got state-of-the-art equipment and pots of money. But practice? No. It's a lousy health-care system and the patients treat you with either adulation or suspicion.''

''As well they might. Many an operation has been performed to finance a tennis court.''

His face looked as though he were taking the Boy Scout oath. ''I'd never do anything like that.''

''I know you wouldn't, Tas.''

His apartment in Nedlands looked, from the outside, like the residence of a fairly well-to-do man. Inside, it looked as though it belonged to an absentminded college student. As he opened the wine she took in the print of the Manhattan skyline, remembering that first day they'd spent together in Central Park. ''Do you ever miss New York?'' she asked as he handed her the glass.

''I dunno. When I was first there I filtered New York through Perth eyes—it seemed exciting, yes, but also outrageous, filthy, overwhelming—then when I got back I filtered Perth through New York eyes. It was small, isolated, provincial. Ever since I've lived away it seems that life hits me at a slant.''

''The perennial discontent of the expatriate. I was well into that when I was just a kid. Where I wasn't always seemed the most desirable place.''

"Maybe we're both discontented by nature.''

"I feel very contented just now.''

"So do I.'' There was a pull between them, strong and pleasant as a current that moved you when you were floating in warm water. At another time, in another place, they would have floated into the bedroom.

"Your hair looks like hell,'' he said by way of compliment, touching it lightly.

"And you're a silly bastard,'' she retorted. And each understood what was really being said: We might have made a go of it. They moved away from each other and sat on the couch, careful that their legs didn't touch. They watched the sun go down over the river and talked about the wine, his fourteen-year-old patient, the film festival. She thought it was like that Woody Allen movie where Woody and Diane Keaton chatted self-consciously about politics and art while their real thoughts (Would she go to bed with him? Would he make a move?) appeared as subtitles. He asked her about her work.

"It's always a circus,'' she said. "Budgets, logistics, the sheer number of people involved. And I have my own ego problems. One day I think I'm great, the next day I think I'm lousy, the third day I just slog on.''

"I think that's the definition of a professional.''

She laughed, a little too heartily, her mind still on their subtitles. "It always seems like a matter of life and death to me, but yours is the real business of life and death.''

"I wouldn't be a damned bit of good if I let myself get so poetic about it.''

"But it does cross your mind.''

"A lot of things cross my mind.''

They looked at each other. She could see that his desire both surprised and confused him, that in a moment he might sweep both aside and she might be towed under. As she stood, the couch creaked in protest. "I'd best be getting back.'' A swift move to the door was in order, otherwise . . .

He got up, pulling out his shirt to cover his erection. "I see you've still got a good circulatory system,'' she said lightly.

"You were the one with cold feet. Do you still wear socks to bed?"

"Thick, woolly ones."

She turned and hurried down the passageway, catching a glimpse of the bedroom. The unmade bed decided her. Even if she could rid herself of visions of Greta—and during the last half hour Greta had been the last thing on her mind—there was Naomi.

He opened the door, then closed it. "Megan . . . I'm no good with words, but . . ."

You don't have to be, she thought. Open the damned door before we both say devil-take-the-hindmost and start ripping off our clothes.

"It's been good to see you again, Megan. I like you better than any woman I've ever known."

"And I like you better than any man, with the possible exception of Thomas Shelby."

"Who?"

"But I never really knew him." She pulled the door open and by the time she'd reached the elevator felt relatively calm. "We got through the day. No mishaps. No repercussions. It was good to see you again . . ."

"Who knows, maybe we'll meet again."

"Who knows."

"Good morning. Wake up call. It eleven o'clock."

It was the Asian receptionist at the front desk. "Thanks, I'm already awake," Toni said, replacing the receiver and nuzzling in for another few minutes of indulgence. This was the big day. She would nurse Megan through a predictable case of the willies and then tonight *Chappy* would screen—to resounding applause, she had no doubt. Then they'd go with Victor to the party on Dennis Danher's yacht and Megan would be charmingly persuasive and clinch the deal. She felt confident of that. Confident about everything, including herself, which was due in part to her date the previous evening with Matthew White, the assistant director she'd met at the party.

For the first several hours it had seemed more like a guided tour than a date. He'd driven her up to King's Park for a view of the city, telling her that Western Australia was the last state to be settled, mostly by free settlers though using some convict labor, that Perth had seen a boom with the gold rush in the 1890s and another big leap forward during the 1960s when iron ore, nickel and the like were discovered and created a crop of millionaires. The city was the preferred place to live for Aussies with money, with more millionaires per capita than any other state. Though it now had an international skyline, it retained a leisurely, small-town, almost resort atmosphere, snuggled as it was amid river, sea and bushlands. After a drive to the beach they came back to the city's equivalent of Restaurant Row, once an immigrant neighborhood that now blossomed with Chinese, Thai, Indian, Greek and Italian restaurants.

It was at the restaurant that the outing took on the feeling of a date. Unaccustomed as she was to small gallantries, she almost opened the door for herself. She paused to let him pull out her chair and smiled at his chivalry if not his accuracy when, in ordering, he referred to her as "the young lady." With wine flowing and candles glowing and Matthew giving her his undivided attention, it was all lovely, except for that nagging question she hadn't dealt with for decades: Will he make a move and how will I handle it? She glanced around at the other couples. She could spot those on dates; they dawdled over the food, the men seemed to be doing most of the talking and the women smiled a lot. The married couples ate more and talked less, but that didn't mean they weren't communicating. A telepathic language of gestures, grunts and half-finished sentences developed over the years. She often chided Joe for being uncommunicative, but if he did no more than talk to the waiter she could guess the color of his mood, know if he'd had a good or bad day and whether his stomach was acting up. She found herself ordering the calamari, one of Joe's favorites.

When Matthew asked her to tell him all about herself, she looked at the married couples with envy. It was one thing to talk about yourself when you were twenty, but giving your history when you really had one was like talking about America with someone who wanted you to start with Plymouth Rock. She turned the conversation to the movie business and ploughed into the calamari. It was really a pleasure to watch her eat, he said.

People didn't let themselves go and really enjoy things enough. Was she imagining it, or had that been a verbal pat on the knee, implying that a woman who indulged her gastronomic appetites would indulge others? She said something about no diets on holidays, but when she got back home . . . He leaned closer, offering her a forkful of his veal and saying that women "with a bit of flesh" had appealed to him ever since his days as an art student. At least she had to give him points for trying. If she ordered the crème caramel would that mean she was a pushover? She settled on the fruit and cheese and turned down a liqueur. But she took his arm on the way out, thinking how nice it was to walk along the street without seeing homeless people or being asked for a handout. As his arm snaked around her waist, she launched into a discussion of New York's social problems. As he pointed out the moon, she told him about her son and daughter. He said that he had grown children, too, and wasn't it a relief that responsibility was over and they could really start living their own lives. No question about it. He was going to put the moves on her.

She tried to say good night in the lobby but he insisted on seeing her to her room. What now? she thought as he stood next to her in the elevator. His hand was only casually draped around her shoulder, but she could feel the heat of it through her dress. Make up your mind. Be prepared. This was the main chance— the fling with an attractive stranger in another city, better yet, another country. This was romance, the sort of thing she read about, even fantasized about. And some of her friends had actually done it and didn't seem the worse for it. Easy on, easy off. Possible orgasmic bliss. To refuse implied a low libido or no sense of adventure. And, to be brutally realistic about it, at her age how many more chances would she have? They reached the door.

While muttering the obligatory "had a wonderful time" he put his arm on the wall above her head and she felt a queasy but not unwelcome sense of being cornered. She echoed that it had been fun. He moved closer, his chest coming up against her breast. What a curse to be bosomy. She felt she had a protective barrier. Had she worn matching underwear? Yes. The Christian Dior beige bra with the front clasp she'd bought at Daffy's Discount especially for the trip. Joe had never mastered front-clasp bras, but Joe didn't undress her anymore. But, if she remembered correctly, letting the man undress you was part of the foreplay, at least in initial encounters. As Matthew's nose furrowed her neck, she wondered if he had mastered front-clasp bras. The confident way he'd taken possession of a buttock while simultaneously moving his lips from neck to ear made her think that he had. He could probably even handle pantyhose. She could feel a stupid expression on her face, as though she were waiting to have her picture taken and had been told to "just say cheese." No, nowadays they said, "Just say sex." His thigh moved between her legs, he was nibbling her ear and, as was usually the case when her picture was being taken, she moved at the wrong moment so that his open mouth landed somewhere between eye and ear. Her earring dropped off. He either didn't notice or didn't care. She closed her eyes as his lips found the target, then peeked, seeing part of his forehead, moist around the hairline, and beyond that the EXIT sign. She thought about Joe. Matthew's kiss, which had been vaguely stirring, seemed not quite right, like brushing your teeth with someone else's toothbrush. She disengaged herself and muttered something about getting enough sleep. No nightcap? he asked in a low voice. Nightcap. Now there was a euphemism. She turned her key in the lock. Not tonight. But surely, he persisted, they'd get together again? They were bound to run into each other, she assured him; after all, they were both at the festival.

She waited on the other side of the door until she was sure he was gone, retrieved her earring from the hall carpet and went to the phone, catching a glimpse of herself in the mirror and noting that her eyes were bright and her cheeks flushed. Eleven-thirty P.M. here; 11:30 A.M. in New Jersey. Joe should be in his office. As she waited for the operator to place the call she knew what she would say: Joe, I just went out with a very attractive man and he likes a woman with a bit of flesh and he wanted to go to bed with me but I didn't, and I want some credit for that and I want you to tell me that you love me, because I love you and damn it, you'd better shape up. No, that was a bit too head-on. How about: I miss you and I hope you've kicked Mario and

Mary Lou out by the time I get back because I want you to chase me around the furniture again.

"Sorry, your party doesn't seem to be answering."

Well, that was the way things go. She undressed, thinking, Joe's centerfolds be damned. She was going to ditch her nightdresses because she liked sleeping in the nude.

She'd slept the sleep of the innocent. Now it was time to get up, go downstairs and get the papers and a cup of coffee before she woke Megan up.

The desk clerk greeted her with a bizarre combination of Oriental dropped consonants and nasal Aussie twang that sounded like a toy whose battery had run down. The clerk had already opened one of the newspapers and folded it on top of the pile. "You flen, Miss Hanlon, she be please she get in paper, yes?"

Toni eyeballed the photo. "Oh, shit. I mean, sure. Sure. Any other messages?" While the girl checked the boxes Toni looked at the photo again and read the caption. Maybe she could make one of those "first the good news, then the bad news" jokes when she handed it over to Megan. But hand it over she would. Megan always wanted the bad news.

Megan took a long time answering Toni's knock. "I figured it was you," she said.

"I guess you did," Toni answered. Megan wore only a pair of cotton panties and wrapped her arms across her chest. She looked both wan and puffy. The room was dark except for a light coming from the bathroom.

"Don't open the shades yet," Megan said, staggering back to the bed and dramatically pulling up the sheet to cover her head. "I feel lower than whale manure. Couldn't sleep all night. Reread the screenplay about three o'clock this morning. It's lousy. No one will ever finance it." Toni ignored all this and crossed to the windows. "This is the big day. *Chappy* tonight. There's a message here from Victor. Said he'd tried you all day yesterday. He's ordered a car to take us to the screening. Be ready by seven."

"I don't want to go to the screening. Couldn't you just write me a note: 'Please excuse Megan as she has the mumps' or something."

"It didn't go well with Tas?"

"I don't want to talk about it."

"How about the visit to the convent?"

"I don't want to talk about that, either." She threw back the sheet, sat up, pressing her fingers to her temple, and said, dramatically, "I have a feeling of great foreboding."

"Get up, will you? You look and sound like an ad for a witches' Sabbath. I'll order some breakfast. Here are your other messages and . . ."—she put the newspaper on the bed and tapped it with her index finger—"this little dog turd was also left on your doorstep."

Megan squinted at the paper, slowly lowered it from her face, brought it up again, then sank back into the pillows. "That bitch!"

"So what are we going to do? Report her to Accuracy in Media? Come on, get up. I'll get us some coffee."

"I'd like a Bloody Mary."

"Megan, it's only noon. You can't start . . . chances are his wife won't even see it. Coffee?"

"I said a Bloody Mary."

Trouble. She couldn't say she hadn't seen it coming: Megan on a slide and predictably greasing the slope with booze. "Hey, the Chinese symbol for crisis is the same as the symbol for opportunity," Toni said.

"Will you stop sounding like you're from southern California? I'll say an act of contrition. And I'll pour my own damned drink."

Loukia's Toyota bounced over the ruts in the dirt road leading to her sister's farmhouse. She knew her husband, Alex, would be furious with her for leaving that girl who never bothered to clean the celery strands from the juicer in charge of their Subiaco shop, but she'd simply had to come. Stranded out here as Greta was, never taking much interest in the world, she might not know what was going on. Worse, some outsider might tell her. It was her duty to protect Greta from that. Her sisterly concern was buoyed by a rising sense of expectation: she felt like the detective in the final reel of the thriller. At last the evidence was in her hands, or, more precisely, on the seat next to her: today's paper, opened to Merle Jaunders's feature, "Tittle Tattle." There was a whole page of photos of the beautiful people, feigning surprise or disdain as the camera caught them sipping drinks, hugging each other, showing off their clothes and their celebrity. At the bottom of the page, not the largest but by no means the smallest photo showed Megan and Tas in a clutch, lips so close they had either just met or were about to. They were the only ones who truly didn't seem to be aware of the camera. She turned her eyes back to the road. She didn't have to read the caption because she'd already memorized it: "Tall Poppies Reunited," and under that, "Fast-track director Megan Hanlon let Perth's famous surgeon, Dr. Tasman Burke, take her pulse years ago in New York, and it's still beating fast. 'Just friends,' the redhead said before they hurried to her hotel room for a private showing. Hanlon's film *Chappy* will screen at the festival tonight, but it won't be as hot as this reunion."

Loukia had expected she would have to go to the outbuildings and track Greta down at one of her many chores, but as she pulled up she saw her sister on the veranda in an uncharacteristically relaxed pose, her feet up on the railing, sipping a cup of tea.

"Whatever are you doing here?" Greta asked as she swung her legs down. "Mama called about an hour ago and said you'd called her to say you were going to her house for lunch because you had some important news. But why did you drag all the way out here first?"

"I had to see you."

"But why?" There was something about Loukia's expression, a glint of satisfaction in her eye, which the grim line of her mouth did not altogether deny. Even before Greta took the newspaper that was thrust toward her, she knew that there was something in it she didn't want to see.

CHAPTER
THIRTEEN

IT WAS AFTER TWO IN THE MORNING AND THE CONVENT
was quiet as a tomb. Joan stood at the open window of her room
and stared out into the garden. The lawn was white in the moonlight, and if she craned her neck she could see the blue-black
sky pricked with stars. If only she could be outside under those
stars she might be able to think more clearly. She was dizzy with
fatigue, but there was no chance she could sleep. Not after what
had happened today. She glanced at the narrow bed, icy-looking
in the moonlight, the wooden crucifix. And James's Panama hat
sitting on top of her desk. She picked it up, smelled the sweat
and hair tonic on its band and carried it back to the window.

After teaching her morning classes at St. Brigid's she'd driven
to the university, ostensibly to use the library. She'd gone straight
to James's office, so eager that she'd forgotten her manners,
knocking and opening the door without waiting to hear the invitation to come in. The electric fan didn't do much to dispel
the lingering smell of the cigar James usually saved till the end
of the day. He didn't look up immediately, but finished making
a correction, then swiveled round. "Sorry," she said. "I was
wondering if you . . ." What was the pretext? Yes. ". . . if
you'd managed to get a ticket to that film showing this evening."

"And I was wondering why you don't wear blue more often.
Suits you, you know."

She did know, but it was only recently that she'd thought about
such things. "Did you manage to get a ticket for Megan Hanlon's film?"

"That I did. Will you sit down or shall we take a walk? It's
an exceptionally beautiful day." She nodded. "Better yet," he

went on casually, "why don't we play hooky and take a drive to the beach?"

She couldn't remember voicing her desire to go to the beach and for a moment, as she formulated then brushed aside excuses, she imagined he'd intuited it, before remembering that he often said how much he liked the beach. "I'd . . ."

". . . love to." He finished the sentence for her, putting on his Panama and getting Belle's leash before she could change her mind.

They drove off in his car, a disreputable fender-dented Ford with piles of books, papers and empty carry-out cartons in the backseat. Belle, as though anticipating their destination, stood up amid the mess, paws gripping the open rear window, head in the wind. The Mozart flute sonata on the tape deck soared and trilled as if in joyful accompaniment to their escape. They stopped to buy meat pies and peaches and drove along the shoreline, looking for a "dog beach" where Belle could run free.

The sun was like a blessing on them as they sat on the concrete steps leading to the shore, barely talking except to accuse Belle of being a beggar or to say how blue the sky was, how delicious the peaches. When there were no more crusts to be begged, Belle trotted off to the water. James took off his shoes and socks, rolled up his pants legs and, saying that she was already getting pink, insisted that she wear the battered Panama. As she slipped off her sandals he watched, his face as pleased as a parent watching a child master some task. He put the hat on her head, told her she looked fetching, took her hand to help her up and didn't let go of it as they walked to the water's edge. The sun seemed to penetrate her clear through, and that wonderful smell of surf and seaweed, and the sand, both hard and soft, deliciously warm beneath her feet.

"Can you surf?" he asked as they watched a lone surfer take a spill.

"I never tried that, but I used to be a bonza swimmer."

"I'd guessed that you were," he said. Their attention was taken by a young couple who took turns dipping an infant, squealing with fear and delight, into the waves.

They walked on, Belle dashing ahead, then darting back to make sure they were following. A wave caught them, taking

Joan's breath away, drenching her skirt. He laughed as she let go of his hand, moving crablike away from the water. She gave him an I'll-show-you smile, hoisted up her skirt, tucked it into the waist of her underpants so that her legs were bare above the knees, then waded back in.

She took his hand again and they walked on for a mile or more, silent, until they came to a little cove, deserted and sheltered from the wind. They sat down, she putting her legs to the side and tucking her skirt around them. Still silent, they gazed out at the ocean.

"I don't think we've ever gone this long without talking," she said after a time.

"One of our problems. We talk too much. Cooped up in classrooms and offices. Have to talk to convince yourself you're there. Out here you feel alive. There's no need to talk. You can feel the presence of . . ."

"God," she suggested, tilting her head.

"I'd say . . ."

"You'd say 'nature.' "

"Shall we agree to disagree?"

"We shall."

Belle, who still wanted to run, nosed a bit of driftwood James had picked up. He gave it a powerful toss and watched Belle lumber after it. "You know I have a sabbatical coming up next year," he began.

She nodded. She had already wondered how she would cope with his being away.

"I've been thinking of going back to Greece. There was a little village I visited. A hotel with a main building but separate bungalows. Fresh fish, lots of quiet. Just the sun and the Aegean."

"That place in the picture on your desk?"

"That's it. Might be totally changed by now, crawling with tourists, but when I was there they didn't even have electricity so you didn't get the mobs. Students mostly, or people who really wanted to fish, or couples who didn't need outside entertainment. I've written away to find out if it's still in operation and how much their rates have gone up."

She pulled up her legs, dug in her toes and rested her chin on her knees, idly tracing circles in the sand. "Who took that picture of you?"

"The maid. She came over to the bungalow once a week to sweep up and change the sheets. She was a shy little thing, very pregnant and missing a front tooth. She was afraid to use the camera."

"Oh, I thought . . ." This must be one of the unpleasant by-products of infatuation: she'd imagined the photo had been taken by some woman with whom he had been traveling and she'd already endowed the imaginary woman with long, straw-colored hair and a golden tan.

"No. I was alone. Though I didn't mind that at all. I enjoy my own company and have an abiding mistrust of people who don't. Shows want of character." This was pronounced in his I-brook-no-disagreement lecture-hall voice. He tossed a stone from hand to hand. "It was all right being alone after the divorce. Margaret, my ex-wife, talked a great deal. At first I took it for vivacity, then I realized she talked out of nervousness. She had to keep unpleasant things at bay. Or perhaps my silences made her nervous. Doesn't matter much now, does it?"

"I've never asked you before, but were you the one who . . ."

"No. We said it was mutual and by the time we actually parted it was. I don't think she liked me much anymore. But then, I'm not, in many ways, a likable man. No," he insisted when she raised her head, ready to protest, "I'm not easy. But then neither are you. Your ardor, your seriousness about life— well, you know as well as I it frightens as many as it attracts. But your vocation has kept the reins on your ego. I know sometimes I'm a petty tyrant—a university is an easy place to get away with that. Ah, you asked about my divorce . . . it shook me up terribly for a while. Men are more addicted to routine than women, don't you think?" He was drifting into the theoretical and another level look from her made him aware of it. "Of course," he continued, "the ideal would be to be with someone you're so comfortable with that you can have conversation but never feel the need for it." She nodded and closed her eyes. The rosy glow she saw seemed to suffuse her entire body.

"No, lack of company never bothered me. Except at mealtimes. I started out driving into town, buying provisions, making proper meals for myself, but by the end of my stay I was reduced to wolfing down bread and cheese. I could have gone up to the hotel's main building but there's something about a waiter saying 'one for dinner' without a question mark that makes you acutely and uncomfortably aware of your solitary state.''

Belle returned with the bit of driftwood and dropped it by James's side. He picked it up and tossed it again. ''I've found myself hoping . . .'' His next words were almost drowned by the sound of the waves. ''. . . that when I go back, you would come with me.''

Her heart did not knock against her ribs nor did the color rise to her neck. She sat very still, visualizing the bungalow—the whitewashed walls, the primitive kitchen, the pots of red geraniums on the balcony. They would read and write in the mornings, swim before lunch, nap or explore in the afternoons. In the evenings they might stroll to the dining room and have a glass of retsina, making friendly conversation with other couples. As they walked back to their bungalow, they would see the fire the young people had made on the beach and hear them singing. She would hold the flashlight while he opened the door and lit a candle. They would undress by candlelight and settle into the rough-hewn bed with sheets made soft from many washings. He would take her into his arms . . . They would fall asleep listening to the susurrating sound of the sea, wake when the first light slanted through the shutters.

Belle waited for the driftwood to be tossed, then settled down between them. All three looked straight ahead.

Finally, James got to his feet. He brushed off his pants and reached for her hand, releasing it as soon as he'd helped her up. But as she stood, immobile, he wrapped his arms around her. She put her head against his shoulder, her arms slowly moving from her sides to encircle his back. His hat tipped off her head but neither of them moved to retrieve it. One of his hands, dry and warm, moved to the nape of her neck, his other arm moved to her waist and pulled her to him. His bulk surprised her, and his smell—a combination of freshly laundered cotton, cigar smoke and sunlight. Could sunlight have a smell? So this is what it's like, being held by a man, by James, she thought as Belle's tail wagged against her leg. Not a shock at all, but a deeply pleasurable awareness of her body and an expectation of relief, like getting into bed when you were bone-tired. She could have wept at the comfort of it. Gradually he released her, clasping his hands around the back of her neck. When their eyes met there was no avoidance, no shame-faced pause.

"Your face is dear to me," he said.

"And yours to me," she answered.

He reached for the hat and put it back on her head. They turned, walking back along the beach in silence.

Once in the car they began the sort of conversation they might have had in his office. The Mozart was almost too energetically joyful. Did she think Jean-Pierre Rampal's rendition of the allegro was a mite too quick? No. Had she finished the book yet? Yes. And what was her opinion of the chapter on John Stuart Mill? Belle, exhausted, settled into the books and papers on the backseat and dozed. Joan put her head back, the Panama cocked over her eyes, and made desultory replies to his questions. When they'd stopped talking, she reached for his hand and held it for the rest of the trip back.

He pulled up to her car in the parking lot but neither of them made any attempt to get out. Belle, coming to, got up on her hind legs and nosed their necks. James opened the back door, letting Belle out, and she wandered a few feet from the car, then looked back, confused.

" 'Let me not to the marriage of true minds admit impediments,' " he said at last. "Though in our case impediments are so overwhelming that we'll have to admit them."

She stared at the tape deck. "I've been in the Order since I was eighteen."

"I know. For you, it would be worse than a divorce." He passed his hand over his forehead, then put his head on the steering wheel, raising his eyes to look out through the windshield. "You should leave. You should come with me, Joan. We could make each other happy. You don't doubt that, do you?"

She shook her head. A chemistry professor drove by and waved.

"I don't want to pressure you. No, I do want to, but I won't. I simply had to let you know how I feel."

"Yes."

"So . . ." He turned on the ignition, the Mozart started up. "You'll let me know," he added as casually as if he were talking about a lunch appointment.

As she started to get out, he seized her hand, drawing her back into the car, nodding to indicate the hat. "You won't want to waltz into the convent in this, will you?" He touched the tip of her nose. "We'll have to carry a gallon of sunblock for you. Then again, I might like you with freckles."

"I don't freckle." She leaned into him, quickly surveying the parking lot to make sure there were no cars pulling in or out, closing her eyes. He did not kiss her, but gripped her upper arm so firmly that she could feel the imprint of each finger, then, quickly, he reached across her, his chest brushing her breast as he opened her door. Belle followed her to her car. She bent down and took the dog's muzzle in her hand.

"Go back," she told Belle. "Go back and tell him it's been one of the most wonderful afternoons of my life." Belle trotted off and climbed into the passenger seat. James drove off without looking back. She reached up and realized she was still wearing the hat.

She drove as though she'd been traversing the Nullaboor Plain since morning, dazed by limitless horizon and sun. At an intersection, she sat while the light changed to green and the driver behind her swerved around her, yelling, "Wake up, you silly bitch!" before she could get the car into gear. Cresting the hill leading to the convent, she knew she couldn't go back yet, couldn't formulate excuses or answer questions. She pulled into the almost deserted bank parking lot, then went in through the side door of the church, grateful for the comparative darkness and the familiar smell of incense and candle wax. She knelt at a side altar before the statue of the Virgin. She prayed, but the image of James, not as she'd seen him last, but in the photo taken at the bungalow with the wash of the sea behind him, kept intruding. Bringing her folded hands to her lips, she tasted salt on her fingertips and found she was humming Sister Ursula's favorite: "Hail, Queen of Heaven, the Ocean Star, guide to the wanderer here below . . ." Rising, she crossed herself, walked to the center aisle and genuflected. As she turned, she saw Greta Burke kneeling in a back pew.

She thought it strange that Greta should be in the church at this hour but, not wanting to interrupt her meditation, began to walk past. There was something about Greta's posture that suggested pain rather than adoration. Her arms were on the pew in front of her, her head sunk low between them, her body almost doubled up.

"Greta?"

Greta raised her head, wiped her eyes with the back of her hand and muttered, "I came to see Father Celebrizzi."

Joan checked her watch. "It's not quite six yet and he doesn't start hearing confessions till six. And he's usually late." She slid into the pew. "Are you all right?"

"No. I don't think I am." Greta pulled herself up into a sitting position, gingerly, as though she'd been knocked down and wasn't sure if bones had been broken.

Joan put her arm around her. "Is there anything I can do?" Greta shook her head, then crumpled onto her, her hands clutching Joan's shoulders. "Oh, Sister. I'm so unhappy." A single wracking sob went out into the quiet of the church.

"There, there. Whatever's happened? Are your children all right?"

"It's Tas."

"Your husband?"

"Yes . . . Tas . . . he doesn't love me . . . I love him so much and he . . . they both . . . both lied to me and . . ."

Joan looked around, wondering what to do. "Would you like to come to the convent?"

Greta shook her head. "No. I can't see anybody. I don't really want to see Father Celebrizzi. I just didn't know where to go."

The side door creaked open and old Mrs. Feeney, in the black coat and felt hat she wore even during the hottest weather, dipped her fingers into the holy water and blinked about. Mrs. Feeney was always the first to appear for the evening confessions and the subsequent Stations of the Cross.

"Perhaps we could go up into the choir loft," Joan suggested. They moved out of the pew and walked, heads down, while Mrs. Feeney peered after them.

"I hope the loft door isn't locked," Joan said as they ascended the stairs. Mercifully it wasn't. She took Greta's hand and guided her down the risers to the organist's bench. "Sit down," she said softly, taking a place on a riser, her back to the stained-glass window. "Now tell me what's happened."

"I went into the city. I drove by Tas's office but I just couldn't bring myself to go in. Then I drove by the hotel . . . I was going to confront Megan. I'm such a coward."

"What's Megan got to do with . . . ?"

"She's having an affair with Tas."

"Surely not," Joan said, and to give some rationale to her disbelief, "Megan's only been in the country for a few days. Why would you think . . . ?"

"Before. When Tas was in America, and now here, again."

"What would lead you to think such a thing?"

"It's all here." Greta fumbled in her purse and brought out a crumpled piece of newspaper. "Here is a gossip column. My God, everyone knows about it. I won't even be able to hide it. Chrissie . . . I can't . . ."

"But something in a gossip column . . . these things . . . you can't give any credence to . . ." Joan looked at the picture, read the caption, looked at the picture again. "These gossip columnists will print anything," she said with disgust. "It's no proof of—"

"But don't you understand? That picture was taken days ago and when Megan came out to the farm she and Tas pretended not to know each other. I know you're fond of Megan, so you don't want to believe it. I was fond of her, too. I thought she was so wonderful, so honest. I was so flattered when she befriended me."

Joan's disbelief was giving way to misgiving and disappointment. "Where did you get this?" was all she could think to say, wanting to tear it up but handing it back to Greta.

"This morning . . . Loukia brought it to me. She said it was for my own good that she show it to me."

Joan looked grim. Most things that were done "for your own good" rarely were. Loukia had always been a meddler.

"And I suppose Loukia is right. That everyone has known about Tas except me. I'm so stupid. I've known for ever so long that he didn't love me. We haven't slept together in ages and I know he wants a divorce, but I just thought if I could hold on. I've done everything wrong. Everything. Just the other day when

Tas and Megan drove off, I called after them. I could hear it in my voice, a horrible sort of pleading that I know drives him away, but I couldn't stop it. *Couldn't* stop it." She began to weep again, emitting horrible gasping sounds. She threw her head back. The waning light from the stained-glass window turning her face into a red mask of anguish. "You can't know, Sister. You can't know what it's like to love a man and know he feels nothing for you. Guilt perhaps, and pity, but nothing else. Mother of God, what will I do?"

The lights came on in the church below. "Shush . . . shush," Joan said, half in comfort, half warning that they might be overheard. She got up and went to the railing. A few more people, mostly older women and children, had come into the church. She turned and sat beside Greta on the organist's bench, putting her arm around her.

"How could she do this to me?" Greta sobbed. "I trusted her."

Joan still couldn't bring herself to believe that things were as they appeared, and if they were, she thought Greta was placing far too much importance on Megan's role. Even now, in the depths of her despair, Greta seemed to find it too painful to blame Tas. Greta turned her head away and put her inhaler into her mouth. "I can't . . ." She placed her other hand on her chest.

"I know, dear. Just relax. Just breathe slowly." Had this poor girl ever in her life had the breath to yell or cry out in pain, to accuse or shout?

"I'm so stupid."

"No, you're not," Joan said firmly. "So stop saying that. And tell me, quietly, tell me when things started to go wrong with your husband, and what you propose to do."

By the time Greta had finished talking they were sitting in darkness. Greta was so calm she almost seemed anesthetized. She had gone down the long trail of tears, blaming herself for taking all the wrong turns. It was too much to hope that she had any plan of action. Greta blinked into the darkness. "It's late. I didn't realize . . ."

"Will you be all right to drive home?" Joan asked, wishing she could provide a haven.

"Yes. I'm all right now. See, I'm even breathing regularly.

This afternoon I thought I'd have a real attack and have to be hospitalized, but I'm all right now. I just feel . . .''

"Exhausted," Joan supplied. "Yes. You must. Go home and get some rest."

Greta started to get up and sank down again. "I just don't want to live without him."

"From what you've been telling me it seems you've lived without him for a long time. Do you want to talk to Father Celebrizzi?"

"No. I think I know what he'd say."

Joan nodded. She thought she knew, too: Greta should hold on, pray and forgive, accept her lot in life. But perhaps she was not giving Father Celebrizzi credit. Perhaps he understood that sometimes a divorce, or even breaking your vows, was not giving in to the loose moral code of the modern world, but a desperate attempt to be responsible, to find the path for which you were truly intended. "I can't advise you," Joan said, "but I think that first you must talk to your husband."

"And Megan?"

"Forget about Megan. Leave her to heaven."

But that was easier said than done. She had not been able to get either Megan or Greta out of her mind. As for herself . . . she pressed her forehead to the window, remembering how, as a girl, she would leave her parents' house, sleeping bag under her arm, and go into the bush. Her favorite camping spot was the pond. Fancy and superstition told her that there was a spirit in the pond and if she made a sacrifice, threw in pennies or marbles, or the ring she'd won at the Royal Show, the spirit would grant her wishes. The caw of a bird, the sound of wind in the trees had assured her that she had been heard. It was a primitive but deeply satisfying form of worship. But who would hear her now?

"Oh, God," she began, but it was no prayer, only a cry of pain and confusion.

CHAPTER
FOURTEEN

HIS HAND MOVED FROM HER RIBCAGE TO HER HIPBONE, clutching her away from waves that threatened to swallow her up. She could hear the cries for help, smell the chlorine . . . Chlorine? She tried to force her eyes open. He threw his leg over hers and slid it down till their feet touched. She felt as though she were being rubbed with fine-grain sandpaper. A musky sex scent mingled with the chlorine. With a gasp she opened her eyes.

She was not on a raft in a stormy sea, but on a bed, in a hotel room. Not hers. Sunlight invaded the edges of the blinds, the shouts and the smell of chlorine came from a swimming pool that was just outside the window. Her mouth was so dry she couldn't have spit if her life depended on it. She must have some water. She inched away from him, pushing back her hair, making sure the floor was solid beneath her feet before she stood up and turned to look at him. Victor.

Images surfaced, she could even remember snatches of dialogue: "No one's been better than you, baby," and "Carry me over the threshold, you never did."

She'd started to unbutton his shirt in the elevator and once at the door, at her suggestion if memory served, he'd hoisted her up, more or less throwing her over his shoulder while he turned the key. He'd thrown her on the bed while she'd made jokes about cavemen and they'd kept it up, growling, laughing, grinding into each other, all hands and mouths, going at it as though life depended on it. Jungle love. And lots of it. Her skin felt raw and there was a pleasurable heavy feeling from her waist to her knees. She watched him now as he pawed the space she'd left, found a substitute in the pillow and hugged it to his chest. She felt her way to the bathroom. Scooping water into her mouth, the kaleidoscopic images of the previous night began to settle.

With the help of well-spaced Bloody Marys she'd maintained a numbing buzz all afternoon. She'd dressed—perhaps with a foreknowledge of disaster—in a black tubular shift with a businesslike jacket. Against Toni's advice she'd fortified herself with another drink before they'd gone downstairs to meet Victor and Deirdre. Anxiety and anticipation about the screening kept her quiet for most of the ride out to Fremantle. Victor sat up front with the driver; she, Deirdre and Toni sat in the back.

"What's your movie about?" Deirdre wanted to know. Apparently Megan's criticism had hit its mark because Deirdre had taken off her heavy makeup. She looked about eleven, the same age as the movie's protagonist.

"It's about a hundred minutes," Megan said, staring out the window.

"Don't tease her," Toni admonished and proceeded to fill Deirdre in. "It's a coming-of-age movie," she explained, and when Deirdre looked blank, "That's a turning point in a young person's life. The girl in the movie is the daughter of a rodeo rider. It takes place back in the 1950s when rodeos were still a big thing. We shot it in Arizona and New Mexico. Anyhow, the girl's parents have a shiftless sort of life and a pretty shaky marriage and during the course of the movie she begins to see how precarious their life—her own life—is, how alone . . ."

"Don't tell her the whole thing," Megan said. Toni started talking to Victor, and Megan absolved herself from participation.

"I know how it is," Deirdre whispered to her. "Dad gets uptight just before a screening, too."

Megan nodded, and though she thought dark glasses were an affectation, put on a pair. She felt very much removed as the car turned off the Stirling and onto the West Coast Highway, as though she were watching a movie she'd seen before.

Fremantle itself looked rather like a set. Its turn-of-the-century character had been partly restored and the buildings painted in soft pastels for the America's Cup. Since it was an hour to screening, Toni took Deirdre for a cappuccino while Megan checked in with the projectionist. Toni and Deirdre reappeared just as the house was filling, Deirdre carrying a large stuffed kangaroo, which she sat on her lap. Megan took a seat between Toni and Victor and wished she were invisible.

As the title appeared on the screen her skin got itchy all over and she had to pee. Toni grasped one of her hands, Victor patted the other. "Written and directed by Megan Hanlon" was the last thing to appear before the shot of the father astride a bronco, waiting for the doors of the stall to be opened, then a wide shot of the stands, zooming in on the girl's face, proud and expectant. This was all done without a soundtrack, but as the doors of the stall flew open and the horse bucked wildly into the arena, the soundtrack—the burst of country music, shouts and neighing—came up. It was a terrific mix. Megan was glad she'd been able to get the composer (a country-and-western star who was a serious druggie and going through marital problems to boot) to work for scale because he'd liked the script. The opening shots worked. So did the next scene in the bar. She went on like this—riveted but grading herself, remembering the difficulty she'd had getting a particular shot—for at least fifteen minutes. Then she became aware of the audience. They were involved enough to be vocal during the action scenes and tensely quiet during the dramatic ones. She felt her shoulders relax. She was going with the flow now, actually caught up as though she'd never seen it before until . . . she froze. A scene had been cut. The father did not hit the mother before he went off, leaving the girl and the mother in the grungy motel room. Toni let go of her hand and gave her a quick look as she stiffened. The movie got back on track, as she'd directed it. She relaxed. But then another omission, just a few moments, but extremely important ones, where the drunken cowboy slaps the girl's ass and the girl, humiliated but flattered by the male attention, begins to feel herself a grownup woman. That bastard producer! He'd edited it out. She was on the edge of the seat now—but only figuratively, literally she pulled back, like an animal about to strike. Another forty-five minutes, pretty much as she'd shot it, as she'd intended. She watched now with head slightly down, galvanized but horrified, like a passing motorist seeing an auto accident.

She expected the worst, but how could she have been prepared for the final butchery? Her closing shots had been of the girl riding in the backseat of the beat-up Chevy, the played-out mother now driving and saying, "You wanna run away? You got all this to run to," the pan of the vast, flat and lonely desert, then the close-up of the girl's trapped face. Freeze-frame. Instead she saw discarded footage spliced in: the mother, father and daughter driving along, all singing, slogging through, making it as a family unit. This altered the entire thrust and intent, changed it into a warm and runny puff piece about surviving rough times instead of the harsh reality of blighted lives she'd intended. It was worse than a nightmare. It was on film. With her name attached to it.

"Stand up." Toni pried Megan's hand from the armrest. The lights had come up, the audience was applauding as though nothing were wrong. Applauding enthusiastically. She felt the pressure of eyes on her and though she thought she was speechless, Toni hissed, "Not now!" and she realized that she was sputtering curses. She stopped her mouth and did a half turn. Emile, the French director, was two rows back and gave her the thumbs-up salute, the woman in front of him said, "Not many directors could get that sort of a performance out of a kid." The man sitting next to Toni leaned over and flung his arms out. "Great action shots. Great!" A tough little smile that advanced her age immeasurably creased her lips. She sat down.

"That's right, lady," Victor whispered, his breath hot in her ear. "Leave 'em beggin' for more." The applause crested and died away. People began to collect themselves. Toni and Victor spoke at the same time: "Hey, sweetheart, you sick?" and "For God's sake, Megan, don't . . ." She crawled over Victor's legs. "I have to go to the bathroom. Excuse me."

She sat in the locked toilet stall, elbows on knees, head in hands. When someone knocked or leaned down to see if the stall was occupied she brought her feet up to the sides of the commode and stayed perfectly still. Women flushed and brushed, talked about the film, men, their periods, where they were going for drinks. Someone bashed at a jammed Tampax machine and, getting no satisfaction, took her friend's advice and plugged herself with toilet paper from an adjoining stall. At last it was quiet, except for running water from a tap someone had neglected to turn off.

"Megan, it's me. Toni."

She brought her legs down and winced at a charley horse.

"You gotta come out. Everyone's gone now and the custodian wants to lock up. There was some funny-looking guy who said he was a professor who waited for the longest time to meet you. *Yoo-de-lay-he-hoo!* Come out! We've gotta get over to Danher's party at the yacht club."

Megan flung back the door, walked to the sink and spoke to Toni via the mirror. "That unprincipled, slimy bastard! The no-nuts wonder! He reedited the entire goddamn thing without letting me know. I swear, if he was in front of me now I could run him through and not feel anything but joy. How could he! I'll kill the son of a bitch. I swear I'll kill him!"

"I don't suppose you noticed that the audience loved it."

"I don't give a shit. Don't tell me the goddamned audience goddamn loved it. A year and a half of my life to make this and he reedits it into a piece of candy-coated dreck, and you say don't feel bad?"

"All right. I know. I know. Don't you think I know? I'd like to take out a contract on him." She was angry, too, though she knew that her shock and rage couldn't even come close to Megan's. Megan's version of the film was immeasurably better, but probably would have doomed the movie to art-house distribution. With the producer's reedit and sugar-coated ending it would probably be more successful commerically. This could maybe, maybe, be pointed out a week from now. If she said it now she'd be worse than Judas. "We have to go to this party, remember? You're finally going to meet Dennis Danher, and if you go there mouthing off you're gonna make a fool of yourself. So just don't do it. Here, fix yourself up." She fished in Megan's purse for a brush.

Megan clenched her fists and raised them above her head, looking for all the world like some grieving relative in an earthquake disaster photo. She picked up the brush and began whipping it through her hair. Like a nurse assisting at surgery, Toni silently slapped first lipstick, then blusher into her hand. Megan applied them deftly and more heavily than usual, layering on the protective never-let-them-see-you-down hide. "Okay," she said when she was finished. "Okay. Okay. Okay. I will not shriek. I will not curse. Certainly I will not cry. I will go to the party."

Victor and Deirdre waited at the doors along with a man in overalls who impatiently jiggled a set of keys. "Toni told us it was different from what you'd done," Deirdre said. A look of concern wizened her face. "But I still think it was awesome."

"It was . . ." Victor put aside the superlatives and sought something believably concrete. ". . . very good, Megan. Very good."

"Don't be a hypocrite, darling. You'd probably have done just what he did."

Another smattering of applause greeted her as they walked into the yacht club. She accepted it with the tight little smile and helped herself to a drink from a passing tray. A circle of well-wishers converged. She finished the drink in two gulps. ". . . and a great sense of period," a man with an egg-shaped head was saying. "Americans are usually sloppy about period detail."

"That's true," Toni answered for her. "But Megan has an incredible eye for detail. Did you notice the Indian costumes? We got those from an Indian museum. Megan got friendly with this . . ."

"I just lost it when the father fell off the horse and didn't win the prize money," a woman with frizzled hair said.

Someone else asked, "How many of those actors were amateurs?"

"Congratulations, Megan!" a voice brayed from the periphery. It was Merle Jaunders.

"Steady," Toni cautioned, giving Megan a humorless wink and waving back at Merle.

Megan asked the waiter for another drink. Victor touched her elbow. "Want some hors d'oeuvres?"

"I want another drink. I believe I just ordered one."

"Fasten your seat belts," Toni whispered to Victor, "it's gonna be a bumpy ride."

He nodded. As soon as there was a lull in the conversation and Megan had taken possession of her drink, he said, "I think you should meet Danher and his wife now. Or would you rather wait until this reception's over and we go out on their yacht?"

"Now," Megan said. She was just drunk enough to have the illusion of control. As they moved through the crowd she saw everything in sharper focus, observed the little gestures that captured character, the male guerilla skirmishes that passed for kidding, the female subtle and not-so-subtle sizing up, the deal-making and oneupsmanship. Victor touched her elbow and indicated a couple standing near the buffet table.

"That's Danher and his wife, Annette."

Danher was taller than average, robust and freckled. Only his eyes, slightly bulging and unpitying as a Pekinese's, prevented him from being good-looking. His wife, reported in the press as a homebody who enjoyed occasional charity work, was a conservatively groomed, sweet-faced blonde. They held hands loosely, because they were supposed to, like the girls at St. Brigid's.

"Dennis, Annette, good to see you again. This is Megan Hanlon." Megan offered her hand. Dennis Danher disengaged his, passed it over his diminishing hairline, and thrust it forward. Even multimillionaires can't stop their hair from falling out, Megan thought. But no need to feel sorry for him. Not with those eyes.

"Dennis just got here." Annette smiled. "But I was at the screening and I really liked your film, Miss Hanlon."

"Call me Megan."

"For a while there," Annette said, "I was afraid that it wouldn't have a happy ending. I'm a sentimentalist, and I do like things to have a happy ending. Or at least a hopeful ending."

"That cuts out *Romeo and Juliet* and—"

"Don't we all." Victor cut Megan off.

Annette turned to Dennis. "It really was very good, dear. I wish you'd seen it. He never has time for any relaxation except sailing."

"I'm sure it was good. Tell you what, Megan, why don't you send round a print and I'll try to take a look at it before our meeting."

"Well, sure . . ."—and since he'd used her first name—"Dennis. Though I'd like to talk to you about it first. There've been some changes . . ." Victor's fingers tightened on the fleshy part of her arm.

"I think the children would like it," Annette said. "It's the sort of film they'd enjoy."

"It is now," Megan said tartly.

"I didn't mean it's a children's film. Our oldest is seventeen and she wants to be an actress."

"If at all possible, discourage her," Megan said. "Though I guess no daughter of yours would be exposed to the usual propositions and penury." Victor squeezed her arm in warning again, but she didn't give a damn.

Annette smiled as though Megan's remark were a compliment to the protection of their wealth. "The little girl who took the lead was wonderful. In that scene where she leaves the motel and walks into the desert alone, she just broke my heart."

"Yeah. She was an amateur when I found her, but her mother has the morals of an alley cat and thinks the kid's a meal ticket."

Annette's curiosity shriveled. "You don't say."

"The scene you're talking about, I had a helluva time with it. The girl, Charlene, just couldn't cry. I didn't want to resort to glycerine tears, so I took her into one of the trailers to talk with her. Her mother was right there, and after a while she said, 'Don't waste time talkin' to her. You want her to cry, just slap her one. I give you permission.' "

"You must be joking. What did you do?"

"I wanted to slap the mother, or at least turn her over to some child-protection agency, but when I saw the look on Charlene's face I hustled her out of that trailer as fast as I could and got the cameras rolling."

"I suppose you had to," Annette said dubiously.

"I did have to. We were going into overtime."

Danher looked at Megan with new respect, and Annette asked, "Where's the girl now?"

"Probably hooking on Hollywood Boulevard. The mother packed her into the car and headed for the coast the minute I said wrap."

Victor laughed. "My grandfather always said, 'Never make a movie with kids or animals.' " A surge of voluble guests had converged on the buffet table, causing Dennis and Victor to take a few steps to the side. Megan heard Victor say, "I knew Megan way back in film school. Knew then that she had it," while she shifted to let a couple pile up their plates.

"Tell me about your new film." Annette's tone was encouraging. "Dennis's secretary said she'd read the screenplay and she loved it."

Thank God for literate secretaries. A piano started up, or maybe it had already been going and she just hadn't noticed it. She didn't want to talk to Annette Danher, she wanted to dance. But she shouldn't pass up an opportunity to pitch to a would-be producer's wife. Annette seemed more than politely interested when Megan began to talk, but then her attention began to waver. I know I'm not boring, Megan thought, I'm never boring three drinks in. Maybe Annette wanted to dance, too. But no, Annette was magnetized by something that was going on directly behind Megan. Megan turned her head and saw what had so galvanized Mrs. Danher's attention: Naomi Tishman, in a yellow backless dress, standing between Victor and Danher, her head moving from one to the other as though watching the championship match at Wimbledon. Naomi laughed at something Victor said, then reached up to touch Danher's lapel. Unaccustomed to such familiarity, he pulled back, then decided he liked the attention and smiled down at her. Megan turned back to Annette Danher. "I wouldn't worry about Naomi Tishman. I happen to know she's otherwise engaged."

Annette played the innocent. "Why would I worry about Naomi Tishman?"

"I guess if I believed in happy endings I wouldn't worry about anything, either."

Annette soured as fast as only the superficially sweet can. "You were saying . . ."

"Ah, yes, I was saying . . ." But the trio joined them, Naomi flashing her perfect teeth. "Megan! I absolutely loved *Chappy*!" Her voice was so girlish that Megan could easily imagine it turning into a childish whine. Tas was an idiot. "I laughed and cried in all the right places, just like you told me to. At least . . ."—and now Naomi turned to Victor—"I hope they were the right places."

Megan said, "I'm glad you enjoyed it."

"Oh, I did. I truly did. When we get away from this impossible crowd and out on the yacht I want to have a good, long talk with you." She looked at Megan with the focused intensity she usually reserved for men. He's told her, Megan thought. Tas has told her about us. There they'd be, out on the high seas, Naomi shifting the good, long conversation to Tas. It would be like some rotten French novel—she could either play the sophisticated, discarded mistress sharing advice with the younger one, or jump overboard. She scanned the room. "Have you seen Toni?" she asked Victor.

"I think she's over near the door."

"Please excuse me." She was Princess Di at a press conference. "Such a pleasure to meet you. Annette. Dennis."

"But we'll all see each other on the yacht," Naomi insisted. "A midnight cruise. Dennis, what a lovely idea."

After they'd moved away Victor said, "You might have spent a little more time chatting up Danher."

"I don't want to chat up Danher. And I'm not looking for Toni. I'm looking for the bar."

" ' . . . with a wishing well, I wish that we were there together,' " Megan crooned. The room had started to empty. But she was so content, so happy there on the piano bench.

Deirdre looked at her with the unpitying judgment of youth. "She's drunk."

"So it would appear," Toni said as they moved closer to the piano.

"Do you know 'Wild Colonial Boy'?" Megan asked the pianist. "Or how about 'Patriot Game'?" He shook his head. Three choruses of "Small Hotel" were enough; he didn't propose to venture into Irish ballads. "It starts, 'Come all ye young rebels, and list while I sing . . .' You must know it." He shook his head. "What's your name?" she demanded.

"Kevin McCarthy."

"I thought so. Kevin McCarthy. And you don't know 'Wild Colonial Boy'? You must be pulling me leg. You must know it. And you must know some hymns. How about 'Hail Queen of Heaven'?"

"She's *very* drunk," Toni said as the pianist shook his head more vigorously. She spotted Victor across the room and motioned for him to come over.

Victor touched Megan's shoulder. "The people who are invited on the cruise are getting on the yacht now. Are you up to it?"

"I'm up to anything. We'll all die game." She got to her feet and looked at Victor as though seeing him for the first time. "Victor. Victor," she said sadly, putting her arms around his neck. "I wish I liked you, Victor. I still love you a little bit, but I wish I liked you."

"I don't care if you like me—if you love me, even a little bit."

"That's where you've always been wrong." She swayed against him. "And as you told me the other night, I really only loved my idea of you. You are nothing but an illusion."

"But I'm right here. In the flesh." He pulled her closer.

"Maybe a few whiffs of night air . . . ," Toni suggested, but Megan and Victor were oblivious.

"They're both disgusting," Deirdre muttered.

"They're gonna sail away without us," Victor warned in a barely audible voice.

"Sail away," Megan said dreamily. "I'd like to sail away. . . ."

And that was the last she remembered clearly. She turned on the bathroom light and forced herself to look in the mirror. Why did she always expect the worst, the wages of sin? Despite dehydration and a crushing sense of remorse, she looked flushed and content. Never underestimate the curative power of good sex. They must've been at it most of the night. Another image flashed, so compelling that she saw it in black-and-white: she straddling him, her hair falling onto his face as she rocked and goaded, "Come on, come on, baby, I'm gonna get you," while groans of satisfaction came from his open mouth and his eyes rolled up in ecstasy.

She crept back into the bedroom. He was dead to the world. She spotted her dress in a pile with his clothes. Her bra was flung over a chair. Her underpants must be lost in the bedclothes. And her shoes . . . where the hell were her shoes? She shivered as she pulled on the dress. Kneeling, she began to scrounge around under the bed. Then she felt him awake, watching her. "Megan." She ignored him. "Megan." He sighed. "What are you doing? Saying your prayers?"

"I'm looking for my shoes."

"We wake up together for the first time in seventeen years and you're looking for your shoes?" She continued the search. "I think you left them in the car," he said. "Or maybe you took them off at the party. Toni might have them."

She sat back on her haunches, wiping carpet fluff from her hands. "Where's Toni?"

"Toni took Deirdre back into town. She's something. If you don't get the money for your next movie I'm gonna hire her."

"Fat chance. And where are we?"

"Someplace called the Esplanade Hotel in Fremantle."

"Oh, God."

"Your choice. I thought we should go back into town but we were . . . how can I phrase it so as not to offend your sober sensibilities? . . . in a hurry. You complained that they'd put too much chlorine in the pool. That was the only thing that stopped you from taking a dip without your swimsuit."

"Oh, God." She pulled herself up and sat on the edge of the bed, fumbling with her zipper. "Just help me zip up, will you?" She straightened her spine and held the sides of the dress against her ribs. His hand was warm as it slithered down her back. "Don't tell me you don't remember anything."

"I remember everything." His touch produced more blue-movie images, wild protestations of love, his assurances that he'd never been with another woman like her.

His hand stilled. "You're not sorry?"

"Of course I'm not sorry." It was a point of honor not to be. She was responsible for her actions drunk or sober. She wouldn't disgrace herself with morning-after whining or disavowals. If only she could find her shoes. But he'd said she'd left them in the car, hadn't he? She had to be perfectly still, still and quiet, and think it through. She sat back on the bed, pushing her spine against the wall and looking straight ahead. He put his arms behind his head and stared at the ceiling. The children's shouts from the pool were piercingly shrill.

"What are you thinking about?" he asked after a time.

"A Dorothy Parker story called 'You Were Perfectly Fine.' A drunk's friend tells her all the details of what she did the night before and begins each horrendous revelation with 'You were perfectly fine.' What else did I do?"

"You made me give the piano player a twenty-dollar tip. And you wanted to go after that columnist—Merle What's-Her-Name—but fortunately she'd already left. Who was that Burke guy in the photo with you anyway?"

"I'm sorry Deirdre saw me like that."

"She's seen worse. She's been worse herself. But since alcohol isn't her generation's drug of choice she gets very self-righteous about it." He sat up and pulled her to him. She sank down, resting her head on his lap. "Do you feel bad?" he asked, smoothing the hair back from her face. She nodded. Mostly she felt bad about Deirdre, even worse about Chrissie Burke.

"I'm sorry," she said.

"You needn't be."

"I'm sorry about everything."

He slid down and repositioned himself, so that they were eye to eye, belly to belly, saying, "So am I, baby, so am I." They made love again, slowly, with bruised tenderness.

He went to sign for the bill, she went ahead to the car, moving through the lobby with emperor's-new-clothes oblivion. How else could she get through the lobby, barefoot, in a rumpled black cocktail dress, and whisker burns bright as raspberry stains all around her mouth? The chauffeur opened the door for her but she leaned on the car roof, hot metal burning her bare arms, staring across at the marina.

"I went on holiday from here once," she told Victor as he came up beside her. She squinted against the sun. "Over to a little island called Rottnest. With Uncle Mick and Auntie Vi and all the cousins." She took a deep breath. "I'm going to leave the festival."

"That's not a good idea. Why don't we have some breakfast, take a nap, see how you feel?"

"No."

"The reviews will be in the papers. I know they'll be good."

"I'll hate them. Even if they're good I'll hate them."

"I thought we could . . ."

"Just take me back to the hotel. I'm going to collect my things. I'm going home."

CHAPTER
FIFTEEN

"MICK. HEY, MICK!" VI CALLED FROM THE VERANDA. "GET a move on, will you? She's here."

"Hold your horses," a voice bellowed back.

Megan looked beyond the vegetable garden, the yard littered with grandchildren's toys, the brick barbecue, the chicken coops, the dunny with the sagging door, and into the dense tangle of trees. A dog of indeterminate breed trotted out and moments later Mick appeared. He carried two large plastic buckets and was dressed in shorts and singlet, high-topped boots with the laces partially done up and a battered hat. His steel-rimmed glasses caught the afternoon sun. She was struck by how much alike Mick and Vi had come to look. Both had faces deeply grooved by a lifetime spent out of doors and their bodies had the same stringy musculature that, from a distance, gave the lie to the fact that they were in their mid-sixties.

"Look at the silly bugger," Vi said, running her hand through the last of a disastrous home perm. "He's got a crook back but he insists on lugging those buckets." Mick reached the veranda, put the buckets down and stared up at Megan.

" 'S'truth," he said as his eyes began to mist, "it's hotter than the hobs of hell, i'n't it?" Megan ran down the steps and threw her arms around him. He gave her a rough, self-conscious hug.

"She looks well, doesn't she?" Vi asked, swatting a blowfly with a rolled-up newspaper.

"Turned out better than I thought she would," Mick said. "She used to be plain as a picket fence." Megan laughed. She had left the world of caviar canapés and darling-you-look-divine; here it was two veggies and a hunk of meat for dinner and she was plain as a picket fence.

"How's your mother?" Mick asked.

"I saw her in Los Angeles. She's fine. Well . . ." No more than a shrug was needed to convey Irene's discontents.

"Right. And your brother, Michael?"

"Haven't seen him in ages. He's working in a parish in New Mexico."

"And your father?"

"You mean George?"

"No, I meant Tom Shelby."

"You know I haven't seen him since I was in college. God only knows where he is."

He nodded, working his tongue around his teeth. "They could have made a go of it if they'd come back here. This was where a bloke like your father belonged, out here in the bush where he wouldn't have to take orders from anyone."

She disengaged herself and looked at the plants swaying in the buckets of water. "What're these?"

"Mick's raising tropical fish and aquarium plants," Vi explained. "It's his new hobby."

"It was supposed to be a business," Mick said, "but she's right to say it's a hobby. Sell 'em to a chap in the city. So far we haven't made a brass farthing."

"Keeps him busy. That and keeping the bush away from the door, which is about as hopeless as bailing out the ocean with a spoon. He's too old for it, but try and tell him."

Mick ignored this. "You change out of those fancy boots of yours, Megan, and I'll show you the fish ponds, walk you around the property."

"Don't worry about the boots. Let's go," Megan said. "Unless you want me to help in the kitchen, Vi."

"No. You go on with Mick. Our mob will all be here soon and I don't have to bother with much. They'll all bring something."

"Just as well." Mick winked at Megan. "If you remember, Vi cooks with religious devotion: everything's either a burnt offering or a bloody sacrifice."

Vi smacked him with the newspaper. "Get on with you."

When Mick and Megan came back the place was swarming. One little girl pushed another in the rubber tire swing, two older boys were chopping wood, an infant was chasing a chicken, a teenage girl sat on the veranda reading a book. "This is your cousin Megan from America," Mick announced and all save the infant, who found the chicken more interesting, trailed into the house after them. There were kisses and hugs, exclamations and questions as Megan went round to her cousins Moira, Jeremy, Daniel and Sean, and was introduced to their spouses, whom she'd only seen in photographs. Moira held a newborn. Daniel's wife, Muriel, was pregnant with their third. Megan was introduced to the children, marveled at the genetic permutations, tried to keep their names straight and quickly forgot who belonged to whom.

"All right," Mick ordered. "Kids out of the house now. You big boys get the trestle set up on the veranda because you lot are eating out there. The rest of you off, and if I catch any of you mucking about in those fish ponds I'll have your guts for garters."

The women congregated in the kitchen, unwrapping sponge cakes rich with passion-fruit icing, lamingtons, jam tarts and Pavlova, gossiping about kids and recipes. The men grouped around the barbecue, laying out prodigious amounts of the chops and sausages that Moira's husband, a butcher, had brought. They squinted at the smoke, knocked back the beer, cursed the heat and talked in the laconic, cynical but good-natured fashion that Megan remembered from her childhood. The topics were also similar: the Americans and the Japanese were taking over the country; Labour was in bed with the Liberals so you couldn't expect any help from the government; if the weather held good the farmers could make up last year's losses; old Mr. So-and-So down the road had died. Jeremy's youngest fell out of a tree, was told not to make a to-do of it and bundled off to the bathroom for first aid and a hug. The dog got hold of a link of sausage and ran off into the bush.

A meal that would have made a health food faddist faint dead away was piled onto the tables. The children ate on the veranda. The adults sat in the dining room at a large table whose scars had been camouflaged by a crocheted cloth, beneath a gallery of tobacco-colored family photographs. The largest of these was of Great-grandmother Kathleen and her first husband, Gareth.

Though Kathleen was not a pretty woman, her face was made beautiful with shameless love. But it was another picture that captured Megan's attention: Kathleen astride a horse that wore a wreath of wildflowers and drew a little cart loaded with pots and pans. Kathleen's eyes were sharp in this one, her mouth drawn down in fierce determination.

"Lillypond," Megan said.

"Right." Mick nodded, spearing a pickled onion. "Lillypond was the real love of Kathleen's life."

"How could you love a horse better than a person?" asked a girl who'd wandered in, hoping to be first in line for dessert. It was obvious she'd heard the story before and her question was a prompt to hear it again.

"We aren't responsible for what we love," Mick told her. "Might as well blame a compass for pointing north as blame people for what they love. Lillypond was Kathleen's hope of having a business of her own, so she loved him."

"But start with how she loved Gareth," the girl, who had more conventional ideas about love, demanded.

"Well . . ." Mick pushed back his plate. "Gareth was a fine cut of a man and he'd raised horses back in Ireland. He came to Australia in a bit of a hurry and in reduced circumstances, having escaped from the Cork constabulary. Kathleen's parents ran a boardinghouse in Sydney, the Harp of Erin it was called, and that was where Gareth stayed. Kathleen was only sixteen at the time and she was horse mad. Gareth took her for buggy rides, he took her to the races, he promised her rings on her fingers and bells on her toes, said she'd be a fine lady upon a white horse."

"Did he own stables?" the girl asked.

"No, luv, he was a bookie. And he ran into some troubles with the Sydney constabulary, so it was off to Western Australia and Kathleen running along with him. They were up against it, short of cash, and Gareth took a job felling trees at the lumber mill in Mornington. They were still planning to raise horses, you see, but then Gareth was killed by a falling tree. So Kathleen was left with three kiddies—my mother, Henrietta, and two boys—one died with diphtheria and the other with scarlet fever." The moon-faced infant who'd been chasing the chicken toddled in, studied Megan for a moment and crawled up onto her lap. "Now," Mick continued, "after Kathleen's widow's pension ran out she went off with a woman friend and set up a little shop in the bush. It was only a couple of miles from the single men's settlement, so rumors started that they were running a brothel."

"What's a brothel?" Jeremy's eldest boy, who was scraping passion-fruit icing from the side of the plate, wanted to know.

"You'll find out when you're older," Jeremy said.

"I should hope not," his wife scolded.

"A brothel is a capitalist enterprise employing women," Mick told him. "Now let's get on with it, who's telling this story?"

"You are, as usual," Vi yelled from the kitchen. "Not that we haven't all heard it before."

"You remember Kathleen," Mick said to Megan. "Anyone who knew her would split his sides at the idea of her running a brothel. Holy as a month of Sundays she was and you'd have needed a crowbar to pry a smile out of her."

"If I'd lived that life I don't suppose I'd be smiling much either."

"Yes, she was a battler. Not like you lot." He stared at his sons and daughter disparagingly. "Union wages and worrying about your VCRs. If it hadn't been for men like Gareth you wouldn't have any unions."

"Ah, the unions are what's keeping the country back," Daniel, who owned a small appliance store, protested.

"Get back to the horse," the girl reminded him.

Mick paused until he had their complete attention. "So there she was, out in the bush with her girlfriend and the kiddies, trying to make a go of it, and one day Lillypond and One Lamp Louie wandered by. Louie, called 'one lamp' because he'd lost an eye, had a gypsy cart. Louie took a shine to Kathleen and Kathleen took a shine to Lillypond. She saw an opportunity to take the goods to the customers instead of having the customers come to the goods. So she promised to honor and obey . . ."

"And had no intention of doing either," Vi hollered from the kitchen.

"And they lived happily ever after?" the girl, who'd now draped her arm around Megan's shoulder, asked.

"Not exactly. But they made a go of it. They collected bottles and sold pots and pans, cigarettes, newspapers and homemade plonk. At last Kathleen had her nest egg and wanted to settle down. She bought this property we're on now, but without letting Louie know. Louie was a traveling man, he was in love with long distance. Kathleen called him the Wandering Jew and there's a possibility he might have been of the Hebrew persuasion, at least that was Kathleen's explanation of the fact that he had a wanderlust, never went to Mass and accused her of being priest-ridden. Anyway, he went off to Kalgoorlie to pan for gold. Kathleen always said she didn't miss him, but she did pine for Lillypond. When she heard Louie had died she went up to Kalgoorlie to look for the horse but couldn't find him. So she had a headstone made with a man and a horse on it and the inscription 'Whither Goest Thou?' I don't know if that was about Lillypond being lost or her comment on Louie's chances in the life beyond." Everyone laughed. "You've never seen that headstone, have you, Megan?"

"No."

"I'll be driving up that way next week," Jeremy said. "You could come along."

"I'd like to, but I can't. I'm only staying here for a couple of days, then I have to go back to town. I have a meeting with Dennis Danher."

"Why would you want to meet with him?" Mick asked. "He prints nothing but rubbish, pictures of bare-breasted women, and crime and drug nonsense."

"Have a brain, Mick," Vi said as she carried in the pot of tea. "She needs money to get this next film started. She wouldn't be likely to get it from any of us."

"You'll want to watch your step with a bloke like Danher," Mick cautioned. "He'd take a worm off a sick hen."

"Does it cost a lot of money to make a movie?" the girl at her side asked.

"Yes. Lots and lots."

"As much as to build a house?"

"A lot more."

"I'd rather build a house," the girl said.

"Don't be dumb." Her brother punched her. "I saw *E.T.* three times. It was better than a house."

"Even when we were little I knew you'd do something special," cousin Moira told her.

"And Mum told us you're up for an Academy Award," Sean put in. "When will that be?"

"A couple of weeks from now. But I don't expect to get it."

"Why wouldn't you get it?" Sean's wife demanded. "You're as good as any of them. Better."

"Don't be telling her that," Mick said. "She'll be putting too high a price on herself. She's always been cocky as a dog with two tails."

Ah, the Aussie psychic balance: you're as good as anybody/ don't put too high a price on yourself. Megan smiled in recognition. Though she hadn't planned to discuss it, she found herself telling them about the reediting of *Chappy.* They were instantly indignant. They might not gush and tell her that they were proud of her, might never bother to see her work, but if there was a hint that someone had done her wrong they would close ranks, give her unconditional loyalty. It made her feel like the kid who'd fallen out of the tree and had his cuts bandaged up, had it kissed better. Vi poured another round of bladder-distending tea while they asked her more about the movie business and what it was like to live in New York, then Vi ordered the children out and the women began to clean up. Megan volunteered to help but the women turned her away as though someone of her accomplishments shouldn't be bothered with household chores. She sat on the veranda with the men and the children, watching the last golden glow of sunset tint the tops of the trees. Daniel mentioned that a unit had become available on their block and urged Mick to sell up and move into town.

"You hear that, Mick?" Vi, whose hearing was amazingly acute, yelled over the clatter of dishes.

"I hear it but I choose to ignore it," Mick yelled back. "But if you want to live cheek by jowl and look out on nothing but a garage and a mangy rose bush, you're free to go. I'm not stopping you."

"He's stubborn as Paddy's pig," Jeremy whispered to Megan. "His back gives him pain all the time but he won't admit it.

And they're too old to be out here in the bush. We'd all feel better if they sold up and moved in closer to us. The real estate market is good now and . . .''

Mick growled, ''Bugger the real estate market. Where would the lot of you congregate if we didn't have this place? It's family property, you all have a share in it.''

''And we could use that share in cash,'' Jeremy said.

''You have money, you'll just spend it. You have land, you always have it. You take care of it,'' Mick declared.

''Will you give us a poem, Uncle Mick?'' Megan asked.

''Which will you have?''

Daniel suggested ''Andy's Gone with Cattle.''

Moira came out of the kitchen and wiped the mouth of the squirming infant with a wet cloth. ''Do the one about the aborigines, Dad. 'The Last of His Tribe.' ''

''No, that's too sad.'' Sean's wife joined them and sat on the steps.

''Right. It'd remind me of m'self,'' Mick said.

Megan suggested, ''How about the one about the kookaburras?''

The kitchen tap was turned off, the dishes stilled. Vi came out with another pot of tea. Moira went to the end of the veranda and gave her baby the breast.

'' 'Fall the shadows on the gullies; fade the purple from the mountains . . .' '' Mick began, and Megan let her head loll back, watched the enveloping darkness and felt content, with just a touch of sadness. When Mick went, all the stories and the poems would go with him, their history would become a blur unless Moira or one of the cousins' wives took up the current fad of researching the family genealogy. But a family tree on a piece of paper wouldn't be the same thing. That wouldn't tell you that Kathleen had fallen in love on a buggy ride and was horse crazy, that Kathleen's grandfather had been an emancipationist who'd won the Harp of Erin in a card game, that his brother had died on the gulf expedition with Burke and Wills, or his sister, Henrietta, had been so ashamed of her flaming red hair that she'd cut it all off and had to wear a bonnet, that Uncle Jack had come back from the First World War without his legs and finished himself off with a single bullet. She loved these familiar ghosts. Had they not fought and gambled, birthed and buried their young, cleared the bush and battled the bosses, none of them would be sitting here now. It was this connection with the past, her sense of gratitude and debt, that made her want to make the movie, to honor and give life to what had come before.

Mick answered another request, and then another, his voice becoming less expressive as he struggled with the marathon task of getting out the long verse stories. Daniel found an ashtray and, over his wife's objection, began to smoke. Sean nodded off. As Mick got a run on "The Man from Snowy River," Jeremy's son, who sat cross-legged at Megan's feet, grumbled, "I wish we had a TV." Reciting poetry was a form of entertainment that belonged to another century. The other children became restive. Finally the women gathered up shoes and toys and went back into the kitchen to claim foil-wrapped leftovers. The men went to the cars. In the glare of impatient headlights, they hugged and said good-bye, good luck and when would they see Megan again?

"I'll show you the bathroom." Vi yawned. "We thought about you when it was being built on, how you used to whine about emptying the chamber pots."

Megan was given fresh towels and shown to her room, which was already occupied by Daniel's oldest girl; she'd convinced her parents to let her stay the night.

Mick leaned against the door frame. "It's good to have you back," he said.

"It's good to be back." Megan yawned and, kissing him, closed the door. She pulled off her clothes and slid into bed in her panties and T-shirt, careful not to wake the sleeping girl. She could hear Mick and Vi in the adjoining room, still grousing at each other as they undressed, then Vi's quick, muffled laugh, and the squeak of rusty bed springs accepting their weight. What would it be like to sleep with the same person for your entire adult life? That was almost as outdated as reciting poetry. It was completely quiet except for unidentifiable bush sounds and the sounds of the house itself, contracting from the heat of the day, the walls and floorboards creaking, settling in for the night. She stroked the girl's head, turned on her side and slept.

When the phone rang she reached for it, her hand dropping

through space to hit the floorboard. She thought she'd imagined the ring and went back to sleep. A shaft of light from the door brought her to. "Tell 'em I'll call back," she muttered.

"It's your mother," Mick said. "You'd better get up. Your father's been in an accident."

She sat on the veranda nursing her second cup of instant coffee, listening to the bush wake up, watching the light change the trees and bushes into recognizable shapes, smelling the bacon and toast she'd refused but Vi had insisted on fixing anyway.

"I can't possibly go," she said, and when Mick said nothing added, "My chances of getting a booking and making connections on the airlines . . ."

"Surely the people who arranged the festival could arrange a flight for you," Vi suggested, setting the plate before her. "You could call your friend Toni now. She could be on to them by the time you got back to town."

"And there's the meeting with Danher. I can't miss that." When neither Mick nor Vi deigned to comment, Megan's voice hardened with self-justification. "And I've told you I haven't seen Thomas Shelby since I was in college. I simply can't imagine how Irene knew where he was. She's never let on that they were in touch, so how could she possibly have found out that he was in this car wreck in Arizona?" Even in shock she'd had the presence of mind to ask that question but Irene had ignored it, giving her a list of Thomas Shelby's injuries instead, saying that she was catching the next flight out of L.A. to go to him, then Irene's voice had trailed off with "I don't suppose you could come," to which Megan had said, "Probably not," though the hopeless way Irene had said it, the very absence of a plea, forced Megan to add, "But I'll see about it. I'll call you back."

She picked up a piece of bacon, shaking her head, first with incredulity, then with conviction. "I simply can't go." Then she added, though it had nothing to do with anything, "What time is it?"

"She said the doctors said he may be dying," Mick reminded her. When she said nothing he got up, took a rasher of bacon from her plate and chewed on it as he looked out at the bush. A peal of kookaburra laughter rang out.

"It's going to be another scorcher," he predicted, then, "Tom Shelby helped me clear that patch down near where the fish ponds are now. I thought he was just trying to impress Irene at first, but he seemed to like it. He wasn't afraid of hard work."

Megan drew in a breath, ready to explain herself again, but Mick, without looking at her, issued a couple of simple sentences that sealed the issue: "She'll need you. He's your father."

Megan was absolutely still. "Yes." Simultaneously issuing and obeying her own directive, she got up from the chair. "I'll call Toni. I'll get my things."

CHAPTER
SIXTEEN

GRETA SAT IN HER ROCKING CHAIR, HER BREATHING shallow but regular, her detachment disturbed only by a desire to paint the light that washed the bedroom wall. It had changed from rosy gold to blue-grey. Lovely really. But she couldn't get up and paint because she had to wait for Tas. She didn't mind waiting now that she knew everything would be all right, or at least that things would be as they'd always been, which amounted to much the same thing.

Her actions of the previous day seemed unreal. Had she driven into town to seek out Tas, gone to Megan's hotel, broken down in church, with a nun, no less? She hoped she hadn't upset the children. She must stop calling them children. David and Colin were grown men and had treated her as such when she'd finally come home, ignoring the fact that she'd missed dinner and that her eyes were all but swollen shut. Chrissie had sighed, asked, "What's he done now?" and offered to make her tea, but had seemed relieved when Greta had told her to go back to her homework. She'd told Chrissie to turn off the TV, but after putting ice on her eyes, she herself had sunk down in front of it. It was an American movie she'd already seen, about a woman who'd "found" herself (and a rich, younger lover) after going through a harrowing divorce. Discarded movie wives always bought a new wardrobe, discovered their identity and their libido, and rose phoenixlike from the ashes of failed marriages. It was so unreal as to be comforting, and she was watching, so zombie-like she half expected drool to dribble out of her mouth, when the phone rang. Chrissie grabbed it before she could and had the sense to tell Loukia that Greta was already asleep.

She wanted to go to bed but she was afraid that if she did she would start crying again. She cleaned up the kitchen and went out into the garden, grateful for the darkness, feeling the tomatoes for ripeness and wiping her tears with the back of her hand. Back in the kitchen, she began to make tomato-and-passion-fruit jam. She was stirring the pot when Tas finally called. Perhaps influenced by the TV dialogue, she said, "I know about everything. You have to come home. Now." He didn't question or deny. He just said it was impossible. It was already after eleven and he had surgery the next morning. The soonest he could get out would be the following evening. She said all right and went back to stirring the pot, her rage as scalding as the bubbling jam. Why was she tied to him by this tight cord that vibrated to his needs, never to hers? She would like to poison the jam and watch him writhing in slow and painful death, begging her forgiveness. David came in, said she was mad as a hatter to be cooking at that hour, patted her shoulder and went off to his room. When she heard him turn off Pink Floyd she showered, her sobs drowned in the rush of water, avoided looking in the mirror as she toweled herself, and went to bed.

After all the years of sleeping alone, she still reserved the larger space for him. Thinking about this, she moved from "her side" to the center of the bed, lying on her back with her hands crossed over her breast. The position reminded her of pictures of saints in coffins. All I need is a lily, she thought. She could imagine Megan Hanlon at her screening, looking sleek and triumphant, acting gracious and democratic. Easy to be gracious and democratic when everyone was telling you how great you were. Probably Tas was with her, on the sidelines, giving her bony little elbow a squeeze when no one was looking. How she hated women like Megan Hanlon. Women who aged as only successful women can, who insisted on being called Ms. and talked about sisterhood, but thought other women's husbands were fair game, women who had manicures and bank accounts, who wanted abortion on demand, who had never gagged at a smelly diaper but got on famously with your children and made them think you were inferior. She felt fat and old and lonely there in the middle of the bed. She rolled over to her side, curling up like a fetus, and began to recite the Hail Mary. ". . . Holy

Mary, mother of God, pray for us sinners (wasn't she a sinner to feel such hatred for a woman she barely knew?) . . . now and at the hour of our death (she wanted to die, except for Chrissie, she wanted to die) . . . Amen.''

By six, harsh reality and sun had invaded the room. Her night-dress clung to her, her skin looked dry and flaccid. Chrissie tapped on the door and asked if she'd like a cup of tea, but she stayed in bed until they'd all gone, then went into the kitchen. The table was littered, the sink full of dishes. She should do a painting—congealed egg yolks, discarded crusts, jam-smeared knives, soggy cereal bowls, greasy water—and call it ''Moth-erhood.'' The geranium she thought she'd destroyed when Me-gan had come to lunch had survived. Better yet, she should let rip and smear a canvas with the brilliant red of that geranium, the color of anger, blood, life. But . . . there were beds to be made, animals to be fed, the garden to be watered. If she did all that it would seem like any other day: just time to be gotten through until Tas arrived.

Edgar, the hired man, came by in the early afternoon. She wanted to hide and pretend she wasn't there, but her car was in the drive; besides, where else would she be? She brought him into the kitchen and offered him a cup of tea. He reeled off the things that needed to be done the following week and asked her to give them priorities, watching her as she did so, his eyes grazing her breasts that hung, loose and braless under one of Tas's old shirts. She hadn't bothered to comb her hair and her eyes were still puffy. His eyes, she noticed, not for the first time, were kind, inviting her to tell him what was wrong but showing no reproach when she couldn't. He might even have understood. His own wife had left him a couple of years ago not, as he was now able to joke, for greener pastures but for concrete side-walks. He had a workingman's arms and chest. How comforting it would be to rest her head on his chest, to feel strong arms around her. She poured more tea. He thanked her and said he would show himself out. She stayed where she was, sitting and staring at the linoleum until its pattern blurred. The phone rang. She picked it up before thinking that it might be Loukia, oozing concern and wanting an update. It was a woman's voice, but with an American accent. It was perhaps the strangest phone call she'd ever had.

"Hi, this is Toni Massari, Megan Hanlon's assistant. I'm sorry but the desk clerk got your number but neglected to get your name. May I ask to whom I'm speaking?"

"Greta Burke. Tasman Burke's wife." She couldn't remember leaving a message at the hotel, but clearly she must have. She'd had fire in her belly then, knowing that Megan would best her in any confrontation, but believing that when confronted, Megan would not lie.

"Yes, Mrs. Burke." There was a pause. "We met briefly when you picked Megan up to visit the nuns." Another pause. "Megan's not here. She's gone out to visit relatives."

A mumbled "I see."

A businesslike "May I help you?" but with an underlying concern in the voice.

"I saw the newspaper," Greta blurted.

She could not remember the conversational bridge that had taken them from awkward introduction to free communication, only that she could feel the other woman's confusion and fundamental honesty. And Toni said what she wanted to hear. Yes, Tas had come to the hotel—well, there was photographic evidence of that. Megan had agonized about coming out to the farm (Toni's words were "felt like shit") but, Greta must believe her, Tas and Megan had not resumed any "prior relationship"; that was all gossip-column drivel. She was further relieved when Toni assured her that anything they said would be strictly confidential and that Megan would be returning to New York in the near future.

As she'd hung up, she was foggy, but felt a sense of deliverance, as though she'd been lost in a strange and dangerous city and a Good Samaritan had come along, taken her by the hand and told her in which direction she should go. Whatever had threatened her was in the past.

She called the mother of one of Chrissie's classmates and asked if Chrissie might stay the night. When Chrissie came home, she told her that she was taking her to Muriel's because she and Tas had something important to discuss.

Why should she be packed off? Chrissie grumbled. "You and

Daddy never talk to each other, and even if you did, nothing would change.''

That, Greta secretly agreed, would be a blessing that Chrissie couldn't possibly understand. When she drove back home, she washed her hair and took up her place near the bedroom window.

She was so calm now, rocking in the growing darkness. When Tas came she would forgive him. They would make it up. Perhaps—though this was too much to hope for—they would even go to bed.

''They're all gone. We're alone,'' she would tell him. The words took her back decades, to when they'd wrestled on her parents' couch beneath that garish painting of the Acropolis. How had they managed to feel desire while always tuned to an opening door? But she'd been the one who'd always been nervous, opening her arms and legs to his urgency, always afraid of interruption or, worse yet, pregnancy. (How could little pills in pretty pastel packets prevent it?) Tas had never heard a thing.

It was only in the brief period after they'd married and before she'd started to swell up with David that she'd really enjoyed it. They'd been happy then, on the pull-out bed, planning their future, Tas praising her breasts and hair. They had both been inexperienced, though Tas had the benefit of his biology books. Tas had suggested she get a mirror and look at her clitoris, and she'd almost died of embarrassment. It wasn't until years later, when he'd come back from America, that she'd been ready for exploration and experiment. But by then, they were strangers. She remembered a quote she'd thought cynical but now understood: ''Love is not so much a sentiment as a situation.'' Their situations had always been wrong: no privacy, money worries, his long absences, the children's needs. If only . . .

His arrival was almost an interruption of her reveries. She heard his car and saw its headlights simultaneously. He did not slam the car door as he usually did, nor did he call out when he came through the kitchen. She could feel him standing in the living room. But surely he knew where she was.

It seemed a long time before the passage light was switched on and he stood at the bedroom door. ''Don't turn it on,'' she said, seeing him reach for the bedroom switch. He looked around as though he didn't know where to put himself, then sat on the bed. She would let him speak first.

He held his elbow crooked on his knee, his head in his hand. "I'm sorry I didn't get back to you until last night. I had a helluva day yesterday. Had a helluva day today. I . . ." No. No excuses. No backing away. Not this time. "You saw that damned picture in the paper."

"Yes. Loukia showed it to me."

"That meddling cow."

"Yes, she is." Her unexpected agreement caused him to lift his head, but it was too dark to see if there was anger or contrition in his eyes.

"Someone showed it to me." He couldn't bring himself to say Naomi. He wanted to say he was sorry, sorry that she, such a private woman, should suffer such a public humiliation. Sorry that he . . . but he'd been the guilty boy for years, she the forgiving mother. The pattern was worse than shameful, it was as boring as a chronic illness. He had to make a good clean cut. "I've been trying to tell you for years . . ."

"Trying to tell me you were having affairs?"

"I think you knew, Greta. You knew."

"I suppose I did. Was that my responsibility? To know and not do anything about it?"

"You didn't want to do anything about it. I asked you for a divorce when I first came back from the States."

"Yes. After your affair with Megan."

"Megan's got nothing to do with this." No equivocating. "All right, it happened. I should have told you way back then. I should have told you when you met her at the Tishmans' party. But it was in the past. I thought it meant a lot to you to have her come out here."

"Oh, it meant a lot," she said sarcastically.

"And more than that, I always considered her a friend."

"You're very sophisticated people, you and Megan, aren't you?"

"By your standards. We're just people."

"No, you're different. You're both the center of your own world." She had not meant to sound bitter, to chastise.

"Everyone's the center of his own world. Even you. It's just that you've shrunk your world to this farm, this house. Sometimes I think you've shrunk it right down to that bloody rocking chair.''

She had not realized that she was rocking. She put her foot out to steady the chair. ''The farm doesn't run itself, Tas.''

''I know that. I know you've run it, kept it all together. I've been thinking about that all week. The farm was the biggest mistake I made when I got back from the States. We hitched ourselves up like a pair of oxen—so busy, so much to do, so much to worry about that we couldn't speak or think. Good Christ! I've been in harness all my life!''

She said gently, ''You'll always be in harness, Tas. With or without me. With or without the farm. That's the way you are.''

''Look . . .'' His voice was harsh. He wouldn't let her comfort him, or define him, or suck him into her domestic torpor. ''I don't want the farm.''

What was he talking about? ''I understand about Megan. You were young. You . . .''

He hit his forehead with his fist, wanting to shout to her, to the heavens, that he still was.

''. . . you were alone. Men . . .''

''And women, too. Why didn't you?'' His fingers raked his hair in frustration. ''We lie in this bed, pretending to be asleep. We don't touch. We don't talk. It's like being buried alive.'' He thrust out his hand, formed it into a fist. ''Yes, I've fucked other women. Lots of them. Why didn't you fuck other men?''

She inwardly recoiled at the four-letter word. He was trying to shock her. Trying to justify his rejection by suggesting she should have given herself to another man. She stayed calm. ''Tas, I understand . . .''

He was on his feet. ''Why don't you admit it? Why don't you say that you hate me? That I'm a rotten father, a lousy husband, a selfish bastard?'' When she said nothing, he came closer. ''You know, I'm glad that meddling bitch of a sister of yours brought this to a head.'' She had certainly brought it to a head with Naomi. Naomi had not been happy about his affair with Megan, but she'd believed that it was over. She'd also told him in no uncertain terms that she wasn't going to wait around to become a friend. ''Why don't you admit how you feel, Greta?''

he shouted. "You hate me. I can smell it like some festering sore you keep covering up with bandages. You hate me."

"I love you. I've always loved you."

"Good God! You're like some Mexican peasant crawling on her hands and knees to the altar. Can't you see it? Can't you see any of it?" He paced, trapped between bed and wall. "You married me because you wanted to get out of your father's house, because you were afraid to face the world and go to art school, because you wanted the guaranteed love of children. And you can stop goddamn *forgiving* me because I'm not coming to confession in this house anymore. Do you understand? DO YOU UNDERSTAND?" He moved to her, took her by the shoulders and dragged her up. He was ugly, threatening. "I don't want the farm. I don't want this marriage. You must decide for once what you want. Get yourself a lawyer. Then tell me what you want. Tell me what you want and I'll give it to you. I'll give you anything except the rest of my life." He let go of her so suddenly she had to steady herself against the windowsill. Shamed at his violence, he sank down on the bed, making a sound between laughter and tears. "Christ save me from good women!"

"I'm not a good woman," she sobbed. "I know some of what you say is true. I've been a coward and yes, you're right, sometimes I do hate you. But there's still more love than hate. After all this time . . . we do have the children. We have the farm. We . . ."

"I'm in love with another woman. Naomi Tishman. I would leave even if it weren't for her. But I am leaving." He got up. In spite of himself he said, "I'm sorry."

She stood still, but felt a violent internal upheaval, as though her water had broken and she was going into labor—something unalterable had started, something over which she had no power. "No."

He went to the door, reaching for the switch again. "I'll have to turn on the light. There are some things in the closet I have to get."

"Don't." Don't turn on the light. Don't get your things. DON'T LEAVE ME. She flew across the room, hammering at his chest with her fists. He dodged, caught a blow on the neck and spun around, his mouth and eyes wide with amazement. He heaved her off and walked to the closet. She lunged, beating on his back until he grabbed her wrists and held them tight. He let go of her. She fell onto the bed, slid to the floor. He was the one breathing hard, standing at the closet, shaking. He turned and headed for the door. She reached for his ankle, caught it, let him drag her, the carpet burning her elbows, her cheek. NO. NO. NO. He stopped. "Let . . . go . . . of . . . me." He wrenched free with one powerful twist.

She lay crumpled on the floor. This was not happening. He had not walked in, yelled at her for fifteen minutes and left. He was not leaving.

She heard his car start. She pulled herself up and hurtled through the house, knocking against a wall, tearing back the front door, pushing open the screen. "Tas!" she screamed. "Tas. Get back here!" The headlights made an eerie trail down the dirt road. The dog barked furiously.

She went back to the bedroom, felt her way to the rocking chair. She was drenched with sweat. Her lungs felt as though they were filling with water and she would drown, drown in it.

CHAPTER
SEVENTEEN

THOMAS SHELBY HANLON LAY IN A BOWER OF TUBES AND machines. Irene sat by the window, knitting a baby blanket. She registered so little surprise as Megan came through the door that Megan half expected her to finish the row before acknowledging her, but Irene stuck the needles into the pale blue ball of wool and got up.

"You're here," she said as calmly as though Megan had just walked across the lawn for tea, but then she clutched her, held her tight and whispered, "Thank you for coming." She went to the side of the bed and touched Tom's fingers, gently, so as not to disturb the IV taped to his arm. "Megan's here." He didn't open his eyes. Megan walked to the end of the bed and held on to the frame. Her hands were sweaty on the icy metal, her legs felt like feathers. "I don't know if he'll wake up. He keeps going in and out of it. I think they've given him too many shots. I can't seem to get any straight answers out of the doctors."

There was a slight stiffening of his body. His eyelids twitched as though he were struggling to free himself from a bad dream, then slowly opened to look at Megan. "Hiya, kid. Long time no see. Long time no see."

She nodded. Some twenty years in fact. She wondered if he remembered the last time. His apartment in East Los Angeles. His Mexican girlfriend frying tacos. Their argument about Vietnam.

"You were mad at me the last time I saw you," he said.

So he did remember. "That was a long time ago."

"You're . . . ?" His eyes went out of focus. She half expected that he'd forgotten her name.

"Megan," she said.

"Hell, I know who you are. How could a man not know his own daughter. You're . . . you look so much like . . ."

"My mother?"

"Hell, no. Your mother was prettier." He turned his head to have Irene acknowledge the compliment, then winked at Megan. It was his I've-got-the-world-by-the-tail rogue's wink and for a moment it obliterated his receding hairline, shoulder-length grey hair, deep-socketed eyes and leathery skin and transformed him into his younger, wildly handsome self. Then his features hardened and his grin became stoic, as though he understood that if she was here he must be in worse shape than he'd thought. As the realization washed over him, he closed his eyes.

"You're wearing your hair long," Megan said. "I never thought I'd see the day when you . . ."

"If you can't beat 'em, join 'em," he said tiredly, and with his eyes still closed and a half smile playing around his lips, "Don't think I turned into one of your hippies. George Washington wore his hair long, y'know."

Megan waited, trying to find something to say, wondering if the airline had found the bag they'd lost when she'd changed planes in L.A. After a while she realized that he'd lost consciousness.

"He goes in and out," Irene said, picking up her knitting and resuming her seat near the window. Megan sank down in the chair next to her. "You must be exhausted," Irene said, then asked her how the flights had been, how long since she'd slept, how Mick and Vi were. Megan answered, then finally asked the question that had been bothering her ever since Irene's call: "How did you know he was here?"

"We've . . ." Irene counted a row of stitches. ". . . kept in touch."

Megan stared at her. Kept in touch? Since when? And for how long? Had they written or actually seen each other? And how could that have happened without Irene letting her know?

"He must've had my phone number in his wallet because the police called right after the accident. Then I called you. That was . . . was it Wednesday? Must've been Wednesday because I've been here for two days and . . . I'm staying at the Holiday Inn."

"But what about George?"

"You know George. He hates to travel. And he's been having some stomach trouble," Irene said, ignoring the larger implications of the question.

"I meant, how does George feel about your being here?"

The knitting needles clicked on. "And your brother, Michael . . . I've had a terrible time getting in touch with Michael. Well, you know him. He's never around when you need him." This, too, was said casually, as though she were complaining that Michael wasn't around to mow the lawn. "I called the rectory, but they said he was on retreat. One of those secluded places for new priests, so he couldn't be reached by phone. One of the priests sent a telegram, I think. Anyway, Michael finally called. He'll be driving in sometime this evening. It'll be nice that we'll all be together again."

And what could she say to that? "Who's the baby blanket for?"

"A new couple who moved in next door. She's about six months along. They had that new test . . ."

"Amniocentesis."

"That's it. So they know it's a boy. I think those tests take the mystery out of it, but still . . ."

At least you've got someone to knit for, Megan thought. With me as a daughter and a priest as a son you'll never have that grandchild you would have cherished. "It's pretty." She turned her head and stared out into the parking lot where cars baked and a huge American flag hung lifelessly in the hot, dry air.

Tom came to with guttural curses, asking, "Did you get the shot?" He seemed to think he'd cracked his ribs while leaping from a burning car in some long-forgotten movie. Irene bent over him, telling him that it had been another accident, a real one. "You crashed on the interstate, driving back from Texas. You were . . ." She substituted "injured" for "drunk."

"Then you didn't get the shot?" Tom demanded, clenching his teeth. "You mean I have to do it again?"

Megan made a joke about reincarnation, saying they'd all have to do it again, but Irene didn't laugh. Instead she said that Megan must be exhausted and told her to go to the motel. Megan said that *she* must be exhausted and suggested the same. They both sat down again. A nurse came in, checked the dials on the machines and made notations on Tom's chart. Megan said she wanted to talk to a doctor. The nurse said the doctor would be late with his rounds.

An early-evening breeze unfurled the flag in the parking lot just as a man came to take it down.

"Goddamn you, Mario. Haul your wop pussy," Tom muttered. "We can make it. The fuckin' medic is only . . . we can . . ." Irene explained that Tom had carried his best friend Mario on his back through enemy lines. Mario had died just as they'd reached the medic's station. "When we were first married he hardly got through the night without a combat nightmare."

The lights came on in the parking lot. Tom asked for a beer, was given a sip of water and seemed content.

Megan paced the room. "What the hell is this! We've been here all day without seeing a doctor. He's been delirious for hours and—"

"I think that's normal."

"How do we know if it's normal? I've never seen anyone like this, it's—"

"Oh, you talked silly for hours after you had your wisdom teeth out. I don't suppose you remember."

"I'm going to find a doctor. Goddamn it."

"Megan, I wish you wouldn't . . ." Not the time to reprimand cursing. "Better yet, go down and talk to the social services people. There's some sort of problem. I forgot to tell you. They told me they might have to have him moved."

"Why? To where?"

"Some bureaucratic problem. I just couldn't deal with it. But there's a nice man, a social worker, who comes in in the evenings, so if you could . . ."

"All right." Megan wobbled Tom's foot. "Daddy?" The word felt strange. She hadn't used it in years, and then only to Victor, mouthing it sarcastically when he'd tried to tell her what to do. "Daddy, can you hear me? I'm leaving for a bit."

He made no response but just as she was about to walk out he called, "Hey, Tiger, your mother tells me you're up for an

Oscar. Now don't get mushy in your acceptance speech. God only knows you can skip the part about thankin' your old man.''

"And she's going to be making another movie, a big one, in Australia," Irene said. "It's going to be wonderful."

"I don't have the financing yet," Megan began, but changed her mind. "Yes. Yes, Daddy. I'm going to make another movie."

"You gotta give 'em some action. That's what people want to see," Tom instructed. "But you keep at it." His right hand untangled itself from the sheet and formed a fist, thumb up. His eyes held hers. "You do that, right? You do that." It was an order. She was now the keeper of the flame, the one who would signal the future. Her failure would leave them all flat.

"Righto, Daddy."

She found the cafeteria on the ground floor and lost her appetite when she smelled it. Taking a cup of watery coffee, she found the social services office and sat on a bench next to a twitching, chain-smoking vet who told her, though she hadn't asked, about his drug-support group. She accepted one of his cigarettes and found herself shredding it into an ashtray. A belligerent-looking black security guard told her that she was next.

The social worker shuffled through a pile of papers and told her that since her father's injuries were not war-related, there was a ceiling on the amount of care the VA would provide. If Thomas Shelby Hanlon came out of intensive care, he would have to be moved to another facility at his own expense. The "if" short-circuited her brain. She asked him to repeat what he'd just said, and explained that as far as she knew, her father didn't have any money. The alternative, the social worker said without looking up at her, would be for her father to dispose of any assets and go on welfare. He rooted around in the desk and pushed some forms toward her. She heard herself shrieking, "His whole life is a war-related injury, you son of a bitch. He's a war hero. A goddamn patriot. You can't just throw him out. We've been sitting up there in that grubby little room and no doctor has so much as put his head in the door. How dare you! How dare you say that you'll throw him out!"

The security guard opened the door, ready to intervene. The social worker told him everything was under control, shut the door and put his hand on her shoulder. He poured her a glass of water and cleared his throat. Don't say it, she begged mentally, but he did: he didn't make the policy. Personally he agreed with her. He would do what he could. He would talk to his supervisor. She downed the water and carefully placed the cup on the edge of his desk, apologizing for calling him a son of a bitch. He said he didn't take any of it personally anymore.

When she went back upstairs, Tom was still rambling, talking about seeing the ocean for the first time.

Finally, a doctor came in. He answered Megan's questions, then said they'd stayed long enough. Tom was unconscious and didn't notice when they left.

Around eleven, she and Irene lay side by side, fully clothed, on a double bed in the Holiday Inn. How much, Irene wanted to know, did she remember of the early years? "I remember the bedroom in the apartment in Panorama City. How, at night, when I was in bed, I would watch the headlights from cars come along the wall near my door. The sound of the motor was loudest just as the lights hit the window." She did not say that she also remembered the horrible fights or Irene creeping into her bed when she thought she was asleep. "I think I'll take a shower," she said.

After she'd showered she put her clothes back on. She had a premonition that they'd be called at any minute, and wanted to be prepared. She sniffed her dress. The Joy she'd bought at dutyfree almost covered its funky smell.

"I think I'll go the bar and have a drink," she told Irene. She had an upper in her purse and, good sense be damned, planned to take it with a double Scotch. "Want to come?"

"Good heavens, no." Irene had taken off her dress and stockings. She was propped up on the pillow, wearing a mauve-colored slip Megan had given her perhaps ten years ago. The lace on the front had been carefully darned. Thrift and maintenance: habits Megan had long ago abandoned.

"If you're not asleep when I get back, I'll give you a back rub."

"That'd be nice. I won't be asleep. I haven't asked you anything about your trip. Did it go well?"

She didn't want to talk about her trip. Didn't want to talk

about anything. "Too soon to tell. Go on, have a nice bath. That'll relax you. Take your bath and get into your nightdress." Her voice had the same tone, firm but affectionate, that Irene had used with her when she was a child. And Irene responded as Megan once had: she got up slowly and grudgingly, waiting for the touch that would ease compliance.

"Come on." Megan patted Irene's bottom. "Into the bath with you." She forced her swollen feet into her shoes and checked the contents of her handbag. She'd been doing that all day, touching her wallet, keys, passport, makeup bag; then again fifteen minutes later, thinking she'd lost them. "You'd best be asleep when I get back."

"I don't think I can sleep. But you have to. Oh, please check at the desk and see if there's any word from Michael. He was supposed to be here ages ago."

"It's the Holiday Inn, Mom, not the Helmsley Palace. I don't think they're too conscientious about messages."

"But if the hospital called . . . They might at least have the decency."

"I'll call the hospital when I get back." Might at least have the decency. That was something Megan had heard throughout her childhood. Over the years she'd applied it to a steadily diminishing number of people and situations. But, at bottom, Irene was an Aussie country girl. Experience hadn't made a dent in her expectation of decency. Megan looked at her as Irene stopped near the bureau, her hands thrust into her hair, staring at her face in the mirror. "Oh," Irene sighed, "it'd take a bucket of cement to fill these wrinkles." It was true that Irene looked old. Older than Megan had ever seen her look before. But her upraised arms lifted her bosom and flattened her stomach, and in the dim light Megan saw her as a younger woman, pretty and sexy enough to turn Thomas Shelby's head. "You can help me with my makeup in the morning, Megan. It upsets your father if I don't look my best." Megan felt like she was in a time warp, that her mother had obliterated the terrible fights, the divorce, the fact that she had another husband. And why not? He was the love of her life. Again she was tempted to ask how long Irene and Tom had been in touch; instead she asked, "Has Daddy seen any of my movies?"

"He saw a commercial you directed years ago."

"But . . ."

"No. You said yourself that documentaries don't get distribution."

"Right." Megan opened the door.

"He's terribly proud of you. Terribly proud."

"Right."

There was a hand-lettered sign propped up at the entrance to the cocktail lounge, showing a martini glass with bubbles coming out of it and promising that Happy Hour would be extended till midnight. Judging from the noise, a lot of locals had been attracted by the promise of bargain drinks. Megan paused, wondering if she could get a Scotch to go or if she'd just order and walk out with the glass. Looking across the lobby, she saw a tall, bearded man in jeans and cowboy boots filling out a registration form. The clerk leaned across the desk flirtatiously, chin in hand, trying to read his name.

"Michael!"

He turned and opened his arms to her. The clerk, disappointed, looked away. Megan, eyes closed, put her head against her brother's chest. It was hard to believe that Michael had become a priest. True, he'd always gone to Mass, even in those lost years after Vietnam when he'd stayed in George and Irene's garage, drinking beer and watching TV, taking odd jobs, disappearing for weeks in his pickup truck. But he'd been even more critical of the Church than she. She supposed his decision to enter the priesthood was a lifelong penance for whatever he'd done in Vietnam, though she had no clear idea what that was because he refused to talk about it. He'd collected as many medals as Tom had in World War II, and though he'd turned against the war, he still kept them in a velvet-lined box. But he disparaged them, saying that the army now handed out medals like cookies at a kids' Christmas party. But even allowing for their inflated value, he couldn't have been so decorated without seeing a lot of action. He now worked in a miserably poor parish in Nogales, New Mexico. Being his father's son he'd been in trouble with the hierarchy almost from the time of his ordination. Again, being his father's son, that suited him just fine. The last time they'd met, he'd complained that his diocese didn't give enough support to the poor, that the Church was hedging its bets in Latin America and that Pope John Paul and Mick Jagger had the same press agent.

Megan pulled back to look at him. He'd inherited very little from Irene—a few auburn streaks in his beard, a delicately molded nose. Otherwise, he was Thomas Shelby to a tee. He looked more like a trucker or a carpenter than a priest. It seemed unfair that he didn't wear his collar as a warning to interested women. But even in the days when he'd slept with women, none of his liaisons had developed into a real relationship. Irene was the only woman he'd ever wanted to please, though he'd been in constant rebellion against her wishes. He was radical enough to say that women should be admitted to the priesthood, but Megan thought that, at bottom, he was afraid of women, and believed that they would draw him into a vortex of either conformity or lust. They joined hands and moved to the vinyl couch near the potted plant.

"How is . . ."—he couldn't quite bring himself to say Dad—"he?"

"It took all day for a doctor to put his head in the door and I'm afraid I didn't really take in what he had to say."

"You flew in all the way from Australia, didn't you?"

"Yeah. I'm kinda punchy. The doctor said something about a ruptured spleen. Can you die of a ruptured spleen? And several broken ribs—one of them punctured his lung. There's tubes up his nose and IVs in his arms. He's all hooked up to machines. Victor arrives back in L.A. tomorrow. I'm going to call him and see if he can find out the name of a first-class doctor here. Oh, and his heart. His heart's just fine. Would you believe! After a lifetime of nicotine and booze?"

"It's not all in the science books, sister. You mentioned Victor. Do you mean your ex? Don't tell me you're seeing him again."

She shrugged and asked a few of her own questions. Why had it taken him so long to get here? Did he have any idea about their father's finances? Had he known that Tom and Irene had been in touch?

"I'm sorry I couldn't get here sooner," he said, staring down at the ugly gold and brown carpet. "Someone at the rectory told Mom I was off on retreat. That's not exactly the whole story." He lowered his voice. "See, I was really driving this Salvadoran woman to a safe house in L.A. It took the people in Nogales a while to get in touch with me. I don't want to worry Mom by telling her what I'm up to. I mean, what's the point? Ever hear of the Sanctuary movement?" She nodded. Sanctuary brought undocumented political refugees into the country. Several nuns, priests and church members had already been indicted. Don't tell me this, she thought. You're in the right and I'm on your side, but we can't deal with any more complications. "You're just like him," she said as she got up, hearing her mother's voice. "C'mon. I need a drink."

"Maybe you're the one who's just like him."

"Whatever. Let's go into the lounge."

"I don't drink anymore, remember?"

How could she have forgotten the year of AA that had preceded Michael's decision to enter the priesthood? Irene had told her all about it. "Sorry. I . . ."

"That's okay. I'll sit with you." He looked at her dubiously, picked up his bag and followed.

The lounge was so crowded they decided to sit at the bar. She ordered her double Scotch, Michael said he'd take a club soda with a slice of lemon. She rummaged in her purse and found the upper.

"How's Mom?" he asked.

"She's taking a bath." She popped the upper into her mouth and washed it down. Michael either didn't see, or pretended not to. "You know she's still in love with him? After all these years."

"Yeah. Call it love . . ."

"That's what I call it."

"You know there are worse things than him not pulling through. Have you considered what would happen if he lives but he just can't *go* anymore? Who'd take care of him? You think Mom's gonna leave George and play nurse in a trailer park in Phoenix?"

She watched as he up-ended his glass and chug-a-lugged as though it were booze. "Do you still hate him?"

"I never hated him. 'Cept when he hit her. And that's so far back sometimes I'm not sure if I imagined it. I tried to think of George as my father, but George . . ." He took the last gulp. "Naw, George is okay. He's more than okay. But like you said about his heart still pumping away . . . He's like those big old Chevy and Ford gas guzzlers he used to drive: bashed-up body, cracked-up windshield, bald tires, but hey, that chrome, those fins, that power!" He watched the bartender pour out a straight tequila, slid one leg off the stool, so that he was half standing. "If you've finished your drink . . ."

She hadn't, but she did.

As they crossed the lobby, the girl at the desk called after her. "Oh, ma'am? Aren't you in room five-oh-two with Mrs. Shrivers?"

Megan stopped, ready to throw down her credit cards to stop any questions about doubling up on the room. "There's a message for five-oh-two," the girl said, turning her eyes to Michael. "I tried to call but there's no answer."

"She probably in the bathroom." Megan held out her hand for the slip of paper. It was from the hospital. Please call back.

She suddenly felt woozy, though the pill and the Scotch had barely had time to take effect. As they left the lobby and skirted the swimming pool, she stared down into the illuminated water and held on to Michael's arm. She handed him the key, and as he unlocked the door, Irene, who had fallen asleep, her knitting on her lap, automatically reached for the sheet to cover the front of her nightdress. "Oh, son. You're here." She went to Michael and hugged him and began to sob. Megan dialed the hospital. The phone rang at least twelve times before the switchboard picked up. She asked for intensive care, then waited again, playing with the Gideon Bible on the nightstand. It had been a long time since she'd been in a motel with a Gideon Bible. Irene sank to the edge of the bed, watching her. Michael went into the bathroom. A woman's voice came on the line, stifling laughter to say "Een-ten-seef care." Megan explained who she was and waited yet again. She could hear the woman cover the mouthpiece and ask for Dr. So-and-So. The toilet flushed. As Michael came out of the bathroom the woman came back on the line. "You say you're Meester Hanlon's daughter, yes?"

"That's right. Yes. Yes, I am."

"I'm reely sorry. He pass away. Some hour ago."

There were nine of them at the funeral: Megan, Irene, Michael, three men from the funeral home, a priest, and two men from the Veterans of Foreign Wars. Megan had called the VFW because Irene said Tom would have wanted some representative of the military to be there. An old man, probably the same old man who now stood at attention next to the flag-draped coffin holding a Sony tape recorder to his chest, had answered and said that they'd be there.

The place looked more like a neglected golf course than a cemetery. There were no tombstones, only small brass plaques set into the ground. There was no greenery except the shrubbery that separated the grounds from the freeway and somewhat muffled the sound of the passing cars. Michael was wearing his black suit and collar, but looked uncomfortable in them, as though he were an actor priest. Megan also felt like she was wearing a costume. She'd gone to a shopping mall and bought a navy blue dress with a Peter Pan collar, without even trying it on. Irene wore a tailored black suit. She looked calm, even elegant. She had slept for over twelve hours as soon as she'd heard the news.

The priest finished the prayer. The youngest mortician turned and walked to the hearse, taking out a cigarette. The old veteran punched the button on the Sony, and taps drifted out into the hot, dry air. When it was over, he put the tape recorder on the ground and moved to the coffin. He and the other veteran took the ends of the flag. They held it taut, then, like a couple folding a sheet in a Laundromat, they shook it once, then folded it, end over end, carefully, into a triangle. With creaking dignity that brought tears to Megan's eyes, he presented it to Irene. She took it with the slightest nod, like a queen accepting a token from a foreign dignitary.

CHAPTER
EIGHTEEN

TONI PULLED THE PILLOW OVER HER EAR. SOMETHING insistent and metallic was scraping holes in her sleep. "So . . . you're . . . finally . . . awake." Joe was perched on his Exercycle. Physical exertion made his breath come out in angry-sounding puffs.

Toni yawned. "Yeah, but I'm going right back to sleep, if you can put off turning the bedroom into Joe's gym for a couple of hours." He reminded her that it was almost noon. She reminded him that, for her, it was about four in the morning.

Not wanting to lose money by changing her airline booking, and hoping she could salvage something from the trip, she'd stayed on for the extra week in Perth, taking meetings that, without Megan around, were only taking up people's time. The closest she'd got to Danher was a lunch with his secretary, who was none too sanguine about the possibility of Danher's interest. No, he hadn't read the script, but he had met Megan at a party and found her "temperamental." Victor had taken her to dinner before he'd gone off to see about some real estate investment in the southwest, but Deirdre had sulked so much that the evening was ruined. She'd trailed through tourist shops, taken in Nita Narinto's play, met with a union representative and listened to his rules and regulations until her eyes had crossed. By the end of the week, not even room service was enough to cheer her. When she'd looked over their finances, she'd felt even worse. A damned expensive trip to see a bunch of art-house movies. It was GO BACK TO GO. She'd turned down another dinner invitation from Matthew White. She couldn't trust herself to forgo sexual comfort when she was feeling this low. She'd crossed the ocean sitting next to a high school surfing team on its way to competition in California. Needless to say, she hadn't gotten any sleep. She'd stayed only one night in L.A. Megan had decided not to come back to New York before the Academy Awards. Irene needed her. From the looks of her, Megan needed someone herself. But when she'd called Joe, he'd said how much he'd missed her, that they were all expecting her home. So home she'd come.

Joe stopped pedaling and leaned on the handlebars. "All this traveling around, Toni. It's thrown everything out of balance."

She looked at the dirty laundry in one corner, the pile of old *New York Times*es near Joe's nightstand, the dead African violets he'd promised to water. "I can see that it has, but right now, I'm not gonna cope."

"Don't forget that Giovanna and Brad are coming out from the city at three."

"I know. I know." A family dinner had been planned. Apparently no one had thought that she might like to be taken out instead of cooking. She looked past the corpses of the African violets through the window. The sky was pewter-colored, chilly. "It was so warm in Australia," she muttered, pulling the blankets to her chin and burrowing down. From the adjoining bedroom, Mario's electric guitar was tuning up. "Oh, shit. There are worse things than the empty-nest syndrome."

Joe climbed off the Exercycle, pulling his sweatshirt over his paunch, and padded over to sit on the edge of the bed. "They haven't said a word about moving out," he said in a harsh whisper. "You've gotta talk to them."

"Why didn't you?"

"I was waiting till you got back." He grimaced as "Rock Around the Clock" started up. "We dressed that kid in little blue blazers with gold buttons from the time he was four years old. Now he thinks he's gonna be a country-western star."

She wiped the perspiration from his forehead with the hem of the sheet. "Stranger things have happened. Sylvester Stallone was never in the army and he got to be Rambo."

"I remember when Mario was about ten and you bought him his first guitar."

"Yeah, and when he was five I bought him an Erecter set, but he didn't become an architect."

"We should never have let him drop out of college."

"He flunked out, Joe. Two semesters in a row. We lectured, we scolded, we begged. I don't see what else we could've done. But you're right: he's got to see about getting a job. If he's agreeable, I think Johnny can find him some work in his construction business."

"We're not going to give your brother the satisfaction of thinking our son's a failure. We're not crawling to Johnny on our hands and knees."

"I think I can manage it in an upright position." Add that to the list of things to do: get Mario a job. "In the meantime, if they're getting on your nerves . . ."

"Getting on my nerves!" he exploded. "It's like you say, they're playing house, but it's our house. Every time I turn around they're draped all over each other. I don't think either of them has the power to stand up alone. And you know why the house is in such a mess?"

"Because none of you cleaned it up?" she ventured.

"Because Mary Lou was asleep when the cleaning woman came and the doors were locked. I've never seen a girl who could sleep so much."

"It beats the rehearsal sessions."

"And she has the heat turned up to ninety degrees because she's always running around barefoot. You know what our heating bill is gonna look like?"

"That's why I bought her those sheepskin slippers from Australia," she said in another attempt to jolly him out of his foul mood. She massaged the back of his neck. It was sweaty. "Look, why don't you go take a shower, then come back to bed?"

"I don't feel right, getting into bed with you in the middle of the day with them around."

"Tell you what, why don't we offer to let them have the house in Vermont for a couple of months? That would get them out of our hair and maybe they'd get themselves sorted out up there."

"Sure. Sure. Then we'd lose out on the money we'd get if we were renting it *plus* pick up an astronomical heating bill."

"Joe." She sat up, pulling down her rucked nightdress. "You give me a problem, I give you a potential solution, and you don't even consider it before you tell me why it won't work. You think

I'm not worried about Mario? You think I'm not angry with him?
He's not . . ."

"I know what he's not; tell me what he is."

"He's not mean-spirited or greedy. It probably doesn't even
occur to him that we're picking up the tab. We didn't think we
were spoiling him, but somehow we have. I don't know. I don't
know what's wrong with people nowadays. Especially the young
men. Either they're barracudas, or they have no ambition at all.
His whole generation seems colorless. It's like Megan says, after
Spencer Tracy, it was just wimps or bullshit macho."

"You didn't used to talk like that, Toni."

"Like what?"

"Cursing all the time. Using words like bullshit and macho."

"I didn't say you were bullshit macho." Though she sometimes thought it. "Joe, honey. Go take a shower, then come on
back to bed. Screw the kids. Then screw me."

"See what I mean? The mouth you have on you. Tell you the
truth, Toni, I'm just as glad it looks like the deal on this next
movie has fallen through."

"You're *what*?"

"I just told you. I'm just as glad it's fallen through."

"How can you say that! You know how much it means to me?
How much it means to Megan?"

"Megan's a bad influence on you. Being in the movie business
is a bad influence on you."

"What's this crap about bad influence? You sound like I'm
still wet behind the ears."

"You didn't used to be like this. Always running around.
Always flying off somewhere."

"Always? This trip was the first time I've been away from
you for more than a few days in the last quarter of a century."
She put her hand over her mouth, bit her finger and laughed.
"A quarter of a century. Damn, that does make me feel old."

"That's what I mean, Toni. You're too old for all this chasing
around. It's some change-of-life craziness. You've gotta realize
it's too late for you to be trying to get into the fast track."

"You know what your problem is, Joe? You're jealous. Jealous because I'm making my own money and getting out in the

world and having a good time doing it. And because I'm not here to pick up after all of you.''

He gave her the look of hopeless disappointment he usually reserved for Mario. ''I never thought you'd change like this, Antoinette.''

''Change like what?'' Her voice went out of control. ''Rock Around the Clock'' stopped abruptly, then ''Jailhouse Rock,'' with the timid addition of Mary Lou's tambourine, started up. She took his hand, turned it over, smoothed the back of it. ''Joe, I love you. You know that, don't you?'' That coaxed a nod out of him. ''I love you,'' she repeated, waiting for it to sink in, ''but I don't think you're being fair. Try to be fair, Joe. Think about it and try to be fair.''

He chewed his lip and averted his eyes. ''Toni,'' he began, ''the extra money's nice, but do we really need it?''

She flung up her hands. He was the one who was always complaining about money, always comparing them unfavorably to neighbors and friends.

''Toni. I want you to give up work.'' To take the sting out of that, he chuckled and squeezed her thigh. ''You know, you're the one who should get on that Exercycle. There's more than a handful here.''

She was stiff with anger. ''You were saying?''

''That I want you to give up work. It's the only thing that will *save this marriage*.'' His voice had a phony gravity, like a politican's TV ad.

''Joe.'' She removed his hand from her thigh. ''I'm going to take a bath.''

''But I'm all sweaty. I was going to take a shower.''

Count to ten. All right, to twenty. ''You do that, Joe. You do that.''

She leaned on the kitchen sink, taking in the comforting aroma of a garlicky rib roast, contemplating the FOR SALE sign in their neighbors' yard, as Giovanna and Brad came up the path. Brad wore a three-piece suit, Giovanna a tweed blazer, silk blouse and suede skirt in various shades of taupe. Their grooming was in almost comic contrast to Mario and Mary Lou's slovenliness. Bradley knew the best wines but had abominable table manners;

drove a BMW but couldn't change a tire; had a master's degree from Princeton but told ethnic jokes. Though it was on the level of a state secret, Giovanna had found him by placing an ad in the Personals in *New York* magazine: "Slim, extremely attractive, conservative Ivy grad, 24, into the arts, seek affluent male counterpart over 6 feet. No chauvinists or smokers, please." As Toni wiped her hands and prepared to greet them, she wondered what she'd say if she placed an ad. "Chunky middle-aged woman with nice brown eyes seeks virile male with integrity and sense of humor. Height, age, weight and financial status not important." Or maybe she'd substitute "curvy" for "chunky." The ads didn't have to be accurate. Brad had lied about his height (he was barely five feet nine), but that seemed only fair since Giovanna had lied about being Ivy League. But Bradley was Giovanna's counterpart, as surely as if they were twins.

"You wouldn't believe the traffic on the George Washington Bridge," Giovanna wailed, giving Toni a quick peck on the cheek. "So, Mom, how was your trip? What'd you buy?"

"The gifts are on the table in the dining room."

"Nice to have you back, Mom." Giovanna rushed off.

Brad looked around at the dinner preparations. "I'd offer to help, but I know you always have everything under control."

They sat down to dinner at five. Joe brought his Scotch to the table, nursing it and his injured feelings. Brad continued his discussion of junk bonds. Toni carved the roast, realizing that it was too dry because Brad and Giovanna had been late. Mary Lou, barefoot and wearing an Indian print smock, pushed her granny glasses up onto her nose and began to spoon the candied yams (her contribution to the meal) onto everyone's plate. Giovanna said that she hadn't eaten anything cooked with marshmallows since she'd been in the Girl Scouts. Forks were raised to mouths when Mary Lou asked if she might not say a blessing. Brad paused, corkscrew in hand, head lowered to study the $27.95 price tag he'd left on the bottle of Cabernet Sauvignon. After Mary Lou said something about "Dear Jesus," and Giovanna and Brad exchanged sidelong glances, they all began to eat.

"Doesn't seem like a family dinner without Big Toni," Mario said, referring to his grandmother. The "Big" had been conferred because of seniority. Toni's mother was barely five feet.

"She'll join us after dinner if someone will run over to Jersey City and pick her up," Toni said.

Giovanna shook her head. "Drive to Jersey City? You must be kidding. I can't believe she never learned to drive."

"Lots of women of her generation never learned to drive," Toni said.

"But why didn't someone go and pick her up earlier?" Brad asked.

"She's serving meals to the homeless at Our Lady of Perpetual Help," Toni explained.

"That's what you get for being a religious fanatic," Giovanna snorted. "She's eating Wonder Bread and Stove Top stuffing when she could be having . . ."

"You might show a little more tolerance," Toni flashed.

A silence followed, broken only by Brad's audible mastication and Mario and Mary Lou's humming of a song they were working on. Giovanna, finding no need for manners at a family dinner, stared at them in disbelief and pushed the candied yams to the rim of her plate.

"There's nothing wrong with Grandma," Mario said, meeting his sister's glare. "And don't call her a religious fanatic."

"If she's not a religious fanatic, how come she has an altar in her apartment and she thinks the little plaster statues talk to her?"

"You know, sister . . ." Mario ran his tongue over his teeth. "Your attitude sucks."

Giovanna smiled. "Articulate as ever, Mario. But then you never got through freshman English, did you?"

Toni longed for the days when she could have sent them to their rooms. She asked if anyone wanted second helpings.

"Of course not," Giovanna sniffed while Mary Lou piled more of everything onto her plate. Behind the granny glasses Mary Lou's eyes were woebegone and vengeful. "This is just the loveliest dinner," she said between mouthfuls. "I try to cook, but Mario says I'll never be as good as you, Mother."

Knowing Toni hated the generic form of address, Joe said, "Yes, *Mother*. It was quite a meal."

"Maybe I could have a little dessert," Brad suggested, trying to get Giovanna's approval to do so. "You always make the best desserts, Toni."

"The dessert is cheesecake from Giardelli's. I only got home last night so I didn't have time to—"

Joe pushed himself away from the table. "Your mother is a traveling woman now. She doesn't like to cook anymore."

"I love to cook," Toni said evenly. "But I just got back from Australia."

Joe put his arm around her with an amorousness he hadn't displayed in the bedroom. "Hey, Mother, you're testy today."

"She's still tired," Mario pointed out. "Mom, tell us some more about the trip."

She didn't particularly feel like doing so, but at least that might prevent a squabble. She talked and they listened, picking at the remains of the food.

"We saw one of your boss's documentaries on TV," Mary Lou said. "It was kinda depressing."

"Life's like that sometimes." Toni got up to make the coffee.

"Mom," Giovanna called out. "I saw the FOR SALE sign on the Bonnets' lawn. What's up?"

"They're getting a divorce," Joe said.

"No! Well, I'll bet Debbie is real upset. When you guys would fight she always told me her parents were the ideal couple."

"I expect Debbie has other things on her mind," Toni said. "She's pregnant, didn't I tell you?"

"Well, Debbie was always a little flaky," Giovanna replied. "I just don't see how she can afford to have a baby. How much does her husband make?"

"I have no idea," Toni answered coldly. Though bluntly curious about other people's finances, Giovanna never divulged her own. Toni estimated that Giovanna and Brad's combined income must be $150,000 but they always claimed that they were barely scraping by.

"I guess," Mary Lou began, her voice, usually syrupy, tart as vinegar, "that if you want to have a baby you just find a way to pay for it."

Though Toni had just eaten a full meal, she had the light-headed feeling that came from a day's fast. Why hadn't she seen it before? Mary Lou's constant napping and snacks, that listless but contented look that made her seem simple-minded. Why hadn't she seen it?

Mary Lou took Mario's hand and leaned her head on his shoulder. "I guess no one would have kids these days if they added up the bills first. The Lord will provide," she added dreamily.

If not the Lord, then the in-laws, Toni thought, stacking up the plates. She walked to the kitchen, calling over her shoulder, "Giovanna, will you help me with these?"

As soon as the kitchen door had swung shut Giovanna whispered, "Do you think she's pregnant?"

"How would I know?"

"Brad," Giovanna yelled, sticking her head back into the dining room. "You can come and help. Cleaning up isn't just a woman's job."

"Please don't call any of them in," Toni told her. She surveyed plates sticky with glutinous gravy, three rejected vegetables and meat bones.

"I don't want Brad to turn out like Daddy. You've absolutely spoiled Daddy."

Toni turned on the water. "Your father always breaks things in the kitchen."

"You're Big Toni all over. You just let him go on being helpless."

"Giovanna, we'll colonize Venus before your father will learn to operate a vacuum cleaner or wash a dish without chipping it. Besides, I'd rather be out here doing something than listening to the sniping in there."

"Why are you filling up the sink? Why not use the dishwasher?"

"Because it's broken. I've been meaning to have it fixed but . . ."

"Nothing ever works in this house," Giovanna said petulantly and, leaning close enough to be heard over the rush of water, "I'll just bet that little Moon-Pie is pregnant. Mario has to do something to prove his masculinity. Maybe he'll get a song out of it, something like

We're downwardly mobile
But Christianly noble,
'Cause we know the word listless,
Rhymes right well with shiftless,
So if Mom and Dad keep us in shoes,
We won't have no post-partum blues . . .

Ah, go on, Mom. Go on and laugh. I know you want to. But I guess I'd find it hard to laugh if I knew I was going to end up paying the bills.''

Toni plunged her hands into the water, deciding not to remind Giovanna that she and Joe were still paying off Giovanna and Brad's wedding—at St. Thomas's Episcopal, no less—and her thousand-dollar wedding dress, gold cufflinks for the ushers, the photographer's bill. "I don't think I'll mind being a grandmother." She was damned tired of explaining Mario to Giovanna, Giovanna to Mario, Joe to Giovanna and Mario—especially since she agreed with each one's negative assessment of the others.

"Being a grandmother will make you feel middle-aged."

Toni laughed. "I'll be forty-nine next birthday, so unless I live to be over a hundred I guess I'll have to admit that I'm middle-aged."

Giovanna said what Toni had hoped she wouldn't: that middle age was only a state of mind. Toni felt her face flush. Hormones or rage? "I can assure you, Giovanna, that it's also a state of the body."

"And you can't do anything about that?" Giovanna challenged. "There's . . ."

"I know. Dieting, estrogen, plastic surgery, jogging, weight lifting, aerobics, collagen shots, fasting and . . ."

"Look at Joan Collins."

"You look at her."

"All right, that's a gross example. But you're out in the world now, Mom. You're dealing with a different class of people."

"I don't get in front of the camera, Giovanna."

"I know you got a late start on your career. I know you'll never be a full-fledged producer, but . . ." She looked at her as though Toni were a puppy that refused to be housebroken.

"Well, if you're just going to be the Italian mama. If you're just going to *give in* . . ." At which point, Toni did give in. She turned off the faucets and stepped back, flicking water from her hands. "What the hell!" Giovanna shrieked, shielding her silk blouse. Toni took the car keys from the hook near the door and slammed it after her.

She drove through Sunday-deserted streets, imagining the comments that followed her exit, the mutterings that began with "At her time of life . . ." and "You know she's always been . . ." They'd be united for once in their critical nattering. She parked the car near the Palisades lookout and stared across at the Manhattan skyline. Its million lights were just beginning to twinkle. She shivered, turned on the heater, punched "Send in the Clowns" into the tape deck. To remind herself that she really did love her family, she took her mind back to better times. There were those long, lazy summers right after they bought the cottage in Vermont—walks in the woods and berry picking, swimming and canning fruit. And Joe coming up on the weekends, sitting with her on the deck while they watched the kids playing in the sprinklers, Joe caressing her with hands cool from his iced-tea glass, evoking an anticipation that was as insistent but more intimate than their dating days, and she looking satisfied and almost sleek with her tan and her painted toenails. But let's not get too warm and runny, she cautioned herself. Even then . . . even then . . .

A seemingly insignificant incident from a Vermont summer came back to her with the minute detail of her first formal dress: They had been walking in the woods. Giovanna had spotted a turtle crawling on a log and had taken a stick and tipped it onto its back. Mario had inched forward, making gagging noises, then had a poke at it himself. Joe had made a joke about turtle soup. She had scolded them for being cruel and reached to turn the turtle back onto its feet. No, they'd all shrieked and called her a softie; they wanted to watch it struggle. She could see that turtle now, its throat pumping as it rocked exhaustively from side to side, trying to right itself. She knew how that turtle felt.

A couple drove up, the man giving her a nod that barely concealed his annoyance at finding anyone, especially a lonely middle-aged woman, at this scenic, romantic spot. "I got here first," she thought and punched the button to hear "Send in the Clowns" again. No doubt about it, it was all over for her. She was fifty . . . well, almost fifty. A half century old. The heater wasn't working. She was cold and it was dark. They'd all be worrying about her. As she drove off, she looked in her rearview mirror at the couple. They weren't smooching, they were arguing.

As she opened the kitchen door she saw Big Toni, the sleeves of her good navy dress rolled up, scrubbing the grouting around the sink. "Antionette!" Big Toni wrapped short arms around her, holding her close, and said, "Mario picked me up. Where you been?" She placed a hand smelling of detergent on her forehead. "Where you been? You're cold."

"Just needed a breath of air. Just took a spin around the block."

"I been here almost an hour." Big Toni's lips worked through puckered disbelief before they pursed for another kiss. "Anyway, it's good to have you back, my angel. I don't sleep good one night knowing you're all the way across the world. What you doing running around without your coat?" She hugged her again, and Toni looked over her shoulder at the leftovers stacked in the Tupperware, the shining sink, the espresso pot on the stove. "Mama, you don't have to clean up. Especially since you didn't even eat here."

"I don't do it, who gonna do it? Go get yourself a sweater. You don't want this coffee? I make you a cup of tea. Then we sit and talk and you tell me everything you been doing." Big Toni released her and busied herself with the kettle. Big Toni was a feeling rather than a thinking person, and constant activity kept depression and loneliness at bay. Big Toni had never had to search for a role model: she had the Virgin Mary. She believed she was born to serve others, primarily her family, but her serving in no way contradicted her often domineering ways. The home, the neighborhood, the parish, these were her domain. Every woman's domain, unless she was too ugly or too selfish to get and keep a husband. She'd stopped voting for the Democrats when they'd nominated Geraldine Ferraro for Vice President. As Toni watched her give the countertop an unnecessary swipe and fold the dish towel, she realized that her mother was content. But there was no way she could ever go back to such a traditional role. "Where is everybody?" she asked.

"Watching the TV like they got nothing to say to each other. That's why I don't visit Mrs. D'Angelo anymore. She never turn off the TV. She listen to those people on the screen like they in the room talking to her and I'm the one nineteen inches high who can be turned off. She don't bother to cook anymore. She eats from the microwave. At church even strangers talk. Today the priest tell us all to kiss. A man kissed me on the cheek. A good-looking man, too. If your father was alive . . ." She chortled at her wickedness. "Toni, you use a little Clorox with a toothbrush, you can get this grouting around the sink clean. Your cleaning lady, she never going to do it. Nobody take care of your home like you do."

"Yeah, Mama. I'll do that sometime." But just now she had something more important to do. She'd made up her mind. She walked through the dining room as though she were going into a production meeting and stood at the door of the den. "Could you turn off that TV, Mary Lou?" They turned to her as one.

Mary Lou whined, "Gee, we just found a program we all wanted to watch," but seeing Toni's expression, added, "Maybe we could put it on tape" and began to fiddle with the VCR.

"No, just turn it off," Giovanna said. "Now that Mom's back we're going to start back to the city." She nudged Brad and started to get up.

"Please sit down," Toni stopped her, then went to the TV and snapped it off. "I have a few things to say."

Joe looked wary. "Honey, you're tired. Why don't you go upstairs, take a bath . . ."

Toni snapped on the overhead light. "I have a few things to say." And what were they? "I am . . . I am angry and I am sad. I leave for two weeks and come home to a pigpen. None of you expresses the least interest in where I've been or what I've been doing."

"Maybe the others . . . ," Mario began.

"I am sick of your sniping at each other and running to me to complain about each other. We could do with a lot more charity and understanding in this house. And I would like more respect and less advice and criticism." Her eyes held on Giovanna, but when she caught Mario smirking, she turned to him. "Mario, you have to get a job and find your own apartment." Big Toni was leaning against the door, her hands tucked into her armpits, shaking her head. "Don't get upset, Mama," Toni warned, then went back to Mario. "I'll ask . . . No, *you'll* ask Uncle Johnny if he can help you out."

"But I'm working on songs," Mario protested. "I've been promised a gig. I've got three new songs."

"You've got a pregnant wife," she overrode him. "You need your privacy . . ."

"A baby!" Big Toni exclaimed. "Why didn't you tell us?"

Joe eyed Mary Lou for evidence.

". . . *and* . . ." Toni recaptured the floor. ". . . we need our privacy, too. We'll help you get on your feet but we're not going to prop you up indefinitely. I care about all of you but I have a life outside this house. My job means a lot to me. I'll probably be going back to California. When we get financing for the next film I'll be going back to Australia, at least for preproduction." Oh, such a look on Joe's face! "You could come, too, Joe. If we started planning now, you could arrange the time off . . ." But she could save that for the bedroom. She'd delivered the main points of her manifesto and remembering something Megan said about a dramatic exit being as important as a dramatic entrance, she said, "That's it, folks. I think I'll take that bath now."

She was halfway up the stairs when Big Toni called, "Antoinette. Wait up for me. I'm comin' up to talk to you."

CHAPTER
NINETEEN

WAS THAT A NOISE IN THE CORRIDOR? COULD HER DESK lamp be seen beneath the door? Joan got up and listened. Nothing. They were all asleep. She sat back down at her desk and looked at the note James had sent, via Michele, and the letter she was writing in response.

"Watch and pray," she had told herself each morning. She had given Michele a series of feeble excuses for not going to the university—she was working on a syllabus, she had headaches. And today her body had made good the lie by giving her a disabling migraine, though that was no excuse for her behavior in class. "Your answer is so ill-informed as to be beneath comment," she had snapped at one of the girls, and seeing the girl's eyes fill, feeling herself on the verge of tears, had said curtly, "I'm sorry. Excuse me," and had almost run from the room. So she had known, even before getting the note, that she had lost control and would have to see him.

Michele had handed the note to her, almost as an afterthought, at dinner. "Oh, here," she'd said, reaching into the pocket of her denim skirt as stew plates were being replaced with bowls of custard and jam roly-poly. "I ran into Professor Ferzaco today as I was coming out of class and he asked me to give you this." To save Joan any possible embarrassment, he had not sent a sealed letter but an interoffice memo. She'd taken a spoonful of the gummy custard and read, *"Joan, at your convenience, I would appreciate a conference on the project we discussed a week ago last Thursday."* Had it only been a week and a half? But yes. Their separation had produced incredible distortions of time. It seemed she had been trying to write her response for over an hour, and she'd gotten no further than the salutation. She had not had such a difficult time writing a letter since the one she'd sent to Aileen Ingpen's mother after Aileen's suicide. But this was not a letter of condolence. It was to be a love letter. She had never expressed her love, and it seemed essential that she do so on paper before she saw him again. "Dear James . . ."

That *was* a noise in the corridor. She covered the letter, put on her dressing gown and quietly opened her door. There was no one about, but a sliver of light shone beneath Sister Ursula's door. She went to it and tapped gently. No answer. Sister Ursula had probably fallen asleep with the light on. Joan tapped again, then slowly opened the door. A table lamp threw a circle of light on the glass of water, rosary beads, bottles of pills and the little bell Sister Ursula was to ring if she needed assistance.

"Are you all right?" Sister Ursula's head was thrown back, her face and short-cropped hair were almost as white as the pillows, her mouth open, a trickle of drool at one corner. There was not even a slight rise and fall of her chest and for a moment Joan was frightened.

Then Ursula's eyes opened and rolled up to her. "Quite all right, my dear. Now go back to bed."

"Shall I turn off the light?"

Sister Ursula's eyes circled the room, trying to grasp the question.

"The light. Shall I turn it off? Or would you like a cup of tea?"

"A cup of tea? Certainly not. You know what he said . . ." Her voice took on the doctor's clipped and crotchety tone. " 'No liquids after six.' "

"Then I'll leave you," Joan said, only fleetingly concerned over Mother Superior's lectures about the light bill.

"Don't leave just yet. I want to talk to you."

Joan sat on the side of the bed, but Sister Ursula sighed and appeared to drop off again. "When you get as old as I am," she said as Joan started to get up, "you don't really sleep and you're never quite awake. Do you suppose that's His way of preparing us for the end?"

"It may be." Joan took her hand. It was light and bony as a bird's skeleton. She heard the latch of the door release and turned to see Sister Bruno; her face was puffy with sleep, and her eyes swam like tadpoles behind her glasses. She wore a woolen plaid dressing gown and was trying to conceal something behind her back. "There's no need for you to be here," Bruno whispered testily. "Everything's right as rain. You can go back to your room."

"Sister?" Joan looked at Ursula but, either drifting off or dismissing them, Ursula had shut her eyes again.

Sister Bruno held the door open and as Joan inched past her bulk she saw that Bruno was holding a bedpan behind her back. Joan motioned her into the passageway, closing the door behind them. Bruno, caught out, let the bedpan dangle at her side. "I've just been to the lavatory to wash this out," she said, and seeing Joan's expression, explained, "Sister Ursula can't control her water anymore. Please don't mention it because it embarrasses her."

"I didn't know."

"She's been this way for months. Ever since she had that terrible cold. She coughs and . . ." Bruno looked away.

"Do you mean you've been getting up every night? That must be a terrible hardship." She remembered Bruno's weak stomach: the sight of congealed gravy made her blanch, the smell of garden fertilizer gave her the heaves, so emptying a bedpan . . . "You should have told me. I'm usually up late."

"No. You have your studying." This said in a tone of both disapproval and magnanimity. "And I have these attacks of indigestion . . ." Bruno put her free hand to her bosom, her mouth stretching in either a stifled belch or a controlled yawn. ". . . so I don't sleep much myself." She put her hand heavily on Joan's shoulder. "Please don't tell anyone. If Reverend Mother finds out she'll send her to the Mother House because they have a proper infirmary there. It would break her heart to go. She wants to spend her last days here at St. Brigid's. And that's as it should be. So we've agreed not to tell Reverend Mother or the doctor." Sister Bruno lowered her head. It was plain that even this small infraction induced a sense of wrongdoing.

"Perhaps the doctor should know. It might be a bladder infection that could be treated."

"Sure, that doctor is as ignorant as Paddy's pig," Sister Bruno whispered, her brogue thick. "He's already giving her enough pills to choke a horse and if you tell him he'll be pokin' and proddin' and writing up more prescriptions. We want prayers, Sister, not doctors. I'm askin' you to leave well enough alone. Sister Ursula and I may not see eye to eye . . ." That, Joan thought, is a gross understatement. ". . . But we're the only ones left from the old days and we understand each other." Sister Bruno leaned against the wall, her eyes focused on the little leaded window at the end of the corridor. "We understand each other. I'll never forget her kindness to me when I first came out from Ireland. Slips of girls we were then, and I so homesick it would make a heathen weep. There was nothing but an open paddock where the garden is now, and the heat and the flies! Flies as big as rats. And the wild Australian plants I didn't know the names of, and the mallee that wouldn't be uprooted without a man we have come to pull it out with a team of horses. How I longed for a bit of true green! She was the only one who understood. And who would've thought that comfort would come from that quarter? The daughter of the gentry, she is, don't you know, wanting to be an opera singer until God gave her the nod. She gave me a little fan and she used to save her sweets for me at teatime. I never had a powerful appetite until I came out. You wouldn't know it to look at me now but I was a wee thing. And Jude—you wouldn't remember Jude, she was before your time— Jude was Reverend Mother then. She always made her little joke about Jude being the patron saint of hopeless cases. She didn't believe it, but hopeless she was, God rest her soul . . ." Sister Bruno crossed herself. "Stiff as a broom that's been left out in the rain. She called me into her office and told me I wasn't to sit next to Ursula in chapel or at table. She'd been watching us, you see, watching Ursula slip me the sweets at dinner. And she took away the little pink fan with the cherry blossoms on it and told me our friendship was . . ."

Joan mentally supplied the word: "unnatural."

Sister Bruno clutched the bedpan to her drooping breasts, her face confused and angry. Her reminiscence had been too personal, too sentimental, too self-indulgent. She was already sorry for having said anything.

"You and Sister Ursula are survivors of the old order," Joan offered.

"That's it. You won't tell, will you?"

"No. But I want you to let me spell you in checking on her. It's too much of a hardship for you to do alone."

"Sure it's all right. I offer it up."

Joan nodded. Offer it up. Offer up manure and bedpans and crushingly stupid authority that called warmth and consolation unnatural; offer up loneliness and a shrunken self; make the little miseries, and the great agonies that made you stuff your hand into your mouth when you woke up crying, a deposit in your heavenly bank account. Believe your monthly bleeding to be unclean, your desire to call something, anything, your own, unworthy. Let old men who wore dresses and hit the bottle and played politics interpret life and instruct you in morality, and tell you that the yearning, the need to join flesh to flesh was ugly and obscene, and took you away from God.

" 'Grant,' " Sister Bruno intoned, the bedpan dangling at her side, " 'that I may not so much seek to be consoled as to console; to be understood as to understand . . .' "

Joan finished the quote: " '. . . that I may not seek so much to be loved as to love.' " Only natural that Sister Bruno, who had probably never been loved, would forget that part. And now she, too, leaned against the wall.

"St. Francis of Assisi," Bruno reminded her with a touch of caught-you-there. She yawned, widely and deeply, covering her mouth with her chunky hand.

"You're tired, Sister. Go to bed," Joan insisted, reaching for the bedpan. "I promise I won't tell anyone. Now go back to bed." Sister Bruno handed it over, saying, "We keep it in the wardrobe, pushed back so no one can see it and covered with that electric blanket Judith Mosner gave her two Christmases ago. And tuck her in tightly. Not with the electric blanket. She thinks . . ." Bruno smiled to show Joan that though she shared her enlightenment, Sister Ursula was still a captive of superstition. "She thinks that the electric blanket will electrocute her." She yawned again. "Thank you, Sister." She started back to her room, then turned. "You won't tell?"

"No. I won't tell."

Joan opened the door. Sister Ursula was wide awake. "I could hear the two of you out there, nattering away in the corridor."

Joan put away the bedpan and began to tuck the blankets around her feet. "Yes." There was no need to discuss what had transpired.

"You don't look well, Joan. Do you still have your headache?" Sister Ursula asked as Joan lifted her head and plumped the pillows. Joan sat on the side of the bed. "I'm fine. Really I am."

Sister Ursula pondered this. "Then you'll be going back to the university again, I suppose."

"Yes. I'll be going back tomorrow."

Sister Ursula thought some more. "I know you've been . . . ." She struggled to find the right word. ". . . restless lately, Joan. I have been restless myself. I have a great many things on my mind. They dart in and out." She frowned, then chuckled. "Bats in the belfry. I must clear them out before I go."

Joan was mentally composing her love letter to James and did not immediately grasp where Sister Ursula thought she was going. Then she realized that Ursula was talking about her death, preparing herself for it with the same anticipation one might feel when packing for a journey. Joan, who had read the Bhagavad Gita, Lao-Tze, the dialogues of Plato as well as St. Augustine, could not imagine that she would greet death with such equanimity. She had developed stoic resignation without one bit of stoic calm. "What do you imagine it will be like?" she asked.

Sister Ursula chuckled again, immediately grasping the question. "Harmony. I imagine harmony. In heaven that is. But I expect I shall have to spend some time in the other place, and that will be like sitting through an endless recital of Joyce Kirby hitting all the wrong notes. Joan"—she took her hand—"how can we know what it will be like? We must trust in Our Lord. But I don't want to talk about that . . . I'm concerned about what's happening at St. Brigid's. Reverend Mother will be leaving us soon. You must take her place."

"I don't think I'm in favor with the powers that be." She wouldn't be here. She would be in a bungalow in Greece.

"We all go through our periods of doubt, Joan. Our faith would be cheap if it could be had without questioning, and with someone of your intellect, questioning is almost a way of life. But the greatest of the Church philosophers have always questioned. Still they have stayed. Out of love, I suppose. The Church is still here. The Church will always be here. But St. Brigid's cannot survive without someone like you at the helm. There will be opposition to your being the Superior, but even those who don't approve of you respect you. You are the only one who can lead us properly."

"Sister," Joan said in a low voice. "I cannot pray. I can't really say that I believe."

"You'll get through this bad patch you're going through. You have great love, Joan. And you have taken your vows. You will hear God's voice again. You'll get through this bad patch. It's just a storm at sea." She closed her eyes. It was impossible to tell if she was remembering her own storms, contemplating her all-too-brief future, or simply dozing off. "Megan Hanlon," she said. "Megan Hanlon. For weeks I've been trying to remember why she upset me so. Now I remember. I caned her once. I shouldn't have done that."

"I doubt she remembers."

"That would hardly be the point, would it? It's on my conscience. Such a lovely voice she had. And now she says she only sings in the shower. We must pray for her. And for Greta and Mona, too. Pray for all our girls." She pursed her bloodless lips. "Catherine Reynolds is quite a good organist. I know we don't like to turn to the laity, and I know Catherine has two children and holds down a job, but if you talked to her she might be persuaded to accompany the choir. These guitars and sing-alongs are all very well, but a choir and an organ, *that* inspires worship. That gives glory to God and His creation." Her gaze became a stare, losing focus.

Joan sat for several minutes, heavy with this burden of misplaced trust, an ache in her throat. As she got up and reached to turn off the lamp, Sister Ursula came to with the start of a defenseless animal, demanding, "Did you put away the bedpan?"

"Yes. And now it's time to get some rest." Joan gave the blankets an unnecessary tuck. "May I turn out the light?"

"Please do. You know what the electric bills have been like."

Joan switched off the lamp and stood, arms wrapped, hands cupping her breasts, in the silvery light. "Will you be all right now, Sister?"

Ursula's mouth trembled in a yawn. "Oh, yes. God be with you."

"And with you, Sister." As she was about to open the door, Sister Ursula said, "I can rest well now that we've had our little talk. It's in your capable hands, Sister Mary Magdalene. Once you are Reverend Mother I know we'll see an upsurge in vocations and the choir will be lovely again."

CHAPTER
TWENTY

"THEM THAT'S GOT SHALL GET," MEGAN SAID TO HER-
self as she drove Irene's ten-year-old Ford past the hissing
sprinklers, the hothouse, the swimming pool and dressing ca-
baña to arrive at the entrance of Victor's Malibu hacienda. She
walked through a patio lush with hibiscus, dwarf gardenias and
bougainvillea. Birds hung in bamboo cages and she spotted an
Australian bird of exotic plumage whose name she couldn't remember. There were laws against the export of such birds, and
she could imagine that Victor's delight in acquiring it had been
enhanced because he'd bought it on the black market. She
smoothed the skirt of her white linen dress, much crumpled
after the long ride, and raised the knocker on the carved wooden
door. In a tiled alcove near the door sat a Mayan god of the
harvest. An offering of corn sheaves and flowers had been put
at his feet. Only fitting that Victor should be giving thanks to
some god, since his own harvest had been so bountiful. Not
being in the market for pre-Columbian statuary she couldn't
even guess its monetary value. She didn't much hanker for the
standard trappings of wealth; jewelry and furs left her cold,
though she did covet fine, fast cars. Indeed she'd always believed
that too many possessions were a kind of bondage, or perhaps
she'd struggled for so long that she'd ironed the desire for things
out of her soul, just as she'd stopped wanting a lasting love. But
this little Mayan god excited her. She caressed its foot and turned
back to the patio. Its cool and ordered beauty was in such contrast to the smog-ridden, billboard-littered freeways she'd just
negotiated or her own place in New York, where neighbors
chained their bicycles in the hallways and had three locks on
their doors, that when an olive-skinned woman with braids

pinned to the top of her head opened the door, she said, rather formally, "I'm Megan Hanlon. To see Mr. Taub."

"Thees way, please. Mr. Taub expecting you."

Megan stopped on the threshold. Not quite San Simeon, but that combination of indoor-outdoor living with a Mexican influence that was California at its best: adobe walls, a magnificent view of the ocean, glossy plants, tile floors that invited you to take off your shoes, low-slung hand-carved furniture, more pre-Columbian statuary. Victor had abandoned his aesthetic sensibilities in his movies but they were evident in his home. The only exception to this elegant simplicity was a large abstract painting hung over the fireplace. It was all streaks and blobs in angry reds, yellows and purples, like something from an art therapy class for disturbed children. Possibly a leftover from Wife Number Three? As she passed it she glanced at the assertively scrawled signature: Sylvia Taub. So her former mother-in-law now produced as well as consumed "art." She could hear Victor's voice coming from behind a closed door adjacent to the fireplace: ". . . don't shit me about the weather, Jack . . . rushes by Friday . . . crush your nuts." He sounded as though he were doing an impersonation of a gangster, though he supposed it was convincing enough at the other end of the line. The woman glanced back at her and nodded to hurry her on. Megan followed her down a hallway, glancing through a partially opened door to see a room that was a cross between a nursery and a punk disco—stuffed animals, piles of clothes and towels littered the unmade pink canopied bed; a poster of an androgynous rock star clutching his crotch, a giant TV screen and a tangle of sound and video equipment decked a wall that had been painted black.

"And where is Deirdre?" she asked.

"She at school, or somewhere," the woman told her, pulling the door to and adding apologetically, "She don't like me to clean up her room."

They went down steps into a tiered garden and followed a brick path to a small building that overlooked the ocean. "Here the shack," the woman told her.

Shack indeed. A shack was probably where the woman had been born. Was she Guatemalan? Salvadoran? "I'm sorry, what was your name?"

"Maria."

"And where are you from, Maria?"

"Oxnard."

"I mean, where were you born?"

"Oxnard," Maria insisted, avoiding her eyes.

You're from Oxnard like I'm from Atlantis, Megan thought. Michael had told her that many illegals ended up as domestics. But Maria was safe here. No immigration men would dare to enter Mr. Victor Taub's door. Even those goggled robots from LAPD wouldn't come around without checking with higher-ups.

"You need anything, you ring little buzzer." Maria indicated one at the side of the desk. "Mr. Taub be here soon."

Left alone, Megan examined the walls: piles of scripts, books (mainly current best-sellers, tax and business texts, and a "sentimental" shelf of volumes that had been in vogue during their youth: *Siddhartha, Demian, The Stranger*) photos of Victor on location, a commendation from the Film Preservation Society, a picture of him shaking hands with the mayor of Los Angeles, an entire gallery of baby Deirdre (playing in the sand, riding a pony, sitting astride Victor's shoulders) and . . . she stepped closer, scarcely recognizing herself but, yes, there she was, looking impossibly young and open-faced, her arms around the couple who'd been their best friends and upstairs neighbors when they'd lived on Sullivan Street. Natalie and Piet. Piet was going to be a record producer; Natalie an actress. Piet had died of an overdose in an Amsterdam hotel and, last she'd heard, Natalie was living with another woman and running an arts-in-the-high-schools program in New Haven.

She wandered into the adjoining rooms. The bedroom's principal feature was an oversize bed with carved wooden horses from a turn-of-the-century carousel forming the posts. Victor's collection of movie memorabilia was scattered around: a magic lantern, ruby slippers from *The Wizard of Oz*, a camera obscura, the phallic sculpture from *Clockwork Orange*, a megaphone with a tag marked "D. W. Griffith," autographed photos of Mabel Normand and Fay Wray. The bathroom was sleekly modern, with a sunken tub that commanded a view of the ocean. She couldn't resist sliding back a mirrored cabinet to find a cache of bath oils, prophylactics, bottles of Valium and Benzedrine—anything an overnight guest might need. She wandered back into the main room and opened the little refrigerator near the bar: fruit, cheeses, a jar of caviar, chocolates, bottles of wine and champagne.

She popped a few raspberries into her mouth, thinking she must've lost several pounds in the last week. When she was depressed, she usually ate compulsively if erratically, but nothing at Irene and George's had tempted her. Irene was an excellent cook but out of past necessity and now habit she served up the high-carbohydrate budget stretchers—macaroni and cheese, pot pies, and potatoes—that George preferred. There was nothing to drink except Gallo sherry and Budweiser. In the afternoons, when the neighbors came around to get a look at Megan, Irene brought out tablecloth and matching napkins and treated them to homemade cakes and scones. But the neighborhood had gone downhill and Megan could see that the women, with their grubby-faced children, stretch pants and microwave recipes, looked upon Irene's lace-curtain gentility as something of a joke. George watched TV from the time he came home from work until after the eleven o'clock news, at which time he went off—"Because I snore so much"—to his separate bedroom. Megan knew the TV's incessant drone got on Irene's nerves as much as it did hers. She could only imagine the forbearance Irene would have to show when George retired next year and was underfoot all the time. But Irene wasn't about to complain. Not when George was willing to overlook her trip to Arizona.

When she and Megan were alone, Irene talked about the old times, the fun they'd had, the boundless expectations with which she'd started her first marriage. She blamed herself for not having made sufficient difference in Thomas Shelby's life. When Megan tried to comfort her by saying that no woman could have kept him on the straight and narrow, that he wasn't the marrying kind, Irene said, and probably correctly, that women of Megan's generation were too cynical to believe in the transforming power of love and didn't understand the commitment of marriage. "The children of lovers are always orphans," someone had said. Irene, mired in her own grief, didn't seem to notice that Megan, though dry-eyed, also suffered a sense of guilt and loss.

Tossing on the couch that was nightly made up as her bed, Megan recalled how Thomas Shelby would call her "baby bird" and feed her popcorn, how his eyes would shine over the harmonica as he played "Deep in the Heart of Texas" and encouraged her to dance; or the way he'd sit on the edge of her bed, talking to her in that quiet confiding way, as though she were a buddy. All right, he'd been an irresponsible, sometimes violent drunk, he hadn't given a good goddamn about their fate, he'd left her with a lifelong passion and equally powerful distrust for handsome, risk-taking men, so that she wanted to be like them instead of a "good woman" like her mother, but . . . way back then she must've said, "Daddy, I love you." She wished she'd said it again before he'd died.

It hadn't been easy putting up with the constant TV, weeding the garden, having tea with the neighbors, going with Irene to Mass, and today, just before she'd left, when Irene had reminded her for the umpteenth time that the gas gauge of her car didn't work, Megan had exploded, "Don't nag me! I know how to handle things a damned sight better than you do," and stormed out of the house.

Irene, for once oblivious to the neighbors, had followed her, yelling, "You may think you're a high and mighty New York director, Miss. You may think . . ." But then, miraculously, they'd both laughed and Irene, pulling Megan to her, said, "I know it's been hard for you being here. I didn't mean to nag." As Megan drove off, Irene had recovered enough to call, "Drive carefully. God bless you. Remember to check the gas gauge."

Megan opened a window and leaned on the sill, taking deep breaths, enjoying the feel of the sun on her face and thinking that she'd never be able to work while facing such a beautiful vista. She turned her head as she heard Victor come through the door. He was wearing tennis shoes and shorts and looked as exhausted as if he'd just played a game. "Hi," she said. "You've got yourself quite a nice spread here, pardner."

He eyed her backside and joked, "So have you." He raised his arms as though he expected her to come into them. When she straightened but didn't move to him he said, more soberly, "I'm sorry about your father."

"He went fast. I'm glad about that. I don't think he would have dealt well with disability or old age."

"And how's your mother?"

"Taking it hard. All those years I was growing up there was nothing but bitterness about him, at least as far as I could tell. Now we're rewriting history. Maybe one day we'll come up with something like the truth."

He moved to her and put his hands on her shoulders. "Hey, you don't have to tough it out with me. It's always better to talk it out."

"You sound like some shrink on the Phil Donahue show." He understood her vulnerabilities better than most and he already knew the cast of characters, but there was something in his eye that promised more than friendly comfort. To her, their night at the Fremantle hotel had been a one-time thing, an aberration she neither regretted nor planned to repeat. To him, she suspected, it meant territory regained. She'd save her true confessions for Toni. "I do want to talk," she said, "but about my screenplay."

"Right down to business, huh?" His expression told her that he'd taken her refusal to bare her soul as a personal rejection.

She resisted the need to comfort him. "I've gotta get back into harness. I've been moping around for over two weeks. I'd probably still be studying my navel if Toni hadn't called. Thank God, she's coming back out. She got on my case because I hadn't called you. So I did, so here I am. The best therapy for me is to get back to work."

"Right you are." He shifted gears, assuming his harried-and-powerful-man persona, moving to the desk, opening the top drawer to pull out her screenplay, putting on his glasses, all the while muttering that he had a shitload of work to catch up on, that weather conditions in Canada were doing him in, as though she were a girl from office temps and it didn't matter if she overheard him. "Hey," he said, without looking up, "why don't you pour us both a glass of wine." She did so, and lest she feel too much the supplicant, took off her shoes and tucked her legs under her as she sat opposite his desk on the couch. He fished in his shirt pocket, came up with a pack of Marlboros and lit one with guilty speed. "Deirdre's on my case about smoking, so I usually do it out here in the shack."

"How is Deirdre? And how was your trip back?"

"We'll talk about that later."

She nodded and was reminded of advice a friend had given when she'd first started schlepping scripts around to money men: if you could think of the man cutting his toenails or sitting on the john, he wasn't so intimidating. And here was Victor, who had the power to decide a production's fate, who could make heads roll with a phone call, but who was browbeaten by his teenage daughter and had to give his mother's bogus art wall space. He sucked greedily, exhaled a plume of smoke and said, "You're tryin' to make a quantum leap with this. You know that, don't you? I'll give you points for chutzpah."

"Forget the chutzpah, what about the screenplay?"

"You've got a potential winner, Megan. You've got some real good stuff, but . . ."

She was ready for the "but." "Go on," she urged.

"But you've got some problems, too. We never really see Lieutenant What's-His-Name and . . . the convict woman . . ."

"Sarah," she supplied. Great! He didn't remember the central character's name.

"Yeah, yeah. Sarah," he said quickly, as though he'd just had a momentary lapse. "We never see them together."

She was baffled. The lieutenant and Sarah had most of the scenes. "Oh, you mean we don't actually see them making it. But the scene where they wake up together comes immediately after the scene where she finally sneaks into his quarters so . . ."

" 'Fraid we're gonna need a bit more than that if we're going to see any box-office receipts. You wanna go for an R rating right on the edge of an X."

"I hadn't thought about that yet."

"Gotta think about it. Think about it up front. Packaging, rating, publicity—all that—the whole megillah, right up front. You gotta be able to pitch this concept in one sentence, then get straight to the deal."

"I don't want to make a clutch-and-grab in period costumes."

Her voice was frosty. She didn't like being talked down to. She had made a few deals herself in the last fifteen years.

"No. No. I'm just saying expand the love scenes. You ought to be able to come up with something original." Subtle leer.

"Christ, years ago you couldn't show a husband and wife in the same bed, now you're supposed to throw in obligatory sex scenes in anything but a-boy-and-his-dog movies." But this was getting it off to a bad start. "All right, I'll take a look at it."

"And you don't need that riot at the women's prison."

She blurted, "But you do. That riot actually happened. And it shows the conditions that led the women to prostitute themselves."

"Let's leave the history lessons to the professors, shall we? You should also cut the stuff on the journey. Just show them arriving."

"The stuff on the ship sets up the whole thing. When Lieutenant Clarke sees her chained up and bargaining for extra rations she looks like vermin, so when he . . ."

"You cut the stuff on the ship and the riot scene you've saved yourself a shitload of trouble. And you've taken a good hunk outta the budget."

Loaves and fishes, she thought. Maybe she could pull off a miracle, shoot a master, intercut lots of close-ups, make it look like a crowd. Maybe . . .

"And your cast list." He took a sip of wine.

"That's more of a wish list," she explained. "I probably couldn't afford or get most of those actors, I was just jotting down . . ."

"You've got a lot of unknowns here. Who's Richard Maharits?"

"He won a Tony for best supporting actor last year. I've seen him in a lot of Off-Broadway shows and . . ."

"Hey, sweetheart, if I don't know him, you think Mr. and Mrs. America are gonna know him? And Gerald Hughes? He's dead meat. He's . . ."

"Victor, please don't use that slimy Hollywood jargon. Don't say bankable or dead meat, okay?"

He pulled on his cigarette and smiled at her. "I won't talk jargon if you don't get spikey. And Nita Narinto in the lead?

You gotta be kidding. No one's gonna bankroll you with her. Besides, she's too old.''

"She's about thirty-five. A good thirty-five."

"She's not pretty."

"She's a terrific actress. Besides, Sarah doesn't have to be pretty, and having gone through all she's gone through, she'd look older. She's a convict from the London slums, not a beauty-contest winner. And I want an Aussie in the lead."

"Okay. She's good. But no one knows her outside of Australia and maybe the U.K.'' He handed her a paper. "I jotted down some names I think you should consider."

"Kimberly Delsartre! You've got to be kidding. She's all tits and hair. She has as much expression as Little Orphan Annie."

"I'm not saying she's the right choice, but she's been very big on that TV series. Very big. She's made the cover of *People*. She's got out an exercise tape that every other housewife in America is squatting and bending to. And she's looking for a feature. Something she can get her teeth into."

"Without breaking her caps? Why does every glamour puss think she'll really be an actress if she gets a lousy haircut and puts a little dirt under her nails and plays an abused wife or a sharecropper? They equate grubby with serious—no, really, Victor, Kimberly Delsartre is to acting as an aluminum chair is to a Chippendale."

"I once heard you brag you could get a performance out of a rock, so what's the problem with an aluminum chair? Listen, dummy, I'm trying to be helpful here. You can't pay, you can't play, and you can't play unless you get a star. You wanna make this movie or not?''

"Your rhetoric is worse than your jargon. You promised." And she'd promised herself to button her lip and not get angry. "I'll take it under advisement."

"Sure. I understand. It's your baby and you gotta be protective. I've taken the liberty of sending the script to Christopher Leventhal at ICM. Chris is a friend and he's Kimberly's agent. He could package the whole thing from his client list. You'll have to meet the Aussie quota but ICM's got Aussies, got Frogs and Brits, got midgets and trained snakes. Anything you'll ever need."

"They've also got directors. What if they like the script but don't like me as director?"

"I've stretched the truth some—told him you've already got some financing."

And stretching the truth some herself, Megan said, "I do."

"And I've told him I'm interested, so you're protected. And I sent a copy to Melissa McMahon's agent, too. Kimberly and Melissa have a little rivalry going. Seems Melissa once beat Kimberly out of a part, but now Kimberly's ballin' Melissa's ex." He made a circular motion with his hand. "Wheels within wheels. So what could it hurt if they both express interest?" He stubbed out his cigarette, took off his glasses and handed her the script. "I've had it for today. I've been at it since early morning and I'm still on Aussie time. I've made notes in the margins. You wanna look it over later, we can discuss it some more after dinner. You're staying for dinner, aren't you? I told Maria to make paella, and I know Deirdre's looking forward to seeing you."

"Yes. I'll stay for dinner, but then I have to pick up Toni at the airport."

"So. You want to walk on my private beach with me?"

"I don't approve of private beaches and I'd get freckles."

"So. You want to watch a movie?"

"I'd really rather go through your notes. The thing is, Victor, with a period movie, the audience expects certain things: scope as well as costumes, intelligent dialogue as well as first-rate performances. That's the way I've conceived this, and if you get too far away from that original concept . . ."

"Not now, okay? About the Awards . . ." He rolled his desk chair closer to the couch, reached for her foot and began to massage her toes. "I really think you've got a chance. What's the competition? Some flick about ocean pollution . . ."

"Which happens to be excellent."

". . . another one about disabled athletes overcoming the odds, and some Holocaust remembrance. Hey, it's all been done before."

"Teenage runaways aren't exactly flavor of the month."

"I'm telling you, you have a chance. And you know you do. You're not just artsy, you're ambitious, you know what's possible. You have to be grounded in what's possible to be successful.''

"I don't disagree with that.''

The sun slanted through the window, burnishing her hair and turning her eyes a lighter shade of green. "I think of all those years ago when we used to watch the Awards on TV,'' she said.

"And trash them.''

"And trash them.'' They both laughed. He liked her best when she laughed. Laughing made her playful and somehow reckless.

"It'd be great to go to the Awards together, but . . .''

"But you already have a date.''

"Yeah. I already have a date. Who's yours?''

"My producer. Sam Alhauser.''

"I know Sam. He used to be a gofer for my grandfather. He was on his way to the big time when HUAC cut off his water.'' He took her foot in both hands and massaged it gently, his thumbs pressing into her sole. It felt so good she couldn't bear to move.

"I like ol' Sam,'' she said. "I like that certain type of Jew from that generation. He's all cigars and shrewdness, but he's still such an idealist. He told me today when I called him that he'd had his tux altered. He's sure we're gonna win. Then he said, 'So, you darlink girl, if God forbid we don't win and God forbid your Aussie feature doesn't come through, I'm putting together a deal on a documentary about the ACLU so you shouldn't be outta work.' ''

"Why don't you bring him to my parents' for their post-Awards party?'' He'd progressed to her calf now, handling it with the touch of an experienced masseur, pressing and kneading, deep but not too deep, feeling her response.

"I'll be with Toni. And I'm trying to wangle extra tickets for Irene and George.''

"I can get you tickets. Bring 'em along to the party.''

She shook her head. "They'd probably be uncomfortable. I'd be uncomfortable. The last Hollywood party I went to was a cross between a drug dealers' convention and a business college reunion. Talk about dull! And the one before that was even worse. All the old guard. A barbecue at some third-generation director's house in Topanga Canyon. Everyone brought their kids and played normal. It coulda been a company picnic at General Foods except the kids were more obnoxious. No, after the Awards I'll probably just go to the hotel and mourn."

"And you don't have to go to a hotel. You can stay here. Both you and Toni can stay. I won't *bother* you, though I'll admit to a very ripe rape fantasy." His hand encircled her knee. "Oh, how I'd like to tie you up."

"I'm sure you can find someone to accommodate your fantasy," she said, shifting her leg. "I'm not the kind to be tied up." Her tone was lightly derisive but her voice came out throaty.

"You miss the point, sweetheart. It's the ones who won't be tied up who're the most desirable."

As she moved aside her skirt slid up, revealing a moon-shaped scar. Seeing it, he said bluntly, "Let's not walk on the beach. Let's not see a movie. Let's go to bed. Afternoons were always your favorite time."

"You're cute, Victor."

"But not as cute as your Aussie doctor? Maybe I shouldn't be helping you get back over there."

"And why are you? Tell me again."

"Because the screenplay is good."

"You've done nothing but poke holes in it."

"I'm good at poking holes, remember?"

She groaned.

"Walked right into that one, didn't you?" he asked and made his move to the couch. He pulled her to him, one hand firmly on her back, the other pushing up her skirt. "Tell me again how you got this little scar," he whispered, caressing it with his thumb.

"I fell out of a tree at Uncle Mick's and landed on the lid of a can."

As he bent and kissed it, she felt herself about to give way, no longer teetering on the brink but going over the edge, falling into dizzying space. But when his head came up, she saw in his heavy-lidded eyes not just desire but a triumph that bordered on self-satisfaction. Sex would always be a power struggle with them, which, she supposed, was the essence of its allure. But also the worm in the apple. Being literally tied up was a child's game, being emotionally captive was quite another.

She pulled herself free and stood, steadying herself against the desk. He fell back onto the cushions, still eyeing her. "Playing hard to get?"

"Not playing. I am hard to get." Hollow boast. "Want to take that walk now?"

"Just give me a few minutes to . . . subside." He watched her as she collected the wineglasses and carried them to the bar. "How come you don't wear miniskirts anymore? They're in fashion again."

"If you're old enough to remember them the first time around, you're too old to do it again." Which, she told herself, was the way she should feel about him. But was she really getting so old that she could be sensible about sex? She hadn't said no when she'd wanted it since the backseat tugs of war of her virgin years.

"That little scar on your thigh, what'd you use to call that?" he asked laconically.

"When a wound heals without stitches it forms a little white welt and its called proud flesh."

"Proud flesh. That's you, Megan. That's you to a tee." And to restore the balance of power, he said he really didn't want to walk on the beach but had to make some phone calls. She was welcome to go alone if she wished.

She did, walking at first, then running, wanting to think it was the skirt that was slowing her down but finally stopping, breathing heavily, admitting that she was shamefully out of shape. Yet she was in a rare mood of exaltation. The satisfaction of turning him down had been sweet as clear water to a parched mouth. That wasn't an admirable way to feel, but she believed what people like Joan and Uncle Mick had taught her: know thyself, warts and all. She started to run again, imagining the night of the Awards. Even if she didn't win, she was part of the game.

The moon was high, the sound of the surf both invigorating and relaxing. The patio table was set with flowers and heavy Mexican pottery that glowed in the candlelight. The wine was excellent, the paella spicy and succulent . . . and the dinner was a disaster. Victor left the table twice to answer phone calls, one from his mother, another from the director in Canada, who predicted yet another day of rain. Whenever attention drifted away from her, Deirdre became sullen. She dipped her fingers into the candles and rolled the wax into little balls. She tore the petals off a flower. She picked at her vegetarian plate and warned them of the dangers of eating sausage and shrimp. Victor fielded this and other criticisms with a cautious, explanatory tone, but it was clear to Megan that when it came to Deirdre, Victor was strung between boredom and anxiety. When Deirdre got up and went to the kitchen to accuse Maria of putting butter on her carrots and snow peas, Victor whispered, ''I'm afraid she's not eating enough.''

''At her age I thought the worry was with sex and drugs.''

''She's already been through that. She had an abortion when she was fifteen,'' he said, ''and she's been off coke and pills for over a year, at least as far as I know.''

This information saddened Megan so much that she became flip. ''It's like Lily Tomlin says, 'No matter how cynical I become, I still can't keep up.' When did diet replace sex as a source of guilt? Imagine being past sex before you've even reached your majority.''

''She's very concerned with her weight now. With her health.''

''But didn't she have two drinks before dinner?''

Victor was somber. ''I've found some religious tracts in her room.''

Megan rolled her eyes. ''Food faddism *and* religious tracts? Now that's the worst of all possible worlds. But hey, you shouldn't have snooped. Don't you remember how much you hated it when your mother snooped in your room? I do. And kids have some rights of privacy. Anytime you snoop you're bound to find what you've been afraid of.''

''It's easy to tell you're not a parent. It's the food thing that worries me now. Three girls in her class are anorexic.''

This information had the effect of making Megan lose her appetite. She pushed her plate aside and leaned across the table. ''I don't know Deirdre well enough to guess, but might this not be another way of getting your attention? She's desperate for it, and getting attention can be addictive, too. You really should ease up. You've been the absent father all these years. You can't hope that it's going to be smooth now. You'll just have to grin and bear it and hope that when she's in her twenties you two can make a go of it. But that's years off. In the meantime, there's nothing for it but to . . .''

"It's cold out here," Deirdre complained, rejoining them. "Let's go inside."

Victor said, "Maria's about to serve dessert and coffee."

"If you're cold, why don't you get a cardigan?" Megan suggested.

But Deirdre sat back down, wrapping her arms around her chest.

Maria appeared, carrying a tray of flan, guava paste and cheese. Stuck for a conversational bridge, Megan asked Deirdre about school.

"I've already told you." She sighed. "It's a drag. Dad told me you went to a convent school and you had to wear funny uniforms and they were even allowed to hit you."

"Yes."

"Catholics are so weird."

As Maria set down her dessert plate, her eyes met Megan's and quickly lowered. "Coffee, señorita?"

"Yes, please."

"And I'll bet most of those nuns were lesbians."

"Try not to be both scurrilous and clichéd, Deirdre. Any group has its weirdos. Some were suppressed, misguided, hungry for power, ill-informed—all of that, but I don't suppose there was much more neurosis than you'd find at your local shopping mall. I don't regret my Catholic education."

"Weird." Deirdre shook her head and played with her spoon. "No matter what you say, Megan, I bet you had a terrible childhood."

"Not so, but if it makes me a more romantic figure in your eyes, go ahead and believe it."

"I've had a terrible childhood."

"Then why do you cling to it so?" Megan asked. "You know, Deirdre, at some point we have to put it behind us and ask how we're going to get on with the rest of our lives. Seventeen seems like a good time to look forward instead of back."

Deirdre considered this, not sure if it was good advice or a personal attack. "Let's go inside. You could come to my room and see this video I made with some of the air-heads at school."

"Just now I'd like to finish my coffee. And your father looks as though he's desperate for his after-dinner smoke."

"He shouldn't smoke."

"Right. But he does. And it's his house."

"It's my house, too," Deirdre flashed.

"And you seem to do pretty much as you want. Don't be such a tyrant."

"I'm going to my room." This was announced as a threat.

"And I'm going to finish my coffee," Megan said calmly. "I'll come and say good-bye before I leave."

When Deirdre had flounced off, Victor took the pack of Marlboros from his pocket, looked across at her and said, half resentful, half respectful, "You really know how to handle her."

"I didn't mean to overstep"—though frankly she didn't give a damn—"but I won't take rudeness from a kid that I wouldn't tolerate in an adult." She felt some understanding and sympathy for Deirdre, but putting up with her was another thing entirely. They sat in silence for a few minutes. She drained her coffee and shivered. "Deirdre's right about one thing: it is getting chilly out here. And I should be going."

"You said Toni's plane gets in at eleven-fifteen, didn't you? You've got plenty of time. Come on inside. I'll light the fire."

Listening to the distant sluicing of the dishwasher, she watched as Victor set the fire, resisting the impulse to tell him that he wasn't using enough kindling. Maria came in, asked if there was anything else they might need, and went off to bed. Victor twirled a balloon glass of Armagnac and stood in front of the fire, silently ordering it to catch. Finally it crackled into life and he came to sit beside her, staring into the flames.

"You know, Megan," he began, and she rearranged herself to face him, "this afternoon when I came on with you . . ."

Oh, please no, she thought, if we're not going to do it, please let's not talk about doing it. "Mmmm . . ."

". . . I wasn't just trying for a quick fix. I could tell by the way you looked at me that's what you thought. I was trying to get you into the sack because I thought that would be the best place to ask you . . .''

"Ask me what?''

"Want to get married again?''

Her lips parted in incredulity, turned up in a stupefied smile, then she laughed.

"I've never had that reaction before,'' Victor said dryly. "Before you laugh, let's take a look at it. We've both been around. You're not with anybody, at least not anybody serious. I'm not with anybody, though my mother's doing her damnedest to tie me up with this producer I'm taking to the Awards. Can you imagine me being married to a producer?''

"What's she like?''

"Elaine? Oh, she's okay. We've known each other since we were kids. But I was saying . . . I like being married. Essentially, I'm monogamous.''

"You coulda fooled me.''

"I mean I can make an emotional commitment now. Let's get real, Megan, who has the time to fuck around? At our age . . .''

"Only in Hollywood is forty considered ready for the bone heap. If you're feeling creaky, don't count me in.''

"At our age, you want to be with someone who knows you, someone you trust. We talked about having kids once. We could still do that if you wanted. It wouldn't mean giving up your work. I'd never want you to do that. You know I'd be behind anything you wanted to do. And I have the resources.''

"Is this a proposal or a proposition for a business deal?''

"I don't think they're mutually exclusive. I figured you'd appreciate it if I put it to you straight. We did the fools-rush-in bit before. This time we could make a go of it. And we'd never need a sex therapist.''

She traced the line of his jaw with her finger. As a business deal it was not without appeal. She'd never have to worry about money again. She could live in this lovely house, invite the movers and shakers to dinner and make deals poolside. She could have a baby. "This is very sudden.''

"We've known each other over twenty years. And I've loved you . . .''

"On and off.''

"I didn't think I could appeal to your romantic nature 'cause I know you don't have much of it left. Neither do I. But I do love you." He was about to draw her to him when she saw, over his shoulder, Deirdre, dressed in T-shirt and bikini pants, standing at the door. She pulled back. "Deirdre, I was just getting ready to come in and tell you good night."

"Sure. It looks like it."

Megan made a show of looking at her watch. "I do have to go." She got up and went to Deirdre, laying her cheek against hers.

"I'm sorry if I was a shit," Deirdre said. "Are you gonna come back? I mean, no matter what happens with you and Daddy?"

"Sure—"

"And we'll get together after the Awards? To celebrate."

"We'll get together even if there's nothing to celebrate."

Deirdre was mollified. "Okay, then. I guess I'll go to bed. 'Night, Megan. 'Night, Dad."

Victor walked Megan to the car. As she opened the door he turned her and pulled her into his arms. "I do have to go," she said, and with an insouciance that eased the parting, "Besides, me Great-grandmother Kathleen always told me, 'A kiss is more than a handshake.' "

CHAPTER
TWENTY-ONE

THE MORNING OF THE AWARDS MEGAN WOKE UP IN A
fit of itching and scratching. She tiptoed to the hotel bathroom,
flipped on the light and leaned into the mirror. Her neck was
blotched with a bright pink rash. "Oh, shit!"

"Greeting the dawn with your usual lyric cheerfulness?" Toni
called.

"Sorry. I didn't mean to wake you."

"You didn't. I'm like a kid on Christmas morning. I've been
awake for ages, just snoozing here having fantasies." They'd
taken the room together, ostensibly to hold down expenses but
also because they'd wanted each other's company.

"Look at this," Megan came to the foot of Toni's bed and
stretched her neck. "A stigmata. A full-blown case of nervous
eczema. And I thought I felt calm."

Toni pulled herself up into a sitting position, leaned forward
and studied Megan's neck. "Don't it always happen? The pim-
ple before the big dance, the period on your wedding night. It
doesn't look too bad. I don't think the camera will pick it up."

"The cameras may never pick *me* up, but I would like to go
to the Awards without looking like the centerfold of a derma-
tology magazine."

"The choker. We'll go back and buy the choker." They'd
trailed around the shops on Rodeo Drive the previous afternoon,
ogling the latest evening fashions—all sequined and balloon-
skirted taffetas that, Toni pointed out, would make you look like
a lampshade or a chorus girl from *Can-Can*. Megan had decided
to content herself with her little black strapless. Then they had
spotted the choker of jet beads and feathers that could give the
dress just the right festive and sexy touch, but Megan had balked

at the four-hundred-dollar price tag. "Okay," she now agreed, "we'll go back and spring for that choker."

"But first let's call room service." Toni yawned and stretched. "Megan, you've corrupted me entirely. I now know that I was meant to live in classy hotels and only visit my family on national holidays."

After breakfast they went to a Sav-On and bought calamine lotion, then drove into Beverly Hills to get the choker. George and Irene arrived around noon and after checking them into the hotel, Toni and Megan took them to lunch at Musso & Frank's, then drove them through swanky neighborhoods so Irene could rubberneck at palatial homes, mainly owned by Saudis, Japanese and Iranians who called themselves Persians. Back at the hotel, while Toni went to have her hair done, Megan tried to nap. She shifted all over the bed, as though some particular spot or position would offer rest, but was too anxious to sleep.

Toni had already dressed, but Megan was still in her robe, peeling off a pair of false eyelashes she'd taken ten minutes to apply then decided against, when there was a knock at the door. "Oh, no. That'll be my mother. And she'll stand here like some guy reading the newspaper over my shoulder on the subway." Toni, handsome in her green crepe de chine, let George and Irene in and immediately suggested that they all wait in the lobby while Megan finished dressing. But Irene said she wanted a few minutes alone with Megan. As George dutifully followed Toni out, she came to the bathroom door, looking deceptively affluent in a beaded ice-blue dress she'd made for herself. "You'd better get a move on," she advised.

"I know." Megan tissued off the botched eye makeup.

"I spoke to Michael a little while ago. He sends his love and best wishes."

"Good." She threw off the robe and stepped into her dress. "How's he doing?" Irene was behind her, easing up the zipper, and Megan remembered Victor's steady hands performing the same task at the Fremantle hotel.

"How would I know? He's hardly ever at the rectory. I've been trying to reach him for days. I have a feeling he's keeping something from me. He didn't say anything to you, did he?"

"No," Megan lied, imagining Michael on a midnight run

with some terrified illegal crouched on the floor of the car. She'd tried to convince him to come clean with Irene, reasoning that mothers usually intuited when something was up, but he'd clung to his wouldn't-want-to-worry-her defense. She began to dab on the calamine.

"Neither of you ever tell me what's going on." Irene sighed, then: "It's too bad you broke out in that rash."

"Sure is."

"But even as a child your nerves always showed on your skin. I remember . . ."

"Mom!" Megan warned.

"I have some makeup that disguises liver spots. I could get it from . . ."

"No. I've bought this little choker . . ." If she could only get it fastened. "It should cover up most of it."

"How much did you pay for it?"

"Two hundred," she lied again, but Irene was still shocked.

"Two hundred! I could've made it for you for—"

"I needed it in a hurry."

Irene laughed. "It reminds me of a frilled-neck lizard."

Four hundred dollars to look like a frilled-neck lizard? "Mom, if you could just . . ." Irene stepped aside as Megan searched for the eye shadow.

"I only wish . . ."

"That I was three inches taller, with a flawless complexion and a bosom that could do justice to this dress? So do I." Where had she put the green eye shadow?

"No. That you were going to the Awards with someone you were interested in."

Ah, there was the shadow. As she grabbed it she spilled the powder. "I'm interested in all of you."

"I meant a proper man."

"Ah, but I don't like proper men." She winked and held her eye closed as she dotted on the shadow. ". . . any more than you did."

"I only meant, on such an important night . . ."

Shit! She'd smudged it. She didn't need reminders that she didn't have a real date.

"You didn't tell me how it went with Victor."

"He gave me a dose of his hard-bitten commercial advice."

"He is tremendously successful. Or so I hear."

"Yeah. I admire his savvy, but not its products. You ever see any of his movies?"

"You know George won't go to the movies anymore."

"And who can blame him. You know"—Megan waved her mascara wand—"Victor told me he's negotiating for the right to the story of the Hillside Strangler. It sticks in my craw that some psychotic will make money from his crimes." She capped the mascara and hurriedly dabbed a puff into the spilled powder. "Well, you know me: one foot in and one foot out of the polluted stream of commercialism."

"You saw his daughter again?"

"Oh, yes. She managed to make the dinner miserable."

"You usually get along well with young people."

"In short doses. I actually like the kid but she's a very disturbed young woman." She'd given a lot of thought to the emotional obligations of being Deirdre's stepmother. No doubt Deirdre would like the idea, at least initially, but once the novelty had worn off she could imagine herself cast in the unenviable roles of disciplinarian, go-between and rival. She tipped her head forward and began to brush her hair.

"Here," Irene volunteered, "let me do the back."

"No. I can." Christ! Who did she think usually did the back?

"You used to be like this every morning when you went to school. Always running late."

"Mom, if you'd leave me alone, I could . . ."

"I'll be glad to finally meet Victor's parents."

"Wait'll you do before you say that. The father's nice enough. A killer in the business world but absolutely cowed on the home front. And Sylvia? Sylvia has to be seen to be believed." Victor talked a great line about his emotional maturity, but he couldn't stand up to either his daughter or his mother.

"I hope I look all right," Irene said uncertainly. "I couldn't get any stockings that quite matched this shade and . . ."

"You look fine." Perhaps she should've had her hair done, but she couldn't trust a new hairdresser to know how to . . .

"Megan, I'll bet Victor's still in love with you."

"Mom. I'm late. I have to get ready!"

"I worry about you, Megan. After all these years, still not having . . . well, not having any real security and . . ."

Megan slammed down the brush. "Ease up!" She turned to face Irene and was immediately overwhelmed with remorse. What a self-absorbed little bitch she was not to allow Irene a few moments of closeness, not to have taken in Irene's fears about going to the Taubs' party. "You do look classy, Mom," she said tenderly. "Don't be intimidated by any of 'em."

Irene's lip twitched and her eyes filled. "You look very pretty yourself. That black strapless sets off your white shoulders, and the choker . . ."

"Makes me look like a reptile in a defensive display and I lied, I didn't pay two hundred, I paid four." They both laughed.

"Doesn't matter," Irene said. "It gives you just the right air of . . ." She remembered a phrase from a fashion magazine. ". . . frivolous chic."

"I love you, Mom. I really love you." She moved to embrace her.

"No, no. You'll muss yourself." Irene took her face gently and kissed her forehead.

"You made me what I am today. I hope you're satisfied," Megan joked.

"Even if you don't win . . ."

"Shhh."

". . . I'm very proud of you. I'll wait downstairs."

After Irene left, Megan put on her lipstick and looked at herself in the mirror. Fine. Right. As good as could be expected. She slipped into her heels, grabbed her little satin purse and headed for the door, then impulsively darted back to rummage in the pocket of her suitcase. She found the torquoise ring that had been left (along with a silver belt buckle and a wallet containing twenty-seven dollars and an expired driver's license) in the bag of valuables they'd given her at the veterans hospital. The ring was too large to fit her fingers so she slipped it into her bra. She took a deep breath, crossed herself (now where had *that* come from?) and left.

Sam paced the lobby, looking as proud and uncomfortable in his tux as a pudgy bar mitzvah boy in his first suit. The dome

of his head was already shiny with perspiration. When introduced to George and Irene, he seized and pumped George's
hand and kissed Irene's cheek with a resounding smack. He told
Toni she knew how to fill out the front of a dress and boomed,
"What a girl! What a girl!" at Megan, then led them to the limo
as though he were the drum major in a parade. But as soon as
they stepped outside Megan felt her spirits deflate.

Since the Awards were now held in the early evening, to capture the largest television audience, it was still light outside, a
tired sun burning through hazy, soupy air that made you want
to hold your breath. Sam lit his cigar and as they drove past
billboards and pollution-ridden trees, he regaled them with stories of the milk-and-honey land that Los Angeles had once been.
The traffic on the freeway was as thick as the smog and they
advanced and stalled, advanced and stalled, the drivers in other
cars staring at them with unabashed curiosity, sometimes even
pointing at them. What did she really care about the damned
Academy Awards, Megan asked herself. Of course she still
watched them, but cynically, more out of habit than genuine
interest. She knew they were a clubby affair, that members voted
out of sentimentality, or because of an effective publicity campaign, that movies with the latest release stood a disproportion-
ate chance of winning, as though the members had such short
memories that only recent viewing stuck in their minds. And
On the Streets had been released early in the year with an infin-
itesimal publicity budget. The documentary she'd thought most
worthy, a gloomy but brilliantly made exposé of the nuclear-
power industry, had not even been nominated; nor had the
actress whose performance she'd most admired. And the ceremony itself would be a drag, stretched out with interminably
long production numbers of tuneless songs, and shopworn jokes
about some starlet's cleavage or the difficulty of opening the
envelope. She was in such a funk that she started to add up how
much it was costing them to attend, even including the suit Irene
had badgered George into purchasing. Poor George was encouraging Sam's stories (not that Sam needed encouragement)
with a heartiness that was entirely alien to him, and Irene's face
was greenish from inhaling Sam's cigar smoke.

But once they arrived, inching through the police line, seeing the television cameras and the throng of fans, impatience gave way and they were all infected with the crowd energy.

"Isn't that Jack Nicholson and . . . what's her name?" Irene said, staring at the limo in front of them.

"Anjelica Houston," Toni supplied, craning her neck.

The limo stopped to unload Sam and Megan at the main entrance. George offered a stolid "Good luck," Irene said, "God bless you," and Toni gave a thumbs-up salute and growled, "Knock 'em dead," before they were driven off to the audience entrance. Sam held tight to Megan's hand, steering her through the barricaded and noisy fans. His hand was so sweaty that it kept slipping from hers. Or maybe it was her own hand that was sweaty. She had a strong sense of *déjà vu.*

She had been at the Awards before. It had been nighttime then, with great arc lights blotting out the sky. The press of bodies had both excited and frightened her. She'd been high up—yes, on Thomas Shelby's shoulders, her child's arms clasped around his neck, her chin resting on the thick dark hair he combed while wet, so that it had deep, sculpted lines in it. And he had been restless, maybe even angry. Life to him was not a spectator sport and he must have resented being with the viewers instead of the doers, on the wrong side of the barricades. She was on the right side now. But that wasn't enough. A desire made more potent because it had not been fully acknowledged surged through her. Even knowing that the Awards were a sham, little more than a giant publicity turn, she wanted to win. She had to win.

Unlikely because of the crush of people, she saw Victor almost as soon as they entered the lobby. He looked wonderful in his evening clothes. He was with a tall, bosomy, dark-haired woman in a chartreuse balloon-skirted dress similar to the ones she and Toni had made fun of the day before. He spotted Megan and squeezed his way over to shake Sam's hand and bring his mouth close to her ear.

"Why is tonight different from all other nights?" he whispered. "Because tonight you're going to get an Oscar."

Such confident prediction made her nervously superstitious and she started to say so, but he was already gone and Sam was hustling her down to their seats, which were close to the stage but far over on the left. She turned and looked up into the balcony in a futile attempt to locate Toni and Irene, then became absorbed in the faces around her, matching their larger-than-life screen image with the reality. Despite sags and wrinkles, nips and tucks, the oldsters seemed to hold up best. The cue was given for them to settle down, but like unruly children, they all continued to touch and talk. The lights dimmed, the crowd hushed.

"Ladies and gentlemen, the Academy of Motion Picture Arts and Sciences presents . . ." Sam tightened his grip on her hand. Her neck started to itch. The stage lights went up and the MC, a television talk-show hostess with a mean mouth, bustled on to acceptably enthusiastic applause. Megan forced her spine into the seat. At least the award for Best Documentary would come early in the program. She didn't think she could stand it if they'd have to wait until the end.

Production numbers, the Irving Thalberg Award, the award for best special effects . . . would they get on with it! Her backside was numb, she was tired of watching the very pregnant nominee for Best Actress, who was sitting directly in front of them. The actress was making a great show of whispered affection to her date, an English actor the press had fingered as the likely father of her child, though everyone in the film community knew he was gay. Another production number, absurdly combining Best Song with Best Costume nominee, the dancers mincing and prancing about in Lycra tights topped with fourteenth-century vests and cravats. The Best Foreign Film award. She watched this with some interest since, years ago, she'd had a brief fling with the cinematographer, a Hungarian with mournful eyes who'd charmed her with his pronunciation of her name (Mee-gun). He was back in Hungary now, enjoying the thaw of *glasnost*, or so she supposed since she couldn't see him in the audience. Surely Best Documentary would be next. But no. There was a brief nod to social conscience with a word about AIDS. Would they get on with it!

"And in the Best Documentary category . . ." She saw Sam sink back in his seat, his body taut as a dental patient anticipating the drill. Again she became stupidly superstitious, thinking that they would win if their film clip was shown first. It was shown last. *On the Streets*. She watched the clip of the teenage girl—May Beth, was that her name?—yes, May Beth, with her dripping nose, mangy rabbit fur jacket and leather miniskirt—May Beth talking about how warm it had been in her hometown in Louisiana as she huddled against the alley walls of a Broadway theater that was being demolished. The finger-numbing cold of the shoot came back to her. Toni had kept running around to the deli on Forty-forth at Tenth, bringing May Beth cups of watery cocoa. May Beth's pimp had loitered at the end of the alleyway, chatting up the crew with smarmy friendliness, asking if there was any money in this or when it would be shown on TV. Toni had offered to take May Beth home with her, but the girl had gone off with the pimp while Toni stood, freezing and sad, sipping cocoa and saying, "Son of a bitch, son of a bitch," and Megan rushed to the cameraman and hissed, "Get that shot."

And that was the shot on the screen now: May Beth lurching off with her pimp in the whirling snow. Where was the girl now, Megan wondered? Possibly dead. Or turning tricks in a Tenth Avenue fleabag, which amounted to much the same thing.

Lights up. Applause. "And the winner is . . ." The actress and actor presenting the award fiddled with the envelope. Megan wanted to slap them. ". . . the winner is: *On the Streets*, written and directed by Megan Hanlon, produced by Samuel I. Alhauser."

Sam was so excited that he bounded into the aisle before turning to kiss her, and Megan stumbled into his embrace, then moved quickly, leading the way, her shoulders as straight as if Sister Claire were poking her between the blades with her ruler and giving her a lecture about posture. She had to get up there while the applause was still cresting.

As she mounted the steps her heart thumped and she realized that in a stupid hedge against disappointment she hadn't prepared an acceptance speech. She stared into the lights, consciously stopping herself from blinking. The microphone was in front of her and she was saying something about the plight of the runaways, drugs, and America's neglected children, thanking Sam, and Toni, the crew and cameraman, her mother, Irene, and her father, George, while remembering how clichéd she'd always found these predictable expressions of gratitude. The presenting actor's hand was on her elbow and his touch made her conscious of the need to finish up. She took a half step back, then came forward, raising the statuette: "Thomas Shelby, this is for you."

Guided into the wings, the applause still ringing in her ears, she almost tripped over a tangle of cable. Sam steadied and hugged her. "And who's Thomas Shelby?" he asked. She shook her head. Her sobs shocked her. Triumph had released the grief she hadn't been able to express and tears made flaming passage down her cheeks.

"It's okay. It's okay." Sam soothed, ignoring the stagehand who was motioning them to move aside, and wiping her cheeks with his thumb. "We made it. We made it, Megan darling."

Standing in the middle of the crowd in the Taubs' living room, Megan sipped champagne, accepted congratulations and allowed herself to gloat. This was the very room in which Victor had presented her so many years ago, the room in which she'd felt intimidated and rejected by Sylvia, whom she had yet to see, though several of Sylvia's muddle-and-puddle canvases marred the walls. But she knew that her hostess, wherever she was, was aware of her presence and her triumph.

Irene and George stayed close to her, basking in reflected glory and informing well-wishers that they'd always known Megan had a future in movies, a memory lapse for which she was more than willing to forgive them. "A really fine film. Really fine," a stocky man who owned a chain of movie houses told her, and his wife added vigorously, as though contradicting, "I thought it was marvelous." The wife began to talk about a neighbor's child who had run away, but was interrupted by a man with thick eyebrows and a complexion that never saw the sun. He introduced himself as Christopher Leventhal. This was the agent Victor had told her about and, judging from the deferential behavior of those around her, he was an important one. Where was Victor? She craned her neck but couldn't see him. "And here . . ."—Christopher Leventhal nudged a young blonde forward—"is Kimberly Delsartre. She's been anxious to meet you."

Kimberly was as perfect as a mannequin in a Saks window but without the look of aggressive hauteur that was molded on those faces; indeed, she seemed genuinely shy, speaking so softly that Megan had to incline her head to hear her. "I'm so glad you won, Miss Hanlon," she said with the trace of a lisp. "Chris arranged for me to see *On the Streets* last week because I loved your new screenplay so much."

"Thank you."

"I really identified with Sarah and those other poor convict women. Before I read it, I didn't know much more about Australia than the Qantas ads."

"*The Fatal Shore* is a great book for historical background."

"I'll remember that. But listen, when Sarah first has sex with Lieutenant Clarke, does she love him?"

"No. Not at first. She does it because she knows that if she becomes his mistress she'll get extra rations and have some protection from the other men."

"That's what I thought. Sometimes, when people are in a tight spot, they'll do anything . . . they'll . . ." As Kimberly struggled to express herself, a look of baffled determination sharpened her features.

"Yes," Megan helped her out, aware that those around them had stopped talking. If she could get Kimberly past what "people" did and down to the raw nerve of what she'd probably done, it might be possible to pry, goad and cajole a performance out of her. Of course there was that lisp, but that was probably an affectation, and a full-time dialect coach was already written into the budget because if there was one thing she couldn't abide it was a babble of different accents.

"Maybe we could have lunch and talk about it. Just the two of us," Kimberly said, with a sidelong glance at Leventhal.

"Yeah," he assented, "let's get together."

"There's no need for you to be there, Chris." Kimberly asserted herself with a touch of resentment. "We'll just be talking about the script and the character motivation."

So, Megan thought, at least she's in some acting class. But she was no Nita Narinto, and never would be. They were making arrangements to meet when Sam came up, put his arm around Megan and told her there was someone he wanted her to meet.

She made the date with Kimberly and excused herself. They walked past the den where a bevy of guests were watching a video replay of the Awards. No, she would not bring herself down by seeing her acceptance speech. And she had to get some food into her stomach. She was already a little tipsy. Strange that she could exercise control in success, but never in defeat.

They stopped by the buffet table and she fixed herself a plate of finger food. Toni sidled up to her and said, "Ah, sweet smell of success. I'm workin' the room and they're asking me what we're going to be doing next." An actor who'd lost out for Best Supporting was slumped near the buffet, glass dangling from his hand, his face dangerously close to the chopped liver. Megan paused long enough to praise his performance.

"Don't shit me," he grumbled. "I'll probably never work again."

"I hate a sore loser," Sam said as he guided her to the patio door, though she wondered just how magnanimous they would have been in defeat.

They were stopped again on the steps and after more congratulations and introductions, Sam led the way down to the pool. "Megan, I want you to meet a very old friend." Sam indicated a wizened man who'd been all but swallowed up by a deckchair. A shock of yellowish white hair stood up from his monkey-bright face. "This is Sol Taubinski. He gave me my first job sweepin' up the sets, so you can imagine how old he is."

Sol croaked, "Sure. I got one foot in the grave and the other on a banana skin, but I'm not dead yet. I still know a pretty woman when I see one." His eyes glittered in the network of wrinkles. "But hey, don't I know you?"

"I'm Megan Hanlon." And more softly, "Victor's first wife."

"Sure. Sure. Now I remember. Abie's Irish Rose. I think I liked you."

Sam was exuberant. "What's not to like? She won me an Oscar. An Oscar I've wanted all my life. She's got looks, she's got smarts, she's got everything but a good pair of knockers." He added a quick but amused "Sorry" in answer to Megan's warning look, then went on, "And you know what else she's got? She's got integrity."

"Not to worry." Sol smiled up at her. "That affliction is so rare in these parts that they don't worry much about the symptoms because they know it's not catching."

"She's on a roll now. I know it. Someday I'm gonna say I knew her when."

"I did know her when. I figured she must be all right because my witch of a daughter-in-law never liked her. And speaking of trouble . . .'' Sol's eyes roamed to the steps. "Here it comes."

Megan popped a piece of cheese into her mouth and turned. Sylvia Taub stood at the patio door in a gold pantsuit. From that distance she appeared not to have changed at all, but as she came closer, on heels so high they made her ankles wobble, the illusion was shattered. She lacked the texture of youth. Her hair, though subtly colored, was brittle and her scalp peeked through the artful arrangement of curls and ribbons. Her skin, stretched too tight by too many lifts, was coated with moisturizer that floated on it like a film of oil.

"Megan, how wonderful to see you again!" She clasped Megan's hand, and her rings, decorations for a lifetime of successful marital campaigns, felt like rocks. "I haven't seen your film, but congratulations. It's always wonderful to see a woman win." Megan smiled at the generic compliment. It was, she thought, less an expression of Sylvia's newfound sisterhood than a way of minimizing her individual accomplishment. "Yes, always good to see a woman win," Sylvia repeated.

Sol sucked his teeth in disgust. "She'd congratulate Imelda Marcos just because she was born with a puss—"

"Cigar, Sol?" Sam put in quickly.

"Sol," Sylvia flashed. "I wish you wouldn't smoke. It smells so terribly, and you know the doctor said it would shorten your life."

"Shorten my life? Shorten my life? At ninety-two I say, 'From your mouth to God's ear.' Who wants to stick around anyway? Pollution and television, and the Arabs and Japanese buying up the city, producers who aren't dry behind the ears stuffing their lunch up their noses, Ted Turner playing with his Crayolas and ruining the best pictures ever made . . .'' His list of complaints was interrupted by a spasm of coughing, but he reached for one of Sam's cigars and continued, "You see what won Best Picture tonight? A piece of dreck. Now in 1939—what a year!—you remember it, Sam. You probably remember it, Sylvia, though you wouldn't admit it. In 1939 *Gone With the Wind, Ninotchka, Stagecoach, Wuthering Heights, Mr. Smith Goes to Washington, The Wizard of Oz* . . . They were all nominated.'' He sniffed the cigar and thrust his face out for a light. Sam, balancing precariously on the edge of a deckchair, obliged. Sylvia made a moue of distaste and turned again to Megan. ''As I was saying, Megan, congratulations. I know it's been a terrible struggle. Women are always kept back. I know that from my own painful experience. Where did my life go? I often ask myself. Who knows what I could have done if I hadn't been forced to be concerned with family? If only I'd put my own talents first.''

''Talents?'' Megan heard Sol snort. ''Shopping is a talent? Having lunch is a talent?''

''Of course,'' Sylvia went on, pretending not to hear him, ''you've never had to cope with the burden of a family. You've never had any children, have you?''

A rhetorical question, delivered with such reproachful sympathy that Megan didn't deign to answer. ''And, of course, I still have family obligations,'' Sylvia went on, looking at Sol as though he were a stain on a carpet that countless cleanings had failed to banish. ''It's too late for my career as a concert pianist, but I suppose Victor's told you that I've found my métier in art. I have an almost uncanny visual talent, but I couldn't unleash it until I'd had a workshop in assertiveness training.'' (As necessary to you as it would have been to Genghis Khan, Megan thought.) ''And I've already had several showings. But as in so many other fields, the woman artist is at a disadvantage.'' Sylvia sighed. ''I suppose you could say I'm a survivor.'' (No, Megan thought, munching another piece of cheese, a survivor is someone who's been through a war, a revolution, a major illness, or is working at a soul-destroying job because her husband has skipped out on the child support.) ''The trouble with women,'' Sylvia droned on with unctuous certainty, ''is that we've always been too modest, not sufficiently assertive.''

Megan couldn't stop herself from saying, ''I suppose that beats immodest and gratingly assertive.''

"The trouble with women," Sam announced, "is that not enough of them will look at an alter cocker like me."

"I'll look at you, Sam." Megan broke the lethal exchange of glances with Sylvia. "I'll even sit on your lap." She did so, putting her arms around his neck as Victor walked up.

"I told you so. Can I say I told you so?" he asked. He was drunk but not offensively so, just enough to make him expansive.

"All you should say to her is *'Mazel tov!'* " Sol told him.

Victor bowed from the waist, said it and took her hand. "Come on over here with me. I want to talk with you alone."

Sylvia said, "I think Elaine was looking for you, Victor."

"Hey, Mother, you fixed me up, you entertain her for a while." Then, placatingly, "It's a good party."

"Is it? I'm too worn out to enjoy it, I suppose. The caterers were late, the bartender can't speak English, the florist—"

"It's a good party," he reassured her, pulling Megan up. "C'mon, sweetheart, or I'll throw you in the pool with your clothes on."

Sol stared wistfully at his cigar smoke. "I remember when we threw 'em in the pool with their clothes off."

As Megan and Victor walked away, Sylvia called, "Megan, if that rash on your neck doesn't clear up, I know the name of a wonderful dermatologist."

Victor pulled back, studying her neck. "Yeah, what happened to your neck? I didn't notice it before."

"You know me. Nerves." She started to take off the choker, which had been driving her crazy all night.

"We could cut out real soon. There's a party at Spielberg's and another at Bobby Duvall's. I talked to Elaine and she doesn't mind if you come along."

"That's nice of her, but I've got the parents in tow. Besides, I want to get back to the hotel and call the Aussie relatives."

"Then come and sit with me for a few minutes. Away from all this."

He led her around to the side of the house where chauffeurs lolled, chatting and smoking, against the limos. "Can't remember which one is mine. Don't suppose it matters. This one'll do." He opened a door and they got into the backseat. "*Mazel tov* again.'' He gave her a long, warm kiss, which she reciprocated. He sighed with satisfaction and sat back, his arm around her shoulder, looking out the windshield. ''I feel like we're at a drive-in movie. Remember them?''

''Uh-uh. I used to have to crouch on the floor in the backseat with a blanket over me so they didn't have to pay my fare and sometimes, when they thought I was asleep, they'd neck.'' She played with the feathers on the choker.

''Are you happy?''

''Yes. I think I am.''

''What we were talking about the other night . . .''

''My movie?'' she purposely misunderstood.

''About getting back together.''

She looked into his face. She had admitted, the night they'd gone to bed, that she still loved him a little bit, but that she didn't like him. Now she even liked him, or rather, she'd come to accept him for what he was, so yes, she even liked him. But apart from his business savvy she didn't respect him. How could any marriage survive if not founded on mutual respect? But she hadn't the slightest inclination to inform him of that; indeed she was inclined to protect him from such a painful assessment. ''The thing is . . .'' She took his hand. ''Did you ever see a remake that was as good as the original?''

He studied her, gave a little snort and shook his head slowly.

''Are you still interested in helping me get my movie together?'' she asked after a time.

Whether out of genuine interest or because he still hoped to impress her with his magnanimity, he said, ''Hey, I called Dennis Danher today to push him to read the script.''

''Thank you.'' And now she felt the urge to kiss him. ''We'd better get back to the party.''

He opened the door and stood, offering his hand to help her out. She grasped it and gave it a firm up-and-down shake. ''Great-grandmother Kathleen was wrong: sometimes a handshake is more than a kiss.''

CHAPTER
TWENTY-TWO

SHE'D SEEN THE SUN COME UP OVER THE INDIAN SUBCON-tinent, a magnificent red-and-gold orb that had inspired religious awe, and she'd been awake ever since. They were twenty minutes away from touchdown on the London-to-Perth journey now, and all but a few of the passengers had succumbed. Megan glanced into the dimly lit cabin and saw the expansive rear end of a woman who'd curled into her seat, a young couple who slept holding hands, the spill of light on the plastic tray of the workaholic who'd been doing accounts since the Singapore stopover. Her mood was one of such exuberant expectation that she even felt affection for these strangers.

She was coming back. And this time with the means to realize her dream. She could already hear, "Rolling . . . sound . . ." the slap of the clapboard, "Take one," though there was another month of preproduction ahead. No matter. She would settle in, have a chance to see those she loved. She crossed her foot over her knee and massaged her pins and needles before pulling on her boots, then got out her mirror and repaired her makeup. She was grateful that Tas was picking her up. Being greeted would make it seem more of a homecoming. She was eager to see Tas himself. If anyone had told her that she and Tas would become more intimate than they'd ever been during their affair through that old-fashioned and neglected form of intimacy, letter writing, she wouldn't have believed it. But they had. And she might have guessed that Tas, so reticent in conversation, could better reveal himself in correspondence.

He had written soon after she'd returned to New York, a long and confiding letter, apologizing for what had happened, telling her that he'd moved from the farm and was getting a divorce,

335

and asking about her progress with the movie. She had answered almost immediately and, over the following months, his letters had taken on the intimate confiding tone of a journal. Everyday events ("will have to have this bugger of a wisdom tooth out") were mixed with deeper concerns: his relationship with his children, the disparity between what he'd set out to be and what he had become, the dissolution of his partnership with Herbert Tishman. Her own letters had taken on a similar "Dear Diary" mix of practical concerns ("Heat off again. Will have to take the bastard landlord to court") and soul searching ("Now that it appears I'll get the financing, I'm awash with self-doubt—stupid, I know"). She'd had to read between the lines to understand his breakup with Naomi, not, she believed, because he was holding out on her but because he hadn't yet achieved the distance of understanding. After the divorce, he hadn't followed the all-too-familiar pattern of male neglect; indeed he'd tried to become more involved with his children. That had not pleased Naomi. Nor had his refusal of a lucrative offer to join a Houston practice. And, Megan supposed, the idea of marriage, so appealing when Tas and Naomi had been confined to illicit meetings, had palled once they'd had the freedom and burden of unlimited time together. Megan had restrained herself from saying he was well out of it.

Months after his breakup with Naomi, he'd mentioned, casually, that he was seeing other women. She'd mentioned, just as casually, that she was dating an entertainment lawyer by the name of Steve Holliman. It wasn't just her growing attachment to Tas (all right, she did wait for the mail) that made her consign Steve to a mere footnote. Steve simply didn't occupy much of her emotional life. He was that rare New York breed, a heterosexual bachelor in his late thirties who was looking to get married, yet he wore an invisible sign that said "No disruptive emotions." At first she'd thought that perhaps he was shielding a broken heart, but after a few months she began to suspect that Steve's emotional closet was too small and well-organized to permit any skeletons. That he had never been married or lived with a woman seemed a liability rather than an asset. There was something missing in a man who'd never cared enough to hurt or be hurt. It was Toni who had, quite unintentionally, crystallized Megan's doubts, not because she'd said, after meeting Steve Holliman, that he was a better-looking, richer version of her son-in-law, but because, with a slip of the tongue, Toni had called Steve "Mr. Hollowman." That was it. Hollow Man. What was the point of meeting, carefully groomed as dogs for a show, for expensive dinners, agreeable conversation and mutually satisfactory sex when she knew that there would never be love? She'd never be able to explain that to Steve and, fortunately, she wouldn't have to. The affair would peter out because of distance. They'd never even have to say good-bye.

Judging from Tas's letters, his involvements with other women had been as unemotional as hers with Steve. Like her, his time might not be his own, but his heart was. She hoped the closeness of the correspondence would carry over once they were face-to-face, but the fact that they now knew each other intimately might prove inhibiting. That would be a disappointment, but one she would accept. Hadn't George Bernard Shaw said, when confronted with the fact that his lengthy and passionate correspondence with Mrs. Patrick Campbell had never been consummated, "Some of the greatest love affairs have taken place only on paper"?

The lights came on and, simultaneously, the pilot announced that they were about to land.

Customs and immigration were briskly efficient. She wheeled her luggage trolley through the doors, scanning the waiting crowd. No Tas. She was swept along by other passengers. "Miss Hanlon," a woman called. "Welcome back to Australia." The woman waved and the photographer next to her started snapping away. She shouldered her way over to Megan. "Hi, I'm Diane McRobb. Don't s'pose you remember me. We met in New York and I did an article about you that came out last year, just before the festival. Could you spare me a few minutes of your time?"

"I do remember you, but . . ." She dodged as a child ran into the arms of his father. "I think we're blocking traffic." She looked around again. "A friend was supposed to meet me."

"Why don't we go over near the entrance? You'll be bound to see your friend from there." The photographer took over Megan's luggage cart and she followed McRobb to the line of bucket chairs near the front doors. Where could Tas be?

"Awfully nice of you to give me the time," McRobb said after they were seated. "I know it's inopportune when you're just getting off a long flight, but I have a deadline for the Arts supplement. Now. When do you start shooting?"

"The twenty-third of next month. I haven't checked with my astrologer but I hope it's an auspicious day."

"And where are your locations?"

"Western Australia and Tasmania, with pre- and postproduction in Sydney. I'll also be doing some final casting in Sydney—oh, don't put that in, please, I'm already deluged with actors." She smiled and looked around, past the gift shop with its kangaroos, koalas, boomerangs, opals and posters of animals and flowers. She could hear the distinctive Aussie twang, see distinctive Aussie types—the pair of older women, arms linked and purses dangling, hair in sausage rolls, bosoms trussed in hand-knitted cardigans; a sunburned young couple, with shaggy hair and backpacks, their short shorts showing off powerful legs; newly rich women, aiming at high fashion and mostly missing the mark; healthy-looking kids in school uniforms with knee socks and sandals. There were well-groomed airline stewardesses and their male, mostly gay, counterparts, known as "trolley dollies," farmers, surfers and factory workers, with a lone Indian in a sari and the ubiquitous Japanese businessmen thrown in. A bustling crowd, but no sense of the oppressive crush of Kennedy or Heathrow. Here, you felt you could breathe. And where was Tas? Diane McRobb reeled her back in with "There's a bit of flak because you aren't using an Aussie actress in the lead."

"I had to have an actress with international box-office appeal. The male lead will be Australian. And, I'm happy to say, Nita Narinto will have a large supporting part." She was going to wind this up and get a taxi. "I'm very excited to be back. Part of me never believed I'd get this off the ground."

"But you've had a lot of successes in the past year. The Academy Award, and I hear *Chappy* fared well both critically and at the box office."

"I've been lucky."

Diane McRobb cocked her head. "Just lucky?"

"Not just. But there are many talented people who don't get

their main chance. My ego's not so fragile that I have to assume total credit for my good fortune.''

"Frankly, I don't know how you got a bad rep for being uncooperative with the press.''

"When I was here last, I had a little problem with—what's her name?—Merle . . .''

"Merle Jaunders. You wouldn't be the first. She's in Sydney now. You might run into her there. She's working for *Women's Weekly*—actually it's a monthly magazine, but for obvious reasons it can't be called *Women's Monthly*.'' Megan's laugh encouraged her to go on. "Between you and me and the lamppost, Merle got the sack because she wrote a squib saying that Dennis Danher was paying too much attention to a local socialite by the name of Naomi Tishman.''

This was a quick and unexpected plunge into pertinent gossip. She gave way to base impulse and asked, "Any truth to that? I met Naomi Tishman a couple of times.''

"Who knows? Danher has always cultivated the loving hubby and dad image. And he was her boss. So it was an extraordinarily stupid thing for Merle to do. Anyway, Naomi Tishman isn't here anymore. Danher got her a job with some South African paper. She's writing reports from Jo'burg. If I could get over my prejudice at seeing the idle rich take someone else's job I'd have to admit that her columns aren't half bad. She isn't as dumb as she looks.''

"I never thought she was dumb.''

"I've been looking for a slant on this interview and I think you may have given it to me a minute ago. You said that you feel lucky, or that you attribute part of your success to luck. There was a recent psychological study that said women who've made a name for themselves attribute their success to luck far more frequently than do similarly successful men. What do you think about that?''

"Any director . . .'' The words came out and, she assumed, they made a modicum of sense, but she was thinking of a hot bath. Better to think of that small pleasure than to dwell on her disappointment. Perhaps Tas had been in an accident. Ridiculous. But a sign of her attachment. She looked out of the plate-glass window to see if the taxi stand was nearby. Yes, a hot bath.

And then she saw him, moving through the crowd so quickly that he was standing in front of her before she'd had a chance to take him in. She stood up. She'd lost the thread of what she was saying but wound up with "I think I'm both deserving and lucky. Hello, Tas."

Diane McRobb told Megan thank you and had the grace to excuse herself without waiting for an introduction. Megan and Tas just looked at each other, the impulse to embrace and simultaneous embarrassment making them both stiff. Finally she pecked him on the cheek. "Was that one of your show-biz kisses?" he asked.

"It sure was. Wonderful to see you, dah-ling. Don't you look marvelous! Not a day older!" She kissed his other cheek, then said, "Where were you, you bastard? I thought you'd forgotten me."

"Get away with you, woman." A slow smile creased his mouth and eyes. He had one of the truest smiles she knew because he smiled rarely, and never as a social obligation. "Sorry I'm late. Where's your friend Toni?"

"She can't come for another couple of weeks. Didn't you get my last letter telling you that?"

"No. I'm late because I knew we couldn't all fit in the Porsche so I arranged to borrow a friend's car and the bugger was late dropping it off. Come on. Let's go." He picked up her bags.

She walked quickly to keep up with his long-legged stride, and she talked too quickly, to dispel nervousness. "Yeah, Toni's coming later. And when we last talked she was pretty ambivalent about coming. Much to her surprise, but not to mine, she's the doting grandmother. She and Joe are up in Vermont now, visiting the son and daughter-in-law and the baby and overseeing construction of some cabins on their property. The son's a no-hoper, and Toni feels that if they build a couple of cabins and Mario, the son, maintains them it'll give him enough work and income to keep him out of trouble. Having met Mario, I wouldn't count on it. Oh, and her daughter and her husband are splitting up and the daughter's moving back in. My guess is that in another few weeks Toni won't be so ambivalent about coming. In the meantime I'll just have to soldier on by m'self."

"Any chance she won't come?"

"Uh-uh. I got her an associate producer status on this one and she's talked her husband into taking six months off so he can join her. I'm not too happy about that, but we'll fall off that bridge when we come to it." The sliding doors opened, they stepped out and she stopped. "Ah, air. Real fresh air. And that sky. Look at that sky. Too bad we can't have the Porsche with the top down."

"Too bad we aren't in the bush."

"Do you miss it awfully?"

"Yes, Lady Megan," he drawled. *"Awfully."* They crossed the parking lot.

"You could come up to the bush with me. Next Saturday. I told you Mick and Vi are moving down to the city, didn't I? Poor Mick. It'll break his heart. But his health hasn't been good. They have to do it. Seeing that place go will break my heart too. This Saturday will be the family's final corroboree up there. Can you come?"

"I'm to see Chrissie next Saturday. It's taken a long time for her to get to the point where she's willing to see me."

"Bring her along." She stood back while he unlocked the trunk and hefted in the bags. He was so intent on this job that she sensed the shadow of depression. "Am I being too pushy? I just thought . . ." But in all likelihood Chrissie wouldn't want to see her again. The circumstances of meeting the girl came back to her, darkening her mood. "No, I don't suppose she'd want to see me."

"You're wrong. I told her you were coming back. She'd love to see you again." He slammed the lid of the trunk and wiped his hand over his face as though to erase his worried expression. "Greta never let on to Chrissie about us."

She leaned against the car, crossing her arms over her breast. How easy and understandably human if Greta had told Chrissie, turned the girl against them in order to bind her more closely to herself. Would she, in similar circumstances, have had so much understanding and restraint? "Greta is . . ."

"Yes. She's decent. She's always been decent."

And what greater praise from an Irish Catholic? She was tempted to ask how Greta was doing but stayed still, eyes on the ground, offering no more than a "thank you" as he opened her

door. As they drove off, they started to talk again, but with a
tentative politeness. She debated about asking him up to her
hotel room. When she did he was deferential, suggesting that
she might want to rest, even though he'd taken the entire day
off. No, she said, all she needed was a shower to revive her,
then they could have lunch.

Once they reached the room, he asked to read her screenplay
and settled into a chair while she went into the bathroom and
closed the door. Hearing the rush of water, he was reminded of
that first morning in her apartment, how he'd made instant coffee
and decided not to see her again. And the night before, when
she'd strode ahead of him, already stripping off her clothes. That
night had been like being caught in a hurricane—irresistible,
amazing. But she'd been little more than a desirable, albeit too
opinionated, redhead then. Now they truly knew each other. It
could never be that easy if you knew the woman, and respected
her. And, more to the point, if she knew more about you than
anyone else ever had. He put aside thoughts of what state she
might be in when she emerged—would he even be up to Venus
on the half shell, knowing it was Megan?—and concentrated on
the screenplay.

She came out, toweling her hair, barefoot but otherwise fully
dressed in a rumpled skirt and sea-green blouse. As she'd stepped
out of the shower, it had crossed her mind to present herself
naked and dewy. But it couldn't be that simple now. They had
a history.

She started to speak, but he raised his hand and said, "Wait'll
I finish this scene." So she went about, silently unpacking and
hanging up her clothes. Her actions seemed to have great pre-
cision and meaning, as though in a dream. He was acutely aware
of her every gesture, though he glanced at her only occasionally.
She sat on the bed, wanting to lie back, but afraid a seductive
gesture would shatter the mood. "You can take that copy with
you," she suggested.

"Right." He continued to read.

"Shall we go downstairs to lunch?"

"If you like."

"Or we could drive someplace by the river. Seems a shame
to be indoors on such a lovely day."

"Right."

All the outpourings in the letters, she thought, and now he's lapsed into monosyllables. Not that she could think of anything to say herself.

He closed the script. "I'm no judge, but so far it seems pretty good."

"Pretty good. Pretty good!" she demanded, before getting up and sinking to her knees in an elaborate curtsy. "Why thank you, Dr. Burke."

"I expect you're used to a lot of palaver. But you're home now, girl. You get to be too much of a tall poppy, they'll lop your head off."

She got up, feisty as a hen with ruffled feathers. "I expect I can handle it. Lunch?"

He nodded.

"Good. I'll go fix my hair."

"If you're going to bugger around with that rat's nest of yours . . ." He wanted to lift that tendril that trailed her cheek, curl it around his finger, train it back behind her ear. ". . . then I might as well get on with reading this spectacular! Box-office bonanza! Superb! screenplay of yours."

She shrugged and looked him in the eyes. "Suit yourself."

"Go on then. Get a move on." But as she stepped away he reached, reflexively, drawing her to him.

She bent her head to his chest, turning her ear so that it was close to his heart. Such a fearful pounding. Her arms circled his back. What sort of future could they possibly have? But she said, "It was good of you to pick me up. I come and go so much. It was good to have someone I know, someone I really know, pick me up at the airport." She raised her face to his, pecked him on the cheek, but he held her fast. Their kiss was more tender than urgent, and she pulled away from it, but again put her head on his chest. He rested his chin in her springy, sweet-smelling hair and felt as though he were running on the beach, pulling cleansing air into his lungs. Easy. So easy. Undeniable. "Can we put off lunch," she murmured.

"We can put off everything." He lifted her up and moved toward the bed.

CHAPTER
TWENTY-THREE

SISTER BRUNO SAT UNDER THE JACARANDA TREE, HEAD bowed, rosary beads in her lap. Seeing her, and not wanting to disturb her prayers, Megan stopped abruptly, reaching out to the upturned hand of the Virgin to steady herself. She looked down at the flower bed that encircled the statue. The soil had been turned over but nothing had been planted and the clods of earth baked in the sun. She'd been shocked just now as she'd walked by the old school. She'd known that it was scheduled to be torn down but the sight of its partially demolished walls and the dumpsters loaded with broken bricks and shattered lumber had jarred her as much as if she'd seen a once vibrant friend propped up on her deathbed. She raised her head and looked at Bruno again. Her glasses had slid down her nose, her hands had fallen away from her beads, her feet, which poked through a pair of sturdy men's sandals, were yellowish and lumpy. Perhaps it was the exposed feet that made her look so vulnerable, or the fact that, Megan now realized, she was not praying but had fallen into an afternoon snooze.

She tiptoed past and knocked at the convent door. She could hear hammering inside and, after a time, the door was opened by the same young woman—Michele, wasn't it?—who'd been there when she and Greta had visited. "Oh, Miss Hanlon, sorry it took me so long. I was up a ladder." Michele wore a plaid shirt and jeans, and spatters of blue paint flecked her arms and her cheerfully bland, athletic face. "Joan called to say she'll be a bit late. Won't you come in? Joan said Sister Bruno and I should entertain you till she gets here. As if we could. We're all at sixes and sevens here. See," she said, leading Megan to the right as soon as she'd stepped into the vestibule, "We're redoing the parlor. Turning it into a community room for our lay teachers and the Marist Brothers.'' She gestured through the door, hailing her co-workers, one of whom was pounding together a bookshelf while the other knelt on the floor touching up the baseboards. ''This is Megan Hanlon. She's our most famous alumna.'' Both women gave friendly but distracted acknowledgment and went back to their work. ''We've been in chaos for months,'' Michele said as she led Megan back into the vestibule. ''The entire place is being overhauled. I guess you know we're merging with the Marist Brothers and going coed.''

''No, I didn't know that.''

''And now Joan's our superior. You did know that, didn't you?''

''Yes. She dropped me a note to tell me. But we haven't corresponded recently.''

''Well, now she's in charge she wants everything redone. I think it's going to look great when we're finally finished. But poor Joan! She's been flat out. We're really strapped for money and Joan's had to go to all the parishioners who have businesses and hit them up for donations. She just hates it. Well, you can imagine Joan having to ask anybody for anything.'' Michele's eyes creased with amusement. ''She told Mr. Johnston at the paint store that if he donated everything we needed she'd see to it that he got two weeks off his sentence in purgatory. He was quite offended. Not everyone understands Joan's sense of humor. But she can squeeze blood out of a turnip. She's got everyone doing something, and we aren't working under union regulations, let me tell you. Piety, she says, is no substitute for elbow grease.'' How lucky, Megan thought, that Joan had found this disciple who brought the enthusiasm of the hockey field to religious life. ''If you'll just wait here for a tick,'' Michele continued, ''I'll go and get us some lemonade. Or would you prefer a glass of sherry?''

''Lemonade will be fine.''

''Righto, I'm off.'' Michele scooted down the hall and Megan was left alone in the vestibule. The heavy draperies had been removed, giving the room a sense of space and light. A vase of eucalyptus leaves was on the table. The painting of the archbishop had been removed and in its place hung the school crest, a quotation from Albert Einstein ("The whole purpose of art and science is to awaken the cosmic religious feeling") and a restored photograph of the sisters who'd founded the school, eight in all, straight of spine and serious of mien.

"I'm back." Michele carried a tray with glasses, a large pitcher of lemonade, a plate of arrowroot biscuits and a piece of crumpled needlepoint. "Joan's so excited that you've come back. Well, we all are. You're going to shoot your movie here, aren't you?"

"Yes, here and in Tasmania. We start in a couple of weeks."

"And Kimberly Delsartre is going to star. Tell me, what's she really like?"

"I don't think Kimberly herself could answer that question," she said, then amended, "She's very nice." Surprisingly, Kimberly *was* very nice, eager if vapid, and if Kimberly's fame had made it to a small convent in Western Australia then she wasn't a bad choice, at least in terms of box office.

"Hiring any extras?" Michele laughed. "Just kidding." Megan held the door open and they stepped out into the garden. Michele put the tray on the old wooden table and tapped Sister Bruno on the shoulder. Bruno started. "Sister, look who's here."

Sister Bruno stared up at her. "Megan Hanlon, is it? You must've sneaked past me while I was saying my beads." Her eyes peered out accusingly from behind her thick lenses. She had lost weight and her sagging flesh made her face seem more relaxed and less formidable. She tried to hide her feet beneath her habit. "My arches have fallen, Megan, and I have these fearful bunions, so I can't wear proper shoes and I can't be on my feet too long. That's why the garden isn't as it should be."

Megan sat down. "It's nice to see you, Sister."

"So yer back, are y'?"

"Remember, she's doing her movie here. We put the articles up on the bulletin board," Michele reminded her.

"Sure, I'm not senile, Michele. I was the one to spot those articles." She folded her hands in her lap. "So, Megan, how are your father and your mother?"

"My mother's well. She and my stepfather hope to visit Australia later this year. My father passed away about a year ago."

Sister Bruno crossed herself. "God rest his soul."

"Yes," Megan said. "God rest his soul."

"And your brother? The one who's the priest?"

"He's fine." For someone who'd had a gag order from the Sacred Congregation of the Doctrine of Faith—formerly known as the Holy Inquisition—and was under investigation by federal authorities besides.

Michele handed around the lemonade and took up the needlepoint, first showing it to Megan. It said "God make me faithful, true and plain" but was surrounded by a busy border of flowers and ribbons. "I've been working on this for six months, but I'm nowhere near finished. I'm not much good at this sort of thing."

"All it takes is patience," Sister Bruno told her.

"I was never much good at that sort of thing myself," Megan said.

"It was Sister Ursula's idea as a gift for Joan. It's a quote from Thomas More. He's Joan's favorite saint."

"How is Sister Ursula?"

"Didn't you know?" Sister Bruno said. "She passed on."

"No, I didn't know. Oh, I'm so sorry."

Bruno crossed her arms under her bosom and nodded. "It was a peaceful passing. In her own room and in her sleep."

"It must've been hard on you, Sister."

"God's will be done. It was Joan who took it hard. So upset she was. God took Sister Ursula in His infinite wisdom. She's up in heaven now, looking down on us all. She wouldn't have been able to survive the changes we're goin' through, let me tell you. Hammering and sawing all through the day and into the night, the practice rooms being turned into offices, strangers invading the place! It's the Lord's sweet mystery how any of us will survive it. I can't help but feel that I'll be called to m' rest soon, and not before time. I won't want to be here when those ruffians from the Marist Brothers come howlin' in. Cats and snails and puppy dogs' tails. Nothing but a trial and a distraction they'll be. Sure, the girls won't be able to keep their minds on their books or their prayers."

"You're probably right," Megan agreed, and Sister Bruno, surprised at this unexpected concurrence, shifted her weight and, just to be argumentative, said, "Of course it has to be done. We're out of cash and if we're to keep on we must pay the piper. We must take in the Marists and their hooligan boys.'' She shook her head again. "Ah, it's almost too much for a body to bear. All these changes! Do you know what we had for dinner last night? Grass soup!''

Michele laughed. "We're not that broke. One of the new parishioners comes in once a week to spell Janette with the cooking. She's a refugee from Vietnam and she makes the most incredible dishes. It was lemongrass soup, Sister Bruno, and if you'd given it a try you would've found out how delicious it was.''

Bruno hurrumphed. Megan opened her bag and took out a box of Cadbury's. "Perhaps you'll be glad to see these,'' she said, offering them. Bruno eyed them greedily but shook her head. "I've given up sweets for Lent. Perhaps some of the younger nuns can make use of them.''

"You could save them till Easter,'' Michele suggested. "We could put them in the fridge till then.''

"No, no. I won't have them, but it's the thought that counts. Thank you, Megan. You know, seeing you again puts me in mind of Mona Gallagher. She was here when you last visited, wasn't she?''

"Yes, she was. How's she doing?''

"You'll never believe it,'' Michele told her. "Mona's married.''

"To an Englishman,'' Sister Bruno added sourly.

"Just imagine, getting married at her age,'' Michele said. "We all thought she was bound to be an old maid.''

"That's not a charitable way to put it, Michele. Mona was devoted to her mother and father. She chose the single life. Many women do. Megan, for instance.''

"But I can't believe Miss Hanlon hasn't had lots of offers.'' Michele turned to her expectantly, asking, "Haven't lots of men—?'' But Bruno interrupted, saying, "Poor Mona's mother got so bad that she required a doctor's care. Mona had no choice but to put her into a home. But it seemed to send poor Mona mad with grief. She threw up her job at the bank, though she'd had it for almost twenty years and—''

"She went round the twist,'' Michele said, rather cheerfully.

"So off she went to Singapore for holiday. And while she was there she stayed at this hotel and that's where she met the Englishman. He was the manager and he'd been recently widowed, so they fell into each other's arms . . ."

"They married after a brief courtship," Bruno corrected. "And now they're back here. They've opened up a restaurant at that new marina out at North Beach."

"That's wonderful," Megan exclaimed. She drank down her lemonade and tried to tease a thread of truth from this seamless weave of gossip. Had Mona's mother really gotten worse, or had Mona snapped and packed it in? Had her married lover of many years really become a widower, or had he finally gotten a divorce? Not that it mattered. At least Mona had made a U-turn in her life.

Michele giggled. "We met the husband once. He looked like a walrus. Mona was taking him to a convert class and he didn't look too happy about it."

"And while Mona was away her mother's condition took a turn for the better, so now that Mona has a proper home and a husband to help her, she may be able to have her mother live with them," Sister Bruno said.

Well, perhaps not a complete U-turn, Megan thought, replacing her glass.

"And Greta," Michele said. "You came with Greta last time, didn't you? Have you contacted her yet?"

"No."

"Poor Greta Burke." Sister Bruno sighed. "Though I suppose you know she's not Greta Burke anymore."

"She's resumed her maiden name," Michele supplied.

Bruno lifted her bosom and pursed her lips. "Not that it was her idea."

"The divorce wasn't her idea," Michele said. "She looked just terrible for a while there. But now she looks better than she ever has. You know that nervous habit she had, always touching her clothes, so that she made you feel how uncomfortable she was?" Megan looked at Michele more closely; she hadn't imagined that Michele was capable of such acute observation. "Well," Michele continued, "she doesn't do that anymore."

"Because she wears these artist's weeds—funny skirts and

all," Bruno interjected. "And her hair frizzed out in one of those wild permanents that look like . . ." She glanced at Megan's hair, then said, with the hint of apology, "Well, some were born with it."

"She's ever so much better off than she was before," Michele said. "She's taking art classes at the university and Joan's talked her into being a lay teacher next year. She's so good with children. Infinite patience. Which is more than I have." Michele tossed the needlepoint aside. "You may have a chance to see her. She's supposed to come by this afternoon to paint. Not to paint pictures, but to paint *paint*. The walls in the parlor."

"The poor dear," Bruno said, "married one minute and divorced the next."

Michele rolled her eyes at Megan. "She was married for ages. Her sons are grown men. Even Chrissie's almost as tall as I am, and she's ever so much better in class. Not that she wasn't always clever, but now she's more open and friendly. No. Greta is definitely better off. You said yourself, Sister, some women don't want to be married."

"Greta Papandreou is not one of them."

"Be that as it may . . ." Michele sensed a change in Megan and, taking her discomfort for impatience, said, "Joan should be here any minute. She said she'd only be twenty minutes late. Here we are, nattering with all this gossip, when what we really want to hear about is your movie."

"No," Sister Bruno corrected. "We want to hear about your father. Was his being called to his heavenly rest expected, or did he go suddenlike?"

Megan was deciding whose curiosity to satisfy, while surreptitiously looking at her watch, when they heard Joan's footsteps on the gravel.

Joan wore a grey summer suit with a boxy jacket. Her hair had been cropped to a no-nonsense length, had more streaks of grey, and the lines from her nose to her mouth had deepened. Her walk, Megan thought, seemed to have lost its bounce, or perhaps the large purse thrown over her shoulder and her armful of books had given it that fatigued but determined forward tilt. Megan got up and put her arms around her, then pulled back to look into Joan's deep-socketed grey eyes. Joan squinted against the sun. She had the beginning of a sty in her left eye. "Megan, how lovely to have you back. And how well you look. Much more rested than when I saw you last."

"I'm well rested now. Check me out in a coupla weeks. I'll already be a wreck by then."

"Lemonade, Sister?" Michele offered.

"Yes. Thank you." Joan sank into a chair. "I'm parched."

"And I suspect you've missed lunch. Could I fetch you a sandwich?"

"No. Thank you, dear. Don't bother. I'll just wait for dinner." Joan put her purse on the table and turned to Megan. "Sorry I'm late. I had a meeting with Father Celebrizzi. It started late and dragged on."

"Father has so many things to do," Sister Bruno said, excusing him.

"The one thing I wish he would do is remember to wind his watch," Joan said tartly. She took her glass of lemonade and drank it thirstily. "Now, Megan, tell me all about yourself. I've been looking forward so to seeing you. When does your filming begin? How long are you going to be with us? And will you be staying in Perth? Excuse me." Joan dabbed her lips with a handkerchief and the tense muscles on either side of her mouth relaxed into a smile. "There I go, asking you several questions at once. Just begin anywhere you like." She leaned forward, always the attentive listener.

"Ah, where to begin?" Megan hunched her shoulders and made her eyes wide. "I can start off by saying that I'm much more hopeful than I was last year."

"That's certainly understandable," Michele said. "After all, you won the Academy Award and Dennis Danher's giving you pots of money and the movie's starting soon. You're rich and famous, so why shouldn't everything be fabulous and marvelous?"

"Worldly riches are not a measure of all things," Bruno reminded Michele. " 'What shall it profit a man if he gain the whole world and lose his immortal soul?' "

"I know that, Sister, but Miss Hanlon's not in danger of losing her soul." Michele got up. "Well, Joan's back and my break's over. I'd best get back to work."

"And I'll come along with you." Sister Bruno placed her arms on either side of the wicker chair and it trembled as she struggled up. "I did have it in mind to get to those flower beds this afternoon. A bit of green, some growing things . . . not that I suppose so much as a weed will be safe now that those hooligan boys will be invading the place."

"No need for you to come in, Sister," Michele said quickly, thinking that Bruno would play overseer in the parlor.

"No," Sister Bruno insisted, "I'll be coming along. Sister Mary Magdalene and Megan have always found things to talk about. I'll sit in the chapel for a while. It's cool in there, and away from the noise and the confusion. Sure, Australia's a most regretful country. Sun burning down on you like a rich relation's judgment." She reached for Michele's arm. "And bring the chocolates along, if you will. Not that the heat hasn't destroyed them already. God bless you, Megan. I'll remember you in my prayers."

When they'd limped off, Megan said, "It was thoughtful of them to leave us alone."

"Yes. Michele's a kind girl, and she takes in more than you'd think, though her excessive use of superlatives is rather tiring. She thinks everything's marvelous and wonderful. Still, preferable to a nay-sayer. There are plenty of them around. Sister Bruno . . . well, the changes have been hard on her."

"Congratulations on your election as Superior. Just when I think the Church will stay bogged in the mire, it does something right."

"Sister Ursula was my campaign manager, before I even knew I was launching a campaign. The Order has some autonomy, at least insofar as our elections go. I wouldn't say the bishop is pleased with the choice." She clinked her glass to Megan's. "And here's to your film. Now tell me how it all came about."

"That's a long story . . ." But she launched into it with enthusiasm, adopting the accents and personalities of various producers, distributors, union officials, agents and actors. Joan was thoroughly entertained. She'd forgotten what a talented mimic Megan was, and she delighted in her pungent turns of phrase. "So I wouldn't say I've lost my immortal soul," Megan concluded, "though I have put it in danger with more than a few white lies and some murderous rages."

Joan refilled their glasses. "I've been teetering on the brink of some sins of distortion and omission myself." She pulled a face of exaggerated piety. "All to the greater good, of course. Now, tell me about your father. I was sorry to hear of your loss. Your letter was brief, but I sensed that you were very upset."

"Yes. It shook me up. I knew I should've made more of an attempt to be in touch with him. Why do we always put off reconciliations until the very passage of time becomes the obstacle? Ah, well . . ." She put her head back and looked up through the leaves. "I was sorry to hear about Sister Ursula. How old was she?"

"Eighty-six."

"I suppose that only leaves Sister Bruno from the old gang?" Joan nodded.

"I thought she'd be the most upset by Sister Ursula's death, but she said you were."

"Yes. I suppose I was. I still am. My conscience bothers me . . ." Joan wrapped her hands around the books on her lap. "Sister Ursula . . . I was closer to her than I was to my own mother. And it wasn't an easy passing."

"But Sister Bruno said . . ."

"Not quite true. Sister Ursula should have been sent to the mother house where they have a proper infirmary, but she didn't want to go. It was my, what do they say in business?—my judgment call?—to let her stay here. Her life might have been prolonged if she'd had more intensive care."

"But at eighty-six . . ."

"Yes. But she was in a good deal of pain. I read all the books on dying, but . . ." She stared into Megan's face. "I suppose reading books about dying is rather like reading books about the nature of love or how to swim. It doesn't really prepare one. And as I said, she was in considerable pain. A friend loaned me a small tape recorder with earphones. The music did seem to calm her. I'd always thought her faith was unshakable, but at the last she became very frightened. She'd already received Extreme Unction and seemed quite peaceful when the priest left. But at the very last she was frightened. 'Do you think God will welcome me?' she kept saying, and once, just once, 'Do you think He's there?' At the very end she was peaceful. She died with her earphones on.'' Joan allowed herself a rueful smile. ''I believe the last thing she heard was one of those New Age tapes . . . whales calling to each other off the coast of Alaska.''

Moments drifted by. A bee hovered on the rim of the pitcher and Joan shooed it away. Megan reached into her bag. ''I've brought you a book. I got it from my brother. It's the gospel painted by the peasants of Solentiname, a Christian commune in Nicaragua. See . . .'' She put the book on the table and opened it. ''Here's the Annunciation, but with Mary as a peasant woman sitting in a hut at her sewing machine. And here . . .''—she flipped through the pages—''. . . Jesus is being taken into captivity, but the soldiers are wearing National Guard uniforms and Jesus is wearing glasses and jeans. All the old stories revitalized.''

''How lovely. Thank you, Megan.'' Joan bent forward to examine it and one of her own books fell from her lap. As Megan bent to retrieve it, a postcard fell out. It showed terraced, seaside bungalows against a backdrop of a brilliantly blue sea. Greece, she supposed, turning it over to see before stopping herself. ''Sorry. Just reflexively nosy,'' she said, handing it to Joan.

''No. Go on. Read it. In fact, read it out loud.''

This seemed not just a courtesy but a real request. Joan settled, her head resting on the back of the chair, as though waiting to hear a favorite poem. Megan checked the postmark. It was from Greece. The sender's bold hand resisted the cramped space, so it wasn't easy to read. '' 'Congratulations,' '' she began slowly, '' 'on your election. This place is, as I'd hardly dared to hope, unchanged, except for the addition of electricity. Peace, quiet, natural beauty—everything I'd wanted. With one painful exception.' '' It was signed ''Your colleague, James.'' Megan looked at Joan. Her eyes were closed and the corners of her mouth had turned up in a pacified smile. ''This is the professor you told me about?''

''Yes.''

''Your . . . friend.''

''Yes. Listening to it is satisfying but hurtful, rather like probing the socket of an extracted tooth with your tongue.''

"I half thought I wouldn't find you here."

"I half thought so myself. But only half." Joan thought for a long time, her eyes moving beneath her closed lids. When at last she spoke she seemed to be talking to herself. "There isn't much evidence that the future will hold years of plenty for Catholic education. Young people, particularly young women, are subject to so many pressures and are so confused. Society and traditions offer so little in terms of support or guidance. Well." She opened her eyes. "You know about all that, though I don't suppose you run around Hollywood and New York saying you're a Catholic."

"But I've told you, Joan. I'm not a Catholic."

"You're not a *practicing* Catholic. But the traditions you were raised in cannot be altogether denied. They're too powerful. And an enrichment to us if we don't cling to them rigidly or take them as the last word. You share those traditions as surely as you share ribbons of DNA from your parents and grandparents. Forgive me, I'm proselytizing. You see, I have to refine my pitch since I'm dealing with the Marists and the diocese and the concerned laity, not to mention the bank and the parents. I'm beginning to sound like one of those hucksters on television. But would you concede that you are, culturally, a Catholic?"

"How could I deny that?"

"Good. These days we take what we can get."

"But you've dropped the subject of James. Do you ever see him?"

"No. He's still in Greece, but even when he comes back I doubt . . . I don't have many dealings with the university anymore. I gave a guest lecture there a few months ago, appropriately enough about the history of celibacy in the Church. But now that I'm in charge here there's no possibility that I'll get back to scholarship, at least in the foreseeable future. When someone else takes over . . . when I'm an old woman . . . I imagine a retirement filled with little else than reading and writing."

" 'Stranger, tell the Spartans that I lie here, obeying their orders.' "

"What?"

"It was a quote you had us memorize when we were studying the Peloponnesian War."

"It's better that I don't see him. I love him, you see." Joan smiled. "I'm very grateful to have known that kind of love. I feel it has enriched my understanding and . . ." She shook her head. "And it was wonderful to be loved in that way. It's made me feel stronger and—how shall I put it?—more worthy. I suspect, but I still only suspect"—and now her eyes were mischievous—"that under the right circumstances sexual love can be an ennobling experience."

"I'll never understand why or how you stay on."

"Did you get out of the movie business because you have to deal with thieves and charlatans?"

"It's hardly the same."

"No, of course it's not. Let's just say that when the time came for me to leave, I simply couldn't do it. Perhaps if I'd been younger, or if the school hadn't been in such dire need of leadership or if James himself had been more insistent. But he would never have pressured me. Our relationship was always one of respect and free choice. Oh, I've thought about all of this. I'll think about it till I die. But when the time came, my vows were simply more important. It's enough for me to have known love. I expect I seem tired and overwrought—well, I *am* tired and overwrought—but it's not just because I didn't go with James. I've heard through the grapevine that he's met an American woman, an academic from the University of Michigan, and that he's angling for an appointment there next year. I hope he gets it. Life is so much easier when he's half the world away. I miss talking to him so much, you see, that if I did see him, I just might weaken. It's funny, when I heard about that American woman I had such a twist of jealousy. It was an emotional charley horse that I just couldn't ease. It made me understand how miserable and crazy those feelings can make you. I know what a struggle Greta had to put up, about you and that other young woman her husband almost married."

"You knew about all that?"

"Greta doesn't confide easily. She's always been a lonely and essentially untrusting person, but yes, she and I have become quite friendly."

Megan felt the color rise to her neck and cheeks. "I'm not ashamed of my affair with Tas. Though I wish I hadn't tried to cover it up with Greta. The circumstances . . ." No, she would not become apologetic. "I never meant to hurt her."

"I understand that. I think you should tell her so yourself."

"I'm not up to that. I don't go to confession anymore, even with ex-wives. And I plan to see him again."

"Do you love him?"

"Oh, Joan. I'm very cautious about that word."

"Perhaps too cautious? I can still say I love God though His nature and meaning are often hidden to me."

"Just now the movie's the first thing on my mind. In fact—" She looked at her watch. "I'm meeting the costume designer for drinks in another hour. I should be getting back to the hotel."

"I trust this won't be the last time we'll be seeing you?"

"Of course not. If you can break free we might go to dinner."

"How about a nice drive to the beach? I've been promising myself that for ever so long. James's dog Belle is staying with some friends of his who live out near Rockingham. We might go there and visit Belle along the way. We could have a good long chin-wag and I could see Belle as well. I have no inhibitions about petting Belle. A transference. Isn't that what the psychiatrists would say?"

They both laughed, Joan's chuckle diminishing into a satisfied sigh. They got up and put their arms around each other. "Ah, Megan, it's been lovely seeing you again. It's such a deprivation not to be around someone who shares your sense of humor." She cupped Megan's chin in her hand. "Thank you for the book. A picture book is about all I'm up to these days. And do call when you are free, and we'll see if we can't arrange that outing. I just might be able to squeeze it in, though I can't promise." Her eyes filled. "This sty," she said impatiently, touching her handkerchief to her eyes, and then, almost curtly, "God be with you."

"And with you, Sister." Megan walked away quickly, afraid that her own emotion would spill over.

She had almost reached her rented car when she turned to look at the ruins of the old school and couldn't resist walking back to it—what was it Joan had said about the compulsion to probe the socket of a lost tooth?

White dust rose and settled on her legs as she stepped into the ruined space that had once been the entrance. She picked her way through a heap of shattered planking, careful to avoid the protruding nails. There, to her right, were the remains of a brick wall, its rusted and broken pipes exposed. She stepped through the doorway and stood beneath a dangerous-looking ceiling now water-stained and cracked. This was the room in which she'd learned her catechism, said her prayers, been punished, swapped homework and secrets, daydreamed about her life as a grown-up woman, pondered right and wrong, guilt and forgiveness, free will and the mysteries of sex. She stood motionless, almost hearing the voices of the past, until the sound of a car motor broke her reverie. She walked back, reached the dumpster and quickly moved behind it. A pickup truck had pulled in next to her car. A man in work clothes was at the wheel and Greta was at his side. They chatted for a moment, then he patted her hand and she got out.

As he drove away, Edgar stuck his head out of the window and called, "Mind you don't work too hard. See you at six." Greta waved and smiled. These small reassuring gestures she found so comforting came naturally to Edgar. Perhaps, she thought, it wasn't so much that he anticipated her needs as that they simply reflected his own. He liked the reassuring pat, the promise made and honored, of when they'd next meet. He worked steadily but never compulsively and always had time for a cup of tea, a chat, a silent contemplation of the sunset. He'd even kidded her into a pride in her appearance, saying that she should at least give herself the time and care she gave the garden, and noticing when she did. And that had given her confidence. She wasn't the sort of woman who had enough ego to believe she was pretty unless she saw it in a man's eyes. She had gone through the better part of a year doubting that she would ever have the desire or energy to function, enrolling in the art classes only because she was afraid of losing Joan's respect if she didn't rouse herself to some sort of action. Initially the classes had felt as though she were going through some painful treatment necessary to prolong her life, and there had been times when, had it not been for Chrissie, she wasn't sure that she'd wanted to prolong it. But gradually, almost imperceptibly, she had started to mend. Fear of failure still slowed her hand when she was at the easel, but she'd kept at it. She'd even sold a few landscapes, though she knew the violent abstracts that no one could associate with such a seemingly ordinary woman were her best works. And she'd started to enjoy the farm again, to accept some credit that it was thriving. She knew a large part of her recovery was due to Edgar, though he dismissed the credit, saying she was "just naturally on the mend." What she felt for him was so different from what she'd felt for Tas that she wouldn't call it love, but at least it was a fortuitous combination of mutual concern and ease, and she'd begun to reconsider—perhaps that was love. She shook her head and picked up the bag in which she carried her work clothes. She was late already, and Joan wasn't someone to be kept waiting.

Megan's first impulse was to remain hidden, but as Greta hurried across the parking lot and reached the path to the nuns' quarters, she stepped out. Greta stopped. They stood for a moment regarding each other, then advanced with steps that were measured, almost ceremonial. When they faced each other Megan thought, I must let her speak first.

"Hello, Megan."

"Hello, Greta."

A pause. "My friend Edgar just dropped me off. I'm going to help with the painting."

"Yes. Seems like there's plenty to do. All these changes . . ."

"Yes. Chaos."

"Changes are always hard, but that's the nature of life." She wished she hadn't said that.

Greta held her ground, saying no more than "Yes." What could this supremely confident woman know about change or chaos? Had she felt grief and loss? Had she woken with her fist in her mouth, crying out for God's help and afraid that she would not be heard, or been frightened at a new man's touch even though she ached for it?

"But it should be good when it's finished," Megan said lamely.

"Yes, it should."

Another pause. "How's Chrissie?"

"Oh, she's fine. Going like a house on fire. She thinks she wants to be a doctor now, so she's studying very hard."

"That's good."

"And I hear you're back to do that movie you talked about. Congratulations."

"Thanks. I hear you're studying art at the university."

"Well, if you've already visited the nuns, you know all the gossip." Greta stuffed her hand into the pocket of her skirt, then raised it nervously to her hair.

"You've got a new hairdo." Megan smiled. "It's becoming."

"Yes. I like it. Though yours . . ." Who could deny that tangled radiance? ". . . yours is a natural glory." She remembered the very first time she had seen it, here on the playground. Megan had been kind to her then, had offered to trade her a biscuit for grapes. And who was she to judge what was now in this woman's heart? Charity. Charity was required. "For which"—she could almost hear Sister Bruno's voice instructing—"you can gain a special indulgence."

"Greta . . ." Megan knew that she had to say it now, no matter how painful, even if it was rejected. "I never meant to . . ."

"Yes. I know."

Their eyes held, then looked away. They might have been twelve years old. The power and forgiveness of the moment astonished them both.

"Well," Greta said finally, "I'd best be getting inside. I said I'd be here twenty minutes ago and a promise . . . well, best of luck with your new movie."

"Best of luck to you, too."

Greta nodded, began to reach out her hand, but decided it wasn't necessary. Their eyes had told the story. "God bless you, Megan Hanlon."

"God bless you, Greta Papandreou."

Greta walked away. Megan turned and went to the car. As she put it in gear she looked once again at St. Brigid's. She checked her watch, looked right and left, humming nervously as she pulled out into the oncoming traffic. As she crested the hill she realized that she was singing "Hail Queen of Heaven, the Ocean Star'' at the top of her lungs and the driver in the next lane was looking at her as though she were mad. Bugger him. Sister Ursula had said it was a sin not to use God's gifts. She let her voice ring out.